The Taming of the Oligarch

D A Latham

DEDICATION

To my dearest, darling, Allan.

ACKNOWLEDGMENTS

With thanks to
Penny Restorick
Michael Harte
Amy Watton
Penny Harrison
Tomme Darlington
And
Gail Hayward

CONTENTS

ISBN-10:1494757184
ISBN-13:978-1494757182

CHAPTER 1

I sat through yet another business lunch, discussing the same boring subjects, with boring, grey men. I'm sure the food was exquisite, as it was one of the top restaurants in Canary Wharf, but I could barely taste it, so low was my mood. *I'm working too hard again,* I thought. I had one more meeting that afternoon, so planned to call it a day afterwards, pick up the girls from my flat, and drive down to Sussex. I also decided to give Penny a ring, see if a shag would cheer me up, although she'd proven a bit tricky to shake off afterwards, when I wanted some solitude. With my mind made up, I concentrated hard on what my lunch companions had to say, trying not to allow my thoughts to drift as they discussed emerging markets, and predictions for the telecoms industry on the African Subcontinent. The truth was that it was tedious beyond belief. Idly, I wondered how these men summoned up so much enthusiasm for the project.

My meeting that afternoon was with a pair of young entrepreneurs whose company was intent on developing an extra-tough coating for the cables used in fibre optics. I'd decided to invest in them, as I could see a use for the product worldwide. They'd struck me as a bit naive about valuations, so I agreed to meet them in their lawyers office to thrash out the final price. I hoped to have it all wrapped up, and contracts signed before the end of the day, so I could leave for Sussex with no outstanding issues.

I checked my appearance in my office bathroom mirror. I made a point of always being immaculately presented, as it tended to intimidate lesser men when I swept in wearing my bespoke suits and expensive shirts. I brushed my teeth and combed my hair, just to be sure. Nico and Roger fell into step behind me as I strode out of the Retinski offices, and down to the Pearson Hardwick ones.

"Good afternoon Mr Porenski, your meeting is scheduled in room 3, can I offer you a drink of anything?" Their receptionist was always unfailingly polite and efficient.

"No thank you. Shall I go straight in?" I asked.

"Certainly. Let me show you through." She trotted along ahead of us, past the secretarial pool, and into the meeting room. The others were already there, including a pretty little blonde girl. Everyone was introduced, and sat down to begin negotiations. I had to stop myself from staring at her, and concentrate on the task at hand, namely squeezing the saps for a bit more equity than they wanted to give. I pushed the negotiations forward at a punishing pace, confident I could lose them all in the detail of the deal. When I was certain that their eyes had glazed, I threw in a percentage figure which I'd inflated, which would give me 10% more of their company than I was paying for. *Like taking candy from a baby,* I mused.

"My colleague has indicated a possible discrepancy with the percentage figure," said their lawyer, "we'd like to request a recess to check the figures."

I shot little Miss Blondie a furious look. *How the hell did she manage to keep up?* She looked like a rabbit caught in the headlights. *Yeah, yeah, so I was sharking baby girl. I'm impressed by you though.*

We all took a break while they recalculated. I knew full well that their figures would be correct, and reconciled myself to gaining just 53% of the company. I observed her closely when they all returned. The over-riding attribute I noted was how healthy she looked. Pretty girls were ten a penny, but Miss Reynolds glowed with good health. Her skin was perfect, and her hair shone. Being attracted to women with clear skin and shiny hair was definitely a throwback to my pauper roots, as poor health and weakness was common, and marked you down further into a life of grinding poverty. My first girlfriend, Irina, had been the only girl in my year at school back in Russia with lovely skin, and nice, clean hair. Miss Reynolds surpassed her in every way, with a superior intellect as the cherry on top.

The rest of the meeting passed quickly, and I was forced to acquiesce gracefully on the subject of the percentage figure. I gave Miss Reynolds a pointed look, but couldn't stop the corners of my mouth twitching, seeing how apprehensive she looked. We agreed to meet again on Monday afternoon, and after the usual pleasantries, I swept out, my guards trailing along behind me.

"I'd like a full background check on Miss Reynolds please, I want to know everything," I barked at Roger, just before I bumped into Oscar standing outside reception. I assumed he had business there, and greeted him warmly, despite the fact I was intensely envious of his position in life. I actually quite liked him, once I'd got over just how easily he'd acquired everything, particularly his castle. He had also inherited his position at the helm of his family bank, and was my banker.

"Hello Ivan, how nice to see you. I trust you're keeping well?" he said in his upper class accent. "Another acquisition?" He asked, nodding towards the glass doors of Pearson Hardwick.

"Yeah, although it proved a little tricky. What about you?"

"Here to see a certain lady I'm pursuing. Quite an impressive young lawyer, just started work there."

"Blonde hair?"

"Yes. The one you just ordered a background check on. I take it you met her then?" Oscar raised his eyebrow.

"Hmm, yes. She just put the kibosh on wrapping the deal

today. Called me out on some figures. Just cost me 10% of a tech firm. I wondered who she was."

"She's a lawyer, that's all you need to know. I saw her first, so I'd appreciate it if you stepped aside where she's concerned." Oscar looked impassive, but he wouldn't make a statement like that unless he meant it. I resolved to ask her out for dinner, and discover what had made Oscar lose his usual ultra-detached demeanor. It would be fun to wind him up.

"So, are you taking her out this weekend?" I was curious.

"Hopefully. That's what I'm here for. She certainly knows how to play it cool."

"Oh well, good luck. I'll probably see you Monday. I have some business to take care of with one of your staff. I'll pop by and see how it went." I noticed that Oscar looked a little nervous.

Back home, the girls made a fuss of me, making me smile for the first time since I'd said goodbye to them that morning. They were my saving grace, the reason I took weekends off, and made the drive to Sussex. They forced me to walk through the woods, which did me as much good as them. Those two little spaniels kept me sane, and in return, I kept them safe, loved and well fed. Their unquenchable thirst for fun was the perfect antidote to my rather grey, featureless world spent chasing deals and worshipping the god of money.

I stripped off my suit, and changed into jeans and a thin jersey, ready to begin the process of relaxing. The two spaniels sat on my bed and watched me as I dumped my work clothes in a bag for my housekeeper to dry clean, rolling about for tummy rubs as soon as I was finished.

Each sat on my lap in turn while I fastened their collars and leads, and gave them a kiss on the nose. I packed their portable water dispenser and a rawhide bone each for the journey down, and called Nico to bring the car round.

I called Penny on the way down to Sussex. I figured it was better to see her on Friday night, rather than Saturday, in case she insisted on staying the night. My Sundays were sacred, even more so after getting rid of Dascha, my poisonous ex-girlfriend, I'd vowed never to spend Sundays with anyone who wasn't canine. Penny had sounded pathetically grateful that I'd called, and was delighted to be invited over for what was in effect just a booty call. I'd have to think of a creative excuse to get rid of her afterwards.

She turned up that evening wearing a short, tight dress, clearly thinking she looked alluring. I just thought she looked tarty. I didn't even bother to offer her anything to eat, I just got straight into the shagging. She was one of those insatiable women who wanted it every way it was possible. She begged me to fuck her up the arse, which I declined with a grimace.

Her particular kink was to be tied up. I happily obliged, relatively pleased that her cold, clammy hands wouldn't be running over my skin. On the one occasion I'd fucked her with her hands free, she'd scraped her acrylic nails painfully down my back, which had made me wince, and lose my erection. I was definitely not into pain with sex.

I was grinding away, trying to feel something, anything, when the image of Ms Reynolds inexplicably popped into my head. I closed my eyes, and let myself fantasise about fucking her, instead of Penny, who was yelling her imminent orgasm.

Hmm, silky warm skin against mine, those baby blue eyes filled with lust, begging me to fuck her hard and fast. Her soft little hands caressing my cock, as she wraps those pretty, plump lips around it...

I came with a shout, pumping Penny full of the cum Miss Reynolds should have laid claim to. Without the fantasy I'd allowed myself, I seriously doubted that I'd have been able to come at all. For a fleeting moment, I felt a little ashamed of myself, then shook it off, and turned my attention to getting rid of the limpet-like woman in my spare bedroom. I disposed of the condom in the bathroom, and pulled on a robe. Returning to the bedroom, I took a deep breath. "I have a load of phone calls scheduled for overnight, time differences, you know. It would be better to have Roger take you home," I said, not really caring whether she thought I was a bastard or not. She pouted slightly.

"Means we'll miss out on some morning action," she countered.

"I know, but I have meetings from early tomorrow, and need to leave here by seven at the latest," I lied smoothly. I just wanted her gone, so I could scoff some food cuddled up in my own bed with my girls, and watch some TV. She got out of bed reluctantly, and began to get dressed. I pulled out my phone and called Roger.

When she'd gone, I fixed a tray of snacks, and climbed into bed. Bella and Tania snuggled in, and I watched the news, sharing a packet of cheese straws with the greedy little spaniels. I mused about my naughty fantasy involving Miss Reynolds, and wondered how she'd seeped into my subconscious so quickly. I looked at the clock, and hoped that Oscar wasn't shagging her at that moment. *Jammy bastard gets everything he wants.* The thought of him having the delectable Miss Reynolds grated on me, almost as much as his money, castle and private bank did.

On a personal level, I quite liked him, and enjoyed his company. I could see why women would be drawn to him. On a business level, he was as sharp as his father had been. The late Lord Golding had been complicit in the raping of Russian natural resources, with the help of the oligarchs and the politicians. He had been in cahoots with Vlad, my was-to-be father in law, and the pair of them had set me up to take control of Russia's telecoms industry back in '99. Oscar was one of the few people who knew exactly what had gone on, and it was in all of our interests that it remain concealed.

The next morning, I woke up early, and slid out of bed quietly, so as not to disturb the sleeping spaniels. I cooked some sausages for us all, putting mine in a sandwich, and slathering on a generous helping of ketchup. The smell must have woken the girls, and the pair of them came skidding in, sliding to a halt in front of me, with winsome smiles on their faces. Laughing at them, I cut up their breakfast, and let it cool slightly before putting the bowls down on the floor, only to see the contents inhaled within 30 seconds.

"I don't know why you do that, you should make the most of it," I admonished, as they looked at me expectantly, hoping for more. They knew I always held back a sausage or two for later. I took them straight out into the woods, knowing that they'd need the loo.

Walking through the tree lined paths, I pondered my past week. All the meetings had seemed to blur together, except one. I'd had a few significant wins, namely driving down some staffing costs by outsourcing some call centre work to India, and a significant loss, which was having a certain little lawyer keep up with me during that deal.

As a rule, I never went for intellectual women. I had an image to keep up, so tended to value a woman's looks ahead of her brains. Clever women rarely seemed to take care of themselves as well as airheads, so generally didn't appear on my radar. Thinking about it, I'd never been out with a woman who possessed a degree, let alone one in law. I doubted that Oscar had either. All of his exes had been tall, willowy blondes, usually with a braying voice, and an inbuilt snobbery.

I tended to go for tall, slim brunettes, although my relationship with Dascha had seriously put me off that particular type. I'd also vowed to stick to English or American women, and never ever succumb to a Russian woman's charms again.

I set off after lunch, having appointments with both my tailor and hairdresser in the West End. Bespoke suits were a weakness of mine, and I judged them to be worth the extra time it took with fittings. After my haircut, and a massage, I shopped a little, buying some new underwear, some shirts, and new collars for the girls in the pet department, also picking up new squeaky toys, as they'd destroyed the last ones quite thoroughly.

I arrived back in Sussex around 7, and, after eating, went into my study to check my emails. Straightaway I saw the one from my security company, containing the background check on Miss Reynolds. I ignored the rest of my emails, and opened it.

Background information requested by Ivan Porenski

Name: Elle Reynolds

Address: 14A, 176 Jamaica Wharf, Coriander Street, London E14 2FT

Previous Address: 14b Lovell Avenue, Welling, Kent, DA16 4AH

Mobile Number: 07956 567895

National Insurance number: NR66 01 88 E

Bank Account: NatWest Bank, Welling branch, account number: 26597856

Balance: £3100.34

No other bank or savings accounts found.

Debt: None

D.O.B: 21/10/1988

Mother: Deborah Reynolds 15/3/1967

Father: Unknown (not listed on birth certificate)

Education: Fosters primary school, Upper Wickham Lane, Welling

Bexley Grammar School, Danson Lane, Welling 12GCSEs, 4AS levels, 3A levels. All achieved with A* grades

Cambridge University (achieved first class honours degree in law, highest marks in her year group) Full bursary grant received.

Joined Pearson Hardwick immediately after her year of law practitioners course, taken at Cambridge.

Work History: July 2009-sept 2009 waitress at The Nags Head restaurant, Welling

Sept 2009- June 2011 part time waitress at The Crown Carvery, Porrit road, Cambridge.

June 2011- current Pearson Hardwick law practitioners, corporate law division, Canary Wharf.

Previous Relationships: December 2010- May 2011 Niall Duffy

August 2011- November 2011 Craig Lutey

Property owned: Nil

Social Networks: None

Sexual Orientation: Heterosexual

Sexual proclivities: None known

Criminal Record: none found

Driving Licence: none

Passport: British

I must have read through the report at least ten times. If anything, it made Miss Reynolds even more of a mystery. I printed it out to peruse later, and turned my attention to the rest of my emails, grimacing at a company report on costings for new cabling through downtown Moscow. I then spent a little time researching the information regarding Ms Reynolds. Satisfied that I'd dealt with everything, I switched off my computer.

I lay in the bath that evening, ruminating on that report. *Elle, hmm, the name suits her.* I'd google-earthed Lovell Avenue, discovering that it was a fairly grotty maisonette in South London. Her schools had been state run too. *Miss Reynolds hasn't come from money. In fact, I think she comes from poverty. No wonder she's a closed book. I bet Golding doesn't know. Wonder why they couldn't find all her boyfriends though, that's a bit strange.*

The fact that I was thinking about her so much surprised me. As a rule, women flung themselves at me, and I took my pick. I got bored fairly quickly, took them out for a final shopping trip, then sent them on their way. I didn't usually *think* about them. They were just...there, even Dascha, who was about the nearest I'd got to a relationship, even though it had been largely platonic, thanks to her horrific sexual preferences. She'd been into the BDSM scene in a big way, so we'd agreed early on that we were sexually incompatible, and that our relationship would be an open one, with both of us free to seek sex elsewhere. Even without the sex aspect, I'd disliked her intensely, and could barely be in the same room as her. Great introduction to relationships.

Most women seemed to be happy with a few good shags and a shopping trip or two, and appeared to be quite sanguine about being ditched. A couple had been a bit clingy, but my extensive security arrangements had stopped them becoming a problem. I decided to find out more about Elle Reynolds from Oscar on Monday.

I dressed carefully on Monday morning, conscious that I'd be seeing Elle again that afternoon. I dealt with about a million emails, then caught the lift down to Goldings bank for a meeting at half twelve to move some money into the main Retinski account to cover some acquisitions. I preferred to do it in person, as the web of companies was fairly complex, and required careful oversight. I'd dealt with Mrs Restorick for quite a long time, so she greeted me warmly, and set about enacting my requirements. As I fully expected to complete my deal with the cabling company that afternoon, she set up a new account, and a vast line of credit, ready for my takeover.

I bumped into Oscar on my way out, and, at his insistence, joined him for a coffee in his office. "How was your date with Miss Reynolds?" I asked, trying not to sound too interested.

He pulled a face. "The date was great, then she refused a shag, sent me home, and stormed off at breakfast the next day when I came on a bit strong. Ignored me ever since. She's certainly a feisty one." He looked annoyed.

If I could have punched the air at that moment without him seeing, I would've done. "So she's still a single woman?" I asked.

"Yeah, but I doubt if you'll get anywhere with her. I happen to know she wouldn't date the opposing side. Besides, I think she's a little too ladylike for you Ivan. Let's face it, if she's the first woman to say no to me, she's hardly going to drop her knickers for you now is she?"

"Well, I am better looking than you, Osc, so you never know." We both laughed, but inside I was thrilled. *What is it about her?* "All I can say is may the best man win." I threw down the gauntlet. Probably not a wise move to declare my interest, but I figured that Oscar would back off, having been turned down by her. I certainly didn't expect him to pursue Miss Reynolds, as it would be extremely out of character. He expected women to fall at his feet, and regarded them as playthings. *Rather like me*, the unwelcome thought popped into my head.

"I shall enjoy hearing all about how she turned you down flat," said Oscar, with a slight sneer. *We'll see about that,* I thought. At that moment, I was determined to have Elle Reynolds, if nothing else just to piss Golding off, and wipe the sneer from his face.

"She won't turn me down. I shall dazzle her with my Russian charm," I announced. Oscar started laughing.

"Russian charm? First time I've heard those two words in the same sentence. I haven't given up yet, so calm yourself down, you're up against some stiff competition, and I have a title and a castle up my sleeve." *Yes, yes, I know, you jammy bastard. And I'm just the Podunk with a lot of money, I get it.*

"That as may be, but you've been turned down and ignored. You're already a busted flush, leaves the field wide open my friend," I pointed out. Oscar scowled, which pleased me enormously. "Plus of course, I'm seeing her in..." I looked at my watch, "fifteen minutes."

I arrived at the Pearson Hardwick offices at precisely two o'clock, and was shown straight into the meeting room. I let my lawyer do the talking, and used the opportunity to get a good look at Miss Reynolds. I watched as she sorted some papers, her little blouse draping provocatively over what looked like a perfect pair of C cup breasts. I signed the contract, and the deal was done. Everyone got up to leave, so I seized my opportunity.

"Miss Reynolds, I would like to speak to you alone please." I asked her, fixing her with an intense stare. She looked apprehensive.

"Sure," she said, "here ok?" I nodded, and waited for the rest of the men to leave, before striding over to the door and closing it.

"You are very impressive for such a young woman," I said. Not my most original opener, I admit, but I thought it would flatter her. She didn't look particularly flattered.

"Thanks.......is that all?" She said, a hint of sarcasm in her voice.

"No. You intrigue me Miss Reynolds. Do I intrigue you?"

"Mr Porenski, it's not something I've given any thought to. Now is there anything else? I have a full schedule to be getting back to." *Oh I haven't finished yet, prepare yourself...*

"Would you have dinner with me tonight?" I looked at her expectantly. I fully expected her to smile gratefully, behave all coy, and say yes immediately. Women loved my pretty face, and deep, Russian accent.

"No, I'm sorry but I'm busy." *WHAT? Did she just say no? Maybe she's gay?*

"Oscar was a fool to let you slip away from him. I wouldn't make the same mistake. Now, Elle, take a good, long look at me, and tell me if you see a man who takes no for an answer." *Women just....never say no to me.*

"No means no. I have no idea what Oscar did or didn't tell you, but when I say no I mean it. Do yourself a favour, and accept it gracefully." She said it quite forcefully, and looked a bit annoyed. She grabbed her files, and stormed out of the room. I stood rooted to the spot in shock. *She really is quite magnificent,* I thought.

I didn't see her as I left, and went back to my office to sulk. Galina put a coffee down in front of me, and barely even flinched as I growled at her to leave me alone. She really was worth her weight in gold. Very few secretaries would put up with my moods the way that she did. Half an hour later, Oscar called. "Hello Ivan, just thought I'd find out how your meeting went."

"It went well thank you. Contracts are all signed, and the deal concluded."

"That's not what I meant, and you know it. What did Elle say? Presuming you mustered up the courage to ask her out, that is."

"Of course I did, but she turned me down flat. Were you aware that she's a lesbian?" I heard Oscar chuckle down the phone.

"She's no lesbian Ivan. Guess she's still hung up on me. Hmm, she's quite the ladylike little thing." *Yeah she is, and she's way too good for you, you spoilt brat.* I changed the subject to that weekend. Oscar's family seat was about 10 miles from my weekend house, so we often met up if neither of us had anything going on. We arranged to have dinner Saturday evening, providing that neither of us had anything more exciting come up.

It probably sounds a bit boring, two thirty something bachelors spending their Saturday evenings in the depths of Sussex, but the truth was that both of us were a little jaded with the constant womanising and carousing of London life. We'd both spent our twenties being playboys, sampling the best that London had to offer. Oscar had ended up a junkie, and I'd had a breakdown. Both events had been hushed up, and kept out of the papers, but they were always there, reminding both Oscar and I that peace and solitude were a necessary antidote to the excesses of our business lives. In my own case, I'd worked almost twenty hours a day, to both build the business, and avoid Dascha, and the sense of failure I felt around her. I'd squeezed women into my mad schedule, almost as appointments. It had been a terrible way to live.

As with everything in my life, the stars had aligned to save me. The poisonous ex had tried to kill my dog, and gave me a superb excuse to finally kick her out and send her back to her father, who, as an animal lover, had accepted that she'd done a terrible thing. My breakdown happened shortly afterwards, which I was able to keep secret from both blabber mouth Dascha, and her psychopath father, who would have used it against me. So here I was, six months later, the calmest and happiest I'd ever been, except...I was a little...lonely.

For the next few days, I tried to forget about Elle, and concentrate on business. I was offloading a small company I'd purchased ten years ago for buttons, to Vodafone for eighty five mil. It had definitely proved to be a superb investment in more ways than one, as the technologies it had developed had cut our infrastructure costs by millions as well. My in-house team were handling the sale, with Pearson Hardwick handling the purchase for Vodafone.

I worked my way methodically through all the figures, satisfying myself that we'd left no stone unturned, and had fully disclosed every patent, asset, and liability so that nothing could possibly come back to bite us. I also knew that Vodafone were desperate for the technologies that had been developed, so the price was a touch on the high side to reflect its value.

Figures were my thing, the area in which I excelled. I prided myself on being able to keep up with, and outwit, the best accountants. I'd been taught basic maths back home in Moscow, but it hadn't been until I'd got to the UK, that I'd fully explored my aptitude. Two years of studying accountancy at night school had revealed a talent that I never knew I had.

My only break from working on that deal was a meeting at Elle's offices to map out the timings involved with transferring the company. I felt a pang of disappointment that she wasn't present. I'd been looking forward to seeing her more than I cared to admit. During the meeting, I wrote out a note for her, adding my phone number, just in case she changed her mind, or regretted turning me down. I dropped it into her office on my way out, again disappointed that she wasn't there. She was fast turning into a bit of an addiction, like crack for the soul. Given that she hadn't shown the slightest interest in me, she was a habit I needed to break.

I entertained some business associates that evening, taking them out to the Dorchester grill, and on to Whisky Mist. They were fellow Russians, which meant I could relax a little. I understood them, they understood me, and we had plenty in common. One of them, Karl, was what would commonly be described as a pussyhound, unable to keep it in his pants for any length of time. Fortunately his wife allowed his behavior, thanks to an unlimited credit card, and his blind eye to her preference for the ladies as well.

"So Ivan, who're you shagging these days?" He asked.

"Only some actress, but if I'm honest, she's starting to irritate me. I need to fix up a shopping trip." I admitted. Karl nodded, understanding immediately what I meant. Our other companion, Mika, was a little older, and was loved up with his current lady, a model called Katrina. I noticed he kept looking at his watch, as if was dying to get back to her.

"Mika, if you want to go, we won't be offended," I said.

"Yes we bloody will," countered Karl, "one night out with the boys shouldn't be a problem."

"Ivan can wingman for you tonight," Mika said, "I've got better at home than there is in here."

I looked around, to see the place stuffed full of pretty girls, some throwing glances our way and preening. "Yeah, I'm up for it tonight. I could do with some fun," I told them. Karl looked delighted. With business dealt with during dinner, we were looking forward to some drinking and womanising. With all our security seated on the table next to us, it didn't matter how pissed we got, we all knew we'd get scraped up and delivered home safely, and any girls would be dropped off if need be.

Mika said his goodbyes, and left us to it. "Pussywhipped," declared Karl, "he'll learn."

"Learn what?" I asked.

"Women. They break your heart if you let them. Far better to keep them at dicks length."

"I fully intend to," I laughed. *Apart from Miss Reynolds that is.* I noticed a girl at the bar who looked a little like Elle, with long, fair hair, and similar tits. *I could pretend it's her.* I smiled my best, most dazzling smile, and indicated that she should come over and join us. She smiled back, and grabbed her friend to point us out. The pair of them sashayed over.

"Would you like to join us for a drink?" I said.

"Ooh, lovely, could I have some champagne please?" The Elle lookalike said, before pulling up a chair. Karl ordered another bottle of Krug from the hovering waiter.

"What's your name?" I asked.

"Amy, and my friend is Tracey. What's yours?" *You don't recognise me?*

"Ivan, and this is Karl. I've not seen you in here before." *That's because I've only been here a couple of times, but you don't need to know that.*

"First time here. It's really packed isn't it? How did you manage to get a table?" *They recognised me, dumb girl.*

I shrugged, "just lucky I guess." I noticed Karl smiling at Tracey, like a lion smiling at the zebra he was about to devour.

"I love your accent, where are you from?" Amy asked.

"Russia, Moscow to be exact."

"I thought Russians talked like 'zat', 'zey vont a wodka'," she giggled.

"I took English lessons," I explained, amused at her impression of a Podunk.

"Enunciate the 'wuh' sound, Ivan, your lips should form a kiss," explained Ms Bishop in our English class. I practiced constantly, asking the staff at the home to correct any mistakes I made with my grammar or pronunciation. I was determined to be able to say 'the' like a Londoner, and be able to keep up with any conversation in English, without being left behind. A bit of an accent was ok, sexy even, but sounding like the vampire in a cheesy horror film wasn't, so I worked hard.

Another bottle of Krug later, the two girls were giggly and clearly up for anything. We ended up booking rooms at the Dorchester, under the premise of carrying on the party. They appeared too stupid to notice that we took them into separate rooms.

Amy turned out to be a surprisingly good shag, and a bit of a tiger between the sheets. She got a couple of orgasms, and I was able to indulge my fantasy that I was shagging Ms Reynolds, thanks to some low lighting and a bit of imagination. When we'd finished, I took her number, and arranged a car home for her. I was after all, a gentleman.

CHAPTER 2

I woke up with the thickest head ever the next morning, with Bella standing on my chest and licking my face, clearly concerned by my failure to wake up at the normal time.

Feeling rather bleary, I let the girls out onto the balcony to use their loo, and made myself a strong coffee. I had no meetings booked, so didn't have to race into the office. I sat out on the terrace to drink my coffee, and check my emails. My company, Retinski, had many myriad arms, and a fairly complex array of industries that we operated in. I'd started off in telecoms, which had made me wealthy, and still did, but as technology moved forward, Retinski had kept up, and even been in the forefront at times. We were operating the 3G network across the whole of Russia and the Ukraine, and most of Africa. Having had the foresight to install easily upgradeable infrastructure had proved to be an extremely good move. It had meant buying, and investing in numerous tech and engineering companies along the way, leaving me with a complex web of companies, which would confuse even the most determined tax official. Couple that with worldwide retail shops, handset production, and SIM card sales, and even my mind occasionally boggled with the amount of companies I controlled. I also bankrolled various venture capital enterprises, as it made good business sense to capture up and coming young entrepreneurs.

I was extremely proud of my achievements, especially given

the poverty I'd been born into. All too clearly, I could remember the hardships that my parents and I had endured.

"Ivan, finish your food. I won't have you wasting it." I looked down at my bowl, the soup looked watery and slightly grey, with bits of vegetable floating in it. It tasted as foul as it looked. I knew my mum had been down to the market that day, and suspected the soup had been made from the rotten odds and ends thrown away by the traders. I also noticed that she hadn't eaten, serving the food to my dad and I instead.

He mopped up the last of his soup with a little bread, and indicated that I could have the last bit. "It's ok, I'm full, mum can have it," I said, trying to make sure that she at least had something. At school that day, I'd at least had lunch provided, even if it had been pretty vile. I couldn't wait to leave school and start work. I wanted to earn money, and help provide for our family. The fact that we were poor grated on me constantly, like a nagging, gnawing inside that ate away at me.

I shook myself out of my daydream, and back to the reality of my beautiful penthouse. I'd come a long way from West Biryulevo, and the shame of poverty and ignorance. My entire life since leaving had been devoted to never returning to the deprivations of my roots. I'd had to do some things that I was ashamed of on the way, but as far as I was concerned, the end had justified the means. Nowadays, I visited Moscow as an Oligarch, part of the capitalist royalty whose excesses intrigued the world. I was happy in that role. Alongside fellow Oligarchs I was well educated and urbane. It was only in the company of the British elite that I still felt gauche and ignorant. If I was truthful, I'd love to have their easy acceptance of their place in the world, and the security that a first class education gave them.

All I'd had was state schooling in Moscow until the age of 15, and a combination of night school and the Russian Mafia once I'd arrived in London. It was only the good fortune of being introduced to Vladimir Meranov that had opened my eyes to the possibilities that the old Soviet Union presented. When his daughter and I started dating, he had taken me aside, and told me that I would need to become a wealthy man if he was to sanction the relationship between Dascha and I. He introduced me to the right people, gave me enough cash to start up, and helped me scare off all rivals. The most important lesson he taught me was that ownership was everything. I should always aim to own the companies I ran. It was good advice, and a lesson I took to heart.

He also taught me the art of being ruthless. In hindsight, we raped Russia for her resources, helped by the banks, who smoothed our way in order to reap the enormous benefits. As capitalism took hold, we made sure we were the ones holding the reigns.

I finished my coffee just as my housekeeper, Mrs Watton appeared. She'd been looking after me for around five years, since I'd moved into my apartment, and was one of those middle aged, motherly women who seemed to make 'keeping house' look effortless. She was also a great cook, as well as a superb organiser.

She greeted me cheerfully, and started preparing my breakfast while I went for my shower. My morning routine was fairly straightforward, and rarely varied. She made me bacon and eggs, and cooked two sausages each for the girls. She was able to time it to perfection so that it was ready as soon as I got out of the shower. I liked my life like that, precise and well organised.

I went into the office around ten, and read through the memos that Galina had put on my desk. She came in bearing my morning latte, and her tablet, ready to take down her instructions for the day.

"Tell Oleg I want a full list of all our bank accounts showing the cash balances held, and a full list of liabilities to the end of the month. Has legal checked over that sale contract yet? I want to see it before it goes over to Pearson Hardwick on Monday morning, and it must be treble checked."

"Yes Ivan. I'll get on it straightaway." She said meekly before scurrying away. I was interrupted by my mobile ringing. It was Karl.

"Hey Ivan, how was your shag?"

"Not bad at all. Quite the little tiger. How was yours?"

"Bit uptight if you ask me. Nice enough girl, small tits though." Karl preferred his women to be stacked, as did his wife. "You gonna see yours again? Or should we go and find some fresh ones?"

"I'm not up for a late one tonight, but we could try a new stomping ground. How about the bar at the Mandarin Oriental?" I liked a shag every day if I could.

"Good choice. I'll book us dinner at seven in the restaurant there first. I can't shag on an empty stomach."

"Can you invite Dmitri? I need to speak to him about permits for siting some masts in Moscow. I believe he has contacts." I could kill two birds with one stone.

"Sure. See you at seven in the hotel bar."

I returned to my screen, waiting expectantly for my email from Oleg. It was my little Friday ritual, to work out exactly how much cash I had. Silly, I know, but it made me happy.

The rest of my day was spent dealing with the various issues and details that plagued my working life. Problems with planning officials, lawsuits we were working on, the list went on. I wrapped up at five, and went back to the penthouse to get showered and changed.

The girls seemed totally unimpressed that we weren't driving down to Sussex, as was usual on a Friday, and Tania sulked a little. They had a security team of their own who accompanied them down to the garden square at the side of the apartment block where we stayed during the week. They still preferred being with me though, and played up when I went out. Their 'nanny' was babysitting them that night, and was busy preparing their dinner when I left, causing them a confused conflict, as to whether or not to get upset at my leaving, or excited at the prospect of food. The food won out. As usual.

Karl and Dmitri were already there when I arrived with my guards. We ate, sorted out business, then retired to the bar to check out the local fauna. Karl hooked up with someone straightaway, a pretty brunette with enormous tits. Dmitri went for her friend, who was a little plain for my taste. Dmitri was a fairly unfortunate looking man, with a large nose and a weak chin, so wasn't generally quite as picky as me. I decided to give Amy a call.

I sent a car to pick her up, and bring her back to my penthouse. I said my goodbyes, and left them to it. I'd barely got back when Amy was brought up. Within half an hour she was naked and in my sex swing, being pounded into ecstasy. This time, even with the lights down low, I just couldn't pretend she was someone else, and it took me ages to come. At one point I nearly gave up, figuring I'd be better off having a wank. *What on earth is wrong with me?* In the end, I got there by closing my eyes, and visualising Elle in her place.

"I'll organise a car for you while you dress," I said to Amy. Her face fell.

"Is that it? You just brought me here for a fuck, and now you're dismissing me?" She challenged. *Well, yes.*

"I'm sorry, but I have calls coming in overnight, so it's better that Roger takes you home. Where did you say you live?" *The old 'overnight call' excuse always works.*

"Battersea. Why do you have calls on a Friday night?"

"Business. It's a 24 hour type of thing. I have calls through the night sometimes due to time differences. It's still Friday morning in America you know."

"Oh you poor thing. It's not good for you to work so hard." She looked sympathetic.

"I know. I'm used to it though." I pulled out my phone and called Roger. I put on a robe and watched her get dressed. Idly, I wondered if Elle's body would resemble hers. Elle would be a little smaller waisted, I mused.

With my rather disgruntled booty call safely dispatched, I showered again, wanting to get her smell off me. The fact that I hadn't really enjoyed the sex, and my skin had crawled a little at her touch, disquieted me. I considered myself an intensely sexual man, and had always enjoyed plenty of variety in my sex life. Now I was feeling a bit ashamed of myself, and just a little grubby.

Dinner at Oscars was always an extremely refined affair. He always served the most exquisite food and wine. Having seen his cellars, I'd immediately started learning about fine vintages, simply so that I wouldn't feel like such a philistine around him. I couldn't muster up the enthusiasm to build a huge cellar though.

I was intensely jealous of his castle. There, I've said it, I was green with bloody envy at its massive, grand, proportions. Its collections of artworks provoked an almost covetous rage within me that I felt ashamed of. I could afford works of art and beautiful things, but didn't have enough confidence in my own taste to spend millions on a painting. Oscar's collections had been built over generations of well educated, wealthy family members. He appeared to barely notice the extreme luxury he lived in, and only used a small portion of the castle as an 'apartment'. In my mind, it was totally wasted on him.

"So, what are you working on at the moment?" He asked me.

"Upgrading the Russian systems to carry 4G, and extending our reach across Africa mainly. There's a vast, untapped market there, and we beat Vodafone to it."

"How come?" He frowned.

"We bribed all the village leaders, as well as the politicians. No other company dares set foot on half the continent. We got there first, and tied it all up. Tricky fuckers to do business with." *Yeah, we bribed them with buttons, then put the fear of fucking god into them if they so much as spoke to another phone company. Suckers.*

"Hmm. Agreed. We issue the money supply to most of the African countries. Terribly corrupt. Most of it sits in our Swiss arm in numbered accounts. Don't listen for one moment when they tell you they're poverty stricken. Some of those African dictators are nearly as wealthy as you."

This was part of my problem with Oscar, he knew pretty much how much money I had. Compared to the other Oligarchs, I was up there with the wealthiest. In front of Oscar Golding, I felt like the poor relation.

"So have you seen any more of our favourite lawyer?" I asked, partly to change the subject, and partly because I'd been dying to ask all evening.

"I've seen every bit of our favourite lawyer. Finally got it together with her. Hard work groveling and trailing around after her, but well worth it." *WHAT? Why Elle, why?*

"You groveled? After a woman? Have you gone mad?" I sneered.

Oscar grinned, and looked a little embarrassed. "Yeah, she's no pushover in any way, but, well, I won my friend."

"How come she's not here then?" I demanded.

"She had something planned for tonight with her flatmate. She's coming next weekend. I've got a shooting party going on, friends over, that type of thing."

"Does your mother know you have a girlfriend?" Oscars mother was legendary for being brutally nasty to the women he'd brought to Conniscliffe. She'd even been quite unpleasant to me, called me Mr Podunky, and I didn't even fancy her precious boy.

He shook his head and pulled a face. "I won't introduce her as my girlfriend, better to say she's a friend. She's way too lower class for me to consider partnering permanently. I do quite like her though."

I felt a murderous rage rise inside me. Indignation on Elle's behalf burned like a furnace, shocking me with its intensity. She was way too good for this spoiled mummy's boy, yet by sheer virtue of an accident of birth, he'd deemed her unworthy, despite her intelligence and polished beauty. I resolved to stay close to her, knowing that at some point she'd need my help. He was going to really hurt her.

"I wouldn't call her lower class. She's got a degree in law from Cambridge University. Hardly 'common' is she?" I snapped.

"True, but she works for a living, has no title, and I have no idea about her family." He said, looking amused at my defence of her.

"Call her middle class then, but not lower class." I actually hurt for her. I was pleased that Oscar didn't know the truth of her background, as he'd be treating her like a servant girl.

"Ok, ok, I'll refer to her as a young professional if you prefer. She's nice for a little affair, but not really wife material. Is that better?" *No, not really.*

I changed the subject to the building repairs that Oscar was doing to the castle. I needed to get off the subject of Elle Reynolds before I felt compelled to punch Oscar for being such a wanker.

Monday afternoon I had the meeting with the CEO of Vodafone to hammer out the heads of agreement, which concluded quickly, and without issue. The sale contract drafted by my legal department would be sent over and signed without delay. A good result. I also got to see Elle for a full hour, which pleased me enormously. I wished that she'd come and work for me. She seemed so precise and quick witted.

"One day, it would be nice to be on the same side," I said to her, smiling my best, most dazzling smile.

"Engage us as your lawyers then," she shot back as quick as a flash. *That's actually a brilliant idea.*

The lawyer that had headed up my in house legal team had just retired, and with over seventy separate companies in our stable, I either had to recruit more lawyers or use a legal firm. I used Pearson Hardwick for my personal affairs, mainly my will and a couple of property purchases, so it wasn't a huge stretch to engage them for some of the company work as well. I generally preferred to surround myself with other Russian speakers, but my English was pretty perfect, so I figured it wouldn't matter.

Back in my office, I barked at Galina to find out who was the managing partner in charge of corporate, and to get him on the phone for me.

"Mr Porenski, how nice to hear from you. What can I do for you?" Said Mr Carey, the top man in Elle's department.

"I'm looking for a legal firm to take over some of my corporate work, contracts, that sort of thing. It's getting too much for my in house lawyers, and I've been particularly impressed by one of your staff."

"Good to hear. Well, we can certainly assist you with any work that needs doing."

"Excellent. There is rather a lot of it, I'm looking at some restructuring work, some acquisition projects, as well as patents and litigation. I would need some assurances and assistance from you before I proceed, as I'm sure you realise, this would be a large amount of work." *I bet he's salivating...*

We arranged to meet the following morning to discuss my requirements. I figured it would be a great way of keeping her close, and keeping her safe from Golding.

I worked late that evening, compiling a list of requirements for my meeting the following morning. Under the guise of my requirement for complete confidentiality, I hoped to get Elle an executive office and her own assistant. Far nicer for her than the cubby hole she had to share with three others. I decided to let them handle the purchase of Derwent engineering for me. It was a medium size factory in Sussex which made the heavy duty cabling I currently used by the mile. By owning the company, I'd get a huge cost saving, and by teaming it with the company building the new coatings, I'd make a killing worldwide. *Simple.*

Next morning I met with Mr Carey and Mr Jones. I outlined my requirements and spending projection for the year, and waited expectantly. As I'd envisaged, they agreed immediately to all of my wishes, welcomed me as a client, and told me they would have everything organised that day.

I bounced into my office, and shocked Galina by smiling at her, and thanking her for my coffee. I called Paul Lassiter, a head hunter I used, and arranged to meet him for lunch.

Over Japanese, I told him I wouldn't need him to search for a head of legal anymore, and that I'd found an alternative solution. He smiled when I told him what it was.

"So this young lady convinced you to engage her company? How much are you projecting to spend with them?" He asked.

"A few million or so."

He whistled, "what's so special about her that's made you do a complete turnaround?"

She reminds me of Irina. "She can keep up with me on figures. Not many people can do that Paul."

"True. She must be quite something for you to be impressed. Can't you entice her to work for you?"

I shook my head. "She's ambitious, I doubt if she'd want the confines of a legal department. She made it to the most prestigious department of the top law firm in London. She wouldn't want to give that up to run a company legal office."

Paul gave me a hard stare, and frowned. "So she's quick with numbers. Is that the only reason?" *Oh you know me so well.*

I smiled, "of course."

"Why don't you just ask her out?" *Am I that bloody obvious?*

"She said no. Besides, she's seeing Golding. He got to her first." I scowled at the thought.

"I see. I shall have to make sure that I meet this miss..?"

"Reynolds, Elle Reynolds."

"And find out what's got you in such a tizzy."

"A tizzy? Who uses words like that these days?"

"An apt description I think. I'm quite intrigued by this young lady myself if both Golding and yourself are so taken by her. I need to find out what all the fuss is about."

"Don't you dare.. If I find out you've so much as sniffed in her direction...." *Damn, he's staring at me again.*

"Interesting."

Back in my office after lunch, I dealt with some issues regarding the Derwent factory purchase, as my legal team had discovered an anomaly with the directors loan accounts. In short, the figures they'd declared to me didn't match the ones they filed on their last end of year accounts. Either they'd been paid back, or they were attempting to conceal something, and hoping I wouldn't notice. I decided not to tell Elle, but wait and see whether or not she'd spot it.

A flunky arrived with a sheaf of NDA's, signed by the hand-picked team at Pearson Hardwick who'd be dealing with my account, and a sheet detailing Ms Reynolds contact details. I decided to give her a call. She sounded quite composed on the phone, confirming that she had a nice new office, and thanking me for insisting on it. I liked her good manners. We arranged to meet for breakfast first thing the next morning, when I'd give her the task regarding the factory. When I put the phone down, I was beaming.

My final task that day was to call the chairman of the board at Derwent, and arrange for a meeting at my offices for four o'clock the next day, ostensibly to sign the contracts and complete the purchase. He agreed a little too readily, probably thinking I hadn't spotted the accounting anomaly.

Like a silly schoolboy, I stayed in that evening, as I wanted an early night, ready to see her the following morning. I sprung out of bed, did a little exercise, and took a long, careful shower before dressing in a new suit and shirt. Satisfied that I looked my best, I handed the spaniels over to Mrs Watton, and got into the waiting Bentley.

I spotted her the moment I walked into Smollenskis. She looked breathtaking in a little skirt and blouse, and her hair looked as though it had been washed only an hour before. She shone with vitality. She chose her breakfast, and allowed me to order for her. I outlined the task I had for her, namely the Derwent contract. I explained all the terms of sale that I wanted, and watched as she wrote her notes in neat handwriting.

Oscar must have told her about the background check I'd ordered on her, because she quizzed me on it, trying to find out exactly how much I knew. I decided to be honest with her, and confessed that I knew about her background. Seeing her face fall, I told her that I too had come from a poor background, and it was nothing to be ashamed of. It broke my heart when she asked me not to tell anyone what I knew, and that she'd had to conceal it to get her job.

She seemed quite shocked that I'd also started out poor, telling me she thought I was very urbane. That pleased me a lot, and put me in a good mood for the rest of the day. *She's not immune to me then.*

I waited in my office with baited breath when the contract was delivered. Within half an hour she'd spotted the accounting anomaly. I let out a sigh of relief. She'd passed the first test. Fifteen minutes later, she called again to tell me they'd uncovered an issue with the property itself. It was only a lease, which was ending next month, and the freehold was owned by a separate company, with two of Derwent's directors owning it. *Why the hell hadn't my own team picked that one up?* An email containing the documents popped onto my screen as she was telling me. I recalculated, and called her back, explaining that the other directors were coming for a meeting.

When everyone was assembled in the conference room, I let the directors have it, making them squirm. I even caught a couple looking nervously at Roger and Nico, as if they were going to attack at any moment. In the end I asked for the whole factory, rather than the 70% I was originally getting, plus freehold for a slightly lower price than agreed initially, as the directors had already helped themselves to three quarters of a million quid.

Afterwards, Elle and her boss sat at my computer, and quickly amended the contract, while I listened in on what was happening in the conference room.

"Did you really think they wouldn't spot that loan account? This is all your doing, and I hope he sacks you for it."

"He could sack all of us, if he knew we all had a hand in it."

"No, he needs us, he'll sack George, Barry and Julian, the rest of us will be safe. He won't want to take it over with no directors at all in place."

"Yeah, I'm sure John's right. I think just you three will get the push, and it really is your own fault. He's not as stupid as he looks." *Cheeky bastard.*

"That's not fair, you all had a share of it, didn't hear anyone objecting at the time."

Elle finished re typing the contract, and handed copies to Galina to take in. I grinned at her, and carried on listening.

"Well, I suppose we don't have a choice. We need to offload before it goes tits up, and quite frankly, I don't give a shit if those three get the push."

"Yeah, me too. As long as I get my salary, my missus won't moan too much, although she was looking forward to us having a bit extra every month."

"Julian did tell us it was foolproof, and I guess he was wrong. Serves you right if you get the push, just don't drag the rest of us into it."

"So are we all in agreement? We sign this one, throw those three wankers out, and let the Ruskie bail us out?"

"Yeah" "Agreed" "I think so."

I pulled out my earpiece. "I think they're ready for us." Two minutes later, Galina came to call us in. All contracts were signed, and I fired the board, before sweeping out. Nico knew the drill, and sent security teams with the directors to clear them out, change the locks, and let Sergei, my most trusted takeover manager, have a look around. I ordered a bottle of Champagne to toast Elle's first success.

When she'd gone, I poured Lewis, her boss, another glass of champagne. "She's really rather impressive, isn't she? Tell me, is there a policy in place that would prevent me taking her out for dinner?"

"No, not as such. Clearly we have to protect our staff from being coerced by their clients, but if it was her own choice, then it's none of our business what she does in her own time, as long as there's no detrimental effect on her work or reputation."

"Good to know."

"I do happen to know that she's currently seeing Lord Golding though."

"Yes I'm aware of that."

He finished his champagne and left, and I went back to the penthouse. I'd not long been in when Sergei called. "Boss, this is appalling. The records are all paper based, and a complete mess, the place is in uproar, and right now, I can't see how we can organise payroll at the end of the month. It's all done in fucking ledgers. You're gonna freak out when you see it. It'll take weeks to sort out, and apparently some mad old woman deals with it, and won't let anyone touch it. We had to actually break into her office to even see it."

I groaned. "Ok, get IT in overnight, and have them set up our Gravidlax system. I'll work on it tomorrow to get it sorted. Are there contracts of employment in place?"

"Nope, not that I can see. It's a total fucking mess. I'll send you a video. Have to be over 3G though, as they haven't even got fucking WIFI. Can you believe it?"

"Tell IT we need WIFI there too then. No wonder the company's in shit state. I'll get a legal team down there as soon as poss to sort it out."

I sat and watched the clip of film showing the mess that was the HR department. With over a thousand staff to sort out, and only three weeks till payday, it would be a Herculean task to get it sorted. I called my HR director, "How long will it take to process an employee, enter their details and sort their contract?"

"Hello Ivan, about half an hour per employee usually, longer if it's more complicated. Why?"

I told him what had been discovered, and what I planned to do about it, then asked him to call our IT guys and get them to install around fifteen computers, all linked. As I put the phone down, I glanced at the clock. It was one in the morning. I quickly emailed Elle to meet me at Smollenskis first thing, and went to bed.

She appeared quite sanguine the next morning when I outlined the task I had for her. She made copious notes, asked some questions, and told me she'd get on it straightaway. With Ranenkiov and Elle dealing with it, I relaxed a little. I'd invited her to use my house the following week, rather than stay at a hotel. The thought of her sleeping in my guest bed kind of excited me, although I'd have to remember to lock up my study. I didn't want her looking through my computer, and seeing all the shrink sessions I did online. I'd carried on with the sessions as part of my recovery. I preferred sessions by email, as I'd found it uncomfortable to talk face to face with a therapist, particularly about my parents, which may have been a Russian thing, or a male thing, but it's how it was.

I also made the decision to say goodbye to Penny. She kept trying to call me, and was really starting to irritate, so I made arrangements to take her shopping on Saturday afternoon, and say goodbye on Saturday night. It would take my mind off Elle being at that damned castle with wanker Golding.

I'd arranged for Roger to drive Elle, and look after her as well. I didn't anticipate there being any problems, but I felt happier that she had some security, and I effectively had my eyes on her at all times.

She made a start the next morning, getting there bright and early. From the reports I had back from Roger, the mad old woman was giving her a hard time, and Elle had made the old bag cry. I loved getting little updates on her, although my stomach sank when Roger text me to say that Golding had picked her up. He dropped her suitcase off at my house for Mrs Ballard to sort out, which was also quite exciting. When my housekeeper had left, I checked out her clothes, looked at her knickers, and examined her bras. I truly was regressing into stupid schoolboy territory.

Chapter 3

Penny really irritated me all of Saturday afternoon. I treated her to some new outfits, a handbag, and a few pairs of shoes. Not much really, yet she seemed pathetically grateful. I took her out for dinner afterwards, then back to Sussex for the big goodbye.

Only I couldn't seem to shake her off. She begged, pleaded, shouted and swore at me. By one in the morning, I was losing patience, and was just about to call Roger to remove her and take her home, when he called me with the news that Elle was lost and wandering the lanes, having walked out of Conniscliffe.

Roger dispatched Penny with no further argument, and I set off to get Elle, waving off Nico after he'd got a fix on her mobile. Her face fell when she saw it was me in the car instead of Roger.

"Are you alright?" I asked, concerned by her reaction.

"Ivan? What are you doing here? I thought Roger was coming to get me," she said, looking embarrassed that I'd arrived instead.

"He told my bodyguard that you called, and he needed a GPS pinpoint, so I decided to come and get you, and reassure myself that you were in one piece. Jump in." She threw her bag on the back seat, and got in the passenger side. "What did Oscar do to make you walk out in the middle of the night?"

"Nothing that I wish to divulge. Suffice to say I won't be seeing, or speaking to Oscar, or his friends, ever again." My stomach leapt.

I paused, before replying; "I knew something would happen. He lives in a different world from the rest of us, with different rules. You are far too good for him."

We drove along in silence, before she spoke, "they weren't horrible to me, well his mother was at first, but we got over that. I just really want to go home, and forget about it all. I can get a taxi if you know a cab firm round here."

"Elle, it's nearly two in the morning, stay at mine tonight, I promise you'll be safe. You can meet my girls, sleep it off, and if you want to go home in the morning, Roger will take you. Women shouldn't travel alone in taxis at night, it's not safe."

She didn't reply, and seemed very quiet all the way back to the house. I introduced her to Bella and Tania, and watched as she made a fuss of them. I sat her in the kitchen and made her a cup of tea."You look like you just got out of bed," I said, seeing her wild hair.

"That's because I have. I was fast asleep about two hours ago. I'm really sorry about disturbing your Saturday night, I didn't think Roger would tell you." She stared into her tea, looking embarrassed about needing to be rescued.

"What exactly would you have done if I hadn't been around?"

"I don't know, walked probably, or called my flatmate in the states to see if he could google a cab."

"In Sussex in the middle of the night?"

"Well, I don't know. I'm a city girl. I'm not used to there being no street names, and no passing taxis. I would have carried on walking northeast until I got to civilization." She began to get annoyed. "I can call a cab now if you would prefer me to go," she snapped.

"Don't be silly. Mrs Ballard, my housekeeper, already has the guest room ready for you, and your clothes hung up. Roger's busy driving my date home, so I'm afraid I don't even have a spare chauffeur to lend you."

"You were on a date? I'm so sorry for interrupting you." I saw her blush.

"Nobody of consequence. If I'm truthful, I was pleased to have an excuse to shake her off. Now, shall I show you to your room? You look exhausted." I stood up, and placed our cups in the sink. I led her upstairs, and stopped at the guest room door, pushed it open, and gestured for her to go in.

She looked around the room. "Do you think you'll make it up with Oscar?" I needed to know.

She shook her head, "no, I don't want to ever speak to him again."

I didn't really know what to say, so I left her to it, pulling the door to behind me. Back in my own room, I stripped off, and was about to get into bed, when I realised that the girls weren't with me. I padded down the hall to look for them. I saw straightaway that her bedroom door was dog-tummy width open, and stood silently, listening as she sobbed her heart out.

I was at a total loss. I wanted to go in there, and wipe her tears away, but stopped myself, reasoning that she was crying for another man, and my presence might not be welcome. I slipped back to my own room, and went to bed. That night I dreamt of Irina and Russia for the first time in years....

That day at school, there was huge amounts of chatter about the coming strike. Almost everyone's parents worked in the factory, so it was big news. I was walking into the lunch hall, when I was stopped by Irina, who I had a bit of a crush on.

"Hey Ivan, I hear your dad's the new union leader. My dad told us he was going to stand up to the factory owner, and force him to pay everyone. Is that true?" It was the first time she'd really spoken to me, and I was a little tongue tied. She flicked her long, fair hair, and looked at me expectantly.

"Erm, yeah. They all had a meeting last night." Even in a worn, frequently mended school-dress, and shabby shoes, she looked amazing. I could feel the blush rise up my neck.

"Did you go to it?" she asked. I wished I had, as most boys my age would accompany their fathers to such things, have a little vodka, and join in with the men. I'd been quite content to stay home with my mum, and do my homework. It wouldn't sound

terribly cool to admit that. I just mumbled something, and turned to leave.

"Come out this evening? We're all meeting by the riverbank." She smiled as she said it. I didn't usually join the others when they just hung out, as I preferred to read, and concentrate on my schoolwork. It was my exam year, and I was determined to do well. The other girls all liked me, but seemed to look so unhealthy that it was off-putting. I couldn't bring myself to kiss anyone with a sore on their mouth, or lice in their hair. Irina had clear skin, and shiny hair.

"Maybe," I replied. I'd wait and see if I had homework first before committing to anything. Just hanging out wasn't productive, and while fun, wouldn't help prevent a life shoveling chemicals.

After school, I did my homework at the table during dinner, so that I could go out afterwards, but was drawn into the conversation between my mum and dad. "We were told we could be paid tomorrow if we all agree to a pay cut of five hundred roubles a year," my dad told mum, looking grim, "with prices rising as quickly as they are, there's no way we can agree to that."

"There'd be nothing to stop him cutting pay again if we agreed to this," counseled mum, "we have to say a collective 'no', people are poor enough as it is. The letter came today saying the rent is going up. It would barely leave enough money to eat, let alone pay for heating and clothes. If anything, wages should increase."

"The other men said the same. He only has two more days, and he won't have a working factory, so he should take heed of the worker's voices."

"Kaparov refused to even see me today, his assistant said he was busy, although I could see into his office, and he was only on the phone. I'll try again tomorrow." Mum said, slicing the cheap black bread thinly, and dividing it between dad and I.

I finished my homework, and packed my books into my bag. "I'm going out for a while," I said.

"Where to?" Mum demanded.

"Just by the river. Irina invited me."

"She's the pretty one that you like, isn't she?" Dad said, winking at me.

"Yeah, she's alright," I admitted, feeling a bit embarrassed. "Well, you be careful son, I don't want you having to get married at sixteen," he replied. I shuddered at the thought. As pretty as Irina was, the idea of tying myself to the same person, the same home, and the same job, for my entire life at age sixteen, was horrifying, even though it was probably my reality. I'd been given a packet of condoms at the health centre, so I slipped one in my pocket, just in case, and then felt a little stupid for being so optimistic.

I quickly brushed my teeth at the kitchen sink, and went out onto the street. The evenings were light until quite late, so there were lots of people out and about. I hurried down the main road, and down the alley between two grey tenement blocks to the scrubland behind. Hidden behind a hill was a secluded area with a small brook running through it, away from the prying eyes of our parents. It was the local hangout for the teenagers in the area.

"Hey Ivan! Your mama let you out?" A male voice called out.

"Andrei! My mama always lets me out, but it's my exam year, I have to put the work in."

"I don't know why you bother. It'll be the factory for you, along with the rest of us. Might as well have a good time and enjoy yourself."

I sat down with them. Irina wasn't there yet, so I chatted with the others, mainly about the impending strike, and their parents attitudes to the requested pay cut. It seemed as though everyone was indignant, and ready to refuse. We all believed that the businessman would have no option but to pay up. One of the boys produced a tiny bottle of cheap vodka that he'd stolen from his dad. We all took a sip.

Irina arrived about half an hour later, arm in arm with her best friend Sofia. They giggled when they saw me, then sat down, with Irina sat beside me. She looked lovely in a pink top and skirt. Her mother was a seamstress, and had often made clothes for the neighbours during better times. Irina had always been the best dressed girl in the village. Her hair shone with gold glints in the evening sun. I was transfixed.

"Hi Ivan. Don't often see you over here," she said softly, so that the others, who were laughing loudly at a joke, couldn't overhear us.

"No, well, it's exams soon, and I want to do well," I explained, "which subjects are you doing?"

She laughed, "not many, not much point is there? I learnt to sew, my mother taught me, and I can read and write, I can't see the need for much else. I just want to marry and have a family."

"Is that all?" I asked, curious as to why she didn't have any other ambitions.

"Well, yes. I'd like a flat in your block, as they have the biggest rooms. Your parents were so lucky to be housed there." Lucky? I wouldn't call us that.

For the next couple of hours, we all chatted, laughed, and Irina and I flirted shamelessly. Inside, I was puzzled as to why my father becoming the leader of the trade union should suddenly make Irina aware that I existed, but I didn't question her. I was simply grateful that she'd noticed me.

As the others began to leave, I offered to walk her home. Andrei jeered at me, commenting that Irina shouldn't trust me, but she placed her soft little hand in mine, and we began to walk. She seemed happy to walk the long way back to the flats, and we meandered slowly through the scrub that covered the wasteland.

"You're very good-looking," she said, "how come you don't have a girlfriend?"

I shrugged. "I don't know. There's not many girls at school that I find appealing I suppose. You're very pretty though." She glanced up at me, and smiled a shy smile. Eventually, we reached the block where she lived. We stood at the door for a while, while I plucked up the courage to kiss her goodnight. I think she must have gotten fed up with waiting, as she leaned forward, and asked me if I was going to kiss her.

I bent down to her upturned face, and our lips met. I pressed mine to hers, softly at first, until her mouth opened slightly to let me in. Her tongue felt warm and gentle as it grazed mine in an erotic dance. I instantly became aware of my erection, and tried to keep my body away from hers, in case she felt it.

Her hands reached up to caress my shoulders, running over the muscles, and sending a little shiver down my spine. I pulled away slightly to look at her face, and stroke the silky skin of her cheek. "You are so pretty, you know that don't you?" I told her. She shook her head and smiled. "Meet me tomorrow evening?" I asked.

"I'd like that. Down at the river?"

"About six?" She nodded, and I kissed her again, before pulling away, and turning to walk the short distance to my own block, wondering how I'd get through school the next day without daydreaming about her.

Mum and dad were watching the tiny TV when I got in. Our bigger, better television set had gone back to the rental shop the previous month, and if things didn't improve, it was only a matter of time before the little one got sold.

"Nice evening?" Mum asked.

"Yeah, fine," I said, rather abruptly. I didn't want to tell her about my kiss.

The following evening, I met Irina again down at the riverbank. We chatted with the others for a while, before I summoned up the courage to ask her to go for a walk with me. We meandered through the scrub for a while, talking about *nothing in particular. When I was sure we couldn't be seen, I pulled her close for a kiss. I stroked her tongue softly with mine, pressing firmly, as I'd seen the movie stars do on TV. Eventually, we lay down on the grass, and I kissed her a bit more, slyly moving my hand to get a feel of her breast. She didn't seem to mind, so I fondled her a little more firmly, before sliding my hand under her top to feel her properly. It felt amazing, all warm and soft, with a hard little nub at the top. She wriggled slightly.*

"Ivan, have you ever made love to a girl before?" She asked. Instantly I was worried that I'd done something wrong.

"No, have you done it with a boy before?" She shook her head.

"No, but I want to." My stomach leapt. This was it! I slipped my hand down between her legs, thankful that she was wearing a skirt. I pressed my fingers under her knickers, pushing them to one side, and slipped a finger into her. She felt warm and wet. I knew from listening to the other boys that this meant that she was ready and willing.

"Have you got a johnny?" She whispered. I fumbled around in my pocket, taking out the foil packet and opening it carefully. I took a deep breath and undid my trousers, sliding them off one leg so that I had freedom of movement. She looked a little scared when she saw my dick for the first time.

With shaking hands, I unrolled the johnny over my cock, praying that it wouldn't break. When it was on, I pulled down her knickers, and settled myself between her legs. I nudged into her slowly, scared of hurting her. She inhaled sharply as I pushed in the final inch. "Is that ok?" I asked, concerned, despite my excitement.

"Yes, I'm ok," she said softly. I began to move, managing exactly four thrusts before I lost control and came, shuddering as my body twitched and pulsed. I kissed her with gratitude, thrilled that I had become a man, and experienced my first fuck. I wanted to do it again almost immediately, but only had one

condom with me. I pulled out of her, and took off the rubber, throwing it into a patch of grass.

My dream woke me up. It was still dark outside, and I rolled over to look at the time. It was 4am. I strained my ears to hear if Elle was still crying, but the house was silent. My erection was straining, and would keep me awake, so I had a quick wank before rolling over and going back to sleep.

I woke early the next morning, strangely excited about spending a Sunday with Elle. I hoped that she didn't insist on returning to London for the day. I made us all some breakfast, then did her a coffee, and took it up to her, pretending to shield my eyes in case she was in the nude. She looked beautiful, all mussed up and sleepy. I noted that the girls had slept in with her all night, and looked quite comfortable.

"Come on lazy girls, we're wasting the day," I announced. I told her that her breakfast was ready, and waiting for her downstairs.

She seemed fascinated as I fed the girls their morning sausages, and appeared surprised that I'd made her breakfast. I explained that Sundays were for my girls, and was my day off from staff, apart from security. I was delighted when she agreed to stay for the day.

I loved showing her the woods, watching her relax and interact with the dogs. Even washing the stinky fox poo off them afterwards was fun, because it was with her. I was a little shocked that Oscar hadn't called her to make sure she was alright. I added 'callous bastard' onto my list of his failings.

I cursed myself for falling asleep that afternoon while watching a film, but the late night caught up with me, and I felt so relaxed that I drifted off. When I woke with a start, she was sitting watching telly, completely unfazed by the girls and I having a nap in the afternoon.

Rather sneakily, I suggested a swim while it was still warm. Truth was, I was dying to see her in a swimsuit. She came down wrapped in a towel, as if she was ashamed of her figure. When she unwrapped herself, I nearly choked. She was a vision, long, slender legs, peachy arse, and a tiny little waist with the most perfect, perky tits. *Control yourself.*

She was also the fastest swimmer I'd ever seen. I wasn't bad, but she beat me easily, and made it look effortless. She was also super-bloody-fit, and was barely out of breath at the end of our race. To serve her right for beating me, I swam up underneath her, and launched her into the air, to come down with a big splash. Laughing, she dived under the surface, like a water baby, and grabbed my feet, causing me to flail around wildly to stop myself sinking.

She popped back up, pleased with herself, and laughing at my flailing. With her hair slicked back from her face, and not a scrap of makeup on, she looked....beautiful, a completely natural beauty that could rival Aphrodite herself. I stared at her, unable to drag my eyes away. "You are so beautiful, you know that don't you?" I told her.

"And you're very handsome," she replied.

"But?" I asked, thinking there had to be a 'but' coming.

"But nothing, you're handsome," she said, before stepping out of the pool.

The god of Russian perverts answered my prayer. The moment she stepped into the cool air, her nipples tightened, and stuck out through the flimsy material of her costume. My cock immediately sprang to life, and I couldn't help myself. I stared shamelessly. She looked mortified, and quickly wrapped her towel round herself, but I already had enough material for the wank bank.

"Are you getting out?" She asked. *Erm no, I have a stonking big hard on.*

"Not just yet, in a minute."

She smiled a rather knowing smile, and sashayed into the house. It took another five minutes for me to be able to get out of the pool. I went straight up to my shower, desperate to get a little relief.

I had to have two wanks, due to the image of her nipples burnt into my retina. The first one just made me even hornier than before. I wondered if I should make my approach, then dismissed the idea. I didn't want her walking out on me as well. I decided to bide my time, and pick my moment. She hadn't given me the come on, and, unlike most women who threw themselves at me, didn't give me any signals that my overtures would be welcomed.

I made us both a tray of snacks, which we shared with the greedy spaniels. I found her company surprisingly easy, normally spending a whole day with a woman was torture, but with her, it just left me craving more. Watching her sitting in her pink pyjamas engrossed in Top Gear, kind of warmed me inside.

Leaving for London the next morning made me feel bereft. I wouldn't see her again until Friday, although the little updates from Roger helped. I had a heavy week ahead, full of meetings, dinners and paperwork, so it was probably better for me to be able to completely concentrate.

I think I discussed, and recommended Ms Reynolds, and her firm to everyone I met with that week. I reasoned that if I couldn't have her, I could at least assist her professionally, and I did believe she was a truly outstanding lawyer. I was a little concerned when I received a text from Roger telling me that Lady Golding had turned up to see Elle. I called him back immediately to find out if he could listen in on their conversation, but he informed me that he'd tried, and couldn't hear what they were discussing. I was keeping away from Oscar, unsure if I'd be able to keep my opinions on his behaviour to myself. I was burning with curiosity as to what had actually happened on Saturday night, and it was clear that I wouldn't be able to get any information out of Elle. It was a shame really, as I would've loved to have something to hold over Goldings head, as he was holding enough over mine.

Apart from a boozy night out with the boys on the Wednesday, my week was all about work. I refused to answer calls from Penny or Amy, and had barely even bothered to listen to their whiny voicemails. I had my sights very firmly set on Miss Reynolds, and no other woman would do.

She called me on Friday morning to tell me that she'd uncovered a scam involving fake employees, convinced that the fraud had been perpetrated by the mad old woman who ran the personnel office. I was delighted to finally have an excuse to go down and see her, so I immediately jumped into the car, and made my way to Sussex.

I have a real hatred of being stolen from. Now this old lady hadn't exactly had the chance to steal from me, as I'd only just taken over. In fact she'd done me a favour by pushing the factory to the edge of bankruptcy, which had allowed me to buy it for thruppence. Even so, she had to be stopped, and punished for her wrongdoing.

As soon as she was challenged about some fake payroll, she cried, confessed, and pissed herself. My guards weren't even pointing Kalashnikovs at her, so I didn't understand why she was so scared. Even so, I wasn't entirely happy about Elle seeing me scare an old woman half to death. I guess I could have approached it slightly differently.

She said as much in the car on the way back to London. I'd decided to lay my cards on the table, and tell her that I wanted her, even tried to kiss her hand. I thought my standard line of 'I'll make you come so hard you'll forget your own name,' would make her all horny and pliable. Instead she snatched her hand away and told me 'no thanks'.

So instead of a long journey spent creating wonderful sexual tension with her, I ended up dealing with phone calls, while she stared moodily out of the window. After taking a call from Vlad, pestering me to discuss a deal with him, I was pretty annoyed as well. I dropped her off at home, and went into the West end to meet Vlad as he'd requested.

Chapter 4

Vladimir Meranov was an imposing man, a powerful Oligarch himself, he emanated cruelty and domination from his every pore. I wasn't scared of him, but I did treat him with respect. It was safer that way. We'd met after I'd joined the Russian Mafia, mainly for the purposes of self preservation, and because my English at that point hadn't been good enough to get a regular job.

It had been a little strange, I'd been taken to see him personally, and asked to join his personal staff. I'd been under the impression that it took years to be trusted enough to work directly with an Oligarch. I'd been concerned that it would affect my studies, I'd been learning English and accountancy at night school, but he'd encouraged me to continue, and altered some staff rotas to allow me the time off I needed. He also introduced me to his daughter, Dascha, the apple of his eye.

She was sweet sixteen, and extremely pretty, if a little spoilt. I was instantly dazzled by her looks and sophistication, and, encouraged by Vlad, began to date her. In hindsight, I should have questioned the situation, I mean, most men don't want a randy 19 year old anywhere near their daughter, but Vlad seemed delighted.

He'd taken me aside and told me that if I was going to look after his daughter properly, I'd need to be wealthy, and he would assist me. He gave me some seed money, took me to Russia, and between us, and his thugs, we blackmailed, terrified and schmoozed our way into taking over the whole of Russia's telecoms networks.

Riches had come at a price though, I was effectively tied to Dascha for as long as she wanted me. She was a sadistic bitch, and took delight in making my life a misery. As soon as I was in her father's pocket, she'd changed towards me, initially enjoying inflicting physical pain, then progressing onto emotional damage after I refused to sleep with her. It was only when she'd tried to kill Bella that I'd finally snapped and sent her back to her father.

Thankfully, he'd been fairly understanding, as my spaniels had been the puppies of Olga, his personal favourite. He took Dascha into his home, told her off, and I was off the hook. So when he called, asking to see me, I went along with armed guards. I hoped enough water had passed under the bridge that he wouldn't bear a grudge, but Vlad was a classic psychopath, and having witnessed him personally killing a man, I put nothing past him.

We met in a private room in Claridges. "Security outside," he barked at all our guards. I watched as they all trooped out. It was highly unusual. Thankfully I was wearing a gun under my jacket, and would be faster than Vlad if the need arose.

"Ivan, how lovely to see you my boy," he said, shaking my hand warmly.

"Vlad, you're looking well. Been keeping busy?" I replied, relaxing slightly. He didn't usually touch the men he was planning to kill, it was a quirk of his...

"Of course. I have a little venture I'd like your help with. It is of course completely confidential."

"Of course."

"It's regarding Dascha, she wants her own business, and at thirty years old, I feel that she has the maturity now to run a company."

"I see, do you have a company in mind?" *She's as useless as they come Vlad. Don't ask me to invest.*

"I do. She rather likes fashion, as you well know," *yeah, she spent enough of my money on it,* "but it's rather a closed club. I'd like to buy her a fashion magazine to run. I approached her favourite, but they refused to sell to me. I had a bit of a run in a few years ago with a member of the family that currently own it, so they won't deal with me. I'd like you to buy it on my behalf."

"That's all well and good Vlad, but I don't want a magazine, and how would I give it to Dascha?"

"Oh that's easy, buy it, get back together with her, then give it to her as a parting gift."

"No way Vlad, I'm not getting back with her under any circumstances. Sorry, you'll have to get someone else to front it."

Vlad looked surprised, "Ivan, I don't see the problem. I don't expect you to actually get together again with her, and it's not as though you have a girlfriend to upset is it?" I shook my head. "Golding will take care of the bank transfers secretly in Switzerland, so nobody will know about our agreement apart from him, and we both know how discreet he is."

"Vlad, I don't want to front this for you. I'm sorry." *I don't want Elle seeing me have anything to do with Dascha.*

"Oh Ivan, when will you learn? I'll be in touch..." He left the room, leaving me wondering exactly how he planned to force me into his stupid scheme.

I spent the whole weekend brooding about my meeting with Vlad. I hoped to god he'd find someone else, and leave me alone. The only good news I had that weekend was an email telling me that a pair of wide boys who had started up a business comms company years back, were in a cash flow crisis, and were prepared to take an investment from me, which would give me a great excuse to call Elle, and arrange to take her out to dinner to discuss the negotiation.

I ended up having to email my shrink, the meeting with Vlad had unnerved me, and I hadn't been able to sleep afterwards. I couldn't tell him truthfully what had upset me so much, so I just called it a business deal.

From: Ivan Porenski
To: Carl Verve
Date:25th May 2013

Subject: Can't sleep

Carl

Can you help? I'm insomniac again, worried about a deal, tried writing stuff down as you suggested, but it's not helping.

Regards

Ivan

From: Carl Verve
To: Ivan Porenski
Date:25th May 2013
Subject: Coping strategies

Ivan

Perhaps you could give me a little more information. For example, why is this deal so important to you, and why is it playing on your mind? Another thing to consider is; what would happen if it fell through? Would it impact on other areas of your life?

Kind regards

Carl

From: Ivan Porenski
To: Carl Verve
Date:25th May 2013
Subject: deal

The thing is, it's a deal I've been asked to do for someone else. I don't want to do it, not because it's illegal or immoral, it just involves me having to see the poison ex. There's someone I want to get together with, and I couldn't see her being too impressed at me meeting up with the ex, even if it was just business. She's too clever for me to just pull the wool over her eyes, and I'm scared to risk that her opinion of me would sink if she knew the type of people I had in my past. She only knows me as a legit businessman.

Ivan

From: Carl Verve
To: Ivan Porenski
Date:25th May 2013
Subject: Concealment

Ivan

It sounds as if this lady's opinion of you is a primary driver? Would it not be better to be open and honest with her, especially if you hope to build a relationship with her? You wouldn't be able to conceal your past involvement with organised crime forever, and if she was aware of your internal struggles with your past, she may well be sympathetic. I would go so far as to suggest that your obsessive need for secrecy from someone you are in love with is probably the cause of your distress.

Carl

From: Ivan Porenski
To: Carl Verve
Date:25th May 2013
Subject: sweeping statements

Carl

I'm not in love with her, I've not even slept with her, and on Friday when I told her that I wanted her, she said no, and told me that I scared her. She's my lawyer, so I don't think confessing that I used to be a thug would be an option.

I will be seeing her this week as we have another deal we're working on. By the way Carl, she's a superb lawyer, if any of your CEO clients need a good corporate. Works for Pearson Hardwick, names Elle.

Ivan

From: Carl Verve
To: Ivan Porenski
Date:25th May 2013
Subject: Now we're getting to the truth

Ivan
So this lady said no to you? Have you ever been turned down before? Have you considered that this may be the cause of your insomnia, and you're just projecting onto the deal? I know we've talked at length about your relationship with your mother, and I'd be interested to find out if Elle resembles her in any way, or stirs up any feelings you have regarding your mother. As your lawyer, does she make you feel protected?
Carl

From: Ivan Porenski
To: Carl Verve
Date:25th May 2013
Subject: No!

Carl
She reminds me of Irina, not my mother. Irina, but with ambition and intelligence to go with the physical attributes and sweet character. In answer to your question, no I've never been turned down before, but Elle just split up with Oscar Golding (owner of Goldings bank) who followed her round like a puppy. Let's face it, I can't compete with him, and she wasn't impressed enough by all his money to stay with him.

She doesn't make me feel 'protected' as such. She's not a criminal lawyer or litigator, but I know she's as quick witted as me, and has picked up on things I've missed, so I suppose in some ways you're right, it feels like she has my back. I engaged her company purely to get her working for me.

Ivan

From: Carl Verve
To: Ivan Porenski
Date:25th May 2013
Subject: Elle

Ivan

I would go so far as to suggest that the cause of your insomnia is your intense feelings for this lady. The fact that your feelings aren't reciprocated at this moment is a very new experience for you. The fact that you are comparing her to your first love demonstrates that you have deeper feelings than is usual for you.

The fact that she split up with a rich man only tells a small piece of the story. If she's a lawyer, she probably earns a decent living, and there's the possibility that she embraces the feminist ideal of not needing a wealthy man in order to survive. You may want to consider that to her, your money may not hold the same importance that it does to you. Perhaps you could consider approaching her in a different way if she has already turned you down?

Carl

I sat back and thought about it, my main worries with Vlad's proposal were that Elle would see me with Dascha and assume that I'd gone back to her. Carl was right, the actual 'deal' part was inconsequential. I ran through some of our conversations from the previous weekend, one in particular popped into my mind. She'd told me that Oscar hadn't taken her shopping, and had only bought her some flowers and a few meals out, and that she wouldn't have asked him for anything else. I decided that I would take her shopping, spoil her a bit, show her what she'd missed out on.

With a plan in place, I switched off my computer, and went to bed.

I called her first thing on Monday to organise a meeting. Unfortunately, she had a packed week, and could barely fit me in

I took her to Claridges under the guise of running through the details she'd need to draw up a contract. It also gave me the opportunity to ask her to accompany me to a gala fundraiser at the weekend. I saw her hesitate, before she admitted she'd struggle to shop for a dress in time. I wasn't sure if that meant she didn't want to go, or that she couldn't afford one, so I offered to take her shopping after we finished on Wednesday. I saw her relax, before she smiled and said that she'd be delighted to accompany me. *She couldn't afford it*, I realised, and decided to lavish some new outfits on her, as well as the beauty treatments that she admitted she'd cancelled to accompany me to dinner.

After we'd eaten, we went back to the docklands to drop her off. She surprised me by inviting me in for coffee. Her apartment was lovely, really neat and clean, and surprisingly expensive. I found out that it belonged to her flatmate, and she just rented a room. She'd surprised me at dinner by asking me if I had a girlfriend, which I'd been able to answer truthfully that I didn't. I turned the tables and asked her if she was involved with her flatmate. She seemed to find that amusing for some reason, and shook her head. She reminded me of the background check that I'd had done.

"Surely your background check told you that the only man I've been involved with recently was Oscar, and you know what happened there. I can't possibly manage more than one man at a time, given that I work stupid hours."

"We only found three men, including Oscar. I'm assuming there are gaps in your relationship history on the check we did," I said.

"No, there's no gaps," she replied, blushing slightly. I was shocked, but didn't say anything. "Where do you live when you're in London?"

"Not far, I have an apartment in Saffron wharf. There's a garden square nearby for the girls. They prefer the woods, but it would have meant a long commute each day." I paused, trying to find the right words. "Elle, can I ask you something?"

"Sure, fire away."

"When I said we would have raw, wild sex, did that scare you off?"

"Yes, it did. It made me feel like a sex object, or a plaything. I'm not experienced enough yet to take on a sex god, and I don't want to sleep my way up the career ladder, I'm sorry." She stared into her coffee, not meeting my eyes. *I'm such a bloody idiot at times, why didn't I realise?*

"No, Elle, I'm sorry if I made you feel that way. Very Russian of me, sometimes I forget..."

"Forget what?"

"That you're not the sharp, assertive lawyer when you're off the clock," I said, "and that you are a lady. I bet I scared the life out of you."

"It sounded...rough. That's what turned me off. I'm really not into the whole 'pain is sexy' thing."

"I see." *Do you realise how perfect that makes you?*

"I'm gonna send you home now. I need my sleep." She said, clearing away our cups.

"Sleep well. I'll see you Wednesday afternoon. I'll make all the arrangements." I gently kissed her cheek, although I desperately wanted to kiss her properly. Mindful that I'd already scared her with my 'Russian' approach, I smiled at her, and left.

The next morning, I was in work quite early to read through some reports. When my email pinged, I was astonished to see that she'd already written up the contract ready for our meeting the following day. I called her to find out if she'd actually slept, and also to hear her voice. *Oh you have it bad,* I thought to myself, smiling at my own adolescent behaviour.

The next day, she came flying into the meeting room five minutes before our meeting, and within moments assumed the cool lawyer persona. It was fascinating to watch the transformation from warm and funny Elle, into the cold, calculating Ms Reynolds the lawyer. She sat quietly making notes as I negotiated with the directors of the comms company. I felt her nudge my foot, and saw her tip her notepad towards me.

120mil is 67% not 60% was written in her neat handwriting. *Fuck me, how did I miss that?*

I corrected the two men on their percentage figure, which they accepted so quickly that I knew straightaway they'd been trying to shark me. *Bastards, as soon as I'm in control you two are getting the boot.*

With the negotiation concluded, Elle and I went to my office to finish the contract. She sat at my desk, typing furiously, while I vented my anger at almost being caught out. *"Does she make you feel protected?"* Carl's words popped into my head, infuriating me. I crashed my hand down on the desk, making Elle jump, and lapsed into Russian; *"For fucks sake, why do I need a little woman to look after me, I'm meant to be a fucking Oligarch, the quickest, most ruthless of all businessmen, and this woman had to save me from a pair of wankers. Probably thinks I'm stupid now."*

"Would you mind letting me concentrate?" She said. I slumped into a chair, and sulked.

Sulking was a particular vice of mine. As a child, my mother used to tell me off for it, which only served to make me sulk even more. I once managed to make a particular sulk last for a whole fortnight, it's a gift I have.

We concluded the meeting, signed contracts, and money was paid across. I dispatched my takeover manager, and prepared to take Elle to Harrods. Instead she grabbed her handbag, and announced that she'd go shopping another day.

I was shocked, and asked her not to leave, explaining that I wasn't angry with her. She countered it by saying I wouldn't be much fun as I had 'a face on', which I thought was quite an amusing description of my sulk look. I told her that she deserved a treat as she'd saved me a shitload of money, and we set off for the West End.

Harrods is always a delightful shop. We were installed in a suite, and I sat on a sofa while Elle tried on various dresses. To me, they all seemed a little staid. I wanted her to have something truly glamorous. She had a superb figure, and the black, rather matronly dresses she was trying on just seemed to cover her up. I asked the sales assistant for something 'extraordinary', and she found two that fitted the bill. When Elle struggled to decide which one she wanted, I stepped in and told the saleswoman that I'd take both, but she needed shoes and a bag for each as well. When everything had been chosen, I whisked Elle up to the day wear department to spoil her a little more.

The minx teased me about her beauty treatments when I asked her which bikini wax she preferred, calling me a nosy bugger, and making me laugh with her announcement that she was having a vajazzle.

After we'd both finished our treatments, we grabbed some food, and I took Elle back to my penthouse. We ate outside on the terrace, as it was a beautiful evening, and the river looked particularly picturesque. I put some music on, doing my best to create a romantic atmosphere. Elle had seemed to relax and warm to me, so I figured it might be the right time to strike.

"So how did you get here from Russia?" She asked, as we sipped our wine. I decided to be truthful with her. I wasn't ashamed of West Biryulevo, so I told her the story.

"My parents were shot by henchmen working for a man we called 'the businessman', and his militia put the fear of god into the rest of the villagers. My only friends really were my then girlfriend, Irina, and her father, who'd been a friend of my dad's too. He helped me bury them, and told me to run for my life. To be honest, we were all slowly dying from the pollution and starvation, so I made the decision to run as far away as possible. I got to Moscow by stowing away on a lorry full of ore, wrapping myself in a tarpaulin to keep me safe from the chemicals. I managed to get onto a train to Poland from there, hiding in a luggage hold, and sneaking around to try and steal a little food once everyone was asleep.

From Poland to the UK was the worst bit, I was terrified I'd be found hiding inside a lorry, so didn't move for several days, even when we were at sea. I was discovered unconscious in the back when they unloaded it in a depot in London.

"Why did you choose London?" She asked, frowning at my story.

"I didn't, I just got on the first lorry that I could hide away on. Then I was too scared to come out. I don't know at what stage I passed out, but didn't wake up until I was in hospital. I was half starved, and dehydrated. When I woke up, I had no idea where I was, but people were so kind to me, that I figured that I was somewhere wonderful and civilised, so I stayed. So what about you? What made you so ashamed of your roots?"

She took a deep breath, and a sip of wine. "I don't have a father, well, not that I know of. My mum was a single parent, desperately poor, and prone to making poor choices. I remember hiding from the rent man, the debt collectors, and even the milkman. She just never seemed to be able to get it together. I remember feeling ashamed when I was selected for the grammar school, because the uniform was more expensive, and she worried that the neighbours would think I'd got 'above myself'. She was right, and the other kids teased me mercilessly, till I was scared to go out.

When I did well at school, she'd complain that I wouldn't find a husband, but on the rare occasions that I didn't get an 'A', she would be almost mocking me, saying I was getting too big for my boots. The only really practical thing she ever did was to sell her jewellery to buy my books for uni. That was a big deal, and a huge sacrifice. I think she was proud when I got my degree, but she never said much. I knew I had to leave, I had nothing in common with the people around me, but then I came here and felt like the poor relation, visiting the posh city people. I had to cover up an enormous amount to even get my training contract, applying from my Cambridge address rather than home, and re-routing the post."

She looked so sad that my heart broke for her. To be as intelligent as her, in an environment where it was looked down on, must have been extremely difficult. "Come here beautiful girl, and let me hold you," I said, taking her hand, and pulling her onto my lap. "Please let me kiss you," I begged. She closed her eyes and leaned into me, lightly grazing my lips, before I deepened the kiss, pushing gently into her mouth, my tongue meeting hers for the first time. I wanted to pick her up and carry her caveman style into my bedroom, but I didn't, I held back, worried about scaring her off by coming on too strong. She felt soft and compliant in my arms, and I ran my hands over her body, hoping for a surreptitious feel of her tits. When she told me that she needed to go home, I immediately thought I'd upset her. She smiled, and said that she wanted me too, but I'd have to wait until the weekend. When I thought about it afterwards, I came to the conclusion that it may have been the wrong time of the month, and she hadn't wanted to spell it out. With the promise of finally shagging her on Saturday, she went home, leaving me with blue balls.

After she left, I had to have another two wanks to get some relief. Afterwards, I sat in my study to plan Saturday night. I emailed Mrs Ballard, explaining that we would be spending the weekend in Sussex, and that she should provide enough food for the two of us, plus I requested that she stocked the guest room with Elle's favourite toiletries, and some clothes for her.

I'd toyed with the idea of booking a room at the Grosvener, to save having to drive, but dismissed that idea. Not only did I want to finally shag her brains out, I wanted another Sunday with her as well.

I also assigned Roger to her personal safety. Although I hadn't discussed it with her, it concerned me that she might be wandering around unprotected. I also loved the little updates that Roger sent me. I liked knowing where she was at all times, and knowing that she was safe.

To: Carl Verve

From: Ivan Porenski

Date: 2nd June 2013

Subject: It worked!

Carl

I thought I'd let you know, I took your advice and changed my approach, and guess what? She's agreed to be my date for a charity ball on Saturday night, and even better, she let me kiss her. I'm on a promise for a shag on Saturday night.

The trouble is that I can't bloody think straight, for some strange reason, I seem to have lost my ability to concentrate properly, which is highly unusual for me.

I'm a bit worried as I've been having some sexual issues lately, not being able to get 'finished' easily. It's happened with the last few women I've shagged. I've stopped taking the antidepressants for two months now. Could they have been the problem? I'm worried that I'll get all excited about shagging her, then not be able to come. I want our first time to be perfect.

Regards

Ivan

I sat back and waited for Carl to reply. He was usually fairly quick. Talking to a shrink wasn't something I'd ever thought I'd do, but after my breakdown it had been a necessity. I actually quite liked having someone to confide in, who I could tell the truth to. Since losing my mother, I'd had nobody. Dascha would have used any weakness against me, and my staff were just that, staff. Even the people I regarded as my friends were all in business themselves, so I was always careful to present my 'persona'. Even my housekeepers, who cleared up after me, and kept me fed, were held at arm's length. Only the spaniels had ever seen me cry, which they'd dealt with in typical spaniel fashion by licking the tears up, and squashing in close. I was glad those spaniels couldn't talk. My email pinged.

To: Ivan Porenski

From: Carl Verve

Date: 2nd June 2013

Subject: pleased it worked

Ivan

I'm pleased to hear that you sound more positive about things. To put your mind at rest, the antidepressants should be out of your system now, and won't impair sexual satisfaction. There's always the possibility that the lack of emotional connection during your casual encounters led to the problem. Given that you appear to have made an emotional connection with Elle, I doubt if the problem will manifest.

I'm more concerned by your last statement, that you want everything to be perfect the first time you make love to her. She is human too, as are you, and human sexuality is an extremely complex subject. Just don't be too upset if it takes a while to learn how to satisfy each other sexually. First time sex is rarely perfect.

Given that you are 'on a promise', I wouldn't get too worried about your inability to concentrate or function at your usual level. Just don't try any complex business.

Regards

Carl

I pondered his words, realising that his insights were correct. I hadn't obsessed this much over a woman since Irina. Our relationship had been cut short by my flight from Russia, and leaving her had been my only regret. I'd begged her to come with me, but she'd refused, too scared to leave her parents and the life she knew. I didn't blame her, I was a fifteen year old boy, with no money, no idea where I was going, and we didn't know if I was as marked for execution as my parents had been. Until Elle, Irina had been the only girl that I'd formed a connection with. After we'd given each other our respective virginities, we'd been inseparable. Sitting next to each other in lessons, and meeting up after school. She had a gentleness about her, and an honesty.

I found out years later that she'd married my friend Andrei, and died giving birth to their first child. I'd still been tied to Dascha at that point, so had to hide my anguish that such a beautiful person should have her life cut short, while an evil bitch such as Dascha was allowed to live a pampered and privileged life.

In my 33 years, I'd loved three people, all of whom were now dead. It was a subject I'd explored at length with Carl, he said I could have survivors guilt, which was a possibility. I just knew for certain that falling in love with Elle would drive me to insanity. If a wealthy, cultured man like Oscar couldn't keep hold of her, I'd have no chance with my rather unromantic approach, and peasant roots. She was well educated like Golding, I had an accountancy diploma from Wandsworth college. I decided to try and be a decent boyfriend to her, and see if that would be enough to hold onto her.

So I made my way over to Bond street on Saturday afternoon to buy her a nice necklace and earrings to wear with her dress that evening. I found out that she was planning to wear the red one, which made it easy to choose a nice ruby set. I took my time, visualising all the various pieces on her, before setting on a pretty combo from Cartier. Pleased with my choice, I tucked the box in my pocket and went home to get ready.

Chapter 5

I really wasn't prepared for how beautiful Elle looked, all done up in her new dress. Her hair was piled prettily on top of her head, and her eyes were made up in smoky greys that seemed to make her cornflower blue irises even more pronounced. I stood in her doorway gaping at her.

How I ever thought models with their flat chests and jutting hip bones were glamorous, I don't know. Elle looked a perfect hourglass shape in her dress, the epitome of feminine glamour with her tiny waist and full, round breasts pushed up into two enticing mounds. I fought the urge to bin the party and stay in and undress her instead.

She was delighted with my gift, and I helped her on with the necklace, my hands shaking slightly at the sensation of touching her bare flesh. Once I'd helped her into the car, I clasped her hand, and told her how wonderful she looked. Her smile looked a little uncertain, but she told me that I looked 'hot' too, which pleased me enormously.

I tried to put her a little more at ease on the way over by telling her about the function we were attending, the charity we would be donating to, (which she approved of), and what to expect when we got out of the car.

The paparazzi generally went crazy when I arrived at these events, whoever I arrived with, and I knew that with someone as gorgeous as Elle on my arm, they'd all be desperate to find out who she was, and get pictures for the gossip rags. The flashes started the moment we arrived, and became frenzied as soon as Elle stepped out of the Bentley. To her credit, she kept her smile going until we got inside, and didn't appear fazed by all the attention. She made me smile by wondering out loud what all the fuss was about, with clearly no idea how many websites she'd be appearing on by the next morning.

I handed her a glass of champagne, and led her into the reception room, where we were instantly mobbed by acquaintances and business contacts. I watched her out of the corner of my eye as she chatted happily to some actor, handling the social small talk with polished aplomb. Just as I began to allow myself to fantasise about us as the 'new power couple', my heart sank as I spotted Golding walk in with Dascha.

I willed the two of them to stay away, but they spotted us quickly and made their way over. "What the hell are you playing at?" I growled at him, hoping Elle wouldn't hear me.

"Same as you. You have a problem?" Oscar growled back. I could hear Elle complimenting Dascha on her dress, which paved the way for bitchface to have a pop at Elle, returning the compliment, but asking if I'd bought it, because it looked like my taste. *Like you'd even know my fucking taste*, I wanted to shout at her. I was even more alarmed when Dascha made a comment about Oscar and I being clients of Elle's, as if she was a sort of hooker-come-lawyer. Thankfully, Elle deflected Dascha by telling her she hadn't known Oscar had such a beautiful girlfriend as they only ever talked business. *Clever girl.* Then changed the subject to some legal issue she was working on for Oscar.

"What the hell are you doing here with him?" I demanded, switching to Russian so that the others wouldn't understand our conversation.

"Ooo, Ivan, don't tell me you're all jealous because I'm here with a richer man than you? And you have to try and pretty up your lawyer to accompany you. Couldn't you get a proper date?" She looked all flirty as she spoke, which made my stomach turn.

"Don't be ridiculous, you can shag who you like. I truly don't give a fuck who you're seeing, but I do want you to leave my girlfriend and I alone." As soon as I said it, I regretted it. I'd just given her ammunition.

"Your girlfriend? Really? A little English mouse like her would probably prefer a little of the *special* chastisement I reserve for her type. The bite of a cane and a dildo up her arse would soon break down a bit of her English reserve. Mind if I try her out?" Dascha smiled, showing her neat row of white teeth, and looked pointedly at Elle's tits.

I could feel my anger rising, and I struggled to keep my temper, and my voice low. "You so much as look at her, touch her, say anything to her, or even breathe your foul breath in her direction, I will rip your fucking head off your shoulders. Now, I suggest you enjoy your evening with Oscar, and leave Elle and I alone."

"Maybe, maybe not," she trilled, delighted to have rattled me.

"Did Golding invite you, or did you invite him?" I asked, suddenly suspicious.

"My father suggested he invited me. Why?"

"No doubt he jumped at the chance. We're you aware that he's only agreed to it because he's trying to make Elle jealous. He wants her desperately, and she's turned him down. Didn't you know?"

She looked disgruntled, "I didn't know he knew her apart from work. I doubt if he'd go for someone like her though."

I laughed, "he's eating his heart out for her. You can't possibly compete. She's beautiful, incredibly clever and well educated. All the areas that you're sadly lacking. Watch the way he fawns over her." I paused, "He's only here with you to keep Vlad sweet and to try and make her jealous. Don't kid yourself that you're in Elle's league, because you're not." I watched Dascha's face harden as my words sank in. *Not everyone likes being beaten and tortured for fun you sick, deluded psychopath.*

We were called into the dining room, so made our way in as

Dascha said; "Ivan, you really need to concentrate on this Conde Nast deal for my father, I mean, I'd hate to put your *girlfriend* in danger over your refusal to do this little deal for us. I even made sure you and your *girlfriend* are seated next to the MD tonight. Introduce her."

"You better not involve her, you vile bitch," I looked round, "where's Elle?" I asked Oscar.

He looked around, "No idea, she was here just a moment ago, while you were busy flirting with your ex."

"I wasn't flirting, believe me. I'll find Elle, and you need to keep Dascha well away from her. Understand?"

Golding nodded, and I turned and retraced my steps out to the foyer. She wasn't anywhere to be seen. *Shit.* I raced into the reception room where we'd gathered for drinks, but apart from a few waiters, it was empty. "Sir," Nico interrupted, nodding towards the doors, where Elle was walking out, looking rather dejected.

"Where do you think you're going?" I shouted, hurrying to catch up with her. "The dining room's the other way."

"I'm getting out of your way, and heading home," she said, "I'll speak to you in the morning."

"Elle, what's got into you? I don't understand why you want to go."

"Ivan, you're not a stupid man. Did you really think you could ignore me to fawn all over your ex, and I wouldn't mind? I might not understand Russian, but I understand flirting. Now I suggest you let me go home, and you can go back in there and spend the rest of the evening with her." *Is she mad? I wasn't flirting, believe me.*

"I don't want her, I want you."

"I'm sorry, I can't do this. Right now I feel bought and paid for, in a dress that you chose, in jewellery that is probably worth what I earn in a year, and that bitch rubbed my nose in it. I just want to go home and take it all off, and be myself again." She looked as though she was trying not to cry. *No baby, don't think like that, you're fucking perfect, and I'm gonna kill that bitch for this.*

"Elle, listen to me, I changed to Russian because I was telling her to behave, and to leave you alone. I told her that I was with you now, and I didn't appreciate her nasty remarks. As for my gifts, there are no strings attached, I bought them because I wanted to make you happy, not because I expected any payback. You are still you, despite how wonderful you look tonight. Please come back inside with me....please."

She looked as though she was thinking about it. "Promise me that we won't sit with her?"

I let out a breath, "I promise." I took her hand and led her into the vast dining room, and through to a round table. I sat her next to the actor she'd been speaking to earlier, while I sat next to Joan Lester, the MD of Conde Nast. No doubt the whole thing had been set up by Dascha.

Thankfully the starters hadn't arrived yet, and we hadn't kept anyone waiting. I picked up the card listing the auction lots, and leaned in so we could both read it. I figured it might take her mind off the earlier events.

Lot 1 A weekend in New York, courtesy of Hilton hotels

Lot 2 A one week stay in the Red Sea resort of Sharm El Sheik, courtesy of Four Seasons Hotel Group

Lot 3 A spa weekend for two, courtesy of Champneys.

Lot 4 A dinner party for six, catered in your home by chefs from Gordon Ramsey, Claridges.

Lot 5 Dinner with Stephen Fry

Lot 6 Lunch with Lord Sugar

Lot 7 A private tour, and lunch at the House of Lords, with Lord Golding.

Lot 8 A helicopter flight over London, courtesy of Battersea Helicopters ltd.

Lot 9 A weekend in Paris, courtesy of Eurostar.

Lot 10 A year's subscription to Quintessentially Yours, courtesy of Quintessentially Yours.

I pulled a biro out of my pocket, and ticked the lots I planned to bid on. Elle seemed to relax a little, beaming a genuine smile when Joan complimented her on her dress. She even made me laugh during the auction, when I got into a bidding war with Golding, telling me I was giving the room a 'my dick is bigger than your dick show', which I thought was quite funny.

Back in the bar, I held onto her tightly as I introduced her as my girlfriend to the various people I was acquainted with. She seemed quite happy for me to call her my girlfriend. She also seemed quite comfortable joined to my hip with my hand clamped firmly round her waist.

I'd been a touch peeved during the week when I found out that both Oscar and Paul had engaged her services in much the same way that I had. I was even more peeved when Paul wandered over and slobbered all over her, making a show of kissing the back of her hand. With Golding barely able to take his eyes off her as well, the thought struck me, *for the first time, I have something that they can't have, and obviously both want.* I noted with satisfaction that Dascha was watching the show as well, and looked murderous. *Good.*

I squeezed Elle a little tighter, and smiled at her, hoping

Golding was watching her give me back a slightly heated 'I'm gonna fuck your brains out later' look. Paul droned on for a while about some executive search he was doing for me, all the while shooting little glances over at Elle, who was chatting to the CEO of a shoe shop chain.

I glanced at my watch, relieved to see it was eleven o'clock, and time to make our escape. I leaned in and whispered in her ear that it was time to leave. Approximately two minutes later we were in the car.

I didn't expect her to be snarky when I announced that we were going to Sussex. She seemed a little cross that I hadn't asked her first. In my excitement at planning our weekend, it hadn't occurred to me that I'd need to run it by her first. Instantly, I felt a bit stupid and gauche.

"So will you come to Sussex with me tonight?" I asked nervously.

"Yeah, ok," she replied, not looking terribly happy.

I was panicking inside a little as I slid up the privacy screen to separate us from the staff. "Tell me honestly Elle, are you pissed off that Dascha flirted with me, or pissed off that Oscar was there with someone else?" I needed to know, as the horrible thought was nagging at me that I was just being used to make Oscar jealous. Maybe he'd dumped her.

"I was pissed off because it looked like you and Dascha were flirting with each other. I didn't give a toss that Oscar brought her." *Ok, I can live with that.*

"That's alright then. I like you being jealous, I wouldn't like it if it was directed towards another man. Oscar in particular."

She changed the subject. "What happened with you and Dascha?"

I decided to be honest, "Not much. Went out with her, let her spend my money, put up with her appalling manners, then finally dumped her when she kicked Bella."

She frowned, "why did she kick Bella?"

"She weed in Dascha's shoe. Bella's way of letting her know she didn't like her I think. Kicked her so hard I had to take her to the vet to make sure there was no damage. Would have killed poor little Bella if security hadn't dragged her off. I couldn't be with her after that."

"I'm not surprised. What kind of person hurts an animal like that?"

"A psychopath. I actually felt quite sorry for Oscar having to spend an evening with her, but she only likes rich men, so she was probably quite happy."

"He was leaning so far away from her, he was almost at the next table," she giggled, "Oscar has a lot of faults, but bad manners isn't one of them. He looked horrified when she insulted me."

"I saw. She was beside herself with jealousy over you, and because she doesn't really know who you are, she threw the only barbs she could find. She figured out that Oscar only invited her to rattle me, and try and make you jealous. She was livid about it, not being the centre of attention. Then when Paul slobbered over you, I thought she would actually turn green."

"Paul did not slobber over me. He kissed the back of my hand, that's all."

"He slobbered, trust me... Elle, what is it you have that makes all us men go so silly over you? Three men at one party competing for your attention, you must be able to see it?"

She frowned, "I think you're reading way too much into it. Oscar maybe, mainly because I'm the only girl to have actually dumped him, but Paul Lassiter is just a client, and would only be interested in me to find out why you and Oscar are so fascinated." *Oh you really have no idea how gorgeous you are, and you just admitted that you dumped him. Interesting.*

"He wants you, I know he wants you, but right now I just want to hold you tight, and kiss you without worrying about smearing your lipstick." I smiled my best, most dazzling smile, and pulled her onto my lap, leaning in to kiss her softly. As her kisses deepened, they ignited my desire, and she slipped her hands under my jacket to feel my torso through my shirt. She pulled back, and slowly undid my bow tie, leaving the ends dangling around my neck.

Undoing my top button, she gazed at me, "you look very hot like this." Her eyes bored into mine, almost daring me to ravish her there and then.

"You've looked hot all evening." I replied. I didn't normally compliment women, but with Elle there was a curious mixture of her uncertainty, and the fact that just being the man she'd chosen, made me feel like a demigod. Her casually dismissive attitude to two other billionaires made me want to worship at her Choo-clad feet.

I could easily have taken her in the back of the car, but I wanted to stick to my plan and make our first time together special, well, in a bed at least. Car sex is ok, but with a long dress to contend with, I thought it would be rather awkward, and I needed her to be relaxed.

Within two minutes of getting home, I dragged her upstairs to my bedroom, and had her dress unzipped, and her bra off. Finally seeing her tits for real after such a lot of fantasising should have been a let down, but they were every bit as perky and full as I'd imagined, with small, pink nips standing to attention. I couldn't get out of my clothes quick enough, and when she slid her hand down to feel my erection through my trousers, I thought I was going to go off there and then.

Thankfully, I've come a long way since Irina, and know how a woman's body works, plus I'm lucky to be able to fuck several times in a night, so I was comfortable admitting that I wouldn't last long, and needed to make her come first. I gently pushed her down onto the bed, and slid her knickers down. Finally, she was totally naked, willing, and as horny as they come.

Her pussy glistened with her arousal. I couldn't resist it, I shoved my face into her, breathing in her wonderful scent, before sliding two fingers in to feel her inside. She was scorching hot, and soaking wet, as I pumped her gently while caressing her clit with my tongue. Her heels kicked at the bed covers, as she fought to keep still. I felt the rippling start deep inside her, as I sucked and licked her. Then she let go, and came, soaking my hand, drawing my fingers deeper into her. I felt her pulsing hard, and watched as her clit twitched and throbbed. *Oh Elle, I love how responsive you are, I bet you're gagging for my big cock aren't you?*

Her eyes widened as she watched me unroll a condom over myself. *Yeah, I'm a big boy.* I took control of her body totally, pushing her legs apart as I eased into her. *Fuck me, she's tight.* I moved at a fast pace, pounding into her, knowing it would be over quickly for me. To my delight, she came again, in an explosive orgasm that shook her entire body. *She loves my big cock, she's totally helpless as I'm fucking her into the biggest orgasm she's ever had.*

She ran her soft little hands over my back, leaving sensuous trails of heat that pushed me over the edge. I pressed deep into her and let go, feeling as though I was shooting a bucketful of cum.

With all my worries about being able to come now a distant memory, I made our next fuck last, stopping every time I felt her close to the edge. I must have changed positions five times, as I wanted to fuck her in every way possible. I must have licked and sucked every inch of her tits, which I discovered, sent her into the stratosphere. Eventually we both came, I just couldn't hold back any longer, especially when her baby blue eyes gazed into mine as she rode my cock.

I was wrung out and exhausted as I flopped down onto the bed beside her. *Ha! Carl was wrong about the first time sex. That was fucking astounding.* As I ran my hands over her soft skin, I heard whining and scratching at the bedroom door. Elle just looked amused, and said I should let them in, agreeing that while an audience during sex would be off putting, she was quite happy for the girls to sleep in with us.

Now, to be entirely truthful, I didn't allow women to sleep over as a rule. Usually one of my team would drive them home after I'd finished. On the odd occasions that one of them had slept over, I'd spent the night on the couch in my study, under the excuse of taking phone calls. I felt different with Elle, whether it was because I'd had to work hard to actually get her, or because she stirred up all sorts of emotions, I didn't know, but I wanted to snuggle into her and breathe in her lovely scent.

The girls were bemused when I let them in, sniffing her, then me, as if they were checking that she hadn't harmed me. They squashed themselves up against me, and dozed off, as did Elle. I lay awake for a little while, watching as her lips parted slightly, and her breathing slowed. By the time I fell asleep, it was gone three in the morning.

She wasn't there when I woke up. For a moment, I panicked, but looked out of the window to see her walk out onto the terrace holding a mug. She settled herself into a seat, and seemed to relax. I jumped into the shower, quickly washing myself all over, before pulling on a pair of shorts and a vest. Seeing that she was still on the terrace, I went down to the kitchen to make us both fresh coffees.

She smiled widely when I took them out, clearly pleased to see me. I gave her a deep, lush kiss before settling into the seat opposite. She looked adorable wearing my dress shirt with her hair mussed up in a birds nest. I told her about the clothes and stuff Mrs Ballard had purchased for her, which seemed to delight her. I was pleased that I'd thought to organise it, women like details like that. She went up to brush out her hair and shower, while I got on with breakfast.

I loved to cook, taking pride in the fact that I could turn my hand to a large selection of dishes with ease, and I adored supermarkets, although I rarely visited them anymore. I could still remember the first time I saw one while I was exploring the area around the kids home I'd been sent to stay in while my asylum application had been sorted.

Strolling around Wandsworth, the area outside the children's home, I found myself outside a large building with bright lettering and open doors. There seemed to be lots of people walking in and out, pushing trolleys full of bags, so I wandered in to have a look around. I was astounded by the sheer amount of fruit and vegetables available, stacks and stacks of things that I didn't even know the names of. The vast warehouse was crammed with every type of food that ever existed. Not one shelf was empty, nothing seemed restricted, and the variety blew my mind. 'I'm going to learn about all this, I'm never going to go hungry again' I thought as I perused the lines of fish and meat.

Even in the kids home, the food was plentiful and good quality compared to what I'd experienced back home. I found out that I liked pretty much everything that was put in front of me, especially white bread, which had no 'bits' in it.

I shook myself out of my reverie and got on with preparing our breakfast. She arrived in the kitchen just as I'd dished it all up, sniffing the bacon scented air appreciatively. The girls sat at her feet while she fed them pieces of sausage, gazing at her adoringly as she gave them almost double their usual allowance. I didn't stop her, thinking it was better that the girls loved her, than worrying about their rather tubby waistlines.

We took a long, cool walk in the woods after breakfast, and I watched as Elle relaxed. Her shoulders dropped, and her hands unclenched as we meandered through the paths. I found her presence strangely relaxing, and just being able to touch and kiss her without barriers or worries about overstepping the mark, was exhilarating and exciting. She told me that she didn't regret our night together, and seemed as happy as I was that we'd finally got it together. Instantly, I relaxed, and began to plan 'round two'.

While we strolled along under the shade of some ancient oaks, I was busy planning a pool fuck, followed by a lovely session discovering how many times she could come. Our night together had simply whetted my appetite for her, and I wanted to spend the whole day exploring her beautiful body. I could barely keep my hands off her as it was.

As we neared the house, I sneakily suggested a swim. I think she caught on to my intentions, as she beamed the sexiest smile at me, and went upstairs to change into one of the bikinis Mrs Ballard had purchased for her. I was already wearing shorts, so just had to throw off my vest. I sat on the terrace to wait for her.

When she hadn't returned after fifteen minutes, I went to see what was keeping her. I found her sitting on the bed in the spare room looking like she'd seen a ghost. I noticed straightaway that she was clutching her mobile. "My mum's been found dead. I need Roger to drive me to Welling, if that's ok."

CRACK, was the noise that pierced the warm evening. I was in our tenement, being held at gunpoint by armed militia. The noise made us all jump. I heard people screaming, as I watched my father felled by a shot to his head. My mother, and another woman were dragged away by four men. I was pulled away from the window by the armed men standing in our tenement. When two more shots rang out, I knew both my parents were dead. I swayed, feeling sick to the pit of my stomach, my spine tingling with fear. 'Not my Mum, anyone but her', I wanted to scream, but I knew it was too late. "He wasn't your father, so no need to mourn the traitor. He brought it on himself, and so did she," said the burly man pointing a gun at me, "although why you're so special, I don't know."

I shook myself back into the present, and looked at Elle's desolate expression. She was clearly in shock, so I wrapped my arms around her, and said; "Baby I'm so sorry, whatever you need. I'll call Roger. I'll come with you." I genuinely felt for her as she began to sob. Anyone who's lost a parent knows just how terrible an experience it is. I gathered up the things she'd need, pulled on some shoes and a T-shirt, and went over to Welling.

Her childhood home was much as I expected, as I'd seen the outside online. Inside it was clean and tidy, but shabby and threadbare. I let Elle sit with her mum's partner while he gave his version of events to the policeman who was there to find out the circumstances. I made us all a cup of tea, listening from the kitchen. It didn't sound as though there'd been any foul play, as he recounted his story. The police obviously didn't think so either, leaving shortly after I carried the cups into the living room.

I looked around the small room, hoping that it would give up its clues as to the particular inhabitant who had grown up there. My eyes alighted on a photograph of Elle in her academic robes, holding a scroll, and smiling happily. Her mother had framed it, and put it on the mantelpiece, in pride of place. "She was very proud of you," I murmured.

"Always said Elle was the brains of the family," her mother's boyfriend confirmed. At the word 'family', I felt Elle's shoulders start to shudder. *She has no family now,* I realised. *Poor girl, I know exactly how that feels.*

I was relieved when Elle told Ray that he could take over the tenancy of the flat. The last thing I wanted was for her to move back there. The area didn't look safe, and the tiny flat was shabby and old. *I want to look after you.* The thought popped into my head unexpectedly. I wanted to gather her up, whisk her home to Sussex, and make sure she never cried again. I couldn't bear the desolate look on her face.

She gathered up some photographs, shoving them in a carrier bag, before disappearing into the bedrooms for a few minutes. "She's taking it badly," said Ray, "I knew she would. Debbie was her only family. Still, I'm grateful for the flat and furniture. God knows where I would've gone if she'd booted me out."

"I'll look after her," I said, "you can count on me." *Not that he seems bothered about what happens to Elle. Loser.*

Elle came back into the room, looking around for items that she should take. I noticed that she had nothing in her hands from the bedrooms, and apart from the bag of photographs, there didn't seem to be anything to take to remind her of her mother. My heart broke for her.

After telling Ray that she would take care of registering her mother's death, we said our goodbyes, and left. "Can you take me back to London please?" She asked, before we got in the car. I pointed out that the Sussex estate might be a better place to grieve, but she insisted that she needed to be alone. I held her tight all the way to London as she sobbed into my chest.

ing out from nowhere just after dawn, I don't know. Usually in these dark moments something inside me urges me.

Chapter 6

Back in her flat, I dumped the bag of photographs on the island, and set about making her a drink. She had barely any food in the fridge, so I sent Roger out to pick up some essentials for her. Elle just sat looking dazed, as I busied myself making her a coffee. "Tell me about your mother, what sort of person was she?" I asked.

"She was fun, had a great sense of humour. Liked music, drinking and the soaps. Made a lot of poor choices in life, narrow outlook. That's it really."

"She made you, so she must have been quite something," I said softly.

"I was ashamed of it, of taking you there. Seeing the cheap, scruffy place I come from. Seeing you drink from a chipped mug. I wanted to hide it from you. I escaped that life." Her tears started to fall again. *Oh baby, don't be ashamed, I don't care where you came from.*

"It's a palace compared to what I grew up in. Your mother did her best for you. Never forget that. She loved you. Be proud of who you are, and where your journey began."

"It's all gone now. Nothing to run away from, I have no family at all now. Nobody, not even a cousin."

"I know how that feels, and believe me when I say you'll survive it. She gave you brains and self reliance. That's a great legacy. Plus you have a knack of pulling rich men." She smiled as I said it. Inside, I was concerned that she had nobody to care about her. Nobody to check if she was alive or dead. Nobody to rescue her from the Sussex lanes in the early hours of a Sunday morning. Nobody but me.

I didn't want to leave her alone, but she insisted on it, saying she needed to be silent and think. I went back to the penthouse and met the rather bewildered spaniels, who couldn't work out why we had returned to London early. I switched on my phone in case Elle needed me. Five minutes later it rang. It was Kristov. "Ivan, have you spoken to Vlad today?" Kristov was Vlad's head of security. For all his brutality, he was really quite a nice man, and had always been kind to me. He'd been the one to offer me a job working for the firm.

"Not today, no. Why?"

"He's just put a contract on a lady called Elle Reynolds. I believe she's your girlfriend? I thought you deserved a heads up."

My blood ran cold. "What sort of contract?"

"We are to kidnap her, hold her alive, but damage her until he says otherwise. I'm sorry Ivan."

"How much is he paying? I'll up the money to keep her safe." I knew it didn't work like that, but well, every man has his price. I thought I'd try.

"Now come on, you know it doesn't happen that way. I'm not even supposed to be giving you the nod about this. I'm putting my own arse on the line by telling you."

"I know, Kristov, thank you for warning me."

I immediately called Nico and Roger in to tell them about the threat to Elle. Nico was ex-mafia too, and straightaway realised the enormity of the threat. We assigned Roger to cover Elle's personal safety at all times, and Nico went off to put a team together to assist him.

"Are you going to tell her about this?" Roger asked.

I shook my head. "With the events of today, I really don't think she needs anything else to worry about. Just keep watch over her." Roger left for Elle's place straightaway. She wouldn't suspect a thing, as she seemed to think that Roger was just a chauffeur, as opposed to ex-SAS, and an extremely highly trained close protection officer.

About five minutes later, Vlad called me. "Ivan, my boy, have you given any further thought to that favour I asked of you?"

"What if I say I won't do it?" I challenged.

"Well, your girlfriend, Elle, is currently sitting in her apartment in Jamaica Wharf, chatting to Lord Golding. Maybe someone should pay her a visit, get her to twist your arm a little. I'm sure that she could easily change your mind. I mean, it's a few days to sort this deal at best. Frees you for the rest of your life. I'd urge you to take that opportunity." *Bastard.*

"Leave her out of this Vlad, she's just lost her mother."

"Nobody to worry if she disappears then," the bastard replied.

"Anything happens to her, and I mean anything, it's a declaration of war Vlad," I said.

"Really? I seem to recall you happily killing Karen Hodges. Didn't worry about killing a woman then, did you?"

"That was different, and you know it." I knew I was losing.

"I see. So this girl, it would upset you to give her up as a surety? I mean, I need to know I can trust you with this deal."

"If anything happens to her, there is no deal."

He chuckled, "Hmm, it sounds as though you are a little.....enamored.....by this lady. So, how about a compromise? I'll call off the dogs....for now, and you do this deal for me. You back out at any point, I take Ms Reynolds. This deal gets done, you get both your freedom, and the girl...intact. Agreed?"

I sighed. "Ok. I'm warning you now Vlad, anything, and I mean anything, happens to her, the deals off. It's in your interests that she stays safe."

"I knew you'd see sense. So, meet me tomorrow at my head office, about eleven. We'll go through the detail of the deal. We've been negotiating on your behalf already, and they're close to accepting. We'll sort the money transfers out tomorrow too. I've already spoken to Golding, I just have to give him the nod."

He ended the call. I sat at my desk with my head in my hands. Fucking Karen Hodges strikes again. The creature was the only woman who had got me praying to my Mama. Even dead, she was still wrecking my life.

I stood in front of Mr Butler, the head of the children's home, with my social worker, Jenny, sat beside me. "Now Ivan, in a couple of days it'll be time to leave us, and make your way in the world. I'm delighted at how quickly you have reached a good standard of English, which will help you enormously. Now, Jenny has arranged for you to rent a bedsit in Lambeth. She will also help you sort your resettlement costs and benefits that you're entitled to. I'd like to take this opportunity to wish you the very best of luck from all of us at St Margaret's."

I shook his hand firmly, and thanked him for everything. The staff had been kind to me, slipping me extra food, pocket money, and even gifts at Christmas. I gulped back a lump in my throat at the prospect of leaving. I was also excited at the thought of being independent, getting a job, and making some money. I was determined to become rich.

My new digs were dire. I had a room in a shared house, with a patch of damp on the ceiling, and the noisiest, most temperamental plumbing I'd ever known, far worse than even the tenement, which was saying something. The landlady was one of those fat, unpleasant looking women, with dyed red, stringy hair, a pasty, sour face, and ridiculously long, painted nails.

She looked me up and down before turning to Jenny, "He'll do," she snapped, before handing me a key. "Does he speak English?" She asked over my head.

"Yes, I can speak some English," I replied.

"That's a shame," she said, "I prefer them when they can't."

I was puzzled by her statement, but re-assured by Jenny, who I'd known since waking up in hospital after my hazardous journey from Russia. After being shown to my bedsit, Jenny explained how my benefits would be paid direct to Ms Hodges for my rent, and the rest would be paid into the bank account she'd helped me set up. I unpacked my holdall of clothes, and, after hanging my meagre clothes collection on the rail, I hugged Jenny goodbye, and thanked her for all her help. I could see the sadness in her eyes as she squeezed my shoulder. "You be careful" were her parting words.

Karen Hodges was, on the surface, a normal member of the community. In truth, she was into just about every illegal or immoral activity there was to try. She rented substandard rooms for inflated rents, sold drugs from her front room, and pimped desperate girls for local men to fuck in a basement fitted out with a dungeon and some sex rooms in the huge rambling house she owned.

At first, I kept my head down, only using the kitchen and bathroom when I really had to. Slowly but surely I began to get sucked into her world. It started when a trick started hitting one of the girls during his session with her. Karen was yelling that if he wanted to beat her, he had to pay extra, and when he objected, one of the girls was sent to get me from my room to eject the fucker. I got fifty quid for throwing him out, and snarling at him to stay out. Easy money I thought.

Within months I was earning great money running drug deals for Karen, and minding the poor girls trafficked into the UK to use as prostitutes. I enjoyed having cash in my pocket, and was able to upgrade my wardrobe, and learn to drive. Karen had to be kept at arm's length though, as she clearly fancied me, making suggestive remarks. She was way too fat and ugly to ever contemplate fucking her, even drunk I'd never be that desperate.

We carried on the drug dealing, despite rivals circling. It soon got serious, and a rival dealer began to take umbrage at Karen's activities, firing shots through the window one night. She dispatched me the next day to see a Russian gangster that she said could supply me with a gun, and show me how to use it.

I was impressed by the sharp suited, sophisticated man, and listened intently to his instructions as he showed me how to use the handgun he'd placed in front of me. "What's your name boy?" he asked as he took me down to the underground firing range.

"Ivan Porenski, sir," I replied. He flinched slightly.

"Where are you from?"

"West Biryulevo, just outside Moscow." He nodded, but didn't say anything. We spent the next hour firing the handgun into a target. I was quite good at it, even if I say so myself.

The following night, it all kicked off. A rival drug gang smashed their way into the house, armed to the teeth. They easily overpowered me, taking my precious gun, and holding it to my head while they beat Karen up, smashing her teeth, and stealing her stash of drugs.

"You fucking loser," she spat at me, "I'll make you pay for not protecting me, useless piece of shit."

"What exactly was I meant to do? There was ten of them, all armed. How the hell did you expect me to tackle them?" She didn't answer, choosing to stare malevolently out of the window instead.

Two days later, it happened. I was dragged out of bed at four in the morning by a group of men, curiously dressed in leather, and studs, who took me down to the basement. With Karen watching, they yanked down my shorts, and raped me. It was the most painful, most humiliating experience of my life. It took three of them to hold me down, I thrashed about so much, trying to throw them off. In the end, they tied me to the whipping bench to keep me still. My ordeal lasted about an hour, with Karen laughing her head off all the way through. The fat cunt even reached down to play with my dick while I was being defiled. "I thought you'd enjoy this, you weak pansy. Even your cocks limp and useless," she taunted. At that moment, I knew I was going to kill the dirty bitch.

They left me tied up until the next morning, when a tiny

Vietnamese girl found me, and released me. I was shuddering with adrenalin and rage, and raced up the stairs to find Karen. Rather wisely, she'd gone out, probably to let me calm down, knowing I'd want to beat seven bells out of her. As it was, I was at a loss, I had to get away, but had nowhere to go, and nobody to run to.

That day, the stars aligned to save me, as sometimes happens in moments of crisis. I'd just got out of the shower, trying to scrub the filthy feeling off my skin, when there was a knock at the door. I pulled on some jeans, and went down to see who it was, only to be confronted by the Russian who had sold me the gun.

"Ivan, I have a message for you. I've been asked to invite you to work for our organisation. It's mainly security work, but it's well paid, with good benefits and prospects. Are you interested?" He looked at me expectantly.

"I'm interested, but I do go to night school two evenings a week, so if it's evening work, that might be a problem." I was only six months away from finishing, so I really didn't want to give it up.

"That won't be a problem. Meet me at one at the fifth floor restaurant, Harvey Nichols. You know where that is?"

I nodded. "Sure." I needed to get away from the fat bitch, and her horrible ways. This sounded ideal.

I arrived a little early, and waited patiently. The Russian arrived, finally introducing himself as Anatoly, with a colleague who was introduced as Kristov. We were shown into the elegant restaurant, and seated at a linen covered table. I read the menu, wondering if we were eating.

"Have whatever you like Ivan, I'm having the soup to start, and the lamb for my main. Are you ok reading in English?" Kristov enquired kindly. He smiled warmly as I said I would have the same as him. "Anatoly told me that you are studying?"

"Yes, English and accountancy. I go to night school at Wandsworth college. I only have six months left though." I

frowned as I noticed a businessman staring at me from across the room.

"Excellent, well that won't be a problem. We can offer a thousand a week, plus accommodation, as you'd need to be based in Knightsbridge. The work is basic security, running errands, that sort of thing."

"Who would I be working for?" I asked.

"We are the private security for Vladimir Meranov, an Oligarch. Have you heard of him?"

I shook my head, "no, sorry."

Kristov smiled at me, "It doesn't matter, I'm sure the others will fill you in. Now, when can you start?"

"As soon as you like."

Within hours, I had moved out of Karen's hell hole, and into an apartment shared with a group of other Russian men, who seemed alright. They soon had the vodka out for a welcome drink. Within hours, we were all friends and compatriots. Taking a deep breath, I told them what Karen had done to me, well, a less embarrassing version, saying I was tortured as opposed to bumfucked. They all expressed their outrage on my behalf, and swore to help.

In the early hours, we went over to Lambeth, got the prostitutes out, and burnt the fat cunt's house down. Karen Hodges died in the fire. I heard her screaming as she burnt alive. We didn't kill anyone else that night, we were gentlemen after all.

I cringed, just remembering that terrible episode of my life. Almost fifteen years on, it was still destined to haunt me forever. I looked at the clock, and decided to give Elle a call. I needed to hear her voice, and wanted to see her, and make sure she was still in one piece. She answered on the first ring, and asked to come over. Overjoyed, I called Roger, and asked him to pick her up in five minutes. I didn't want her knowing that he was positioned outside her apartment, covertly watching her.

She fell into my waiting arms. I held her tight, before leading her into the living room, pouring her a large glass of wine, and settling down next to her. She still seemed fragile, so I talked about the girls as puppies, and their terrible behaviour. Anything really to keep the conversation off her mother, or the threat I'd had in regards to her safety. I just wanted to breathe in her lovely scent, and feel her soft, warm body next to mine.

By ten, she was out cold, no doubt exhausted by the trauma of the day. I gently picked her up and carried her to bed, before slipping off her vest and shorts, and tucking her in carefully. She didn't even wake up. I watched her for a while, as her face softened into deep sleep, her lashes fluttering as she dreamed some unknown dream. I was torn between wanting to slide into bed next to her, and pouring my guts out in an email to Carl. I decided to get into bed, I could talk to Carl in the morning.

She woke me up ridiculously early the next morning, asking how to get a car so that she could go home and get ready. By using my drivers, albeit innocently, I could ensure her safety. I knew we'd kept 24 hour surveillance on her flat, thanks to a camera installed just outside the front door, so I was happy to let her go home and get ready. It was important that she didn't suspect that something was wrong.

"I've identified a weak spot," said Roger in an early morning phone call. "She uses the changing room at her gym, which has a fire exit out onto the street. I can't follow her in there."

"Call Nico to get someone stationed outside for this morning, then I want a female operative engaged for those instances when you can't be present. Totally covert though. Tell Nico I don't want Elle suspecting a thing."

"Will do."

With that matter dealt with, I glanced at the clock. It was only 6am. I marveled at the amount of discipline Elle had, to be up, and at the gym at that time. No wonder she had a great figure. I left the girls sleeping and made myself a coffee, before going into my study, and pulling out my private laptop.

To: Carl Verve
From: Ivan Porenski
Date: 12th June 2013
Subject: oh god

Carl

I thought I'd be writing you a happy email this morning. I finally got together with Elle on Saturday night. It was fantastic, better than fantastic. You were wrong about the first time sex by the way. Sunday began great, then it started going wrong. She had a call to tell her that her mother had been found dead. We went over there to find out more, and deal with her mother's boyfriend. Poor Elle was distraught, embarrassed at me seeing her childhood home, and grieving her mother. I really felt sorry for her.

She needed some time alone, so I dropped her off at her flat. When I got back here, I was told (by phone) that unless I agree to this business deal, that she was in terrible danger. I was told a contract had been taken out for her kidnap and torture.

In short, I've told them that I'll do the deal provided nothing happens to Elle. I feel so responsible for her, she has nobody but me now, no family at all. I can't bear the thought that my dirty past has put her in terrible danger. I feel so guilty about it.

She has no idea about this. I didn't want to burden her further, what with losing her mother. (I had a flashback to the trauma of losing mine), so I've got covert security watching over her 24/7. I just don't know what else to do.

Ivan

I read it through a few times before hitting 'send', unsure if Carl would grasp the severity of the situation. Just writing it all down, made me feel ashamed of the situation I'd put Elle in. I pondered whether or not I should let her go, sacrifice our relationship to keep her safe, then I thought back to Saturday night, and knew the answer would be no. I was way too selfish to give her up now that I had her. I wanted to flaunt her in both Golding's and Lassiter's faces to show them that the peasant from Moscow could win, and hold onto, the grandest prize of all.

While I was waiting for his reply, I purchased a year's subscription to Quintessentially, the concierge service, and the auction lot I'd missed out on, for Elle, both as a little treat, and also to assuage my guilty conscience at putting her in danger.

To: Ivan Porenski
From: Carl Verve
Date: 12th June 2013
Subject: re oh god

Ivan

It sounds to me as if you are experiencing loss of control on several fronts at once, which may or may not be the cause of your distress. Let me expand on this; you may feel as though you have lost control of your emotions re the deep feelings of responsibility and love you feel for Elle. You couldn't control the event of her mother being found dead, which creates a feeling of powerlessness, and, as you pointed out, gave you a flashback to how you felt about losing your own mother, therefore triggering more feelings of empathy for Elle, (a very positive development I think).

The issue with the deal is more complex. You seem to be exploring the possibility of your past dictating your future. Now, this may be true to an extent, however, you have great means at your disposal, and, while I can't give you easy answers, it remains that you are clearly a resourceful and intelligent man, with a deep understanding of how these people operate. You were able to successfully navigate your life away from organised crime. You did it once, have faith that you can do it again.

You may wish to consider that the previous two episodes of loss of control are blowing the third episode out of proportion? Can this deal be concluded quickly? Can you tell Elle the truth of what has happened, and trust her to assist you in dealing with this? Sharing this problem may in fact bring the two of you even closer together.

Regards
Carl

I read the email several times, and while I agreed with Carl on several points, I felt that telling Elle would cause her to run from me, and probably into a less complicated man's arms. The thing that Carl was correct on was that I knew their modus operandi. I knew where they'd target her, how they'd grab her, and roughly where they'd take her. I knew that she'd be safe at work, out shopping, and among lots of people. The Russian mafia weren't terribly skilled, and preferred to get people at home, or during the weekend, when they had their guard down, and were relaxed, especially if she had to be kept alive. A 'hit' was actually a lot easier, as it's quick and quiet. A kidnapping was really quite tricky, especially with armed bodyguards around.

I was interrupted by a call from Nico to tell me that he'd managed to hire the top female bodyguard in London. I knew Gemma Pinfield-Thomas from my mafia days. She was a nondescript looking woman, but the best close protection that money could buy. Vlad had hired her for Dascha once, when there had been a serious threat made. With her trailing Elle, I could relax a little. She'd be in place by mid-day.

I went over to Knightsbridge to see Vlad at eleven, as requested, with a gun tucked into my jacket, as per usual. His office was opulent to the point of vulgarity. He took the overdone Oligarch stereotype to heart, and covered everything with gold leaf and bling. His desk alone made my eyes hurt. "Ivan my boy, how nice to see you again. You're looking well." *Is he fucking joking?* He stood up and came round the desk to shake my hand warmly, as if he wasn't threatening my woman. "Security outside please," he barked. They all trooped out. We sat down, him in his 'executive' chair, which was a giant monstrosity, and myself in an elaborately gilded Louis IV copy, which was equally ugly.

"So Vlad, you have me here. I'm listening..." I stated, letting him see my displeasure.

"Oh Ivan, don't be like that. I'm doing this for you as well. Dascha needs something to take her mind off you, and making her work will give her some direction to her life. Now, we've been negotiating on your behalf. They are pretty convinced they're dealing with you. I gather that the MD is meeting this Miss Reynolds tomorrow to confirm that she is indeed in a relationship with you. Once it's clarified by her, they have indicated that they'll sign."

My ears pricked up, "So you don't want her being kidnapped until tomorrow then?"

Vlad laughed, "No, plus, you get tonight to convince her what a great lover you are." He looked at me shrewdly, "Thought that might please you."

"Who's doing the sale contract?" I asked.

"Breviniov. It's being made out to Retinski holdings inc. that way it's kept separate from your other companies. You just need to gift that holding company to Dascha. He doesn't know you're giving the company away."

"I see. Will she do all the changeovers?" *That would make me laugh, she wouldn't have a clue..*

"No, I'll need you to do all that first, so she has a fully functioning company from day one. She's not....well versed in UK company law.....so I need you to sort all that, hence the holding company. When it's handed over to her, I'll list it as a subsidiary to my Russian companies, just in case, you know." *Yeah I know, low tax, low or no inheritance tax. You ain't gonna make old bones Vlad.*

"This is as much for you, Ivan, as her," he said, "you will be publicly splitting up, giving her a goodbye gift, she can't then come back for more, or try and smear your name. You'll be seen as being both generous and fair to her. It's better than the bad feeling and secrecy around your separation that there is at the moment."

"Look Vlad, I understand all that. My concern is purely for Elle. As I told you, her mother died yesterday, she doesn't need this right now. I don't care about doing this deal for you, personally, although I'm not looking forward to being in the same room as Dascha. What I do care about is the fact that Elle is dragged into this."

"Does she know?" he asked. I shook my head. "Good. Keep it that way. You must understand Ivan, that I've put five billion into your bank account, and I want that company for my money. If you were trusting someone with that kind of cash, wouldn't you want a hostage?" He watched my reaction. I didn't answer him, and just scrubbed my face. "And it appears that I've chosen the right one," he added. "Come, let's have some lunch."

We were interrupted by my phone. Seeing that it was Elle, I answered it. She was at a bit of a loose end, and asked if I had any work for her. "Not now, mad busy. I'll call you later," I told her, under the watchful gaze of Vlad.

Over lunch, Vlad outlined the negotiations and the detail of the deal. Rather grudgingly, I had to admit that he was a master negotiator, and I'd actually learnt a vast amount from him over the years. It appeared that both the sale contract and money were in place, and as soon as we got the nod tomorrow afternoon, the deal would be concluded at the UK head office of Conde Nast.

The plan was to do all the changeover details as fast as possible, and hand over the company as soon as it was ready. A week at most. With Elle safe until after her lunch with the MD, it meant four workdays, and a weekend to protect her. The weekend would be the tricky one.

That evening, I called Elle to ask her out to dinner, and told her about her new concierge service. She was delighted, and used them to find us a table at Quaglinos. With a bar to seat our security just a few steps away from our table, I was able to relax and really enjoy her company. She told me all about her shopping trip that afternoon, including bumping into Lassiter. I pretended that I didn't know, and listened as she mused that there was something 'off' about him. She thought he was some sort of sexual dominant. I didn't tell her that a background check actually showed that he was the opposite, a masochist, who enjoyed the services of a very strict dominatrix based in Chelsea.

All the sex talk was making me a bit horny, and having kept my hands off her for 24 hours, I decided that a good session would cheer her up, and take her mind off things. I decided to have some fun with her, asking her to be my sex slave for the evening. When she agreed, I sent her into the ladies to take off her knickers. She was wearing a demure dress, so knowing she was bare underneath would be a fantastic turn on.

When she returned to the table with a sexy smile, I asked her to give me her knickers. She handed over the tiniest scrap of black lace. I held it up to my face and inhaled. To think. That my lawyer was wearing such things under her clothes! She looked panicked, "what if somebody saw you?" She asked, blushing deeply. Given that we had three bodyguards watching us, I could guarantee that someone did.

"Oh that's half the fun," I told her, amused by her embarrassment. She laughingly admonished me for being 'naughty', then looking rather flustered, demanded that I got the bill. On our way out, we bumped into Ned Miller, chairman of the company I'd bought my plane from. Out of the corner of my eye, I could see Elle fidgeting, clearly desperate to leave. I took my time, chatting about business, letting her anticipation build. I also enjoyed being seen out with her, showing her off. By the time we said our goodbyes to Ned, she was desperate. Her nipples were showing through her dress, and she almost dragged me to the car. "Keep driving," I muttered to Nico in Russian. He nodded, understanding what I meant.

As soon as we were in the car, she pounced, freeing my dick from the confines of my trousers and boxers with an almost animal ferocity. She pulled up her dress, straddled me, and sank down onto my cock, impaling herself, the moment the wretched condom was on. I vowed to discuss ditching the damn things.

She took control, slamming herself down onto my cock as though her life depended on it, pushing herself back to change the angle, and work towards her own orgasm. In the close confines of the car, both almost fully dressed, our fuck felt hedonistic and somehow more intimate. Knowing that our security were aware what we were up to added a frisson of sexiness too. I'd always got off on the idea of fucking in public. What we were doing was as close to it as I'd ever dare.

Elle must have felt so too, as she speeded up, before I felt the familiar quivering and pulsing of the start of her climax. As soon as she'd let go, I held her hips still as I shot my load, marveling at how this sexy woman seemed to enjoy my body as much as I enjoyed hers.

"You can stop driving now," I said into the intercom, before removing the condom and righting my clothes. Glancing over at Elle, I was amused that my horny little tigress now looked a little embarrassed, the realisation that security had known what we were up to, dawning on her face.

Once we were home, I took her up to the room I reserved for sex. It contained my most favourite sex toy, my swing. I'd been introduced to sex swings many years before, by an aristocratic woman who lived near the security flat in Knightsbridge. Mine was a remote controlled deluxe version. I'd been a little nervous about Elle knowing that I kept a whole room for just sex, but she didn't seem to think that it was odd. I usually preferred fucking in the sex room, to using my bed, but with Elle, it hadn't mattered. To be honest, I was just grateful to be shagging her, so wasn't about to complain about my bed being invaded.

I turned the music on, as Elle stared at my swing, looking intrigued. I took off her dress and bra, and helped her into the swing, securing her hands and feet into the cuffs. As soon as she was secured, I began to relax, and slowly undressed. She watched me with rapt attention, gazing at my body with a heated expression, clearly desperate for my cock again.

I raised the swing to shoulder height, so that I could bury my face in her. Lapping at her, and tasting how turned on she was, I could barely control myself. I flicked her clit repeatedly, until she came, then I thrust my tongue into her to feel her pulsate, and taste her juices. As her orgasm subsided, I came up for air, my face covered in her essence. I lowered the swing, slipped on a condom, and grabbed a vibrator from the cabinet. I wanted to find out just how many times I could make her come.

I slammed into her, reveling in the feel of her scorching hot flesh enveloping my cock. I was so fucking hard, it was throbbing. Using the swing, I fucked her hard and fast, *she just loves my big cock, look what it does to her.* I pressed the vibrator onto her clit, and felt her come viciously, her insides pulling up, and rippling around me, as the momentum of the swing impaled her onto my dick. I rode her orgasm without mercy, pushing her into another one. *Go on baby, give me one more,* I thought, as I speeded up. I was mesmerised by her breasts bouncing in time with my thrusts. It had been so long since I'd fucked someone silicon free that I couldn't take my eyes off them.

She screamed my name as another orgasm hit, her body convulsing as she shook uncontrollably. I just couldn't hold back any longer, and thrust into her one last time, pressing in deep while I gripped her thighs to still the swing. I practically poured myself into her, shooting my cum so hard that it almost hurt.

Almost in a stupor, I helped her off the swing, catching her before she slumped to the floor. We lay side by side on the bed, both slicked with sweat, getting our breath back. Referencing my previously unsuccessful chat up line, I asked her what her name was.

"Can't remember," she replied, grinning impishly. *Well played,* I silently congratulated myself.

Chapter 7

I lay awake that night, just watching her sleep, breathing in her lovely scent. I debated whether or not to tell her about Vlad, and the threat to her safety. As she slept, it struck me how much trust she had for me. She looked so small and vulnerable laying in my huge bed. I had an overwhelming urge to protect her. I pulled her into a cuddle, and drifted off.

Next morning, she was out on the terrace sipping coffee when the girls and I got up. They raced off for their morning wee, and I sat down beside her, and asked if she'd enjoyed our wild sex the night before.

When she confessed it was the best she'd ever had, my chest swelled with pride, *suck on that Golding,* and I broached the subject of us both having sexual health checks, so that we could ditch the condoms. She agreed straightaway, telling me that she'd had a birth control shot, which would be effective on Saturday.

After another coffee, she left to get ready for work, with Roger driving her for the day, and Ms Pinfield-Thomas trailing her. Nico had copied her keys, and swept her apartment, so I knew she'd be fine. I sat and braced myself for the day ahead.

The first thing I did when I got into the office was call Golding. "Hello Ivan, what can I do for you today?" He asked in his cut glass accent.

"When you did that secret transfer for Vlad, were you aware of just how much danger you put Elle in?" I spat, barely restraining my anger. The line was silent. "He's put a contract on Elle, kidnap and damage, until the deals concluded."

"I had no idea...." He trailed off. "Ivan, you have to believe me, I had no idea."

"And you didn't think he'd want a hostage? Entrusting me with five billion? Come on Oscar, I know you hate admitting that Elle belongs to me now, but surely you aren't that stupid that you didn't see it coming?"

"I really didn't know. I'll sort it. Does she know?"

"No, hopefully she won't. I'm making sure she has guards with her everywhere. Undercover, of course. With her mother dying, she really doesn't need this," I said, hoping to make him feel as guilty as I felt.

"Yes, quite. Have you got any inside info? You know, where and how?"

"I'm not in the mafia these days Oscar, how the fuck would I know?" *Prick*

"I realise that, but you do know how they operate."

"Not lately, but for a kidnapping, the evenings and weekends are the prime time. Less people around, the subject more relaxed, fewer guards around."

"I see."

"No you don't fucking 'see'. You should have told me about Vlad's request beforehand. I'd already said no to him, mainly because I don't want to Elle anywhere near Dascha. You blew that all out of the fucking water. Now, I've put security in place, and I'll try and get this deal done as fast as possible, but in future, anything like this comes up, you come to me first. Agreed?"

"Of course. Listen, I'll take care of this situation for you. Nothing will happen to Elle, I won't allow it."

"And how exactly do you plan to do that?" I demanded.

"There's always more than one way to skin a cat Ivan. You just concentrate on getting this done quickly, I'll make sure Elle is safe, and that it doesn't happen again."

"Oh, and make sure Mrs Restorick doesn't go home until this deals done today."

After the call, I sat back and ruminated on our conversation. Oscar was a powerful and well connected man, with a link to the British Establishment. Between us, we had to be able to keep her safe. I called my security company, mainly to find out if they'd heard anything on the grapevine. They promised to keep tabs on Kristov and Anatoly, just in case a safe house was being prepped.

I spent the rest of the morning dealing with my own companies, knowing I'd be tied up with the Conde Nast deal for the next few days. I had my head stuck in a spreadsheet when Elle called, furious that Joan Lester had revealed that she had only taken her to lunch to quiz her about our relationship, under the pretence that Dascha had given an interview telling the world what a bastard I was. *Good thinking Joan,* I thought, impressed at her cover story.

Elle on the other hand was livid, and talking about slapping an injunction on the publication. Even my joke about giving an interview telling them what a sex god I was, failed to calm her down. It was gratifying to hear how concerned she was for my reputation, and her readiness to step in to prevent bad press. *Does she make you feel protected?* popped into my head, yet again. *Bloody Carl.*

Vlad called me at four to tell me that the parties were ready to sign. With a heavy heart, I made my way over to Hanover Square. I was greeted upon arrival by the chairman, a distinguished looking Frenchman called André Ruette. He whisked us up to his office, and we sat down opposite each other at his huge oak desk. "Now, Mr Porenski, the family have entrusted me to sign the company over, so I will be signing on everyone's behalf. It's a sad day for us, as I'm sure you understand. With very few outside investors, this has been our family business for many generations. We wanted to make sure that it went to someone who would appreciate it's long, and illustrious heritage."

"Of course André, I can understand that. I'd be heartbroken if someone bought Retinski and broke it up." *And Dascha will rip this place to shreds old man,* I thought, feeling a little sorry for him. "Tell me about the institutional investors."

"They hold about 30% of the stock. Pension funds really. We're a long term investment for them, very few speculators bother with us, being family owned as much as we are...were," he said, correcting himself, "means that the share price is too stable for the city boys, they prefer wild fluctuations."

I stared at this elderly man, who had successfully navigated a vast conglomerate for most of his lifetime, and felt desperately sorry for what I was about to do. Mind you, his family would be around five billion richer. Idly, I wondered whether or not he'd listed in a low tax territory.

"Now, shall we have a little drink before we go through this sale contract?" He offered, opening his drinks cabinet.

We each had a small cognac while we went through the document. Now, to be truthful, I was astonished at just how complex and convoluted the various arms of the company were, as I'd assumed it was just a couple of magazines. By the time we were done, it was almost half seven, and I was interrupted by Roger calling me to see if I'd make my doctor's appointment, and if not, he needed to take Elle home. Glancing at the clock, there was no way we'd be done in time.

I called Mrs Restorick to action the release of funds, and both André and I signed the contract. Five minutes later, she confirmed that the funds had transferred successfully.

While I was waiting for André to confirm with his banker, I called Vlad. "It's done. Money paid across, contract signed and exchanged."

"Excellent news my boy," he exclaimed, "Dascha's downstairs, I'll call her to come up and join you."

Once André had confirmed that the money had been paid, he slid a bunch of keys across the desk to me. "These are yours.

Keys to all the various buildings, this office, the safe, that kind of thing. They're all clearly marked. I'd like to take this opportunity to wish you the very best of luck."

"Thank you André," I said, shaking his hand. At that moment, Dascha came striding into the room. André scowled.

"Why is Ms Meranov here?" He asked.

"I'm Ivan's girlfriend of course, I'm here to celebrate his latest acquisition," she answered, rather dismissively.

He turned to me, "I thought you were seeing somebody else, Joan Lester met with her today to confirm it."

"Oh, that'll be his mousey little lawyer. She's a bit infatuated, deluded sometimes in fact. Tells people he's her boyfriend. I feel sorry for her." Dascha answered. I felt my temper rise.

"If this deal had hinged on who I'm currently seeing, would it not have been better to have asked me directly?" I said to André. He looked furious, and simply strode out of the room without another word.

"Oh well, never mind," trilled Dascha, "now, the press are waiting for us downstairs. Shall we go?"

"I can't get out of here, and away from you, quick enough." I sighed, resigned to the fact that this would be in the papers. We stepped outside to blinding photographers flashes. Dascha was holding my arm, looking triumphant. Even her touch through my clothes made my skin crawl. After talking to the press for a few minutes, she hopped into the Bentley next to me, and we drove off. Straightaway, she slid up the privacy screen.

"Take me to Windsor," she spoke into the intercom.

"What if I wanted to get home? I need to get up early in the morning, unlike you, you selfish piece of shit," I bitched at her. There really was no love lost between us.

"Oh Ivan, don't forget you're supposed to be my boyfriend for the next few days. Now I know your useless, limp cock's off limits, but at least try and make this believable. Otherwise every nasty word will be taken out on your girlfriend."

"You won't get her. This deal will be done, and if there's any further contact, the whole world will know what a cunt you are. I'm not joking Dascha. This whole episode is a declaration of war as far as I'm concerned."

"Really? You'd take on my daddy? Brave words Ivan, but you're no match for him. Just like you weren't man enough for me, you wouldn't be tough enough to go up against him, and we both know it." She sat back to let her words sink in. If it wasn't for the knowledge that Elle would bear the brunt, I would have cheerfully shot her through the head there and then. She always did know how to press my buttons.

I stayed silent all the way to Windsor, preferring to seethe quietly while she rabbited into her phone, discussing my purchase of Vogue magazine with her vapid friends, promising them all free clothes. *Stupid, idiot woman, you have such a fucking shock coming.* It gave me some satisfaction that I knew how complex the companies involved in Conde Nast were, she wouldn't have a hope in hell's chance of coping.

By the time I got back to London, it was nearly midnight. The girls greeted me excitedly as I walked in, jumping up for cuddles. I gave them each a biscuit, and fixed myself a sandwich. I knew that Elle would be asleep, and besides, I didn't really know how to go about explaining the situation to her, so instead, I went to bed.

I barely slept that night, it seemed that every time I closed my eyes, the vision of Dascha kicking Bella seemed to replay in my mind. I'd known that she hated the dogs, hated how much I loved them. I'd been careful never to leave them alone with her, but even with security around, she'd sent Bella flying through the air. I'd heard the dog scream from upstairs in my study. Thankfully, Roger had her in an armlock when I'd raced downstairs, stopping her from inflicting any further damage, and keeping her safe from me. My poor, darling Bella was whimpering in pain, and looked up at me with confused eyes, almost pleading with me to help her.

Dascha, on the other hand, had been unrepentant, only sorry that she hadn't managed to inflict more damage, or kill the dog. After a phone call to her father, I told her to fuck off out of my life. Roger took her to her new home with her father, while Nico got a vet out. I'd always felt ashamed that I'd not been able to keep my girls safe from her, and she was banned from all my homes and offices after that. Thankfully, Vlad had been appalled as well, and had accepted that I couldn't put up with her any longer. God knows why she wanted me, we hated each other, lead separate lives, and hadn't had sex for ten years.

The next morning, I had to explain to the board of my own company how and why I'd secretly bought another conglomerate without their involvement. Understandably, it caused some friction, and in particular, my finance director had been rather concerned about the appearance of five billion quid in a Swiss bank account that he had no knowledge of. I had to tell lie after lie to my own board to cover up the true nature of the acquisition. They were even more puzzled as to why I'd incorporate it into a holding company as opposed to Retinski.

With the changeover to action at Conde Nast, I had to spend the afternoon and evening at Hanover square, sorting the myriad issues that follow a takeover. I worked like a dog to get everything underway. I needed this done fast.

Oscar called to see how it was all going, mentioning that Elle had seen me on the evening news, leaving Vogue house with Dascha on my arm. I groaned, wondering how the hell I'd explain the situation without letting on the danger she was in. Oscar told me that he also had security in place around Elle. Vlad's thugs would be no match for our combined efforts.

I chased my tail all day. By the time I got home that night, it was nearly nine. Roger had text to tell me that Elle was safe at home. Nico had even rigged up a covert camera inside her flat, so we could monitor for any problems. I took a deep breath, and called her.

"Hello Ivan, what can I do for you?" She asked, her voice sounded strange.

"I need to see you," I replied. I wanted to drive her over, and wrap my arms round her, maybe a cheeky shag too...

"Certainly. Would Smollenskis at 8am suit?" She asked. *What? This isn't about work, why is she saying that?*

"I need to see you before that."

"I'm sorry, I'm not available. What's so important that it can't wait till tomorrow?" *You are baby.*

"Elle, don't be like this. I need to explain to you. I'm taking it that you saw the news last night?" I braced myself for her answer.

"Yes I did. Congratulations on your acquisition. So... Do you need me to meet you at eight or not?"

"No. I need to see you now. There's a lot I need to explain to you."

"No need. I understand what happened. You just do as you wish. It's a bit late for explanations." *No, don't say that, you* **have** *to let me explain. Stop being such a bitch.* I could feel my anger and frustration rising.

"You don't get to dictate what companies I buy, where I go, or who I have to see. Now I've asked nicely. If you insist on being childish, then you end up the loser. I said I'd explain to you, so at least spare five fucking minutes to listen to me for god's sake," I was losing it. "At least accept that I wasn't given much time to..." She'd put the phone down on me. Immediately, I rang back, only to discover that she'd turned her phone off. *I guess I could've handled that better.*

I threw my phone down on the kitchen counter, and poured myself a glass of wine. Five minutes later, it rang. I glanced at the screen, and saw it was Dascha. My heart sank. "Yes bitchslag, what do you want?"

"How's my company coming along? Shouldn't your lawyer be

there overseeing stuff?" She trilled, ignoring my less than pleasant greeting. She was used to it.

"Fine. We installed our computer systems today, ran simulations. Had a board meeting to get all the directors up to speed on what needs doing. They seem fairly efficient. I don't think Elle needs to be there."

"I want her there, within reach. If she's not there, we'll snatch her and hold her."

"I'll see if she can do the staff contracts," I said sulkily.

"That's good news. I've been busy too," she said

"That'd make a change. Mind you, your idea of a busy day is getting your nails done." *I couldn't resist a dig.*

"I've been viewing photos of your girlfriend. Thinking up creative ways to damage her. Knowing she's an office person, I thought fingers, and blinding her would have the best effect. Would you still fancy her if she was fingerless and blind Ivan? Igor's really excited, asked if he could fuck her while her fingers are being removed with bolt cutters. He's been walking around with a hard-on just thinking about it."

My stomach dropped, and I went cold. "I would love her no matter what. You, on the other hand, are one sick fucker." I hung up on her, and went into my study to email Carl, and pour my guts out to him.

From: Ivan Porenski
To: Carl Verve
Date: 10th June 2013
Subject: Horrific events

Carl, I can't sleep. I've done the deal, and am racing to get it concluded. The poison ex is around, and Elle isn't speaking to me. I've had dreams about the time Dascha hurt Bella, and I've just had a call from her telling me she plans to cut Elle's fingers off and blind her, mainly to end her career, and inflict the worst damage. I know full well I won't be sleeping tonight for worrying about it.

There's a part of me that feels that Elle would be better off without me. Let her go back to Golding. At least then she'd be safe. I really don't want that though, but think she might well have left me already. I lost my temper with her earlier as she was in 'lawyer mode', and was so cold towards me. I can't live with the knowledge that I've put her in this much danger.

Regards

Ivan

I toyed with the idea of calling him, but dismissed it, the last time I'd tried it, I'd been tongue tied and awkward, plus I didn't want to say out loud the words that Dascha had used.

I took the laptop into the gym to run while I waited for Carl's reply.

From: Carl Verve
To: Ivan Porenski
Date: 10th June 2013
Subject: re horrific events

Ivan

I'm sorry to hear that you're currently in the thick of this issue. It may be worth doing your visualisation exercises to help you get through this. I know it's easy for someone else to say, but I really would like you to concentrate on keeping calm through this crisis. Having another breakdown won't help.

While I can't give you specific advice, I still urge you to tell Elle the truth, and let her help you in getting this problem solved. Trying to do this without her knowledge appears to be risky and difficult, I mean, if she was fully co-operating with your security teams, wouldn't keeping her secure be a lot easier? I'm also concerned that if she finds out about this at a later date, it could bring about trust issues between the two of you. Please give this some thought.

Regards

Carl

I lay in bed that night, my mind racing with ideas of how to tackle the situation. I trusted both mine and Oscar's teams to guard over her effectively, but worried that there was always that tiny window of opportunity that we couldn't plan for, and with Elle barely speaking to me, it would be much harder.

The next morning, after barely sleeping at all, I sat at my desk at five am to compose an email to her, to try and keep her on side.

From: Ivan Porenski

To: Elle Reynolds

11th June 2013

Subject: Explanation

Elle

My purchase of Conde Nast was designed to stop the publication of the article that you were so concerned about. My appearance with Dascha has put paid to her attempts to smear my character, and it also keeps you out of the limelight, so puts paid to the security issues that come with being my girlfriend, and also any rumours among your colleagues that you are only with me to further your own ambitions professionally. I probably should have told you what was going on, but we were working to get the deal done quickly, so I apologise that you had to find out via the evening news.

I didn't appreciate your rather juvenile refusal to see me last night. I would have rather told you all this in person, rather than having to send you an email.

I have some TUPE work I need doing at Conde Nast, which I would like you to oversee. Please contact Mr Ranenkiov for further instruction on that, you have his number.

I should be available this evening, if you would like to come over to my apartment.

Regards

Ivan

I pressed 'send', and went off to do a punishing workout in my home gym. I needed to burn off some of the stress. I got into the office early, to check my own companies, as I'd be over at Hanover square again that day. My heart leapt as my email pinged with a reply from Elle.

From: Elle Reynolds
To: Ivan Porenski
11th June 2013
Subject: your email

Thank you for your explanation as to why I found out via the evening news that you have a long term girlfriend. As I have no desire to be a short term girlfriend, bit on the side, or dirty little secret, it does indeed ensure my safety, as I am no longer involved with you in any other way than my professional capacity.

I will contact Mr Ranenkiov this morning regarding the TUPE work.

Thank you for the invitation, which I will have to decline. In my experience, personal and professional don't mix terribly well.

I hope we can continue to work well together.

Regards

Elle Reynolds

I read it in disbelief. My instincts told me that Elle knew I was lying, but hadn't wanted to directly accuse me, although she seemed to think I was lying about Dascha, as opposed to the deal. At half eight, Ranenkiov strolled in.

"I need Ms Reynolds to attend Conde Nast on Monday and Tuesday to oversee the HR transition. She'll be calling you this morning," I barked at him.

"Good morning Ivan," he said, rather sarcastically, "don't worry, I can do that. It should be extremely straightforward."

"Don't fucking argue, just arrange it," I yelled. *For god's sake, just do as you're told.*

He gave me a hard stare. "As you wish. I'll wait for her call."

I stopped off at the doctors on the way to Vogue House for the check up that I'd missed on Tuesday, wincing as the doctor was rather rough with the swab. It all seemed a little pointless, but was probably a good idea anyway, as I'd been screwing around a bit in the last few months, so it was best to make sure.

I called Oscar to update him, and find out if he had any news on the security situation. "All is in hand. I'm going to invite her to Conniscliffe this weekend, well, mother is. It's the safest place," he said in his snooty accent.

"Safe from who?" I sneered, "I'm not keeping her safe from them so that you can twist this situation and pounce on her. You're as much to blame as I am."

"I'm aware of that. I'll see her after work. I'll let you know if she agrees."

"Just keep your hands off her. I mean it."

After hanging up, I sulked for a while. Just because the fucker had a castle, he didn't need to keep showing off about it, although I rather grudgingly agreed that it was probably the safest place.

Apart from the news that Elle had agreed to oversee the HR on Monday and Tuesday, my day was bleak and grey. Even the little updates from Roger and Gemma did little to lift my mood. When Dascha arrived at Vogue House, I was ready to rip her apart.

"Hey Ivan, how's it going?" She chirped happily as she

strolled into the office without knocking.

"Yes bitch, what do you want?"

"Oh don't be like that. Is it nearly done yet?"

"No. There's operations in five countries to change over, seventeen subsidiaries, and five thousand staff. How the fuck do you expect that done in three days? Stupid slag."

She ignored me. "So when does my little lawyer show up? I told you, I want her in view."

"Monday. She's doing the HR changeover. Although, to be honest, bitch, you amaze me at your stupidity."

She wrinkled her nose at me. "How?"

"Well, if she disappears, you ain't getting this company. So all this winding me up with threats, well, it could backfire on you very spectacularly. I mean, if you can have a hostage, so can I, and right now, this company's in my name, bought with, ostensibly, my money. Golding won't admit to the secret transfers, he's as appalled as I am." I sat back, and watched as she scowled. She opened her mouth, then closed it again, before flouncing out. Five minutes later Vlad called.

"I've just had a call from Dascha, says your threatening to keep the company if we take Elle for safekeeping. Is that correct?"

"Yes it is. I've had your daughter telling me all the vile things she plans to do to Elle, mainly out of spite. I won't have it Vlad. I'm doing this deal for you, and I expect some respect in return. If you have Elle kidnapped, raped, blinded and maimed, the deals off, and Golding and I deny all knowledge."

"Strong words Ivan."

"I told you it was a declaration of war at the start, Vlad. Dascha pushed me way too far. You should have taught her better tactics, as well as better manners."

"She's just over-excited at having her new company. I'll calm her down."

"You make sure you do. I'm trying to get this done as fast as possible as it is, and Dascha is making it slower and more difficult with her behavior. Just remember that this whole deal is to buy my freedom Vlad, you both seem to have forgotten that."

"I haven't forgotten."

"Well, she has. She's treating this like yet another opportunity to torture me. She needs reminding, and putting in her place. Either you do that, or as I said, I'll do it for you."

"Oh, my boy, I taught you well didn't I? It makes me so proud..." At that point, I hung up on him. He must have called Dascha, as she disappeared for the rest of the day.

Oscar called me at around half nine with the news that Elle was staying at Conniscliffe for the weekend. I already knew, thanks to the little camera hidden in her lounge, courtesy of Nico, which I'd been watching all evening. She looked unbearably cute in her pink pyjamas. I'd scowled when she'd told Oscar that we were over, but delighted when she told him in no uncertain terms that it would be separate bedrooms, and that she wasn't going back to him. *That's my girl!*

I tried to call her, wanting to hear her voice, but she didn't pick up. Disappointed, I spent another sleepless night, tossing and turning, annoying the spaniels.

The following afternoon, I had a call from a furious Elle, demanding to know if a maroon van was following her. *Shit, she knows.* Rather than try and blow her off, I resigned myself to telling her the truth, trusting Carl's advice that it would be the right thing to do. Haltingly, I told her the full story. She was livid, understandably, and blamed me for the whole thing. She was also astute enough to realise the gravity of the situation, and agreed to play along, and assist the security team. *Hmm, maybe Carl was right about that bit then.*

Once I'd got a text from Oscar to tell me that they were safely at the castle, a different kind of stress kicked in. Overnight, I managed to convince myself that she'd go back to him, as neither of us had told her that he was as much to blame as I was. He was probably making me out to be some kind of gangster, and he would be her knight in shining armour. I felt outflanked, and depressed. I wanted to call her and warn her that he was a bigger crook than I, and she shouldn't take notice of his high and mighty attitude. To be truthful, I just stayed in and sulked instead.

I couldn't resist calling her the next morning. She was still angry with me, greeting me coldly, and asking if there was something I needed. *I need you to love me.*

"Elle, please stop being so cold. This isn't my fault you know."

"Really? Well it never happened to me before I met you. Now, if there's no legal issues, I'm just about to jump in the shower. Let me know if there are any developments please."

"In three days, this will all be over."

"Provided you sign that company over of course." *Is she mad? I can't get it done quick enough.*

"Do you think I'd renege on this deal and throw you to the wolves? Elle, how could you possibly think I'd do that to you?"

"It's five billion quid Ivan, and I'm just a girl you've known a few weeks. By your own admission, you want to own the world." *Oh baby, don't ever think that. I'd never hurt you.*

"I don't want to own a world without you in it. What's made you think I'd do the dirty on you?"

"You did. I saw you shark a client once. It doesn't matter what you say or do, I saw it, and I know you did it deliberately, so forgive me for not believing that you're always the good guy. You lied to me over this, so I now have to assume that everything you say is a lie." *Hmm. She's got a point. Fucking clever clogs lawyer.*

"Lying to you at the start of this was a mistake, and I wish I hadn't, but I will keep you safe Elle. I look after what's mine." I began to panic.

"I'm not yours Ivan. I don't belong to anyone," she shouted, before putting the phone down on me. I called her straight back, annoyed at her.

"Don't you dare put the phone down on me. I will NOT let Dascha drive you away from me. Let me just deal with this, then I'll figure out a nice treat for you to say sorry for letting this happen to you." *She needs a shopping trip, or a weekend away.*

"Keep your money Ivan, and shower it on your next girlfriend. I don't want any gifts, treats or surprises thank you. What I want is a quiet life, with my peace of mind intact, and a boyfriend who doesn't dump me on the news at ten." She ended the call. I slumped into my chair, and sulked.

Chapter 8

By Monday morning, I was a wreck. Even Carl hadn't been able to calm me down. I must have emailed him a dozen times over the weekend, looking for something to numb the intense pain and fear I felt at the prospect of having lost Elle. Oscar had called me to tell me that all was well, and that he would be placing operatives all around Vogue House and Hanover Square, as well as two close protection officers to guard Elle directly. I had to hand it to him, he was taking no chances. My concern was whether or not he was doing this because she'd gone back to him, or because he worshipped her as an unobtainable goddess.

She knocked on the door to my office shortly before nine. I opened it, nervous at facing her. She still looked like my beautiful Elle, in fact, she took my breath away. "Elle, glad you're here. Security remain outside please." The bodyguards stepped out of the room, and joined hers just outside the door. "It feels like I haven't seen you for ages, I've missed you. Please let me hold you." She didn't reply, just standing stock still. "Elle, what's wrong with you? Come let me hold you." *I need to see your beautiful eyes, and feel your perfect little hands. I need to know you're safe.*

"No, Mr Porenski. I'd prefer not to. Now, Ms Mills appears to have the changeover under control, so what exactly would you like me to spend the next two days doing?" She looked pissed off, and in full lawyer mode.

"Elle, you can sit and read a book, play on the Internet, anything, as long as you are in this building today and tomorrow." I walked towards her, and watched with horror as she stepped back.

"Don't touch me," she hissed, "you want me here, so I'm here. It doesn't mean that I'm happy about it, or that you get to touch me. I meant what I said, it's professional all the way from now on."

"Are you back with Oscar?"

"I belong to nobody." As soon as she said, it, the pain hit me. A horrible mixture of heartache and fear. This beautiful, vibrant woman could walk away from me, as easily as she'd left Golding.

"That's not what I asked. You spent the weekend with him, and he's paying for your security. Are you with him?" She didn't answer. "Has he fucked you this weekend? Dammit Elle, put me out of my fucking misery here. It's bad enough that you're involved with this, let alone leaving me over it. Just...just tell me the truth, did he fuck you?" *Please say no.*

"It's none of your business Ivan. You lost the right to demand answers when you appeared on television with that creature on your arm, and made me a laughing stock, and when you sent an email that was a lie from start to finish, you lost the right to expect the truth from me."

"I will NOT let Dascha drive you away from me, and I will not let Golding steal you. You are mine...please Elle." *I'll beg, I'm not too proud.*

"Ivan, I'm not a possession that can be 'stolen', and you'd do well to remember that. I'm a living, breathing person, who has a say in these things. I'm only here so that this deal happens, and I'm watching you as much as I'm watching the bitch. Now, to ease your mind, no I didn't 'fuck' Oscar this weekend. The last man who 'fucked' me was you, and right now it's something I deeply regret. Now, I'm happy to sit here till five with my security, and read a book, but be aware that there's a bit of me that believes that you'd throw me to the wolves and not give a toss, so think about that when you're shouting at me, and demanding answers." She lifted her chin defiantly, refusing to be intimidated by me.

"I'm sorry Elle. None of this is your fault, I just can't bear the thought that I could lose you over this."

She raised an eyebrow, "Could? Try have. Now, if you'll excuse me, I'm going to have a look at what your personnel department are doing."

"Don't go, not yet," I pleaded, "we need to resolve this."

"I have resolved it. You're free to be with someone else. I do your legal work, and that's all. There's nothing to debate."

"Tell me, did you ever have feelings for me at all?"

"I sobbed like a baby when I saw you on the news with Dascha. So yes, I did, but I'm not dumb enough to think I was ever anything more than a challenge to you."

"Oh Elle, don't let her win. This is exactly what she wants, and what I tried to avoid. Please just have a little faith in me, and let me deal with this, and I'll do anything you want to make it up to you. By tomorrow evening the wretched woman and her slimeball father will be out of our lives."

"Tell me about her father. Who is he?"

"A thug. Huge in mining and minerals. Stole his company really when the old Soviet Union fell apart. Made a hell of a lot of enemies over the years, and is well known for his dubious business practices. Wife was murdered years ago, and Dascha is all he has left. She's almost as unpleasant as him really. They are both bullies."

"Did you love her?"

I sighed, "I was dazzled by her for a while. I thought we would be compatible, both being from Moscow originally, and both being ambitious. Her father liked me, and encouraged me. On paper it should have worked. In reality, I grew to dislike her intensely. For such an indulged woman, she is incredibly mean spirited and envious. The incident with Bella gave me the perfect excuse to end the engagement. If I had told her the truth, that I was leaving her because I felt nothing for her, I would have been killed."

"Is she still in love with you?"

"No. She's not capable of loving anybody but herself. She's a classic psychopath, as is her father. She's currently enjoying tormenting me with what she'll do to you should I renege on this deal, knowing how terrified I am for you."

"So am I being watched?"

"Not as far as I know. I have security all over this building. This deal, by its nature, has had to be totally secret. Only you, me and Oscar know about it. Oscar took care of the money transfers in Switzerland, so there is no money trail. So as far as anyone knows, I bought this with my own money, paid cash, and will give it all to Dascha. If it got out what has really happened, she'd be a laughing stock. At the moment, she has no reason to hurt you, and in some respects, it's in her own interests that you remain safe. She knows that if you go missing before our press conference tomorrow, that our deal's off."

"How come they trust you so much, I mean, it's five billion quid?"

I paused, Carl's advice about telling her the truth, flashing through my mind. I decided to go for it, thinking that it might turn the situation around. "They know I'm in love with you." I watched as my words sank in. Her mouth dropped open, and she looked shocked. *Surely you knew?*

She pulled herself together, and said; "Ivan, let's get through the next two days, and see what happens."

"We can do this Elle. Let's just keep up appearances till this is over, just don't forget how I feel about you." *I have to salvage this somehow.*

"I'm going to check on your personnel department. I'll be in room 7 if you need me." She turned and walked out, leaving me standing in the middle of the room.

I was at a bit of a loss. I wanted to trail around with her, just to reassure myself that she was ok, and to be able to look at her, but I realised that it probably wasn't a good idea, as I had work to do, and it was probably better to give her a little space. I got on with some of the phone calls I had to make.

A little later, Dascha breezed in. "I've checked out my insurance policy. She's sitting in room 7 playing on her laptop. Not very hardworking is she?" I bit my tongue. "She does look rather mouse-like too, although she did come up with a rather good idea about asking all the designers to clothe me, to show off their clothes. It would be great publicity for them."

I smiled inwardly. No doubt Elle had been teasing, but Dascha was far too stupid to realise. "Did you actually want something? Or are you just here because you're bored?" I asked.

"Daddy told me I was to be nice, and that I had to learn about the business," she pouted.

"You should always be 'nice' on the outside at least, people don't like dealing with psychopaths, bitch. Threatening to blind someone isn't usually the way that deals get done, especially in London, so don't go threatening the designers who advertise." I watched as she pouted.

"I wouldn't do that, besides, I don't plan on actually dealing with the day to day stuff, that's what that Lester woman's for. I'll just be at the head, you know, the owner. I expect that I'll have to be entertained out rather a lot and stuff though, everyone will want to be seen with me."

I sat back in my chair, "I've been working sixteen hour days on this since last Wednesday. There are myriad complexities in this company, all of them will need close care. As the owner, it will be down to you."

"It'll be fine," she dismissed.

"This company is approximately the same size as your dads mining company. Do you see him swanning around doing no work?"

"No, but that's boring old mining. This is different, this is glamour and fashion."

"It's a business, just like any other. It's about as complex as Retinski, and I don't mind a bit of complexity in my companies."

"If I get stuck, I can always get your girlfriend to come and sort it out," she spat, getting cross at my smug smile. I was beginning to enjoy myself.

"Well, she would have been the perfect lawyer to help you, she's so clever, none of this would have fazed her. I know for a fact that she'd never work for you, or lift a finger to help you. Just pray that she never ends up on the opposing side, she's terrifying."

"And how would you know?" She sneered.

"That's how I met her. She kept up with me, then slapped me down. Astonishing how masterful she is with figures. Nobody else has ever been able to do that." I watched as my words sank in. For all the hatred between us, Dascha knew that I was bloody good at business, and faster with figures than even her father.

"Everyone has a price, and there's nothing to stop me engaging her company."

"Apart from Golding and I being their biggest clients. If we say no, they'll say no. They don't put their staff in danger, as I said, it's not how things are done here. Now, will you please fuck off for the rest of the day and let me get on? I want you here at nine sharp tomorrow morning for the press conference to hand this over. Don't be fucking late, understand?"

"I won't be. I'll make sure I get up." With that, she flounced out. I sank back into my chair, and picked up the phone to call Mrs Restorick, and check that the bank accounts had been changed successfully.

I couldn't stop myself from going to see Elle. She was on her laptop, and looked like she was doing a little Internet shopping when I walked in. She didn't appear to be concerned about Dascha's visit, dismissing her as 'way too thick to be a worthy adversary', which I thought was brilliant.

We discussed the changeover, which she thought would be done that day, and I asked her to do a contract to give the entire holding company to Dascha.

I took a deep breath, and asked to see her that evening. She didn't seem particularly hostile, so I figured that as she knew the truth, she understood that I hadn't done anything deliberately. She turned me down flat, then rubbed a bit of salt in the wound by telling me that she might invite Oscar round to watch telly with her. *I can watch TV with you, if that's what you want.* She also informed me that she had household chores to do. *I can send someone to do that for you, better than you having to do it.* I wanted to argue with her, but her little jaw had that determined set to it that told me she wasn't changing her mind.

I watched her that evening on the live feed from her living room. She was alone, and pottering around dusting and cleaning. It was stupid, but I was fascinated watching her sort her laundry, and sweep her apartment. When I watched her heat up a tin of soup, I decided to call her. She needed to eat more than that.

She still blew me off, even though I promised her a lovely orgasm. Said she was too jumpy and nervous. She did promise to see me the following night though, once the deal was done. Just hearing her say that relaxed me, and made me feel as though all was not lost. For the first time in a week, I managed to get a little sleep.

I was at Vogue House by seven the next morning, wrapping up the last details before the handover. In some respects, I was sorry to give it back, as it was a fabulous company, and had been extremely well run. To be on the safe side, I'd booked the press conference for ten o'clock. I'd never known Dascha to be on time for anything in her life, and keeping press waiting is never a good move.

I was nervously pacing around, waiting for Elle at five to nine. *I hope to god nothing's happened to her, she's never late. Should I call her?* She flew in at a minute to nine, telling me that the traffic had been horrendous, then pulled the contract out of her handbag, and spread it onto my desk to explain it. As usual, it was perfect. I folded it up, and slipped it into the inside pocket of my jacket.

We made our way down to the press conference at ten. I settled myself in the middle of the table set up in front of banks of press and photographers. The bitch was late. *Fucking typical, probably had a fingernail 'emergency'.*

"Can you tell us what we're all here for?" A journalist called out, "and how much longer are we gonna have to wait?"

There was a collective groan when I said we were waiting for Ms Meranov. She wasn't exactly the darling of the press. Some smart arse made a quip about waiting all day. *I'm as impatient as you are, believe me.* I simply smiled, and reminded myself that in approximately an hour's time, it would all be over, and Elle would be back in my arms for good.

The gathered press began to get edgy, and were murmuring about time wasting, when Nico came flying up to me clutching a piece of paper. He looked so worried, that I immediately glanced over at Elle, to make sure she was still there. She was chatting to her guard, looking amused at something he'd said. I read the message.

* Vlad, Dascha, and Anatoly were killed in a car crash this morning at approx 8am on the Hammersmith flyover.*

I froze, a million questions flying through my mind. "Are you certain? How do you know this?" I muttered to Nico, leaning away from the microphones.

"100% certain. Kristov called me in a panic. The police confirmed it a few minutes ago. I don't know the details yet, I'm waiting on more calls. It doesn't look like a hit though, I think it was an accident."

"Ok, get over to Windsor, and secure it quickly before this gets out," I whispered. Nico nodded, and left. I turned back to the microphone, and announced the deaths to the press, as opposed to the announcement that I'd planned to make. I apologised for having no information, and left the room to a flurry of flashbulbs and questions being yelled at me. *I'm free, she's safe, it's over.*

I jumped into the Bentley and slid up the screen, before switching on my phone and calling Kristov. "Tell me what happened?"

"It looks like Anatoly was driving, and lost control. Two other guards, as well as Vlad and his daughter, all dead. I don't understand it though, Anatoly is a competent driver, unless there was a problem with the car."

"I'm sure it'll be investigated by the authorities. Was it a hit?"

"I don't think so. Too difficult to stage a crash, unless they shot Anatoly while he was driving, but I don't think that happened. I'm trying to find out what I can. It seems that Vlad was killed outright, but Dascha died on the way to hospital. They had the air ambulance out and everything. Nothing about any gunshots though."

"I'm sorry for you, Kristov. I know you worked for him for a long time."

"Don't be sorry, we both know what kind of man he was. I wanted out for a long time. It's time for me to retire. I need to drive over and secure his house though."

"Don't worry, I already sent Nico, he'll sort it, and get rid of the staff. Listen, good luck Kristov, and thank you for everything you did for me. End of an era isn't it?" *Thank god.*

"Yes, I think it is. Well, you have your freedom now Ivan. Use it wisely."

I quickly text Elle to meet me at my penthouse, and called Golding. "Was that your doing?" I barked. There was silence for a moment. "Are you still there?" I demanded.

"Yes, I'm still here. I just saw your press conference. As I said Ivan, there's more than one way to skin a cat." He hung up. *I knew it!* With all threats gone, I sunk back into the car seat, feeling more exhausted than I had in years. All I needed now was to make it up with Elle, and it would become the best day of my life. It also looked like I'd be keeping Conde Nast, which pleased me enormously. Only Oscar and Elle knew the truth, and I doubted that either of them would condemn me for keeping it, although, if Dascha hadn't changed her will, it would've gone to me anyway. I made a mental note to further update my will to include it.

Mrs Watton was busy vacuuming when I arrived home, the dogs chasing her around barking at the Hoover. They stopped when they saw me, and raced over to say hello, before resuming their game. I went straight along to my study to wait for Elle.

I pulled her into a fierce hug the moment she arrived, inhaling her lovely scent. It had been a primal reaction on my part, and I was glad that she didn't try and pull away. She asked me if I had anything to do with Vlad's death, telling me, rather strangely, that she wouldn't judge, she just wanted to know. At least I could say with total sincerity that it had nothing to do with me. After another hug to reassure myself that she really was in one piece, I raised another issue that had been bugging me in the car on the way home, namely, our wills. When we'd got engaged, Dascha and I had both made wills to leave everything to each other, at Vlad's insistence. I'd changed mine the day after she'd been sent back to her father, but I didn't know if she'd changed hers. Given that I was keeping Conde Nast, the rest was just a bonus.

Elle remarked that Oscar's mum knew about the deal, which, to be honest, didn't really matter. Oscar had committed a crime by actioning the money transfer, as well as all the other 'deals' he'd assisted Vlad, and other Oligarchs with, from which he'd skimmed a fortune, and gained a political foothold in the former Soviet Union. I assured Elle that she wouldn't be saying a word.

She went into lawyer mode, calling one of her colleagues at head office to find out when Dascha had last amended her will. When she scribbled the date on my desk pad, I saw straightaway that she hadn't changed it, and had left everything to me. *Good, Vlad was worth a few billion. I deserve it after all the shit I've put up with.*

I was just starting to relax, and smile again, playing with the spaniels, who had put up with my foul mood for the past week, when Elle dropped a bomb, telling me that she wished I treated her the way I did the dogs.

"You want your tummy rubbed too?" I asked, incredulous.

"No, I just wish I was more sure of you. You dropped a bombshell on me yesterday, and it was only a surprise because most of the time you're either barking orders at me, or talking dirty. A bit like when you scared me by telling me we'd have wild sex, rather than just saying you wanted to make love." *Oh for fucks sake woman, I've just spent a whole week trying to keep you in one piece, done a changeover on an entire conglomerate in five days, and you're picking fault?*

"Do I actually get anything right?" *Maybe I'm just not enough for you, like Golding wasn't. Maybe there isn't a man alive who's good enough. I just don't know how to do 'in love', I haven't done it since I was fifteen.*

With that, Elle announced that she was going back to work. She turned tail and left before I could say any more. I slumped down at my desk and sighed, thinking that it wouldn't be quite as easy as I thought to get us back on track. In the meantime, I had companies to run. I logged into Retinski's system, and checked my emails, before making my way into work.

An hour later, Elle called to tell me that the family law department at her firm needed to speak to me urgently, and that she'd arranged for one of them to come to her office. Clearly, it was going to be good news, but I played it cool, and agreed on a three o'clock meeting. I spent the next half hour mentally adding up my new net worth, which put me in a much better mood. Nico arrived back, and confirmed that he'd sacked the rather startled staff, locked up the house, and had a team securing the grounds.

I checked my appearance, and brushed my teeth before strolling down to Elle's office. If my calculations had been correct, my net worth was now just over thirty billion. I was finally up there in the top ten richest men in the world, that people knew of. A few more years, and I'd be bumping Carlos Sim. I knew I'd never catch up with Oscar, but wealth built over many generations was somewhat different in my eyes. I'd built my fortune in just fifteen years, plus Vlad's time in business of course.

Elle's colleague was a pretty girl, but had that air of snobbery that only the English elite can exude, with her slightly braying voice, and overconfidence that the public schools seem to produce. I preferred Elle's softer accent, and her rather reticent manner.

She introduced her colleague as Lucy, and sat back as Lucy droned on about times of death, and police reports. *Get to the point, do I get the money or not?* Eventually it was revealed that Vlad had left everything to Dascha, who in turn had left everything to me. Lucy then told me that she would be the executor, and there would be inheritance tax to pay. *Oh no there won't,* I thought, smiling to myself, remembering our conversation in Langhams one night, when Vlad was pressuring me to marry his daughter.

We were sitting in the elegant restaurant, with its linen covered tables, and sparkling crystal. Vlad liked it there, liked the older, extremely courteous waiters, and the unpretentious food. He ordered steak and chips, a simplistic description of the culinary delight which was placed in front of him. I had the lamb, which was always exquisite.

"Ivan, there are myriad reasons why I think it's about time you married Dascha. I know she wants to, and you've prevaricated for long enough. It's time to get on with it."

"I'm still not sure marriage is a good idea. We don't.....get on quite as well as we should. There are other problems too, not

something I'd want to discuss with you though Vlad."

"I know she's a little spoilt, my fault probably. Since her mother died, I've probably indulged her a little too much...but she's a good girl really, and I know deep down she loves you."

"I don't think she does Vlad. She's not exactly a loving girlfriend."

"I don't believe that for one moment my boy, she told me she'd never want another man but you. Now, back to the engagement, there are some practical reasons, namely the issue of inheritance. I keep everything listed in Russia as you know. I'm fairly sure I won't make old bones, and I'll be damned if the Brits are getting a chunk of anything. Bloody cheek if you ask me, that they expect to take 40% of Dascha's inheritance."

"How's everything kept in Russia?"

"List your homes as owned by your company, which is listed in Russia. Keeps it all out of her majesty's clutches. You see, in Russia, there's no inheritance tax within families, and a lesser 13% to non family. So Dascha will inherit without any tax. If you marry her, you become my son in the eyes of the law, and I can leave you the companies. I mean, she won't want to be bothered with them. The easiest way is for the two of you to get married."

"I see, but married, she'd be entitled to half my fortune."

"Oh, my boy, I'd sort that for you if it ever arose. I'd like to see her settled before I depart this world, surely you understand. I know you'd always look after her. That's as much as any father could wish for."

I shook myself back to the present, and informed Lucy that all the assets were held in Russian companies, apart from some day to day bank accounts. I promised her that I'd get the documents together, and translated before sending them over. She beamed, and handed me a business card.

"Thank you. My secretary will be in touch. Now, I need to speak with Elle about a different matter." She took the hint, and left. "So, are you feeling better?" I asked.

"I wasn't ill, just upset. I'm happy to work with you Ivan, but I don't think I want a relationship with you. I just...." She trailed off. *No, no, don't say that.*

"Just what?" I asked. "Tell me Elle. Tell me what I have to do, because I don't understand you."

"Ivan, I'm scared of you. That's the problem. You scare me, and in my work life, I can cope. In my home self, I can't. I'm sorry. All I know, is that you like to fuck me, have me followed, and put my life in danger for a stupid deal. Hardly romance of the year is it?" I watched as a tear rolled down her face, making me feel like a total shit.

"I don't do romance. I would have thought you were far too logical to do it either." *I don't know how to do romance.*

"Maybe not. I can't be with someone I don't trust though. I was convinced you'd sacrifice me during that deal. Now, I know you didn't, but what I'm trying to say is that I thought you would. That's how unsure I am of you. So it's best you find someone else who doesn't care what sort of relationship you have, as long as you buy her a red dress and some rubies." I listened to her, coming to the conclusion that she wanted out, and this was her way of saying goodbye gently. I still had no idea where the red dress and rubies fitted into the problem though.

"So, you want to run back to Oscar? Is that what you're trying to tell me?" I snapped at her. I needed to know.

"No, I didn't say that. For all his issues, even Oscar sends flowers. I never doubted his integrity, or that he cared about me."

"Cared enough to get Dascha killed? This has all the hallmarks of a British intelligence hit. Oscar is the establishment, he could have done it to keep you safe. Still think he's a man of integrity?" I knew I was dropping him in it a bit, but I didn't care, she needed to know the truth about Oscar Golding, and what sort of man he really was. I mean, I know I have my faults, but I've never raped an entire country of its resources. Elle just shrugged.

"I have no idea what he did or didn't do, and besides, this isn't about him, it's about you. Your assertion that you were in love with me was a complete shock. Don't you see? I didn't have a fucking clue, because you don't show it. No hearts, no flowers, and you can't even say goodbye on the phone, you just slam it down on me. Now, if you want to go through life not doing romance, that's absolutely fine, just be aware that it won't be with me." *Oh, so that's what all this is about.*

"Fine, if that's how you want it." I stormed out, and stomped back up to my office. I sat at my desk in a massive sulk. "GALINA," I yelled. She came scurrying in. "How do I order flowers?" I asked, figuring that she would know.

"To be delivered, or to take to someone yourself?" She asked, looking at me a little strangely.

I thought about it. "I think I'd better take them myself," I replied, and watched as her eyes bulged slightly.

"Well, there's a flower shop in the mall on the ground floor. You just go in there and pick out what you want, and they make them into a bouquet for you, and wrap them."

"Ok. NICO," I yelled, he came in. "We're going to the mall to buy flowers. Get your assistant." Nico nodded and left to get my other guard. With both of them flanking me, we made our way down in the lift. I found the flower shop, and walked in. "I'd like a bunch of flowers please." I said to the assistant.

"Certainly sir, what type?"

I was stumped. "I've got no idea," I admitted.

"Ok sir, is there a particular message that you want to convey?"

With two guards standing beside me, I felt a little self conscious. "I need to say sorry....to a lady," I told her. I heard Nico snigger. *Shut up bastard, or you'll be looking for another job.*

"Ok, do you have a budget in mind sir?" She looked at me expectantly. I could feel myself turn a little pink.

"No, not really. I don't really know how much they cost. A

couple of hundred maybe?" *That bastard's sniggering again.*

"Certainly sir. I can put quite an impressive bouquet together for that. Would you like to wait, or would you prefer them to be delivered?" She asked, handing me a little card and an envelope. "Write your message on that sir." She told me. I quickly scribbled 'sorry' on the card, and stuck it into the envelope, before handing it to her. I watched as she picked out a large selection of flowers, and deftly arranged them into a bouquet, before tying them off with a large ribbon, and wrapping them in some kind of pink fabric stuff. *Perfect, that wasn't too difficult.*

I found out from Roger that Elle was at home, and with Nico holding the huge bouquet as punishment for piss-taking, we walked over to hers. She answered the door wearing her gym kit, and smiled when she saw the flowers. She seemed to soften a little, and agreed to let me accompany her to the gym. I knew she worked out regularly, as did I, but I was keen to see her in action, and exercising together seemed a very normal thing to do with a girlfriend. I thought she might like that.

She was on the running machine already when I strolled out of the changing room. I took the one next to her, and started up. I liked running, and soon found my rhythm, feeling the stress of the past week burning out of my body. I glanced at Elle, seeing her lost in her own world as she set a grueling pace.

I stopped a little while after her, and we moved to the weights machines. I became aware that half the patrons of the gym were watching us, as we tuned ourselves back into each other. I followed her around her usual circuit, simply adding more weight for my sets. We finished off with a swim race, which I put my all into, desperately trying to give her a run for her money.

She made it look effortless as she sliced through the water at an astonishing speed. After twenty lengths, she stopped, and waited at the edge until I'd caught up. "You, darling girl, are a machine, and it's very, very sexy," I told her. She smiled widely.

"I think you got that the wrong way round. Every woman in here has their tongue hanging out, and is holding their knickers up to stop them falling down, especially now that you're publicly single." I grinned at her. I was used to the way women reacted to me, and it would possibly help for her to see it too. I invited her back to my place for some dinner, pretending to be surprised at the news that she'd barely eaten all week. We arranged to meet in the foyer, so I hot-footed it into the shower, and was washed and dressed within five minutes.

Back at the penthouse, she was still giving me a hard time, saying I was controlling, and that I treated her like a man. I listened to her, before telling her again that I was in love with her, and that I needed to know if trying to continue the relationship was futile or not. I put her on the spot a bit, but she admitted that she had feelings for me too, and that it wasn't pointless pursuing her. *Yes!*

She also pointed out that she needed time to recover from the events of the past week, so I pulled out my piece de resistance; I invited her to my villa in the South of France for the weekend. I found it a little strange that her first question was to ask about the dogs. As soon as I reassured her that they'd be coming along too, she seemed to be quite excited.

I had a burning question that I'd been dying to ask, so I dropped it in as a 'by the way', type thing. I'd been a little concerned that she hadn't volunteered the results of her sexual health check, and the doctor refused to disclose them to me.

"Yes. All fine. Did you end up getting tested?" She replied, once I'd asked her.

"Yes. Not the most pleasant experience. That doctor didn't like men much I think, she was rather.....rough in the way she handled 'things'. I'm fine though." She began to laugh at my obvious discomfort. "What's so funny?"

"You. Did you expect her to say a prayer over your man parts?" *Erm, yes. Actually, I expected her to be slightly*

136

overawed.

"Well, I expected her to be gentle, and treat them with kindness and respect, not don rubber gloves, and behave as if she had something nasty in her hand. She was rather brutal with the swab." I shuddered slightly at the memory.

"Poor boy, well if you're good, I'll make it up to you on Friday." *What? I was banking on a shag tonight. You can't do that to me.*

"You're making me wait till Friday? That's.....cruel."

"Anticipation is the best bit, I'm sure you said that once. Besides, you get to go bareback, surely that's worth waiting for?" She smiled, and looked all coquettish. *I bought you flowers, said sorry, put up with a dyke doctor jabbing me with a sharpened swab, and now I've got to wait?*

She skipped off home, leaving me with blue balls yet again. I went into my study with the express idea of finding some good porn for a wank session, but ended up emailing Carl.

To: Carl Verve
Date: 18th June 2013
From: Ivan Porenski
Subject: Back on track

Carl

Thought I'd drop you a line. The deals all over. Everything is fine, and the threat to Elle is over. To say we are both relieved is an understatement. She was, understandably, rather angry with me over the whole thing, so I bought her flowers, and said sorry, because she said that was what she wanted.

She says I'm not romantic enough, and that I treat her like a man. I suppose the lines blur because of our work involvement. I just wish I knew how to handle things better, you know, how to be romantic, and actually show her how I feel. I told her that I was in love with her, which shocked her, as she said she hadn't had a clue that I felt that deeply. Do you think a shopping trip would help? I know women like stuff like that. Beyond that, I feel a bit clueless. I'm not used to feeling so stupid and out of my depth.

Regards

Ivan.

I sat back to wait for his reply, googling 'romantic gestures', and reading up on sappy proposals of marriage at the top of the Eiffel Tower. *Hmm, not relevant.* My email pinged.

To: Ivan Porenski
Date: 18th June 2013
From: Carl Verve
Subject: re Back on track

Ivan

I'm delighted to hear that the source of all your recent stresses has passed, and that you can again concentrate on your burgeoning romance with Elle. As regards your dilemma, you may wish to consider compartmentalising your work and personal relationships, that way the work theme doesn't impinge on your out of work time together. This can be achieved by something as simple as changing out of your work clothes to see her outside of the office, or any kind of ritual to mark the end of your working day. Have a think about that, and figure out what will work best for you.

I don't believe there are any definitive guides to being romantic, and I think we established that Elle is not overly interested in material things, so while she might enjoy a shopping trip, I doubt if it would buy her affections. From what you've already told me, she's more likely to be swayed by having your undivided attention, especially if she is unsure of your feelings or, as you point out, she was unable to successfully 'read' your emotions. It seems to me that you are expecting this relationship to become permanent extremely quickly, so just give her time, care for her, and try your best to communicate how you feel, which I'm aware you find difficult.

Regards

Carl

I read his email several times. Changing out of my work clothes was easy, and no big hassle. The harder part was giving Elle undivided attention. With so many companies now under my control, I could work 24 hours a day, and it wouldn't be enough. I sat and made a plan for our weekend, and emailed Mrs Ballard to call me first thing the following morning. My musings were interrupted by my mobile ringing. Seeing that it was Kristov, I answered.

"Ivan, thanks for taking care of the house at Windsor. I owe you one," he said.

"No problem at all. How's retirement?"

"All good thanks. I understand it all belongs to you now, all the companies."

"Yep, although I need to go to Russia and get a notary to change everything over. I'll do that within the next couple of weeks. Could do without it really, but I need to get it sorted."

"Vlad wanted you to have it. Ivan.....there's something I need to discuss with you."

"Go on." I was intrigued.

"I need to tell you face to face. Can I come over?" I was even more intrigued, so agreed to see him. Half an hour later, he arrived. Nico wasn't terribly impressed at having the head of the Russian mafia in the penthouse, but I felt quite calm around Kristov, as he had nothing to gain by harming me. I still tucked a gun in my pocket though.

Kristov looked extremely relaxed in his grey slacks and casual polo shirt. It seemed odd to me, as I'd only ever seen him in a black suit before. He didn't even look like he was wearing a gun. I took him into the lounge, and poured us each a scotch.

"You needed to see me.." I looked at him expectantly.

"Yes.. When you first met Anatoly, when you bought a gun from him, did he react when you told him your name?"

I thought back. "Yes, he kind of flinched. I don't know why though."

Kristov looked a little uncomfortable. "We were all looking for you. Russian mafia all over the world were trying to find you. Vlad had an alert out." My stomach began to churn.

"I see....why?"

"When you went missing from West Biryulevo, we had no idea where you were. He was desperate to track you down. Wouldn't say why, but I have my own theory that I pieced together from bits and pieces of information I gleaned over the years."

"Hang on, how did he know I'd run away from West Biryulevo?"

"He owned the factory there Ivan, well, you own it now. He sent in his militia to stop the strike by killing the ringleaders, only he knew one of them, rather well it seems." I stared at him, reeling at the revelation. "He knew your mother Ivan, was furious when he found out she'd been executed, I remember him ranting at the man in charge of the militia. Both of you were meant to be spared."

"So he ordered my parent's deaths?" I stared incredulously at Kristov, "it still doesn't account for why he put an alert out Kristov."

"I have a theory. Tell me Ivan, did you resemble your father?"

I thought back. My dad was much shorter than I, with sandy coloured hair, and pale blue eyes. "No, but I think I resembled my mother. She had dark blue eyes like mine."

"As did Vlad. My theory is that he was in fact your father, although I can't prove it. It would account for his search for you, and how he let you into his trusted circle so quickly."

"He wanted me to marry his daughter, which, if your theory is correct, would have been my half sister." All of a sudden, I felt bilious.

"I know, but you have to remember that Vlad didn't have the same....boundaries as the rest of us. He would have seen it as keeping the wealth in the family."

"If that's true, Kristov, that's...sick. Although I did wonder why he was so sanguine about his 19 year old bodyguard fucking his 16 year old daughter. I wonder if Dascha knew?" Kristov shook his head.

"No, I don't think so. Dascha was a lot like him, a bit sick, but I don't think she would have been happy to marry her own brother. She just liked that you were powerful and good looking, plus, for a long time, controlled by her father."

"She was vicious to me, Kristov, we hated each other, couldn't bear to be in the same room." I thought back, we'd never had a good sex life, even at the start. She'd been pretty enough, but I'd always found fucking her....difficult. At the time I'd put it down to still not being over Irina. She put it down to preferring to give pain as opposed to pleasure. We'd agreed to not bother, both preferring to look for our sexual pleasures elsewhere. *I've fucked my sister, shit.*

Kristov looked sympathetic. "We could all see how...dysfunctional....your relationship was. On more than a few occasions I had to take her...partners...to hospital. We all knew what she was like. Even Vlad knew, I mean, he let her build a torture chamber at his home. I doubt if many fathers would be happy to allow that." He looked disapproving.

"So if your theory is true, how do we prove it?" I asked.

"I can put you in touch with an investigator. She can see if there's any of his DNA available. He had a biopsy done in Moscow the last time he was there. He had a dodgy prostrate."

"Ok Kristov. See what you can do, because I'd like this proven either way, and let's hope to God that you're wrong." We shook hands, and he left, leaving me reeling.

Chapter 9

I tried to put my meeting with Kristov out of my mind, reasoning that Vlad and Dascha had had their comeuppance, so there was very little to be gained by getting angry. Instead, I had another Scotch and went to bed to force myself to think about Elle instead.

The next morning, I had a lengthy conversation with Mrs Ballard regarding the coming weekend. She was to spend the day in Harrods purchasing everything Elle could possibly need for a weekend away, then fly straight over in my jet to prepare the villa for our arrival on Friday. She had half an hour to pack her own case before a driver was due to pick her up to drive her into town.

As soon as I got into the office, it was full on. With the added complexities of Conde Nast, it was back to back meetings. I barely drew breath, although, I have to admit, it was quite interesting dealing with top end magazines as opposed to phone masts and cables. I kept tabs on Elle via updates from Roger, and could see that she was working hard too. I called her that night, just to hear her voice. She sounded a little tired, but we flirted on the phone, which left me needing a wank before I could sleep.

I struggled to concentrate the following day, knowing that within 24 hours I'd be making love to Elle. I hadn't told her, but I'd never fucked bareback before, mainly because my dick was my favourite body part, and I'd always felt the need to protect it.

I took a little break to go over to the west end and pick up some sex toys from a discreet adult shop for our weekend. I also nipped into Harrods for some new swimming shorts. I even picked out a couple of new bikinis for Elle while I was in there. I was determined to be a good boyfriend.

I spoke to her that night, and explained that she didn't need to pack anything, as I had taken care of all of her needs. She sounded a little unsure, asking if I was planning to make her go naked all weekend. *Ha! If only!* With all our new sex toys safely packed for Nico to bring onto the plane, I was able to relax, and get on with some work. I was planning a rather whistle-stop tour of all Vlad's companies, which involved a lot of organisation and planning. With a full list of his holdings in front of me, (which included the factory in West Biryulevo), I was able to work out a route that involved the least flying possible.

I was a little worried about flying with Elle. I hated anything to do with aeroplanes, loathed travelling on them, and was terrified when taking off and landing. I decided to try and conceal my fear from her, as I didn't want to appear weak. For that reason, I always flew alone on a private jet, which was maintained to perfection, albeit barely used. Commercial flights were too embarrassing, as everyone could see me shaking, and often puking.

The morning dragged interminably slowly. I had a long, boring meeting with some analysts, who seemed to delight in stating the bloody obvious, as if I were a twelve year old child, as opposed to a seasoned businessman who had built a vast empire. I was probably a little short tempered with them, but when one of them tried to explain the concept of supply and demand in patronising tones, I snapped, and gave him a mouthful. Watching him visibly shrink at my harsh words cheered me up enormously. I enjoyed asserting my superiority in business.

I sat and watched the clock for the last half hour, my

anticipation building with every passing minute. When it was finally time to go and collect Elle from her office, I was actually quite nervous. I needn't have been, she looked delighted to see me, and confessed that the morning had dragged for her too. She only had her handbag with her, which pleased me, as it showed that she trusted me.

As we travelled down in the lift, I couldn't help but tweak her bottom, she glanced sideways and smiled at my naughtiness. I mouthed the word 'bareback' at her, to let her know what was on my mind, which made her giggle. *This weekend's gonna be fun.*

The girls met us at London City, and we were all whisked through the airport, and onto the plane quickly and efficiently. As soon as the aircraft doors were closed, it all got difficult. How I ever thought I'd be able to conceal my fear from Elle, I don't know. She spotted it straight away, and immediately held my hand, telling me that lots of people are afraid of flying. As soon as she told me not to be embarrassed, I blushed, feeling my face turn beet red. When she revealed that she'd thought we'd be shagging on the plane, I had to confess that I couldn't even walk around during a flight, which made long haul particularly difficult, for obvious reasons.

She held my hand until we were cruising, and seemed quite relaxed as she sipped her champagne, and smiled at Bella who had sensed my distress, and clambered onto my lap. With Elle knowing about my flying issue, I was able to relax a little, and drink some champagne, sharing a drop with Tania, who loved it.

With some alcohol inside me, I calmed enough to tell Elle about my villa, which was my pride and joy. I'd bought it about five years before, from a Hollywood actor who had fallen into debt due to excessive gambling. It was perfection itself, completely private, easily protected, and had the best views in the South of France. Best of all, I'd kept it secret from Dascha, which meant she'd never been there, so as far as I was concerned, it was pristine and untainted from bad memories. I'd had a couple of hook-ups there, but nobody who's name I could even remember, let alone have memories of.

I held Elle's hand during our descent into Nice airport, clinging onto her for dear life. In a strange way, just her touch, and her calm acceptance of my fear, seemed to help, and I coped with the landing without being sick.

As soon as we landed, I whipped off my jacket and tie, and rolled up my sleeves. I clipped the girl's leads onto their collars, and we made our way out to the car. During the journey, Elle gazed at the shimmering Cote D'Azure as I told her about St-John-Cap-Ferrat, the small town near my villa.

When she caught her first sight of the house, her jaw dropped open, and she declared it 'beautiful', in her breathy voice. It did look impressive, and seeing it through her eyes was like seeing it for the first time myself. I'd loved it from the start too.

She greeted Mrs Ballard like an old friend, and I briefly showed her around. She liked the infinity pool, and the views, but I dragged her upstairs for a shower before I could show her the entire house. I was a little impatient.

I booted the dogs out of the shower room, and quickly stripped her naked. She attempted to seductively undress me slowly, *I'm already seduced baby,* but I couldn't wait, and practically ripped my clothes off. I needed to shower, as I was sticky and sweaty from the flight, but I wanted my first bareback in a bed, although I was concerned that I wouldn't last terribly long.

She took care of that my giving me a superb blow job in the shower, gently capturing my cock between her lips as she knelt to wash my legs. I watched as she licked every inch of my cock and balls, before cupping my testicles gently, and concentrating on sucking my cock. With the steam from the shower billowing around us, it was incredibly erotic. Her plump lips worked rhythmically over the head, while she gently pumped the shaft. When she looked up at me with those baby blue eyes, I knew I needed to come. I could feel my balls begin to tighten, and knew I was at that point of no return.

I panicked a little about coming in her mouth, and garbled a warning, which she ignored, and carried on sucking. I had no choice but to let go, cringing slightly as I shot a huge load directly down her throat. She didn't miss a beat, and swallowed the lot, seemingly unconcerned. It was the sexiest thing I'd ever seen.

Afterwards, I washed her all over, desperate to run my hands over every inch of her. I wanted her as horny as I felt. I dried us both off, and took her to the bed.

I started off by licking and sucking on her clit, but she begged for my cock. I crawled up her body and nudged into her. *Fuck! That feels....amazing.* She was scorching hot, and soaking wet. For the first time I could really feel it, as her pussy enveloped me in a hot, wet, velvet hug. She must have been as horny as they come, because she came within minutes. I felt every ripple and pulse. It was as if I'd fucked in black and white all my life, and this was glorious technicolor.

I stayed in the same position, savouring every thrust, every moment inside her. When she came a second time, it pushed me over the edge, and I pumped her full of cum, loving the feeling of total abandon that I never got while fucking a hook-up.

I kissed her with the same gratitude that I'd kissed Irina for my very first shag. It had almost felt like I'd lost my second virginity, and I was spoilt for life. I hoped I'd never have to use a condom again.

I dried her off, and flopped down beside her to pull her into an embrace. She felt so soft and warm and familiar snuggled into my chest. I felt....complete, as if I'd found the other part of myself that I'd been missing. Emotion surged through me. "I will make you love me Elle, I promise. I will be the man you fall in love with. I just hope that you will love me as much as I love you, because I love you with every fibre of my body." I held my breath as she digested my words. Words I'd never uttered to another living soul before.

"I think I'm in love with you too. It scares me," she replied, eventually. I moved to look at her face. She looked uncertain.

"Baby, don't ever let it scare you. What we have, we should enjoy. We have to grab this happiness and hold onto it. Now, what do you say we get dressed, and go out to eat? There's the most fabulous little restaurant just on the way to the village." I wanted to change the subject before she changed her mind, either that, or I got ridiculously mushy, and embarrassed myself.

"That sounds wonderful."

I took her to Pierre's place, which was a romantic little restaurant set in a picturesque courtyard in the middle of town. Pierre greeted me by name, and gave us a private table set with a flickering candle. Elle looked even more beautiful by candlelight. I let Pierre choose what to serve us, as he was an expert on the very best fish available from the local market each day. Elle was happy with that too. I loved how easy going she was outside of her work. She seemed happy to just go with the flow, and not make life difficult, which in turn, made being with her easy.

We sipped our wine, and relaxed. We discussed our ambitions in life, which for her, consisted of making partner in a law firm. *That's easy baby, I'll buy you one if you want.* I will confess, I was curious as to whether or not she wanted a family. I quite liked the idea of having sons to pass my company on to. She didn't rule it out, just said that she would have to be very sure, as she was scared of losing her career, and ending up like her mother.

When she quizzed me in return, I confessed that I wanted to own the world. She remarked, rather wryly, that I seemed to own a lot of it already, which made me smile. She seemed to understand my fear of poverty, and reminded me that both of us were never in danger of returning to it. The only difference between us was that she was ashamed of her beginnings, while I wore mine like a badge of honour.

The truth was, I loved being rich. Loved having beautiful homes, wardrobes full of clothes, and millions in the bank. I adored being able to demand the best of everything, and having men envy me. The downside had been never being able to have a normal relationship. I knew women were dazzled by my pretty face, and enamoured by my fat wallet. Until Elle, I'd always questioned their motives, and come to the conclusion that they'd had an agenda. Having seen with my own eyes, her walking away from Oscar Golding, I knew she could have a far wealthier man than I. She'd never mentioned his money, and had dismissed my assertion that he could have given her a fabulous lifestyle. I grudgingly admitted that Carl was possibly correct that she wasn't terribly interested in my money, but in creating her own success. Just knowing that, made me want to shower her with gifts, and heap riches at her feet.

I also confessed that I sometimes felt a little inadequate around more educated people, which she reassured me, didn't show. I changed the subject to sex, telling her I wanted to make mad, passionate love to her again, to which she replied, "great, let's go," which made me laugh.

It wasn't funny getting a huge erection in the car on the short drive home. I complained that, as a grown man, I should be able to control my responses, as opposed to getting embarrassing hard-ons, and being obsessed with Elle's tits. It was like being fifteen years old again. She handed me her bag to hold in front of me as we pulled into the drive, to disguise the tent in the front of my trousers.

I pulled her straight up to the bedroom, desperate to fuck her in every way possible. When I asked her what she wanted me to do to her, she seemed a little stumped, but agreed to try whatever I wanted. I decided to introduce her to some sex toys, so, leaving her on the bed, I went down to the spare room to get a selection.

Now, after my ordeal at the hands of Karen Hodges, it was probably a little surprising that I enjoyed a butt plug, however, the aristocrat who'd introduced me to the sex swing had also got me acquainted with a well-lubed butt plug, and the delights it could bring. I'd bought Elle a tiny 'beginner size' one, so covered it in lube, and laid it on the tray, along with an eye mask, and a wand. I was going to take her to her limit tonight. I stripped off, and made my way back to the bedroom.

She looked beautiful, waiting on all fours, her pussy open, and willing. I started slowly, licking her clit, teasing her pussy, until I made my way up to lick her anus. I wanted there to be no taboo between us, and I wanted to own every inch of her. As my tongue caressed the opening, I felt her squirm a little, so stopped, and nudged my cock into her pussy. *Fuck, that's still fantastic.* I held still for a moment to slide the plug in, which made her gasp. *Hmm, is that good or bad?* She didn't ask me to stop, so I gently thrust back and forth for a little while, listening to her moans of pleasure, before reaching over for the vibrator, clicking it on, and reaching round to press it lightly onto her clit.

With my cock sliding in and out, her clit and arse being assaulted, there was one pleasure zone that was being left out, so I told her to play with her nipples while I fucked her. She had two huge orgasms on the trot, and I felt every ripple and contraction of both of them, like a cock massage. She was practically screaming as her body shuddered and shook. After the second one began to subside, I took pity on her, and dropped the vibrator to power into her. I deserved a big fucking orgasm too, as reward for my creativity, I reasoned. My iron-hard dick rode the last of her orgasm, before practically exploding, and pumping a bucketful of cum into her.

She was so overcome, she barely said a word, as I cleaned us both up, and dumped the sex toys in the bathroom, before letting the spaniels in. She didn't seem unhappy, just dazed, which, I reasoned, was a good thing. The spaniels settled themselves in, and within minutes, all three of my favourite girls were fast asleep. I lay awake for a while, just listening to them breathing, well, snoring in the case of the spaniels, and marveled at how content I felt.

She was already up, and out of bed by the time the girls and I awoke. I threw on a pair of shorts, and padded downstairs to make us both a coffee. After spending a few minutes trying to fathom out the machine, I gave up, and went to look for her instead. She was out on the terrace, crying. Now I knew I hadn't done anything wrong, so asked what was troubling her. It turned out that she was having a sad moment over her mum, telling me that she felt upset that her mother had never experienced such a beautiful, and perfect place. I confided that I'd done the exact same thing.

The interior designer had just left, after her final tweaking of cushions, and checking that the cleaners had done their job properly after the builders had finished. Finally alone, I wandered from room to room, marveling at how lovely it all looked, and happy that it was all mine. I stroked the glossy, white, poggenpohl kitchen, and opened the enormous fridge to see the vast selection of fine foods. Taking a peach, I stepped out onto the terrace to eat it, and gaze at the stupendous view.

For some reason, I thought of my parents, and of our tenement in West Biryulevo, with its tiny rooms, and dank stairwells. 'My father would have adored this place', I thought, 'mum too', although she wouldn't have liked the white kitchen, thinking it would show the dirt. I remembered the tiny TV they made do with, and the rickety furniture, with its frequent mending's, and scratches that were testament to the reality of such cramped living.

I remembered my mother telling me that she didn't need to be rich, that she was happy with my dad and I beside her. I remembered us all being cold when the tenement boiler packed up, and dad moving the telly to the bedroom, so that the three of us could keep warm in bed while watching a Mexican game show.

I'd never actually cried for my parents. Directly after their deaths, I'd been too scared by the need to escape, the journey, and the fear of being alone, to actually mourn them. It was only in this perfect place that a sob finally broke free, and I cried like a baby for the life I could never show them, and my sadness at their life of poverty. The little boy inside me wanted my parents approval. for the success I'd built, buying this slice of heaven, paying cash for it, and making it even more beautiful.

I shook myself back to the present, and stroked Elle's hair gently as she told me how intimidated her mother would've been by the luxury. She smiled when I told her that my mother would've been hanging washing on the balcony, and helping the staff with the housework. As we chatted, I noticed that Elle had made herself a coffee, so I took a cheeky swig, and almost spat it back out as it had no sugar in it. When she objected, telling me it had taken her ages to work out the fancy coffee machine, I admitted that I couldn't use it, and asked her to make us both fresh ones.

After breakfast, I coated her in sun lotion, noticing she'd chosen one of the bikinis that I'd picked out for her, rather than one that Mrs Ballard had bought. I was delighted when she told me that it had stood out to her, and had been her favourite.

We spent a lovely day playing in the pool, fucking in the pool, and laying around on the terrace. It was great to just relax with Elle, she was good company, and enormous fun, with a wicked sense of humour. Best of all, she treated me like a lover, rather than a rich lover. She didn't seem overawed by extreme luxury, or stifled by having staff. She just seemed to take it all in her stride in that funny, easy-going way of hers.

I decided to take her into town to have a look around the shops, which were quite high end for such a small, sleepy place. Truth was, I was desperate to buy her something, as I wanted her to have beautiful things, and acknowledge that I was the only man to give them to her. We passed a jewelers on the main street, and a necklace caught my eye. It was exquisite, made of gold filigree, and studded with diamonds. I pulled her in, and got Nico to translate my request to see it more closely.

It was almost impossibly perfect, delicate, and sophisticated, with impeccable workmanship. Nico informed me that the price was thirty thousand Euros, which I thought quite fair for such a stunning piece, so I bought it, and placed it round her neck. She declared that it was beautiful, and that she loved it, kissing me in gratitude. That was what I loved about her, easy going. If I'd bought it for Dascha, she would have bitched that it was too long or short, and that the diamonds were either too big or too small. Elle just said thank you.

When I saw a pair of cufflinks that I liked, Elle disappeared into the shop, returning a few minutes later holding a little box for me. It was the first time since leaving the children's home that I'd been given a gift. I gulped slightly to stop myself welling up, and admitted that I'd not been given gifts since I'd been 17. Her face clouded a little, and she looked concerned. "Surely other girlfriends have bought you things?" She asked.

I didn't really want to admit that I'd only had two 'proper' girlfriends before her. Hundreds, maybe thousands of hook-ups maybe, but only Irina, and Dascha for any length of time, and Dascha didn't really count. She'd once announced that she was going shopping to get me a birthday present, and come home with armfuls of stuff for herself, telling me she'd forgotten to get me anything.

We stopped for a coffee, and a sit down, and were watching the world go by, when Elle dropped the bombshell that she had a holiday booked with her MALE flatmate. She brushed off my concerns by claiming that her wasn't interested in her, and thought of her like a kid sister. *Yeah, right. When he sees you in a bikini, he's really not gonna notice those tits.*

She started doing that lawyer thing, arguing her point, even bringing up the weekend she stayed at Oscar's house to keep safe, making the incorrect assumption that I hadn't minded that. I corrected her, telling her that I'd in fact been freaked out, and hadn't slept all weekend. She reached over to grasp my hand, and tried to reassure me that her flatmate didn't fancy her at all, and had never so much as flirted with her. She then went on to say, "If I wanted someone else, I wouldn't be with you. I would end it with you, rather than cheat on you."

I regarded her intently, she was a curious mixture of breathtaking naivety, and solid morals. *A rare combination.* "A woman of integrity, a rare and exquisite thing," I said. Her words had, if anything, strengthened my admiration of her. For about the millionth time, I wondered what Oscar Golding had done to cause her to leave him. I didn't want to make the same mistake and lose her. Women like her were few and far between, and had to be appreciated for their strength of character.

I took her out to dinner that night, to the best restaurant in the town. I wanted to show her off, and be seen with her. I even got the chance to show off my new knowledge of wine, choosing a Chateaux Margot to go with our meal, which Elle said was perfect. She seemed oblivious to my lack of confidence when it came to subjects such as fine wines, which meant I could relax with her. I realised that her superior education only stretched as far as the world of law, so somehow didn't make me feel inadequate around her, as opposed to Oscar's well rounded knowledge, and habit of making me feel like an ignorant peasant.

After five courses, and a few bottles of fine wine, we were both sleepy as we headed back to the house. She rested her head on my shoulder in the car, and sighed happily. I took her straight up to bed, and undressed her quickly, before she fell asleep. I made love to her gently, more to just be inside her than anything else, as I didn't think either of us fancied lots of bouncing about.

Plus, I felt as though I'd done the romance part all evening, and wanted to just feel her, connect with her, and love her. I was also getting a bit addicted to bareback sex.

She woke me up as she got out of bed the next morning, so I threw on some shorts, and followed her downstairs, finding her already out on the terrace. She made me a coffee, and smiled when I suggested taking the girls for a walk on the beach, as it was barely six o'clock, and we'd pretty much have the place to ourselves. With Nico, and his assistant Viktor in tow, we drove down to the seafront. The girls loved the beach, playing in and out of the waves, and racing around on the soft sand. Elle had just slipped a pair of shorts on over her bikini, and was looking tanned and relaxed.

As we walked, I told her about the companies I'd be inheriting from Vlad, and how I planned to incorporate them into Retinski. I was just telling her how the notaries worked, when I realised she wasn't standing next to me anymore. I glanced around to see her slicing through the med. Straining my eyes, I saw that she was powering towards a clearly distressed Bella, who looked as though she was going to drown any moment. My heart stopped.

I think Nico saw what was happening at the same moment that I did, as he barked at Viktor to grab Tania and get her on a lead. With Tania safe, I could only watch helplessly, with my heart in my mouth, as Elle raced to get my baby before she perished.

With only a few metres to go, I saw Bella sink beneath the surface, I cried out, my hand flying up to my face in horror. *Not my baby girl, please, don't take her too.* I could only watch helplessly as Elle dived down to look for her, re-appearing moments later with Bella in her arms.

I saw her place my girl over her shoulder, and rub her back vigorously, before flipping onto her back to swim back to shore with Bella unconscious on her tummy. *Please don't let her be dead Mama, please let her stay with me.*

It seemed to take Elle ages to get back to the shore. I waded in to assist her getting out, and laid Bella on the sand. She promptly threw up a load of seawater, and tried to stand up. *She's alive!*

I turned my attention to Nico, barking at him to get a vet to meet us back at the house. My anger began to rise, as it was his job to keep watch on the girls, and I suspected he'd been too busy ogling an early sunbather's tits to actually do the job he was paid extremely well to do.

Elle stood dripping, as I gently stroked Bella, letting Tania sniff her, before picking her up to carry her to the car. *Does she make you feel protected?* Carl's words raced around my head in a continuous loop, as we drove back to the villa. Poor Bella seemed in shock, and was still bringing up saltwater. I worried that she wouldn't recover.

Back at the villa, Elle disappeared to change and dry off, while I waited for the vet. "What the fuck were you looking at on that beach, because it wasn't my dog?" I demanded. Both guards looked sheepish.

"Sorry boss," said Viktor, "I had my eyes on the beach, you know, for threats. I thought Nico was watching the dogs."

Nico was saved by the arrival of the vet, as I needed him to translate for me. He told the vet what had happened, and how long she was under water for. I watched as the vet examined her, checking her heart and lungs with his stethoscope.

"I don't think there's any permanent damage, as she was under only a few moments. The saltwater will make her feel quite nauseous for a day or two, just make sure she has plenty of water to drink, and light, easily digestible food which is salt free. If she's not better in a couple of days, then call me, or her regular vet, and we'll run some tests," said the vet, via Nico.

He checked her gums, telling me via Nico, that she looked ok, but to call if they turned grey or blue. I shook his hand, and said goodbye. Nico showed him out, and presumably slunk off before I could give him a mouthful. I noticed Elle had come down, and was sitting stroking Tania's ears.

"How is she?" She asked. I'd forgotten that the entire conversation had been in French and Russian, so Elle and Mrs Ballard hadn't a clue what had been said. I told them that Bella would be feeling a little sick, but was otherwise fine, and relayed the story of what happened to Mrs Ballard, adding that it was lucky that Elle was such a superb swimmer, as nobody else would've been quick enough to save her. *Does she make you feel protected?*

Mrs Ballard stroked Bella, and turned to me. "Bet it scared the life out of you."

"I'm still shaking," I admitted, "I really thought I'd lost her. Elle, I can't thank you enough, you definitely saved her life." *Does she make you feel protected? Everyone you ever loved has died.* The words played like a continuous loop through my mind as we sat watching Bella.

I couldn't shake it for the whole day. The deaths of my parents and Irina had been a subject I'd explored at length with Carl. I believed that my life had been alternately blessed with great wealth, and cursed with great loss, as if I had to give up the people I loved in return for the blessing of success. By allowing myself to love both Elle and the girls, I worried that the cycle would repeat itself again, and they'd be taken from me. The price for my moments of contentment the last few days had prompted a reminder from the gods that they'd all be snatched away.

My anxiety grew exponentially during the flight home, and by the time we landed, I was tormented by the thoughts that something terrible would happen to Elle and the girls, I tried to shake it out of my mind, but it wouldn't stop. I was desperate to talk to Carl, so when Elle announced that she needed to go home and get ready for work the next day, I didn't argue.

As soon as I got home, I went to my study, and pulled out the secret laptop I kept purely for private conversations.

To: Carl Verve
From: Ivan Porenski
Date: 23rd June 2013
Subject: going mad

Carl

I don't really know where to start with this. I took Elle and the dogs for a weekend away to my villa in France. We grew really close, had amazing sex, and I experienced moments of true happiness and contentment with her. She seems to really understand me, and has told me that she thinks she's in love with me too.

This morning, we took the dogs to the beach. I didn't notice that Bella got into trouble in the sea, but Elle did, and saved her life. I'm not exaggerating, nobody else could have got to her in time, (Elle's an amazing swimmer). Now I have a loop in my head telling me that everyone I love dies, and your words, 'does she make you feel protected' too, as if I'm not capable on my own or something. Is the price of my success the loss of anyone I love? I'm tormented.

Regards
Ivan

I sat back to wait for his answer, which, luckily, didn't take long.

To: Ivan Porenski
From: Carl Verve
Date: 23rd June 2013
Subject: re going mad

Ivan

Lets break this down a little. I'm delighted to hear that you and Elle appear to be forming a very solid, emotionally enriching, relationship. I can understand that this makes you feel exposed to emotional hurt, however, any connection with another person or animal has the capacity to hurt us. I hope as time goes on, you begin to feel more secure that you can have a rich, emotional relationship without fear. Regarding Elle saving Bella's life, I'd suggest that you might like to make a list of her strengths, and a list of your own. Clearly Elle is an accomplished swimmer, in the same way that you are an accomplished marksman. In this case, her strength was put to good use in preventing a calamity. That's not to say that there won't be occasions in the future when your strengths will be needed to assist her. I'm sure from previous emails that you have assisted her career using your contacts and position.

If this episode only happened this morning, there's always the possibility that you're still in shock, as I can appreciate, it must have been a heart-stopping event. These feelings and thoughts will dissipate given time. With a different perspective, it may be possible for you to understand that disaster was averted, and loving or not loving Elle would have made no difference to the situation, except possibly, the outcome.

One thing I'd like you to give some thought to is why you didn't feel able to share these worries with Elle, as she may be the best person to put your mind at rest.

Regards

Carl

I read his email a couple of times. He always made sense, but I knew the thought loops racing round my head weren't something I wanted to share with Elle, she'd think I was nuts or something. My musings were interrupted by a call from Kristov. "Hello Ivan, have you given any further thought to our conversation last week?"

"Not a huge amount, as I've been away."

"Are you going to Moscow soon?"

"Yes, next week, Tuesday to be precise. Just working out an itinerary now. Less flights the better." Kristov knew all about my flying issues, and had thought it was quite funny. *Bastard*

"Of course. I've come up with an investigator based in Moscow. She can dig around a bit, see if she can get the truth for you. I also have to discuss a more delicate matter, mainly the guns. Are you going to be keeping that going?"

Vlad had been involved in drug and gun running routes, namely, controlling them. I had zero desire to be part of that scene anymore, and besides, I made more money out of Retinski legitimately, than could be made out of Vlad's murky activities. "No, tell you what Kristov, why don't you come out of retirement, and take that over? It's not one for me." I heard him take a sharp intake of breath.

"Ivan, are you sure? You're giving away about forty mill a year?"

"Very sure Kristov, have it as payment for your heads up about Elle. I owed you for that. Obviously this buys your loyalty for evermore. Any threats, you tell me."

"Of course, that goes without saying. Anytime you need my assistance, you know where to come."

"I suggest you start a legit security company as cover. Easy to do, just a rented office and a phone. Channel the money through in fake invoices, which cleans it up enough to use for property etc. Just be aware that I don't want that world touching me. My business is legit, and I want it to stay that way." I needed to make it clear that my involvement was over. Kristov would have to deal with any squabbles over the routes, and deal with any rivals trying to muscle in on the action.

"Yes, of course. Nothing will ever come back to you, I give you my word," Kristov assured me. "Just let me know when you're in Moscow, and I'll get Natalya to contact you. Don't be fooled by her appearance, she has contacts everywhere, and is a damn good investigator. She'll find the truth for you."

With my final link to my old life finally severed, I slumped onto the sofa beside Bella, who seemed to be recovering well. I sat and contemplated the day, while Tania, jealous as always, clambered onto my lap. All my girls were safe, I was a rich, legitimate businessman, and had cut the final tie that bound me to my old life. My sulk seemed to dissipate, and I started to feel much better.

I fixed the three of us some food, and turned on the Elle-cam in my office, scowling when I saw Golding sitting on her sofa drinking wine. I heard her ask him who he was seeing at the moment, and him replying 'no-one'. She didn't reply, and I watched her get her ironing board out, and begin pressing her clothes. *I can arrange someone to do that for you baby.* Golding clearly had the same thought, as he seemed surprised that she was doing it herself too.

I watched her work her way through the pile of clothes, and then tell Oscar he had to go home as she needed to go to bed. I noted that she didn't even kiss him goodbye, just held the door open for him. She pottered about for a few more minutes, washing up their glasses, and tidying up, then abruptly turned the lights off, as she went to bed. I'd been so fascinated watching her, that I'd left it too late to call her. *Damn.*

I was at my desk by 8 the next morning. I had a busy day ahead, and had a lot to clear up before jetting off to Moscow the following day. I emailed Ms Pearson, Elle's boss for a meeting to discuss, and amend my will, and also to discuss my request for Elle to become a non-exec at my companies. I called Ranenkiov in to sort out a contract for her. His eyes widened as I instructed him to add a clause saying that she would become MD of Retinski, and chair of Conde Nast, in the event of anything happening to me. "Is that wise?" Ranenkiov asked.

"Absolutely. She has more integrity than any man sitting on either board. She's a highly qualified lawyer, and no slouch when it comes to business and finance. I can't think of anyone better."

"I agree that she's a superb lawyer, and an asset to Retinski, but acting MD?" He replied, pulling a face. "How do you think that would go down with the other, more established board members?"

"I don't really care. All of you combined own less that 5% of the company, so as the owner of the remaining 95%, I get final say."

He nodded, and stayed silent. I got on with an email to Elle, explaining why I went moody on her the previous day, and apologising for it. I also invited her to dinner that evening at my place, and informed her of my trip to Russia. I would've taken her out, but I wanted to spend the bulk of the evening in my sex room, so I figured it was better to stay in.

I didn't have to wait long for a lovely reply from her, telling me she would be delighted to come for dinner, and assuring me that she understood my distress the day before over Bella's incident. She went on to say that she'd be worrying about me, and I should take plenty of security, which warmed me. It had been a very long time since anyone had given a hoot about whether I was dead or alive.

I sent a bit of a mushy one back, telling her I'd worry about her too, and that I'd be back in time for her mother's funeral. It was nice having someone to send soppy emails to during the day, which was an activity quite easy to get addicted to. I emailed Mrs Watton to sort dinner for two, then minimised the screen, and got on with some work.

I met with Ms Pearson at half eleven at her office in the city. She was a sharp, rather ball-breaking woman, who was well known for her brilliant mind, and laser focus. Thankfully, she was also a bit of a sucker for a pretty face, so I smiled my best, most dazzling smile at her as we sat down to discuss my requirements.

"Mr Porenski, nice to see you again. Now you mentioned that you wanted to alter your will, and had a couple of other matters to discuss. Shall we begin with your will?"

"Certainly. I have acquired another few companies since last seeing you, all of which I'd like to add, along with a new beneficiary." I watched as she pulled up a copy of my will on her screen. When I'd altered it after separating from Dascha, I'd left everything to Bella, Tania, and various dog charities. "I would like to leave my entire estate, including all the properties and companies to Elle Reynolds." Ms Pearson's head snapped up from her computer.

"Everything? Without exceptions or residuals?"

"Everything, but there is another request I need to make from you personally," I paused, "I need to make a living will, as part of my contingency planning."

"Certainly. What would you like me to do?" She looked curious.

"If anything happens to me which prevents me from running my companies, you are to disclose the contents of my will to Ms Reynolds. She'll need to know that they'll become hers, so she can act accordingly. This leads me to another question, is there any restriction from you in my adding her as a non-exec on my boards?"

She regarded me intently. "No, if it means she can deliver Conde Nast as a client, and retain Retinski over the long term."

"I think that's a given, plus Retinski has almost doubled in size with the addition of Vladimir Meranov's estate, so should prove even more lucrative for your company. Now tell me, do I pay her direct, or day rates to you for her use?" I planned to pay Elle well anyway, but it was better to clear up any ambiguities.

"Just pay her direct. I'm sure her salary will be more than covered by the extra work she brings in. If that doesn't manifest, we can talk again in say, six months," she said. *You really are no fool.*

"Good, so it's clear, if I'm taken ill, go missing, become incapacitated in any way, you'll pull her in and advise her that she stands to inherit? She'll be acting MD through her non-exec contract as a contingency measure anyway, but she will need to be told quickly."

"Certainly, one thing is unclear, what about your dogs?"

I smiled at the thought of Elle cuddling the two of them on Saturday. "They'll be just fine with Elle, I know she'll look after them."

Chapter 10

Roger brought Elle over at seven that evening. The moment she was in my arms, all my concerns seemed to melt away, and nothing but her hungry kiss seemed to exist. I breathed in her beautiful scent, and relaxed. Nothing in the world could calm me like Elle's touch, even when she was messing up my carefully combed hair.

Eventually, she let go, and we went into the kitchen. I watched as she made a fuss of the dogs, commenting on how well Bella had recovered. Given that the naughty spaniel had just scoffed nearly half a chicken, and ripped up my newspaper only half an hour before, it was safe to say that she was feeling better. Elle perched on a stool, and watched as I poured us both some wine, and dished up our meal.

"So how was your day?" She asked

"Busy, but productive. I met with your boss today to clear up some matters," I replied, spooning vegetables onto her plate.

"Lewis?"

"No, Ms Pearson. I had some of my personal stuff to take care of, and I wanted to ask about putting you on the board as a non exec director." I placed her plate down in front of her.

"Oh? What did she say to that?" She asked, before taking a bite of salmon.

"She thought it was a great idea, especially if it means you deliver Conde Nast as a client. It will mean attending one board meeting per month."

"Ok. As long as she's in agreement, then that's fine."

"Good, because I'm also making you a non exec at Retinski too. That one is probably a little more involved, but it's a great opportunity for you. It also made your boss a little more relaxed that the use of Pearson Hardwick would be a long term relationship."

She put down her fork, and gave me a hard stare. "I see. That makes me an employee of yours though."

"Not really, in fact, it almost makes me an employee of yours as I'm managing director."

"Hmm. How do you think the other directors will feel about this?" *Who cares.*

"Fine. Ranenkiov thinks you're great, and is happy to endorse you to the rest of the board, and we don't have a lawyer present at the moment, so it's a great opportunity to bring you in. Duchovy retired in April, and he not only sat on the board, but also headed up the in house legal team. There was no natural successor until you, so it all fits. With Conde Nast, they don't get a say in it. You will be my representative. If they have any sense, they'll welcome you with open arms."

"Will you have to pay my company for this?"

"No. I made an agreement with Ms Pearson to pay you direct. From her perspective it brings in a new client, plus it's extremely prestigious for your company." *And means I can help you financially.*

"How much will I be paid? And how much work will be required of me?"

"Conde Nast one day per month, plus a few odd days here and there. You'll get 90 thousand a year for that one. Retinski will be nearer two days per month, plus a few odd days as well. You will be paid 250 thousand per year for it." *Ok, about three times the going rate, but you don't know that.*

"Ok, where do I sign?" I handed her the two contracts, which she read while we finished eating.

"There's a clause here that states in the event of anything happening to you, that I assume the role of managing director of Retinski, and chairman of Conde Nast." She frowned.

"Yes, it's one of those 'just in case' provisions. It's so that none of the companies are left in limbo while my estate is sorted out."

"I see, well that makes sense, although I would have thought the other directors have far more experience than me." *Yes, but you're the only person on this Earth that I trust.*

"They don't have your integrity, that's far more important. The others can guide you."

"So tell me about this trip to Russia? I mean, is it safe for you to go there?"

"It's fairly safe, well, as safe as a wealthy man can be. I need to visit a notary and claim Vlad's assets under his will, see the mines, and how they work, grease some palms, and hurry home to you." I was a little nervous about visiting West Biryulevo, not knowing what kind of reception I'd get, but didn't want to concern her.

"Can't you send a representative?"

"Not really. The notary wouldn't accept it. Plus I need to see the mining operations in person. I couldn't afford to show any weakness or nerves. As I said, I'll have a big team around me, so I'll be well protected."

"Good. I'll be worrying about you all the time you're away." We both signed two copies of each contract, and she tucked her copies into her handbag. "Does this mean I shouldn't sleep with the staff?" She asked, pouting seductively

"I think it's positively encouraged. Stay the night? I won't see you till Friday."

"I was hoping you'd ask," she replied, pulling me in for a kiss.

"Pleasure room?"

"Oh yes please."

I dragged her down the corridor, and made short work of stripping her naked. I needed to fuck her hard and fast first, to make way for a lengthier, more intense session afterwards, when I wasn't so turned on. Slipping a finger inside her, I could tell that she was horny too, and panting for it.

I lifted her up, against the wall, and hooked my arms underneath her legs, pinning them wide open, before sliding my cock into her hot, slick, pussy. She gasped as I hit the hilt, and began to move, dominating her body in every way. I used all my physical power to hammer her hard, getting as deep inside her as I possibly could.

Her orgasm hit without the usual warning quivering, and took me by surprise. I could feel her insides pulsing and contracting through my relentless thrusts, which in turn, pushed me over the edge. Knowing that just my cock alone could make her come within minutes, gave my male ego quite a significant boost.

I stilled as I pumped her full of cum, my cock barely even sated. I was thinking about round two even while shooting round one into her. Lifting her away from the wall, I laid her down on the bed, and flopped down beside her to catch my breath, and describe what I'd like to do for round two. When I mentioned that I wanted to use the butt plug on her again, she surprised me by asking if I'd like one too. In the interests of closeness, I admitted that I liked them, not admitting that they drove me to explosive, and intense orgasms of my own, especially if they hit the prostrate just right.

I pulled the toys we needed out of the cabinet, and handed Elle a vibrating plug, and a bottle of lube, instructing her to insert it, and turn the dial to switch it on. I lifted my legs to allow her access to that taboo part of me, and felt her gently slide the plug in, and switch it on. The sensation was fabulous, and immediately made my cock iron hard, and ooze pre-cum.

I stopped her from sucking me to orgasm, as much as it

pained me, as I wanted to watch her riding my cock. She impaled herself slowly, and began to move, adjusting her position to let my dick rub her spot in just the way she liked. I played with her nipples, as her movements got faster and faster, until she was slamming herself down onto me, and her tits were jiggling beautifully. She looked lost in her own world as she worked herself to a frenzy. All it took was a well-timed tweak of her nipple, and she fell over the edge, and into her orgasm.

She soaked me, as her juices increased, and she shuddered and shook. I watched as her face screwed up, and a flush appeared across her chest. I lifted her off me, and put her face down in doggy position on the bed, pulling up her hips to power into her again. I slid in the butt plug, and pressed the wand onto her clit, as I pumped her without mercy. I could feel my own climax begin it's unstoppable rise. With my own butt plug teasing me relentlessly, I knew I wouldn't be able to hold it back for long. "Come for me now baby," I begged, fucking her harder.

She screamed as she came, closely followed by my own orgasm, which seemed to go on forever. I cried out with the intensity, and collapsed onto her, seeing stars in front of my eyes. I don't know if I even blacked out for a moment, but when I came to, there was only the sound of our breathing, and the faint buzzing of my plug. I pulled it out, and switched it off, before flopping down on the bed beside her.

She seemed in a daze as she snuggled into my arms, all warm and languid, nuzzling my chest in post-coital bliss. The moment was broken when I looked down the bed to see two sets of brown eyes gazing at the pair of us in rapt fascination. "How the hell did you get in here?" I yelled, making Elle jump. *Oh this is gross, watching me fuck.* "You are the nosiest, most disobedient little girls in the world," I told them, before turning to Elle, "I wonder how long they've been watching, the little pair of perverts."

She just giggled, and said; "I'm glad we didn't notice them at the crucial point, that would've put you off your stroke." I laughed, and looked down the bed at the two smiling spaniels. They took it as an invitation to join us in our cuddle, jumping up onto the bed with us.

Just when I thought they couldn't behave any worse, Bella decided to start licking the damp patch where we'd been laying. She really was beyond the pale. I resolved to get the dog trainer back in after my trip. "Bella, where are your manners?" I chastised her. She stopped, looking guilty. "We might as well go and get into bed to watch telly," I said to Elle, "it's half nine already."

Elle lay in my arms while we watched the news. It was one of those moments of contentment that I'd been so scared of. We lay in companionable silence for a while, until she asked me what time I was flying out the next day, whether it was dangerous, and if I could have a tracker implanted.

Smiling, I reassured her that I'd be fine, and back in time for the funeral, probably so grumpy with jet lag that she'd want to send me back. I also told her that I'd be going to Vlad and Dascha's joint funeral the following week, but didn't expect her to attend with me. She agreed, saying that there'd probably be press there, and promptly fell asleep.

I lay for a while, pondering my trip. I had Vlad's apartment in Moscow to prepare for sale, although Deripaska had phoned me to say a friend of his was interested. I also had several factories to visit, including the one in West Biryulevo, and the mines in the Ural Mountains. Not having the gun and drug route cartels should make the trip much safer, I mused. I also had a meeting at the Kremlin with the minister for industry, probably to lobby me for infrastructure investment, as well as a donation to party coffers. It would be a hectic few days.

I missed her the moment she left the next morning, as it would be three days without seeing her. I'd toyed with the idea of asking her to accompany me on the trip, but, unsure of the reception I'd get in West Biryulevo, I'd thought better of it.

The flight was horrific, we hit a patch of turbulence, which had me heaving into a sick bag. What with having to pee into a urine bottle, it couldn't have been more miserable. I was pleased that Elle wasn't there to see it. By the time we landed in Moscow, I was a total wreck.

Nico whisked me straight to the hotel to get showered and changed, before I visited the notary in the central district of Moscow. Now, notaries are upright citizens who serve the Russian state rather well, dealing with myriad issues meticulously, and carefully. Knowing that this particular one kept a mistress, and was sympathetic when dealing with company estates, I took a briefcase of cash along, as a gift. He accepted the valuation of Vlad's companies at about a tenth of the true amount for tax purposes, and signed everything over, rubber stamping all the documents we'd prepared for him. I paid a cheque for the inheritance tax, and gave him his gift, tapping my nose as I thanked him for his help. With the bureaucracy out of the way, I headed over to the Kremlin for my meeting with the minister.

He greeted me warmly, and showed me to a seat in his palatial office, before offering me a drink. I asked for a coffee, as I had a vast amount to get done that day, and needed my wits about me. He was a tall, rather handsome old man, with sharp eyes, and a jovial manner.

"Welcome back to Moscow Mr Porenski, I trust business is going well?" He started off.

"Business is good, thank you. Moscow looks different every time I come. Lots of new buildings going up. Things must be good."

"Of course, the licenses you bought for the 4G paid for significant upgrades to the city, as well as some projects in the outlying areas. Tell me, are you planning to move back here now you have inherited Meranov's estate?"

I shook my head. "No, my life is in London, but all my companies are listed here, and pay tax here, even the international ones. Mother Russia is the only beneficiary." We both laughed.

"That's good to know. We do like to see our sons become successful in the wider world, and as a party, we like to support and celebrate your endeavours." *He wants a party donation.* "I wanted to ask you personally if there was anything, that we, as the ruling party, could do to assist you in your business here?"

"Well, it would be extremely helpful if the planning laws could be directed to assist the siting of masts, as opposed to making it difficult. It's important for the city that coverage is good. I know your party is dedicated to Moscow becoming a world class city." I thought I'd chance my arm.

"Of course, quite easy to sort out for you. Tell me, are the banks in the UK as dangerous as they still look? Only after the banking crisis of 2007, we are a little nervous. A lot of people got caught out." He looked serious.

I knew that several Oligarchs had had their loans called in by desperate banks during that time. Some of them had lost entire companies to the banks who had initially backed them. The late Lord Golding had navigated those choppy waters safely, with minimal issues, and I'd been able to buy up a few companies on the cheap. Oscar, for all his faults, had been well schooled in the family firm, and had an amazing understanding of the sector. "I bank with Goldings in London, and it's as safe and secure as it could possibly be." I told him. "I can't vouch for the others though, and I'm sure you have far better information than me."

We chatted a little more about London, and I wrote an eye watering cheque as a donation to the party coffers, which rather pleased the minister. With a parting promise to assist me in any way he could, we shook hands, and I left.

Back at the hotel, I had a meeting with a lady called Natalya Chimneynkov. She was the private investigator sent by Kristov.

He'd already told her everything he knew, so I just answered her list of questions as best I could, while ignoring her outrageous flirting. She was an exceptionally attractive woman, who was clearly used to men falling at her feet. I was too busy missing Elle to be interested in anything she had to offer.

Vlad's flat hit new heights of vulgarity, with an excess of gilded furniture, and painted murals. I searched his office, and found the safe, which only contained about a million in cash. There was also a letter addressed to Dascha, telling her that the bulk of the money was kept at Windsor in the safe in his bedroom. The rest of the apartment was fairly straightforward. It was clear that Vlad had spent very little time there, as there were few of his personal things. I sent the keys over to a high end property broker, who would be selling it for me.

After eating alone in my hotel room that evening, I sat and composed a rather soppy email, telling Elle how much I missed her, and how astonished she'd have been at how easily the notary changed all the companies into my name. I knew she wouldn't get it till the morning, but it was still nice to be able to communicate with her, and show that she was always on my mind.

The following day was earmarked for visiting factories. As all of them were within a drivable distance from Moscow, we set off early in a convoy of three cars. The first three were set in depressing Soviet style towns, all pretty identical to each other. I could feel the animosity radiating from the workers as we toured each factory. I had looked over their accounts back in London, and seen that Vlad had been making almost obscene profits. There was certainly enough in the kitty to give each worker a decent pay rise, to bring them up to a more liveable wage. I communicated this to each factory manager at the end of each tour.

Word must have spread, because by the time I arrived at West Biryulevo, the workers looked happy, and excited to see me. I felt a wave of emotion standing in the same spot my father had done, in one of the vast bays used to store the raw chemicals before they were shipped off for processing. My mother had worked on one of the production lines, making the bags that were used to hold the rough ore. I hoped to feel her ghost, but when I stood in the room, I felt nothing.

"Ivan! Is that you?" Yelled a voice. I turned to see my old friend Andrei. He looked worn out, and had a shovel in his hand.

"Andrei! How great to see you again. How are you? Come have some coffee with me." I took over the manager's office to share a drink with my old friend.

"It must be fifteen years since you disappeared. What happened? Where did you go?" He asked.

"I ran away to London. With no family, I wasn't sure if I was safe here, so I ran. I understand you married Irina?"

"How did you know?" He looked quizzical for a moment. "Yes, she was heartbroken when you went, and to be truthful, I don't think she really ever got over you, but we made a good marriage. When she fell pregnant, I was over the moon. You do know that she died giving birth, don't you?"

I nodded. "I occasionally heard news from here. Did the baby die too?"

He shook his head. "No. I have a little girl, Kristina, she stays with my mother while I'm at work. She's seven now." He pulled a small photo out of his wallet to show me. A pretty little fair haired girl smiled for the camera. She looked more like Andrei than Irina, which I thought was a shame. "Do you have a wife, or children?" He asked.

"No, I have a lovely girlfriend though, in London. She reminds me of Irina in a lot of ways." I had no desire to brag about my life to Andrei, instead I felt mildly embarrassed at my abundance of riches, while he was shovelling chemicals. It so easily could have been me.

"There's a rumour that you're raising wages in all your

factories," he said, not in the least bit embarrassed by the fact that he was wearing a work overall, and I was in a bespoke suit.

"Yes, the wages are far too low, and there's enough in the pot to give everyone a raise, and maybe upgrade some of the local facilities too. After all, this is my hometown."

"Have you driven through the town yet?" I shook my head. I'd driven in by the back route. To be truthful, I was scared to see the tenement, as if I'd wake up, and find out it had all been a dream. I already felt a bit jumpy just being in the factory. "Well, it hasn't changed, well, a bit more run down maybe, but everything stays the same." He seemed quite sad.

"I'll be driving back via the town," I admitted. We were interrupted by the manager, who was keen to show me the rest of the factory. Andrei shook my hand, and said his goodbyes. I resolved to buy him a house for his daughter. I owed it to Irina's memory to help her child.

The manager showed me the loading bays where I stowed away on a lorry, telling me proudly how many tons of ore they could process in a day. With some better technology, and equipment, they'd be able to double that quantity quite easily. I made some notes as I walked around, quizzing him on production methods, and current capabilities. With the technology boom, demand for the metals and minerals processed at the factory would only increase, and they were held back by lack of investment.

I announced the wage increase just before I left, as I had at the other factories. The manager looked stupidly overwhelmed, and was ridiculously grateful on the workers behalf.

"Stop here," I told the driver, as we approached the tenement. I got out of the car, flanked by a couple of guards, and stared up at the window. I was standing on the exact spot where my father had been executed. I strode over to the stairwell, it's stench of damp and piss was strangely familiar, and even a little comforting. I knocked on my old front door, but was disappointed when nobody answered.

Back out on the street, a few people stared, as I walked through the tenements, and out onto the wasteland. I found the brook, looking exactly as I'd left it, although the patches of dirt under which my parents lay, were now grassy, and indistinguishable from the rest of the landscape. I silently said a prayer, and turned tail to get out of there, before I had a panic attack.

We got back to Central Moscow fairly late, and I ate alone in my room. Russian food had improved a vast amount over the years, but instead of tasting familiar, it had that strange twang of foreign flavours that you get when you eat abroad. I was hungry, so ate it anyway. I couldn't wait to get home. Russia was just the Motherland, England, and Elle, were my home.

I spent an hour composing a soppy, mushy, and hopefully, romantic email, telling her how much I loved her. I really tried to put my heart and soul into it, as I'd surprised myself at how much I was missing her, and the girls. The hotel was full of women, and I could've taken my pick, but the idea appalled me. I gather the guards all took full advantage though, particularly Nico, who was well known for being a bit of a pervert.

I woke up to a lovely, equally soppy email from Elle, which made me smile. I had four separate flights that day, so would be making an early start. The final flight was back to London, so would be easier to put up with. Even I could cope with flying if it was delivering me back to Elle.

We checked out, and got to the airport by seven for the first leg of our journey to the nickel mine at the start of the Ural Mountains. The three mines were in a row, almost following the line of the peaks, with five hundred miles between each one. Thankfully, Vlad had built an airstrip next to each one for easy access.

The mines were grim. I'd thought that the factories were bad, but the pits were a whole other level. The equipment was outdated, the safety record appalling, and the miners looked half dead and starved. Vlad had always boasted that he extracted maximum profit from his companies, but having seen the geologists reports that there were massive deposits still left in the mountains, I concluded that with better equipment, and some investment, profits would increase exponentially.

The geologists had reported that Vlad had barely scratched out five percent of what was in there, so I discussed bringing in heavy machinery with the mine manager. We had plenty of space to store the ore if global prices required, so it made sense to extract more at a lower production cost, and give the workers a better life to boot.

As the day wore on, I had a solid plan forming as to what to do. I needed to consult a mining expert to find the right machinery to buy, which could cope with the difficult terrain. As with the factory workers, all the miners got an immediate pay rise, and a new, subsidised, meeting hall.

With all our work done, we made our way back to the final airstrip. The plane was directly in front of us, no more than fifty metres away, when my guards surrounded me, keeping their backs to me, and shielding me with their bodies. Looking past Nico's head, I could see we were surrounded by about thirty men, all holding guns. *Oh fuck, here we go.*

"Drop your weapons," yelled one of them. Given that they were all pointing guns directly at us, and there were three times as many of them as us, my guards threw down their guns.

"Sorry boss," Nico muttered, as we were herded onto a truck, and frisked for weapons as we got in. We sat at the back, with our assailants sitting between us and the exit, their guns drawn at the ready. We drove for about half an hour, before we stopped. One of the terrorists asked for our mobile phones, which he handed to someone outside. We set off again, and drove for at least another twenty minutes.

We were jostled off the truck, and herded into a dilapidated old farmhouse. We were shunted into a room, where the ten of us sat in shock. Soon after, a couple of men came in, and filmed on a mobile as they addressed me.

"We know you have money, we know who you are, and we demand that you share some of your wealth with the people of the Ural Mountains." I was about to open my mouth, and tell him that I planned to, but thought better of it. "We demand you pay us fifty million dollars for your freedom. We know you have it. You have one week to pay us, or we kill you." *Fifty mill? Is that all?* They strode out, and we heard the door lock behind them.

"Jesus, Boss, I should've seen that coming," Nico said, looking distraught.

"How could you have seen it coming? None of us did," I reassured him. For all his faults, Nico was a superb guard, but not superhuman. "I'm wondering how I'm meant to pay them though with no phone, or access to the outside world."

"I'm sure they'll publicise your kidnapping soon enough," growled Viktor, "then they'll tell your colleagues how to pay. Bastards must have been tipped off by someone at one of the other mines that we were coming."

Nico pulled back the curtain, and saw that crude bars had been welded across the window. "First mine probably. They've done this quickly. The welding's fresh." He yanked the curtain back, clearly angry. I sat down on the gruesomely dirty sofa to wait. I was more annoyed that I would be delayed, and miss Elle's mother's funeral. She needed me there to support her, and instead I'd be sitting in a crumbling house in a godforsaken part of the Urals. No wonder Vlad had thought these people were barely animals. I sat and thought of all the ways I could make the miners lives even more miserable than they already were. *I'm cancelling the subsidised bars for a start, and they can fucking swing if they think they're getting that pay rise after this.*

The hours ticked past, the only thing happening being one of the kidnappers throwing a loaf of bread into the room. It was that cheap, black bread, which I declined with a grimace. We could hear people coming and going in the house, laughter, and occasionally shouting. With only a bucket to piss in, and cheap bread to eat, it passed interminably slowly.

I sat and thought about the murkier side of Vlad's activities. He'd operated smuggling routes for arms and drugs, which had generated a lot of cash, but meant that he'd had what was practically a private militia. If they'd have done this to him, he would have had their homes razed to the ground, and their children murdered. They'd have been too scared of him to even try a stunt like this, his reputation had been so fearsome. There was no way I was carrying on with the routes. I didn't need the money, and I was too squeamish to actually kill a man standing in front of me, to have the ruthlessness required. I liked my corporate life, my legitimate wealth, and my position as an upright citizen.

I was woken from my doze by one of the kidnappers, telling me that someone called Marakov had opened a bank account at Bank Ruskia, and placed fifty million dollars in there. As soon as the negotiators had agreed how to do a swap, the funds would be released. My heart leapt. I knew my colleagues would pull out all the stops to get me out of there. They were probably worried sick. I must have been missing almost 24 hours. I wondered if Elle had been told what had happened, and whether or not my contingency plan had been executed.

As the night wore on, we could hear laughter from the next room, and voices saying they'd take the money and kill us anyway. I began to get rather nervous. *You got too content, you know it causes a slap from the gods.* The idea of dying in such a poverty stricken place, terrified me. I wanted to die in a beautiful bed, in one of my lovely homes, surrounded by my world of luxury, not on a sticky old sofa in a room with peeling paint and a piss bucket. I began to panic.

"Nico, you've got to get us out of here," I said. I was worried that I'd have another panic attack, like the one I'd had in my office, which had been the start of my breakdown.

"Just sit tight boss," he said, "try and keep calm, I'll figure something out."

I'd felt strange for a few days. It had slowly crept up on me, an insidious 'not right' feeling. I'd been struggling to sleep, suffering from terrible insomnia for months, even before I'd split with Dascha. I'd thought getting her out of the way would ease things, but it seemed like every day I felt a little worse. With no sleep at all for several nights, I was like a zombie.

Galina had put a coffee in front of me, which I'd drunk quickly, thinking the caffeine would help lift the fog. When it didn't work, I tried a small line of coke, just enough to give me a boost. I tried again to focus on my screen, but the numbers seemed to swim around. My eyes just wouldn't focus.

I took a call from one of the other directors. The phone plagued my life, there was never an hour went by without calls from someone. I must have sounded strange, as he asked if I was alright. My heart was racing, and my chest began to hurt. I couldn't breathe. Through my brain fog, I remember Galina coming in, and dropping some files. I truly thought I was about to die. I must have passed out at that point. I came to in a private hospital, confused as to where I was, and instantly asked for my phone, telling the nurse I had a stack of work to do, and getting agitated when she told me I'd be taking a bit of time off.

I brushed it off as a touch of flu, but she went and got the doctor, who told me in no uncertain terms that I'd had a sort of breakdown, brought on by stress, and without some rest and some help, I'd be in the cardiac ward fairly soon. I shook myself back to the present.

It must have been very early morning when we heard the first shot. We heard screaming, more gunshots, and some shouting. Instantly, all the guards went on alert, standing close to me. The door was kicked open, and a man dressed in black, wearing a balaclava, burst in. "Ivan Porenski?" He asked, looking at me. "Come with me, all of you. Surround your boss in case of stray bullets please. Keep his head down, and covered." *He's fucking English, what's going on?*

Nico leapt into action, and arranged the guards round me, pushing my head down, and leading me out, behind the balaclava clad man. We could hear bullets being fired behind us, in rounds, which stopped abruptly.

We followed him out of the house, and onto a waiting truck, which screeched away quickly. Another one appeared behind, and before we knew it, we were on a road. We heard the house explode behind us. "What the hell just happened?" I demanded, looking around to see four more balaclava-clad men sitting in the truck. The one who had led us out pulled off his headgear, and thrust his hand out.

"Colonel Robert Penrith, special air service. Delighted to meet you." I shook his hand in a daze.

"Ivan Porenski," was all I could reply. He pulled out a communication device, and spoke into it.

"Subject is out, all good on our side. At least five men down on theirs, possibly more. The place of detention has been eradicated." I listened to the reply.

"Excellent work. Penrith, stay with the subject, the others can return by normal means."

I caught Nico's eye, he shrugged, not having a clue either. I just couldn't work out how come the SAS had shown up.

In a better truck than the one we arrived in, we were at the airport within half an hour. Two minutes later, on board my plane, and less than five minutes later, in the air. I didn't even have time to get worked up. "So, Colonel Penrith, would you like to tell me what just happened?" I asked him, as soon as the guards were out of earshot.

He smiled. "Of course, sorry, must have been a bit of a shock for you, us lot bursting in like that. We were sent by the British government to assist in your rescue, with the express co-operation of the Kremlin of course."

I frowned, "Yes, but how come? I mean, I'm Russian, so I would've expected my own government to get me out." *Especially given the donation I made to the party coffers this week.*

"Well yes....they're not terribly good at that sort of thing though, and we are. All I can tell you is that we were sent here as an emergency by someone at the top of MI6. Someone in high places wanted you out quickly. I don't know exactly who, or why, but we had the assistance of the Russian government in executing this operation, so it must have been the top man himself. Now, part of the agreement we made with the Kremlin, is that we make up a story about your escape. We were never here, if you know what I mean. Don't want every rich bugger getting kidnapped now, do we? So, the story is that your guards overpowered the captors, and you all got out. Ok with that?" I nodded, struck dumb. "Good, I'll brief your guards. We'll be landing in Moscow in about 40 minutes for you to refuel. I'm sure they'll want a press conference, so get the story straight in your mind." I nodded again. "Oo, I'll have a scotch please," he said to Nico, who had opened the drinks cabinet on the plane. With a scotch in his hand, he walked down the plane to speak to the guards. *It had to be either Oscar or Elle, or Oscar doing Elle's bidding. Does she make you feel protected?*

Moscow airport was a fucking nightmare. There were hundreds of reporters waiting to pounce, so a press room had been set up. I looked a fucking state, smelt shocking, and, because I couldn't move on the plane, hadn't brushed my teeth for 36 hours. I asked if I could stay on board while we refueled, or at least visit a washroom on the ground, but was whisked out, and put straight in front of the waiting cameras.

I trotted out the version of events that I'd been instructed to tell, although, I'm not sure if it was terribly believable. After answering a few questions, I managed to get away, and straight into the men's VIP washroom for a shit, shower and shave. All the guards had already changed on the plane, and Nico brought some fresh clothes, and my wash bag from the in-flight bathroom. I felt quite a bit better once I was clean.

I had five hours to get myself worked up over Elle saving me, yet again. Five hours on board a metal death trap to work myself into a rage, that she'd clearly pulled Oscar's strings, and he'd jumped, again. It was the only explanation as to how the SAS had arrived so promptly. It became clear to me that Elle had some sort of hold over Oscar Golding, and the fact that she wouldn't tell me what it was, infuriated me.

By the time we landed, I was a tightly bound ball of fury. The sheer embarrassment of getting kidnapped, coupled with the thought of having to be grateful to fucking Golding, was enough to make me insane, especially knowing that given a few more hours, Marakov would have had me freed without all the fuss.

She was waiting at Gatwick with Roger. She looked a little uncertain as I strode towards her. *Yes, you know you interfered.*

"Elle, thank you for coming to meet me. I have rather a lot to ask you on the way back to the house." She looked a little stunned, but fell into step behind me as I strode to the car. She hopped in beside me, and I slid the screen up.

"Did you send in the SAS?" I barked at her. I knew I was being a bit of a bastard, but I was too wound up to care

"Yes." *I knew it! I knew I was right.*

"How?"

"That's confidential. Are you not pleased to be home?"

"Of course I am, I'm just wondering what the fuck happened. One minute Marakov was negotiating, the next, men in black balaclavas burst in."

She frowned. "Marakov wasn't negotiating. What gave you that idea?"

"The terrorists said Marakov put fifty mill in an account for them."

"Oh yeah, I got him to do that, but he wasn't negotiating. He was too busy trying to persuade me to grant enhanced share options and bonuses to the board. If anything, he sounded as though he didn't want you back alive, none of them did. It's why I chose the route that I did."

"He would have dealt with it, I didn't need you rushing in to save me," I told her

"Nobody was dealing with it Ivan. It seemed like I was the only person mildly concerned about you. I'll play you the recording so you can hear it for yourself. Now I'm sorry if I stepped out of line, but you know what? I had a bit of a shit time too. If I did the wrong thing, I can only apologise." *Well that's a first, you saying sorry.*

She looked a bit moody as she stared out of the window, not saying a word to me for the rest of the journey. I was just looking forward to getting home, and putting my feet up for a day.

The house smelt phenomenal when I walked in. When I enquired as to what she was cooking, she told me she was making roast beef. As I was sulking, I snapped that I wasn't hungry, and watched as she turned it all off, got her bag, and informed me that she was going home, in that imperious way that women do when they want you to beg them to stay. *Yeah, I know your game.*

I pretty much ignored her, and went upstairs to change into shorts and a vest. I heard the door slam about two minutes later. I went straight back down, and turned the oven back on. It smelt divine. The girls seemed to think so too, as they danced around my feet, desperate to get to the source of the wonderful aroma. We ended up scoffing the whole lot between the three of us, spending the following hour on the sofa in a food coma. As soon as I'd recovered, I polished off a huge chunk of cheese with some biscuits. With plenty of food inside me, I began to feel a little more human.

I checked my emails, seeing ones from all the board members expressing their relief that I was safe and sound. Marakov confirmed that he'd pulled the money back out of the account he'd set up for the kidnappers, and it was all safely back in the Retinski number one account. There was one from Elle, whining about doing the right thing, I only skimmed it, but she wanted to resign from the board. *Probably sulking as well*, I thought. In a fit of pique, I answered 'fine', and pressed send. I dug out my spare mobile, and plugged it in to charge up.

With no Elle-cam to watch, down in Sussex, I watched a bit of telly with the girls, before having an early night. I was totally exhausted.

Chapter 11

I slept for most of Sunday, only rousing myself for long enough to take the girls for a walk, and fix us some food. I kept my phone switched off, and relished the time alone. I didn't even email Carl, as I wasn't sure what I could say to him, and to be honest, I just needed a good sulk.

Galina seemed pleased to see me on Monday morning, greeting me with a cheerful 'good morning'. I switched on my screen, and straightaway discovered that my password didn't work. *Bloody meddlesome women.* I pulled out my phone, found Elle's email from Saturday night, and read it a little more carefully to find out my new password. I had just got into my computer, when Ranenkiov strolled in. "Nice to see you back in one piece, Ivan, must have been a scary old time out there," he said, pulling up a chair.

"I've had better trips, I must admit. So, bring me up to speed with what's been going on here."

He looked at me a little strangely. "Did Ms Reynolds not tell you what the board did to her?"

"She sent me a recording of something, but I've not listened to it yet. Why?"

"I'd suggest you listen to it before you speak to your board. Left up to them, you'd still be sitting somewhere in the Urals. I don't know exactly what she recorded, but I bet it's pretty damning. They were bastards to her during the board meeting. She was pretty damn magnificent the way she handled them. It's thanks to her you have a company to come back to."

I gaped at him. It really wasn't what I'd expected him to say. I listened as he droned on about an issue we had with one of the call centres, desperate for him to leave, so that I could listen to the recording she'd sent. When he'd finally gone, I barked at Galina to make sure I wasn't interrupted. I logged into my emails, and clicked on the recording. I listened intently as everyone introduced themselves.

"Does anyone have information on what the current situation is regarding Ivan's kidnapping?" *Elle's voice.*

"It seems the group were held at gunpoint at the steps of the plane. We know they were taken onto a truck. We also know that a video message was sent directly to the Kremlin. It shows Ivan, and all ten guards alive, and held captive in a room. Their captors are demanding fifty million dollars for their release."

"Any political demands? Or is it purely money?"

"At this stage, just money. The Kremlin are saying publicly that they won't negotiate, however, they have put a negotiator in place, who has made contact with the kidnappers. He will try and keep them talking for as long as possible, to ensure the safety of the captives, Oleg Marakov, finance director." *She must've forgotten who he was. Good old Oleg.*

"Thank you Mr Marakov, is there fifty million on standby to pay these people?"

"Yes, but of course, we'd rather avoid paying it, if Russian authorities can rescue them by other means. Ivan is a prominent businessman, and as such, this is huge news throughout Russia. If the authorities can be seen to not capitulate to terrorists, it is so much better." *Eh?*

"Clearly. I'm sure the authorities don't want a spate of kidnappings arising from this, but my main concern is getting

Ivan out unharmed. We all know what happened when the authorities tried to rescue hostages in other situations, and ended up killing half of them. I would like fifty million placed into a new, separate, bank account straightaway, just in case. Can you arrange that today please?" *Oh...*

"Consider it done."

"Good, now gentlemen, I will need you all to bring me up to speed on all the current companies, and any projects underway."

"Is there a reason why you have been asked to become acting managing director, when you don't even know our company?" *Sounds like Andrei.*

"I have been appointed to the board already. You have no director qualified in legal matters, so I was asked to join you as a non exec. Ivan appointed me as his nominated second in command, should this type of disaster occur. Please be aware that I will be sitting on this board when Ivan returns, so I would appreciate full disclosure from all of you."

"Ms Reynolds is our lawyer from Pearson Hardwick, and due to her exemplary performance for our company, Ivan invited her to join us." *Ranenkiov sticking up for her.*

"The network of companies is rather complicated....."

"I'm sure I can manage. Gentlemen, I would like a full list of the companies, their structure, and accounts for the last three years please, in English. I'll use this weekend to get up to speed, as I'm sure you can appreciate, this was rather sprung on me. Is there any other urgent business?"

"Yes, we are about to vote through enhanced share options for the board. We are all in agreement, and it was only remaining for Ivan to cast the deciding vote. He had suggested it himself, so it was only a formality. He was planning to cut back on acquisitions, and use the cash to increase dividends and bonuses." *You fucking chancer Oleg, I was gonna do no such thing.*

"I don't think this is the time or place for discussions like that. There will be no enhanced share options granted until Ivan returns, nor will there be any decisions about dividends or bonuses." *Good girl.*

"Are you sure that going against the wishes of the board is a good idea? It would place you in a somewhat difficult position. It would be a disaster for the company if anything was to happen to our interim MD as well." *What the fuck? Who are you? The Godfather?*

"Now, if that's all, I suggest we all get on with sorting the information I'm going to need, and concentrate on getting Ivan back in one piece. Any information or news on the situation in Russia, I would be grateful if you would contact me immediately."

There was a bit of a gap in the conversation. I could hear footsteps.

"You handled them very well. I think they thought you'd be a pushover. The share option thing was a crock of shit." *Ranenkiov's clearly not as stupid as he looks.*

"I know. I wasn't born yesterday, besides, I'm really hoping Ivan comes back in one piece, and I don't think he'd thank me for selling off bits of his company on the cheap. Now, is there anything that needs my immediate attention?"

"Not really. Just be aware that the other directors will begin jostling for position, should the worst happen."

"Do any of the other directors have direct links to the KGB?"

"I do, my brother in law works for them. To my knowledge, nobody else has a direct link, but saying that, corruption is common in Russia, and there's a lot at stake here."

"Am I the only one who actually wants him back alive and in one piece? What all of you seem to be unaware of, is that there is a plan in place in the event of Ivan's death. He dies, most of you lose your jobs. It's in everyone's interests that he comes back." *Clever girl.*

"Have you seen the plans?"

"My boss drew them up for him. As you know, Ivan is the ultimate control freak, and that will extend after his death. The other directors should be careful what they wish for."

"You have my full support, it would be a good idea for me to speak to the others, more privately, and remind them that Ivan would have made provision for this scenario. It would be far easier all round if we all worked together for the good of the company. Call on me anytime, I'll assist in whichever way I can. I'll also contact my brother in law, and see if there's any new information."

The recording ended. I sat reeling at the revelations. I listened to it twice more, to make sure it was actually how it sounded on my first play. If anything, it was worse. Elle had indeed been the only one who wanted me back. No wonder she'd turned to Oscar.

I went up to his office to see him, fortunately he was free. "Oscar, I need to ask you a few questions. Did Elle turn to you over my kidnapping?"

"Hello Ivan, glad to see you got back in one piece. As for your question, yes and no. Yes in that she spoke to me about it. She was rather distraught, and unsure as to the best way to proceed, no, in that I wasn't responsible for your rescue, that was someone else who owed her a favour."

For the second time that day, I reeled with the news that I'd got events totally wrong. "I see, well, ok, thanks for helping her."

"No problem, although I can't take credit for actually doing anything, but as I said, Elle was distraught, and needed a friendly ear to talk to. I gather your board gave her a bit of a rough time, scared her a bit. Your household staff were very good though, took care of her. Your housekeeper even came in on her day off to help. Poor Elle barely slept the night you were missing, by all accounts. I saw her on Saturday morning, she looked exhausted. Still, glad it all ended well."

He clearly didn't know that I'd bitten her head off, and not spoken to her since. *Shit, time to grovel.* "I need to make some changes to my board, particularly in light of recent events. I'd like to know whether you accept non-exec positions?"

"I do, but I'll warn you, I don't come cheap. If it's one day a month, I would expect around two hundred grand a year, which is a little higher than most non-execs, but I do have lots of contacts."

"That's not a problem."

"Good, I'll wait for your formal offer then." We shook hands, and I went back down to my own office to talk to Paul about doing some executive search, and email Elle a grovelling apology. I sent her an email apologising for the behaviour of my board, and thanking her for not allowing them to help themselves to chunks of my company. A few minutes later I got a two word reply, that simply said 'you're welcome'. *She's pissed off with me.*

I decided to take her out to dinner that night to apologise properly. She needed to know that I still loved her, understood how much she'd done to get me freed, and how loyal she'd been. I emailed her an invite. Two minutes later, she sent me an email that made my heart sink. She'd declined to meet me for dinner, saying that she'd said all she wanted to say, and that unless I had a legal problem, I was to leave her alone. I stared at my screen in disbelief. *She can't just leave me over this.*

I spent an hour sulking, before calling Marakov into my office. I played him the recording, watching as he paled at the share options bit, and went a little green at the part about something happening to Elle. "So, would you like to explain to me why you felt you could turn on me the moment I went missing, attempt to plunder my company, and put the fear of god into my lawyer?" I asked.

"I erm, was only joking about something happening to her. You know that," was all that the lame bugger could say.

"No, actually, I don't, and neither did she. There were billions at stake Oleg, and the moment my back was turned, you tried to get your hands on it. You barely raised a finger to get me out of there, and seemed to think my kidnap presented a golden opportunity. Tell me, did you have a hand in my incarceration?"

He looked rather panicked. "No, oh goodness no. I'll admit I was testing her out to see if she'd play along with the share options, but I can't believe you think I'd bear you malice. I've worked for you for five years, long enough to prove my loyalty."

"The only loyal person on that recording was Elle, and possibly Ranenkiov. The rest of you were greedy, thieving bastards, who behaved like a bunch of Mafiosi. You terrified the life out of her."

"She didn't look terrified, looked quite calm to me," he said rather sulkily. *Yes, no doubt Ms Reynolds the lawyer persona.* "She's quite the ice maiden."

"How she 'looked' is immaterial, she's so fucking scared of this place that she resigned her directorship. I won't have behaviour like this in my company Oleg. You are fired with immediate effect. Nico will accompany you to your office to collect your personal belongings, you will be blocked from our systems as of now. Ranenkiov will sort out our contractual liabilities to each other. Now, get out of my sight."

"You can't do this," he shouted, "I've worked here a long time. She just walked in. How's that fair?"

"Fair is what I say is fair. NICO," I yelled, he came running in, "get this bastard out of my sight. He's been fired. Usual protocols."

I spent the next hour contacting the people necessary to cut Marakov loose from all the Retinski systems and bank accounts. I'd checked over his contract, and spoken to my HR director, who'd given me the good news that he would forfeit his shares due to the gross misconduct. He could challenge me in court, but with the rather damning evidence of the recording, I doubted if he'd try.

I met Paul Lassiter for an early dinner that evening. Over our starters, I told him what had happened with Marakov, and that I needed a new finance director, plus a mining expert, and possibly a head of legal, if I couldn't persuade Elle to return.

"Oh dear, she left you as well?" He said with fake sincerity. "Knew she would, let's face it, if Golding couldn't keep hold of her, you had no chance. She's an extremely interesting woman. There's something about her I can't quite put my finger on."

"Do you know why she left Golding?"

He shook his head. "She's never said. He's still in love with her though, so there's always the possibility that they'll kiss and make up. He's considered one of the most eligible bachelors in the world."

"So am I," I pointed out, rather affronted. "She hasn't left me. We'll make it up soon, when she's over her sulk."

"Don't be so sure. There's a lot of men waiting in the wings, I'm sure, who don't walk around with a posse of bodyguards and behave as though she was a possession. Let's face it, Golding has the money, looks, position, to make any woman happy, and she walked away, leaving him trailing after her like a lovesick puppy. She'll do exactly the same to you, especially given the way you treat women."

"What do you mean, the way I treat women?" I demanded, getting more and more pissed off.

He regarded me intently. "My guess is that you have her watched, followed, you try and control her, dismiss her concerns, and behave like an overgrown child when she says no to you," he stated. *Bastard, how did he know?*

"I've helped her career, in case you've forgotten. If I was some kind of Neanderthal male, I would've insisted that she didn't work. You're just saying all this because you want her, and I've got her." He began to laugh.

"Yeah, I can see how well that'd go down. You wouldn't have got off the starting blocks with her. Now, I firmly believe she'll go back to Golding. There seems to be a real, genuine affection between them, and you can't compete. As for me? Yeah, I'd have a go, see what all the fuss is about."

"We'll see." I wanted to close down the conversation, as he was pissing me off.

"We will indeed."

With Lassiter fully briefed on the executives I needed, I emailed Elle to meet me in Smollenskis the next morning, and got an early night. I had Vlad and Dascha's funeral the following day, which I wasn't looking forward to, and I was a bit fed up with being without Elle. I also made the decision to remove the Elle-cam from her living room, as, although I loved it, it was a little bit creepy, and I'd be mortified if she ever found out about it.

My meeting with Elle didn't go terribly well. I told her about Marakov, which she didn't seem bothered about, then argued that she wasn't going to rescind her resignation, no matter what I did. She was pretty stubborn about the whole thing, saying that she wouldn't be playing any part in my personal or business life.

"So that's it, you're just gonna leave me?" I asked, horrified that she'd dump me over such a little spat. It prompted a tirade from her.

"Well imagine if you put up with intense fear on the day of your mother's funeral," *I'd forgotten about that...*"sat awake for a night, listened to others not being fussed if I was alive or not, then at the end of it, I treated you as though you were something on the bottom of my shoe. Would you go back for more?" *Erm...*"I forgave you for Dascha, gave you another chance, which you threw back in my face. So yes, that's it....So is there any work you wish to instruct me on?"

I did a really stupid thing. Instead of grovelling, I brought up her contract, reminding her that she'd need to attend board meetings for the next three months. I can't explain why, I just wanted to....sort of force her, show some power over her, which was really quite dumb. She obviously thought so too, and commented that she'd attend with some security, which she would ask Oscar to provide. She really knew exactly how to press my buttons.

We ended up arguing, with her accusing me of putting her in danger, and loving money more than her. When I protested that I couldn't have possibly known that the board would behave as badly as they did, she changed tack, and told me she was angry because I'd been sulky on Saturday. Rather than talking it out, she stood up, and announced that she had to get back to work. Getting round her wasn't going to be as easy as I thought.

The funeral was unremarkable. I'd left it to Galina to organise, which she'd done perfectly efficiently, but without any panache. The two coffins were placed side by side in the chapel at Slough crematorium, for a rather hasty and generic service. Very few people attended, testament to how little affection either of them had garnered during their lifetimes. Even their household staff hadn't bothered, although Galina had invited them.

I nodded at a few old faces from my mafia days, including Kristov, and posed for a couple of shots for the straggle of press in attendance. When the service was over, I felt nothing as the curtain slid closed across the coffins. If Vlad had indeed fathered me, and those two had been my only family, I'd rather remain an orphan.

"Good to see you back in one piece," said Kristov, outside after the service, "you gave us a bit of a scare last weekend."

"I've had better weekends away," I admitted, "no wonder Vlad hated those miners with a passion. How's the routes by the way?"

"As treacherous as ever, but everything appears to be moving just fine. Had to stamp on a few circling vultures, but that was to be expected after Vlad's death. I think it's quietened down now."

He seemed quite sanguine about the dangerous life he'd chosen. I was delighted to be out of it. "I started up a security company, providing bodyguards, as well as some slightly more...esoteric services, finding people, surveillance, you know. Call me if you ever need me." He handed me a business card.

The wake was held in a local hotel, but, like the funeral, wasn't well attended. Even the other Oligarchs had stayed away. Vlad had had few friends. A couple of Dascha's cronies were there, and tried desperately to catch my attention, flicking their hair so much, they looked like they had nervous tics. I wondered at the morals of flirting at a funeral.

Nico had removed the Elle-cam that day, so I had nothing to watch that evening. I ended up meeting up with Karl, and a heartbroken Mika for dinner at Langhams. We tried our best to cheer him up, but, feeling pretty heartbroken myself, I could empathise with him. "The worst bit is wondering if another man has snapped her up," he confided, "she's so bloody gorgeous, she won't be on the market long." *That's my fear too.*

"Women break your heart," counselled Karl, "always best to keep them at dick's length."

"Oh, I don't know, there are some good girls left out there." I sprung to Elle's defence, even though she had, to all intents and purposes, dumped me. She hadn't left me for another man, or because she was bored, (as Mika's girl had been), but because I'd treated her badly, and without love. It was a bit of a lightbulb moment, in that I'd always treated women as toys, objects without feelings or needs. I'd solved every problem by throwing money at it. Now it wouldn't work, and because of my own stupidity, I'd driven a good girl, who loved me, away from me. I took a large swig of champagne, and resolved to work hard to get her back.

I called Mrs Ballard the next morning, as I usually did on a Thursday, with her instructions on what I'd like her to prepare for the weekend. In a slightly optimistic mood, I asked her to prepare enough food for two. "Have you both recovered now? Poor Elle sobbed like a baby on Friday night. I was ever so worried about her."

"Yes, she's fine," I snapped, wondering if she'd cried over me since. *Probably not, probably too busy snuggling up to Golding,* the little voice inside my head taunted me. I didn't hear anything from her all day, and by late afternoon, I was driving myself mad. I made my way down to her office, and bumped into her in reception just as she was leaving. She told me that she was just on her way out, and asked if there was a problem she was needed for.

"Out? Where?" I asked. *Better not be a date.*

"Oh only the supermarket. My flatmates back tomorrow, and I need to fill up the fridge, and the cupboards. I ate his soup collection," she admitted. *I know, I watched you.* She was quite surprised when I asked if I could join her, so I could talk to her on the way round.

I pushed the trolley, and watched what she put in. She seemed to have a habit of choosing cheaper items, as opposed to the best quality. I began to relax a little, and start enjoying myself, when she piped up; "Did you remember to take all that stuff out of the oven on Saturday?"

I decided on honesty. "Yeah, the girls and I polished it off. Thanks for thinking of making that for me."

"James said he'd make one for me. I can't wait. I've not had a roast since before he went away." She said it without guile, there was no hint of sarcasm or nastiness in her voice. I still cringed a bit, and apologised.

"You're just sorry I'm not coming back to you, yet again," she pointed out. I stayed silent, unsure what to say, as everything seemed to make the situation worse. She finished her shopping, and the guards loaded it into the car.

We bickered all the way back to her flat. She seemed to think I'd be happier with a dim supermodel, who would gaze at me adoringly, and never answer back. *She's got me totally, utterly wrong.*

I sat at the island, and told her, "It was your incredible intellect that attracted me to you. I told you that before. I like that you can keep up with me. I just don't like the way you make me feel...helpless, I'm used to being the strong, capable one, not the idiot who needs looking after."

"I don't think you're an idiot, and you certainly don't need me to look after you. I think you have that the wrong way round. I'm the one who's crying all the bloody time, and you're the one who never notices. Your answer is to try and bully me, which, incidentally, won't work."

"I've never bullied you."

"Breach of contract? You threaten a lawyer who owns no property with that, which, if I lost, would bankrupt me, and end my entire career. You don't think that's bullying? Sending me into Conde Nast as an insurance policy for a psychopath, telling me if I didn't, I'd be killed by the Russian mafia, that wasn't bullying? I've spent half the time I've been with you, terrified for my life. You have me watched, tracked, and guarded, yet you never bloody notice when I'm upset about it. Look, I don't want to keep dissecting why we couldn't make this work, I just want you to accept that it's over, and let me move on." She paused for breath. "Tell me what happened in Russia?"

I was pleased she changed the subject back onto safer ground. I relayed the story of my kidnapping, the house, and finally, my rescue, adding that I'd known it had to be either her or Oscar behind it, and I doubted that Oscar would want me back alive. She jumped in with the news that Oscar had offered to pay the ransom, if the board had refused, which both surprised, and intrigued me. *Maybe he only offered it to get in her good books.*

I asked about her mother's funeral, which she didn't seem to want to talk about, simply telling me it had probably been better that I hadn't been there to see her back in her old life. I tried to reassure her that I wouldn't have judged, but she just shrugged, and told me that her old life was over. She looked a little sad and lost. She was also looking a little pale and thin, so I offered to take her out to eat.

"No thanks, I want to make sure the flat's ready for James, and besides, we're over," she said. I scrabbled around for something to say to change her mind.

"You still see Oscar, despite splitting up with him, so why can't you let me take you out and feed you?"

"Oscar isn't predatory, he's always a gentleman, whatever his feelings. His good manners are very deeply ingrained I suppose. Plus he cares about me." *Yeah, cared enough to order a hit on your behalf.*

"Have I got bad manners now as well? Anything else wrong with me?" I was losing my temper again. I was sick to the back teeth of hearing about how wonderful Oscar-bloody-Golding was. If he was so great, she shouldn't have left him.

"This! This is what's wrong with you! Ivan, you are handsome, sexy, and I fell in love with you. I cried bloody buckets when you went missing, yet the moment I try and tell you how I feel, you bite my head off, and ignore all the things I've actually done to prove how I feel about you. Now I know full well I could go back to Oscar, and you know what? I didn't. Now that may not be enough for you, but to me, actions speak louder than words. You can say the words 'I love you', but your behaviour tells me otherwise. You didn't see me for nearly a week, yet you dismissed me like a servant on Saturday. THAT'S WHY IM LEAVING YOU." I watched as tears started rolling down her face, leaving streaks as they travelled. She was leaving me because I hadn't loved her enough, not because she wanted someone else. I felt like a total shit, as well as a bit of an idiot. She swiped at the tears, as if she was embarrassed to be crying.

"Poor girl, come, let me hold you." I pulled her into my arms, and held her tight. "I'm sorry I'm such a useless boyfriend, I don't mean to do these things to you, I'm just used to being a bit self centred."

"A lot self centred, I told you I was terrified at Retinski, but you didn't listen, and tried to bully me into going back there. Sometimes, just sometimes, it's not all about you, it's about me, and how I feel." Her words hit home. I'd been so concerned with my kidnapping, my rescue, my sulk. I'd failed to think of her, and her fears, and the world I'd sprung on her.

I'd plunged her into becoming the MD of a conglomerate overnight, put her up against greed filled, experienced men, and been angry at her for making the right call, due to my own inadequacies.

"Baby, I'm sorry. I'm sorry I made you cry, and I'm sorry for being a self absorbed idiot. I just want to make you happy, and keep you safe. I think we need some quiet time together, just having fun, without the worries of business, or boardrooms. Tell you what, why don't I rustle you up something to eat, and we can watch a film this evening?"

She seemed to relax a little as I set about preparing us some food. Once she'd eaten, she chose a film, and seemed almost back to normal, as she described the funeral, telling me that her mother's boyfriend had let her old home get filthy, and went to the funeral dishevelled and hung-over. She stretched out on the sofa, resting her feet on my lap, seemingly physically comfortable with me again.

I stroked her leg as she talked, listening to her plans for scattering her mother's ashes, and even offered to accompany her, to support her on that day instead. When the film finished, she stretched, and yawned, before telling me it was time for me to go home. *No way baby.*

"I thought I was staying the night. I want to cuddle you, make you feel cherished." I put on my puppy dog look, and stroked her leg a little more. I wanted to make us 'right' again, and our evening together had brought it home to me how much I'd missed her.

"Smooth, very smooth." She looked amused.

"I mean it, I want to hold you, cuddle you, feel your skin next to mine. I've missed you horribly you know. I know you think I'm a big brute, but I'm not a cold or unfeeling person." *At least, I wish I wasn't. I'm trying not to be.*

"On one condition."

"Name it."

"We talk at the weekend, and you listen without getting cross." *I can do that.*

"It's a deal."

I stripped off quickly, and slid into bed before she could change her mind. She snuggled into my outstretched arms, and stroked her soft little hand over my back. I was unsure as to whether a shag was on the agenda or not, so took it slow, kissing her gently, and stroking her lovely skin. I couldn't help but get a hard on though, which pressed urgently against her thigh, making itself known. Even though I was a horny as a teenage horndog, I held back, and concentrated on making her feel loved and cherished. In the end, she pulled me onto her, clearly turned on by my soft approach. I held back for a moment, worried that I'd only last a minute, but she was clearly in no mood to hang about.

I nudged my cock into her, and paused for a moment to try and calm the testosterone hurtling around my body, urging me to take her hard and fast. I concentrated on her pleasure, licking and sucking her gorgeous tits, while driving her towards her climax with leisurely thrusts.

I was almost mindless with the need to come, when I felt the familiar quivering of her orgasm begin to brew. I hadn't come for over a week, and was struggling to hold back, so it was a relief to follow her orgasm with one of my own, pouring myself into her, and rebuilding our connection.

I must have been exhausted, because, one minute I was nuzzling into her, the next, she was prodding me and wafting a cup of coffee under my nose. I didn't normally sleep that much, or that deep. I took a sip of coffee, and noticed that she wasn't wearing her gym kit. When she said that she was skipping it that morning, I decided it was an ideal opportunity for some wake-up sex, which she seemed quite enthusiastic about, stroking my morning wood, and driving me wild.

Our fuck that morning was more about having fun again. She clearly loved my body as much as I loved hers, and she seemed to get turned on by just the sight of my hard cock, just as the sight of her glistening pussy drove me demented. I also loved how my demure little lawyer seemed to have no shyness with me as soon as we were naked, happily letting me fuck her in every position, and every way I could think of.

Another hour later, She made us fresh coffees, after the first ones were left to get stone cold. I sat at the island to drink mine, while Elle made herself some toast. I decided to try again to change her mind about the directorships. "Paul's doing some executive search for me. I wish you'd change your mind about the non exec positions, at the very least, the Conde Nast one." I wanted to be able to take care of her financially, without offending her. I finally understood that success was important to her, as opposed to just money.

She paused to think about it. "I'd still sit on the Conde Nast board. I don't know why you don't approach some of their board to sit on Retinski, or even merge the two into one, it would kill two birds with one stone. They're well versed in heading up a vast multinational, plus you'd get to integrate the two companies far more effectively than having two boards." *Why the fuck didn't I think of that?*

"You are a bloody genius at times. That's actually a brilliant idea. Would you be prepared to be a part of something like that?"

"Yes, I'd sit on a board like that."

I was delighted. "How's your schedule today?"

"No meetings planned. I'll be helping the others out I should think, as most of my current projects have either completed, or are in progress."

"Good. I'm booking you today. We can sound out some of the directors of Conde Nast, and draw up a planned superboard. Structure it the way we want. I want to look at cost savings that can be gained by fully merging Conde Nast and Retinski."

"I'd keep the names separate, but that's easy to do. Set up a huge umbrella company, and list all the others as subsidiaries, feeding revenue through to the parent company. I did a similar set up for Paul Lassiter's firm. Should save a fortune in both tax and admin." *Oh you clever, clever girl.*

"Sounds like a plan. Can you be ready by ten to eight? I want you to join me at this meeting with Paul, then we can head over to Vogue house. I'll need to book you Monday as well, for meetings with the American directors. I'll pull them over here this weekend." She didn't seem to twig that I'd included her in everything, almost as a partner. I needed to ease her into running a conglomerate a little more gently than I had done previously. Plus as well, I liked having her by my side, as we thought alike, and it was nice having a partner to share with. I also suspected that people would let their guard down in front of her, whereas they wouldn't where I was concerned.

With my mind made up, I went home to shower, change, and deal with the rather disgruntled dogs. They sulked a little that I'd been out all night, but were easily bribed with a cold sausage each. I quickly showered, and dressed, choosing my favourite navy suit, and a crisp white shirt. I liked to intimidate Lassiter, with his off-the-peg suits from Marks and Spencer. A dark blue tie, and the cufflinks Elle had bought me, finished the look.

Elle looked lovely wearing one of the suits I'd bought her. I loved the fact that she'd started wearing designer clothes, as opposed to the mass produced stuff she used to wear when I first met her. I was really quite proud of the way she was evolving to fit into a billionaire lifestyle, knowing that it didn't come naturally. She hopped into the car, and we made our way over to Smollenskis.

Paul was already seated in a booth when we arrived. I ordered our breakfasts, then began to discuss the plans that Elle had suggested that morning, which Paul heartily agreed with. He suggested a super-board of around twenty, made up of predominantly executives, with around four non-execs, including Elle, and Golding, although he expressed surprise that Oscar had agreed to sit, telling me that he was frequently approached, and turned down nine out of ten offers.

During breakfast, he outlined the skills we should be looking for, which we would identify as required once we'd made our selections from the existing executives. We were on our second coffee, when Elle excused herself to visit the ladies, asking me to mind her bag.

The moment she was out of earshot, he started asking me about her. "So you and her an item now?" *Oh for fucks sake, just admit I won, and give it up. Actually, I'm gonna rub your nose in it.*

"She thinks so," I replied, rather flippantly. *I'm gonna make you think she's fucking devoted. Worships me in fact.*

"You hate Golding that much?" *Only if he doesn't keep his paws to himself, actually, yeah, I hate him that much, mainly because she likes him.*

"Jammy bastard gets everything he wants. I enjoy rubbing his nose in the fact that I'm fucking her, and he isn't. I'll keep her out of his reach until he gets bored." *Forever, that is.*

"What if he doesn't get bored?" *He might not, but I need to put a stop to your fascination with her.*

"He will. She's nothing that special. Bit prissy and miss perfect if you ask me. Not sure why Golding's so dopey over her." *Probably for the same reason I am..*

"He thinks a lot of her. You still seeing that actress? I've forgotten her name." *You mean the famous actress falling at my feet? Don't you just wish you had an ounce of my sex appeal?*

"Penny Harrison? Yeah. She's one dirty bitch I tell you. Thankfully lawyer girl isn't too clingy, and I get plenty of time to go over to Penny's place. Makes it easier to put up with the uptight and vanilla I'm getting at home these days." *Yeah, I'm a sex god.*

Paul laughed. "Maybe Elle'll get bored with you, if she's only getting vanilla."

"Nah. She's ecstatic just to be getting a bit of Russian sizemeat. She won't go anywhere." *Certainly not anywhere near you.*

"Shh, she's coming back," said Paul, smirking at me. I hoped I done enough to put him off Elle, as his continued flirting with her was starting to seriously irritate me.

We wrapped up our meeting, and went over to Hanover square for the first board meeting with the Conde Nast executives. They were a sophisticated bunch, all extremely intelligent, and exceedingly well groomed. Elle sat beside me as I took command, outlining my plans for deeper integration between them and Retinski. I could see people start to shuffle nervously, probably worried about losing their jobs, until I announced the creation of a superboard, made up of execs from both conglomerates. The ones who remained at Conde Nast would take on the responsibilities of their colleagues, with an increase in remuneration to reflect the expansion of their departments. Basically, they'd all get a promotion and a raise.

Both Elle and I fielded some questions about the structure, and purpose of the new umbrella company, and I watched proudly as she explained the benefits of the new legal entity in a clear, and concise way, outlining the things that would need to be put in place as soon as it was formed. She really was extremely impressive in the boardroom, her fierce intellect was on show, which, teamed with her calm and gentle manner, was a potent combination. I watched as the older, more experienced executives hung onto her every word, nodding in agreement at her proposals.

With the board meeting concluded, we stopped off for a bit of lunch at La Gavroche, before going back to our respective offices to work on the next steps. I had to call the American directors, and organise to fly them over for a meeting, and Elle needed to start organising the creation of the new company. "What do you want to call it?" She asked me in the car.

I thought about it for a few moments. "I'd like a more English sounding name I think. A merger of both our names maybe? Elive?" She wrinkled her nose. "Ok, a merger of the girls names, Beltan?" She smiled broadly.

"That sounds great. I'll run a search on it as soon as I get back, make sure it's not taken, and buy the web domains." *You think of everything.*

Back in my office, I switched on my screen, and checked my emails. Every single member of the board had sent over their CV. Before I settled down to read through them, I called the chairman of the American board, and invited them all over, telling him I would arrange to send my jet to fly them in on either Saturday or Sunday, whichever suited, ready for a meeting on Monday morning.

My day was going so well, I even managed to smile at Galina as she placed a coffee in front of me, especially when Elle sent over the articles of association that she'd done for Beltan, along with a receipt for the purchase of beltan.com, and the co.uk one, as well as the lesser known .biz. Her attention to detail was astonishing. I called Paul with the news that I'd be seeing the Americans on Monday, so would need to meet him Tuesday morning, once we knew which skills we were still short. He sounded a little odd on the phone, kind of stilted, but I shrugged it off, assuming that I'd caught him at a bad time.

Elle came up to my office at three, holding a couple of files which she placed on my desk, explaining that they were the notes from our meeting with Paul, listing the skills we needed, and some guidance of the formation and structure of an umbrella plc, which she'd be listing in the Cayman Islands, as opposed to Russia, as the tax rates were even lower, and regulation lighter.

We discussed the new board, and Elle listened as I outlined my thoughts on the obvious choices, although, I still wasn't sure about appointing the finance director of Conde Nast, as she was female, and I preferred a man in that position. She seemed a little distracted as I rattled on about the CVs I'd been sent. When I asked her what she'd thought about moving Andrea Mills from HR to Director of Administration, she just stared at me rather blankly, as if she hadn't heard me. I clicked my fingers, rather playfully, in front of her face.

"You're about a million miles away. Come back to the present."

"Yeah, I'm struggling to concentrate today."

"I noticed. Excited about seeing your friend I expect?" Being the good boyfriend, I'd remembered he was returning home that evening. I made a note to put Roger on standby to bring her down to Sussex at the first opportunity. She wouldn't need more than a few hours to say hello.

"Yes, yes I am."

"Look, why don't we wrap up for today? I need to get back and see the girls, get them ready for the drive down to Sussex. You can get back and see your flatmate." She grabbed her handbag, and shot out of my office, clearly excited to see her friend. I read through the rest of the CVs, before switching off my screen, and wrapping up for the weekend.

Back home, the girls danced round my feet as Mrs Watton grumbled about Tania ripping up a kitchen roll and scattering the pieces around the living room. Tania looked unrepentant, and in fact, rather pleased with herself. I made a mental note to contact their dog psychologist, again.

With Mrs Watton placated, Nico drove us to Sussex to begin our weekend. As soon as the gates closed behind us, I could feel myself begin to relax. I'd made no real plans for the entire weekend, well, I planned lots of shagging with Elle, so I didn't want anything else interfering. Roger was on standby to drive her down, and in the meantime, I could have a little catch up with Carl.

To: Carl Verve
From: Ivan Porenski
Date: 5th July 2013
Subject: Catch up

Hi Carl

Sorry I've not emailed for a week or so, but as I'm sure you were aware, I was kidnapped during a visit to Russia. As far as kidnappings go, it was pretty amateur, and they only wanted money. I was rescued pretty quick. So, here's the problem. While I was away, Elle was told she'd been nominated as the temporary MD of my companies. My board turned on her, and me, and it was only through her efforts that I was rescued as quickly as I was. Now, in hindsight, I should have been grateful, but I was angry that my colleagues weren't given the chance to free me without Elle jumping in to look after me...again. When I found out they were too busy trying to carve up my company behind my back, I had to admit that Elle had done a magnificent job of remedying the situation.

I had to grovel, but it seems we are back on track again. I'm trying to ease her into an executive role at my company a little more gently now, as it was all a bit brutal when I disappeared.

I just worry that I'm a bit useless at being the kind of partner that she wants. She says I'm controlling, and treat her like a man.

She also said I was self centred, and I get angry with her too quickly. I just get angry at other men throwing themselves at her feet. Sometimes it seems that everyone she comes into contact with, ends up her devoted puppy, and she just goes along in her own sweet way, totally oblivious. She seems to have some kind of hold over my banker, and just tweaks a string to make him jump. It drives me mad.

I'm also introducing her slowly to a wealthy lifestyle. She's doing ok, and has started letting me dress her, but still insists on doing her own housework, which is silly. I don't want her doing such demeaning things, and can easily provide her with a household cleaner. I hate that she has to fit that into her schedule, as she works too hard as it is.

I'm starting to understand that success in her career is as important as money to her, and have been a little more mindful of that.

The other news is that I was approached by an old friend with a theory that Vlad was in fact my father, and Dascha my half sister. It would explain quite a lot, and I can see why he would think that. Rather than have a meltdown over it, I've engaged an investigator to try and find out the truth. Either way, he's dead, so nothing will change, except that I'll just be even more glad he's gone. In my own eyes, my father in Russia was my dad, and that won't change whoever provided my DNA. My only concern would be whether or not psychopathy is hereditary.

Regards
Ivan

I settled into the comfortable chair in my study to read through some reports while I waited for his reply. I didn't have to wait long.

To: Ivan Porenski
From: Carl Verve

Date: 5th July 2013
Subject: re Catch up

Ivan

Glad to hear you are well after your ordeal. I saw it all on the news, although I was under the impression that your guards had overpowered your captors. Anyway, let's look more closely at your progress since we last emailed.

Firstly, I'd like to reassure you that there have been numerous studies done on the subject of psychopathy, and a hereditary link has never been proven. Having been in contact with you for well over six months now, I can confirm that you exhibit no indicators of a psychopath. I would also doubt that Vlad was a true psychopath, as it's exceptionally rare for them to be animal lovers, and it's usually torture of animals by children which is a first indicator of the condition.

I'm pleased that you've taken such positive steps to find out the truth, as opposed to ignore or internalise the issue of your paternity.

As regards Elle, there still appears to be issues that you may wish to explore regarding your own responses to various scenarios. She sounds as though she is an accomplished and lovely young woman, so interest from other men will always be around. The part that you CAN control, is your response to them. If she is happily ignoring them, then there's no reason why you should be concerned.

You may wish to re-read the part of your email about introducing her to a wealthy lifestyle. I'd like you to try and read it from her point of view. From the outside, it appears that you want her to look and behave in a way that fits your ideal of a wealthy woman. Have you asked her how she feels about that? Maybe open a dialogue with her about having a cleaner, and get her perspective, rather than just foisting your standards and ideals on her. Does she enjoy doing her own housework? Just as you enjoy preparing your own food, it may be a simple pleasure to her, so I would urge you to be cautious in your approach, and communicate openly.

Kind Regards
Carl

I had to agree with a lot of what he said, and be careful of pushing Elle too far or fast into being both a rich man's girlfriend, and the director of a vast conglomerate. The last thing I wanted was for us to hit more problems, as the past week had been torture.

I was watching the news, wondering what was keeping her, when Roger called. "I don't think she'll be down tonight sir, she appears a little.....well refreshed."

"What do you mean 'well refreshed'?" I demanded. "Tell her to get in the car immediately." I glanced at the clock, it was half eleven.

"She's drunk sir, and refused my assistance. Her flatmate appears to be helping her home."

"She better not be. Go and get her."

"Sir, she appears to be a little......strange....ranting about something. I couldn't quite work it out."

"So she's drunk in public, and ranting?"

"Yes sir."

"Ok. Leave her to me. I'll call her straightaway, and make sure that she's alright." I tried to phone her, but her voicemail kept cutting in. I must have tried twenty times, getting angrier and angrier each time. Eventually, I left a voicemail, expressing my annoyance, and telling her that I wouldn't put up with public drunkenness, or her dismissing her security like that. There could easily have been press about, or an idiot with a mobile phone. It was one in the morning, so I assumed she was asleep, and throwing my phone down, I stomped off to bed.

She didn't call until nearly half nine the next morning, probably hung-over, and sorry for herself. She told me that Oscar was driving down, and had offered her a lift. I paced around, working out what I was going to say to her. I slightly regretted my harsh voicemail at one in the morning, but I'd been angry and worried. I decided not to tell her off, as it might come across as a bit controlling, besides, I liked a drink too, and had been carried home on more than a few occasions by Roger, so it would be a little hypocritical of me to forbid her to drink.

I decided to be nice, but remind her about keeping her security close at all times, as the last thing she wanted was some idiot having a pop at raping her. I took a coffee out onto the terrace, and sat in the sunshine for a while, planning how I'd fuck her first. I quite fancied another pool fuck, or even a cheeky shag in the woods.

She arrived around eleven, and was dropped at the gates. I watched her trudge down the drive looking so pensive that I wanted to laugh. No doubt she was expecting a huge telling off for her behaviour. The girls raced up to her for fuss, but I was barefoot, so waited at the front door. I smiled at her, and immediately apologised for my voicemail, admitting it had been rather bad tempered of me. She didn't smile back. In fact she looked rather grim, and didn't even say hello.

We went into the kitchen, and she asked for a glass of water. "You look as though something's eating you alive," I said, "would you like to tell me what's bothering you?"

"Yesterday...in Smollenskis, when I went to the ladies.....I know what you said about me," she said, her voice hesitant.

I brushed it off, telling her that she shouldn't trust a word that Paul Lassiter said. No doubt he told her a version of our conversation. I'd just deny everything. I was feeling fairly confident until she pulled out her iPhone, flicked through the recordings, and pressed play. The whole fucking conversation was played out while I sat there, panicking. Even the stupid lie about Penny.

She switched it off at the point when she returned to the table. "Did Lassiter give this to you?" I asked, my mind racing with possible excuses that might work. She shook her head, and informed me that her phone had been on the table the whole time to record the information for her notes. I remembered that she'd put a file full of them on my desk the day before. *Shit shit shit.*

"I'm sorry Elle, I don't know what to say," I admitted. Listening to it must have been awful. Shit, even I thought it sounded dreadful. She sat, quite composed, then floored me with her next statement.

"Am I really that bad in bed? I need to know." The combination of the daft question, her stone face, and my own nerves, made me burst out laughing.

"Of course not. Hang on, is this why you went out and got drunk last night?" She sat there silent, not answering. I tried to get in control of my stomach, which was churning. "Elle, don't be silly. I said that to put him off you. I just didn't want to admit to being your devoted puppy, as Lassiter keeps taunting me about you, saying that you left Golding and you'll do the same to me." Even to my own ears, it sounded a pretty lame excuse.

"I'm sorry Ivan, but I don't believe you. Firstly, you didn't even admit that we were an item, second, you were totally disrespectful in a way no man would be to a woman he loved, and third, Penny Bloody Harrison. Please answer my question, was I that bad in bed? It's all I really want to know." She spoke deceptively softly, using every ounce of her self control. I could see it in her face. Personally, I wouldn't have blamed her for slapping me, but she kept calm.

I skirted round her question. She knew full well that she was amazing in bed, actually we were amazing in bed, together. "I can't compete with Golding can I? I always knew you'd go back to him, with his top education, society contacts and vast wealth.

He's had everything he's ever wanted from the moment he was born. I wanted to take you from him, have something that he wanted, and he wants you desperately. Lassiter wants you too. I was showing off, pretending I didn't care, that you were just one of many, yet to both of them, you are the grand prize." I allowed her to see my envy, and my frustration, in the hope that she'd understand, and forgive me.

"You haven't answered my question. I'm not interested in your excuses, just that one question." She wasn't letting go.

I decided on honesty. If I was going to lose her anyway, I might as well tell her. "The truth is that I'm in love with you, and I'm terrified of losing you. I'm aware that out of the three of us, I'm neither the wealthiest, or the best educated. I'm not as perceptive as Lassiter or as knowledgeable as Oscar. The only thing I had that they were both desperate for was you, so I made out it was no big deal, that you were nothing special, that I had other women too. It was basically a pissing contest, and the most stupid thing I've ever done." *There, I've admitted that I'm stupid, and inadequate.*

"Answer the question."

She was still grim faced, and wasn't letting it go. "You know you're not boring in bed. Did you honestly think you were?"

"Yes, I did. Thank you for telling me what I needed to hear. I'll be off now." She moved to pick up her handbag. I grabbed her wrist.

"Don't go," I begged, "we need to talk, I need to make it up to you."

"The best thing you can do is make sure this doesn't damage my career." *What is she on about?*

"Why would it do that?"

"Because I've left you. All I ask is that you don't move to another law firm until after I've left Pearson Hardwick. I don't want this tainting my career." *Oh baby, don't do that, I know how much it means to you, I won't ruin it for you.*

"You don't need to do that. I won't move law firms all the time you're there. Look, this is all my fault, and I don't want you to suffer for it, so don't do anything you'll regret."

"I don't want to stay in Canary Wharf. I'm planning to go back into the city. I'm probably going to have to move, so I may as well have a clean break."

"Move? Why?"

"My flatmate is back with his ex, and it's a bit awkward being around them. It's about time I bought my own place rather than living like a student in a flatshare." *You can live with me, let me look after you.*

"I see, you seem to have made a lot of decisions. What about Oscar? Where does he fit into this?" I mentally crossed my fingers, hoping that he didn't fit in anywhere.

"He doesn't. Between the two of you, you've made me the most miserable I've ever been in my entire life. I want out, to get away from all this. Oh, and can you stop tracking my phone please, or I'll change my number." Her beautiful blue eyes betrayed her hurt, making me feel like a total bastard.

"Elle, it doesn't have to be like this. Please don't give up on us. I know I make mistakes, but you know how I feel about you. I'll even beg you, please don't make all these changes, give it a little time. Let me prove how much I feel for you. Please."

Her stony face didn't even crack. "I'd better go. I need to get back to London."

"You only just got here. At least stay for lunch, or a walk in the woods with the girls. If you leave me because you don't feel for me, then so be it, but let's at least try and stay friends, and colleagues. We work so incredibly well together, we should at least try and preserve that." I needed to delay her, as I hoped to be able to reassure her, and fix my mistake.

"I don't know if I can do that. At the moment I can hardly bear to look at you. I mean, how would you feel if you heard me telling someone you were crap in bed, had a small dick, and I had to get it off Oscar to keep me satisfied?"

"I'd be devastated, I know I would, but I'd also know that I don't really have a small dick, and I made you come every time we made love. I'd trust what I know deep down."

"What about Penny Harrison?" *Wondered when we'd get to her.*

"She was the one that Roger delivered home the night you left Oscar. I've not seen her since. That's the truth. She's tried to call me at the office, but Galina filters my calls. She gave up calling my mobile after I didn't answer it when she phoned. I only said I was still seeing her because she's famous, and it would piss Lassiter off." *I know, shallow. I'll put my hands up.*

"You really are a tosser sometimes."

"Yeah, I know." I tried my puppy, sad look, which worked insofar as she agreed to a walk through the woods with the girls and I. She walked at least a metre away from me, lost in her own world. She didn't look happy.

We walked for about ten minutes, in silence, until I saw the forest scents begin to relax her. Her hands unclenched, and her shoulders dropped, as we strolled along. We talked as we walked, but she still seemed adamant that we were over, although she still maintained that she was still in love with me. I felt a little twinge of hope, until she added that she didn't like me very much.

When I questioned her, she told me I was a male chauvinist, controlling, sulky, and tried to buy her off with shopping trips, which sounded about right. She also berated me about my 'inferiority complex', telling me that I needed to let go of the poor immigrant persona.

I turned it back to her, saying that her self-image of the little working class girl wasn't how I saw her. I listed out the qualities that I loved about her, such as her intellect, her femininity, and her innate kindness, and told her that I appreciated them. Instead of caving in, as I expected, she brought up another problem, namely that she'd struggle to have sex with me again without worrying that she was boring, and all the other things I'd described to Paul.

I was horrified, and pointed out that I'd already admitted that I'd lied, and vowed to find a way to make things right, adding that I couldn't bear the thought of never having her again. I loved our weekends together, I loved working with her, and I loved our sex life. The thought of losing her was so incredibly painful, that it felt like a punch in the stomach when she announced, rather abruptly, that she was leaving. *Probably be back with Oscar by tonight.*

I followed her back to the house, and asked if she needed a lift. She shook her head, and twisted the knife by telling me that Oscar was picking her up.

"Is there anything I can do to change your mind, or fix this?" *Please baby, this is just too painful.*

She scanned my face. "No. I don't think there is." *That's it then.*

"So be it. Are you still going to meet me Monday morning to see these Americans?"

"If you want me to."

"Yes. I want it very much. Ten, in my office? Is that ok?"

"See you then." I stood at the door, and watched her trudge down the drive, her head bowed. She looked thoroughly miserable, not happy to be walking into Oscar's arms, just dejected. The look of a woman rejected by the man she loves. I watched her until she'd walked out of the gates, hoping that, at any moment, she'd change her mind, and run back into my open arms.

I closed the door, and turned to see two pairs of accusing eyes. The spaniels seemed to walk off in a huff as well, and appeared to be sulking. I slumped down onto the sofa, and replayed events in my mind. I didn't blame her for leaving me, as

I'd behaved so horribly towards her, due mainly to my desire to be top dog, and rub the other's noses in my superiority. I fully expected her to run back to Oscar, and the two of them to flaunt their relationship around London. Golding would be insufferable.

Chapter 12

The afternoon passed interminably slowly. I tried to fill my time with some work, but couldn't concentrate. I thought about emailing Carl, but decided against it, as I knew it was all my own fault, and really didn't want to have to admit to doing such a terrible thing to the woman that I was meant to love. The girls didn't help, Tania refused a sausage, and wouldn't even look at me. Bella must have barked to go out at least five times, yet as soon as I let her out, she barked to come in. I even ended up shouting at her, which resulted in her slinking off to her basket in a huff.

With the girls not speaking to me, I spent the afternoon concentrating on my sulk. I retreated into that 'woe is me' frame of mind, and had a bit of a wallow in the misery of my own making. I even sat listening to sad music, playing Bruno Mars' 'When I was your man' a few times. The only interruptions were a call from Natalya asking for a quick meeting on Monday to collect a sample of my DNA for testing, and later on, a call from Oscar.

"Wondered if you had anything planned for this evening. I'm at a bit of a loose end," he said.

"I thought Elle was with you," I replied, my stomach leaping.

"She went back to London late afternoon. Said she was going to do some work. Mother's out, and I'm kicking about bored." *I'm not interested in what you're doing.*

"I'm a bit tied up this evening," I lied, "got to get ready for the Americans on Monday. Plus I'm still sorting out Vlad's affairs, which is rather time consuming."

"Not to worry. It was just a thought."

"Thanks for asking though," I said, intrigued as to why Elle had left him and gone home. *Is there a chance I got this wrong, and she doesn't want him?*

After the call, I sat back in my chair, and thought about what to do. I debated jumping into the car, and driving back to London to see her, and continue grovelling. It was either that, or just give up, the thought of which was surprisingly painful. Eventually, I decided to give her a call, under the guise of making sure that she was alright. She answered on the first ring, even though she must have known it was me. My heart started thumping in my chest, as I heard her voice. I started off by asking if she was ok.

"Yeah, I'm alright. Just doing some work." Her voice sounded soft, and melancholy. I was a bit concerned that she was spending yet another night working. Either she had way too much work on her plate, or she was lost for something better to occupy herself with.

"Why are you working on a Saturday night? You sound sad."

"My flatmate's girlfriend's here, so I had to get out of the way. Threes a crowd and all that. I can't spend the entire evening in the bath." *Ah, so she's bored and lonely.*

"I wish you were here," I said softly.

"Do you?"

"Of course I do. I miss you terribly. Do you remember our very first Sunday together? I loved it, and that was before we became a couple." I thought I'd remind her that we could have great times together, even when we'd just been friends. I figured that, as hard as it would be not shagging her, it would be a hell of a lot easier than not seeing her at all.

"Yeah, it was nice, uncomplicated," she agreed.

"What are you doing tomorrow?"

"Flat hunting. I think I need to move out of here. I'm going to see if I can view some apartments."

"Whereabouts? You're not moving away are you?" *Please don't tell me you're moving back to Welling, and that crummy flat.*

"No. If you're not pulling your account, I'm going to stay put. I'm going to look at apartments in this area. I like it here." *Oh, thank god for that.*

"Do you need me to help you out financially?" I really didn't mind giving her a few million if it saved her having to go into debt, and if she wanted her own apartment, I'd make sure she got the best.

"No. But thank you for the offer." *Hmm, we'll see about this.*

"The penthouse of the new building next to mine is up for sale. It's called Cinnamon Wharf. It's very secure. Great river views. It's definitely worth a look. It's on with Savills I think." *And I know full well you'll definitely need my help to afford it.*

"I'll give them a call in the morning, although it's a twenty minute walk from work," she pointed out. I'd forgotten that she couldn't drive.

"I can always organise a driver for you." *Easy problem to solve.*

"Ivan, we broke up. I doubt very much that your next girlfriend will take too kindly to you ferrying your ex around for evermore."

"I don't want anyone else. I only want you. The girls are upset too. Tania's off her food, and Bella won't speak to me." Involving the spaniels was a bit of a dirty tactic, but, hell, I'd try anything.

"I'm sure they'll both recover on sausage Sunday."

"It won't be the same without you here. You left all your clothes behind by the way."

"Yes, I know. I thought it would be a bit greedy to ask for them, especially the red dress."

"Well I'm not going to wear it am I? I bought it for you."

"It's not really your colour."

"Very true....have you eaten this evening?"

"No. James cooked for himself and Janine, and he hadn't made enough for three. He didn't think I'd be back tonight. I'll have a piece of toast later."

"I wish you'd come down here, I could cook for you, and make you sausage sandwiches in the morning. Mrs Ballard left a fillet of lamb in the fridge for us."

"I need to start flat hunting, plus it's half seven now. By the time I got down to you, it would be nine."

"You can view apartments next week. It's not as though you need to move out tomorrow is it?"

"True, I just feel really awkward here with the two of them."

"You can always stay with me if you want to. There's plenty of room in my apartment."

"That's kind of you, but that really isn't going to be an option, given the circumstances now is it?"

"We are still friends though. I can still look after you, and help you. I'm just not allowed to make love to you, is that right?"

"I suppose so. Usually when people break up, they stop seeing each other."

"But we'll still be working together, and seeing each other most days, so spending a Sunday together makes no difference. If you stay there, you'll have to spend all day in your room, apart from the hour that you're flat viewing. It won't be much fun. Roger is only at my London place. He could pick you up in five minutes. By the time you get here, the lamb will be ready." *I'm winning, I can feel it..*

"Separate bedrooms though."

"Whatever you want, your old room is at your disposal. Shall I call Roger, and throw the lamb in the oven?"

"Ok. See you in a while." *YES!*

It was amazing how quickly my sulk lifted. I called Roger to pick her up, then set about preparing dinner. I switched the radio over to Kiss for something a bit more upbeat, and carefully seasoned the joint before throwing it in the oven with some roast potatoes. Even the spaniels seemed to sense that something was up, appearing in the kitchen, and watching as I set the table with glasses and cutlery. I even consulted my wine book to find out the best red to go with our dinner, figuring that Elle was always a little happier with food and wine inside her.

The girls made an enormous fuss of her when she arrived. I wasn't sure whether it was because they loved her too, or because they were being driven mad by the smell of roast lamb, and had figured out that she'd be a soft touch with the scraps. I wasn't sure whether to kiss her hello, or not, so just beamed a smile at her, and poured our wine, before making a start on the dishing up.

She told me about her flatmate getting back together with his ex fiancé, citing it as the reason that she wanted to move out, and telling me that they'd eaten everything she'd bought during our shopping trip, and had barely left her a drop of milk. It angered me that she was being treated with so little consideration, especially after taking so much trouble to get everything ready for her flatmate's return.

We chatted while I dished up, and prepared a plateful for each of the spaniels. Asking how she planned to finance her new flat, she brushed me off, telling me she had savings, and that she didn't ask me about my money. I was a little puzzled until She admitted that she hadn't snooped through my bank accounts while I'd been away, telling me that she hadn't wanted to be nosy, although she knew I had fifty million inside Russia. I smiled at her naivety, as most women would be desperate to know how much I had in the bank, down to the nearest penny. Elle just seemed content to know that I had 'enough'.

She closed her eyes and groaned as she tasted her food, before asking me where I'd learned to cook. I explained that we'd had food shortages in Russia, so when I'd discovered how plentiful and varied the selection was in the UK, I'd set about teaching myself to cook, and I preferred my own cuisine to the rather fancy dishes my housekeepers served up. She took a sip of wine, and asked if I preferred Russian food, clearly having no idea that I was brought up on soup, gritty bread, and gristle.

I smiled as I replied that I liked caviar and blini, but hadn't tried them until I'd been in London a long time. Other than that, I preferred English food. She looked a little embarrassed as she admitted that she'd never tried caviar, and hadn't even eaten in a fancy restaurant until she'd met Oscar, adding that she felt as though there was a huge amount she didn't know. I vowed to take her out to eat at least once a week, and show her all the different cuisines of the world....apart from Ethiopian, which was rank in my opinion.

She changed the subject, asking me what I'd been up to that afternoon, teasing me about my Olympian sulking, after I admitted that had been all I'd been doing. I remarked that nobody made fun of me the way that she did. "That's because women are too busy drooling, and men are too scared of you," she replied, before eating a roast potato.

I smiled, and agreed that not many people had called me a tosser for a very long time. She looked thoughtful, and asked if that was because they didn't dare, or because I wasn't a tosser to anyone else.

I took a sip of wine, and thought about it, before telling her that I tended to keep people at arm's length, adding that I was closer to her than I'd ever been with any woman. She looked surprised. "Even Dascha? You were with her a long time, surely you knew each other well?"

"Not really. I worked seven days a week, extremely long hours, so I didn't actually have to spend much time with her. She had her shopping, her lovers and her hobbies, so as long as she had access to my money, she didn't bother me."

"Did you just say she had lovers?" She looked astonished.

"Yeah, she was into the BDSM scene, which I'm not, and I wouldn't let her tie me up or inflict pain, which she enjoyed. We were sexually incompatible, so she took lovers for all that stuff. It suited me." *I know, it was weird.*

"No wonder you think I'm boring in bed."

"No, quite the opposite. She just wanted to tie men up and whip them. That's not sex. I hated it, let her try it once, and said never again. I just couldn't see where the enjoyment was. I know you and I were a little kinky and adventurous, but it was always sex, you know, with an orgasm at the end of it."

"I thought BDSM was a sex thing, shows how much I know..."

"Dascha used to say that giving pain was sex to her. I told you before, she was a psycho. At some point, I need to go over to Windsor and sort out their house. I dread to think what we'll find there. Would you mind coming with me? I don't really fancy going on my own."

"Just a little game babe, it'll be fun, just try it," she said, brandishing a pair of cuffs. "I'll tie you up and suck you off, in that way that you like." She smiled sweetly.

"Okaaay, but you let me out straightaway if I don't like it?" I was dubious about being restrained. I still had flashbacks to that terrible night in Karen's place, and Dascha was a nasty cow at times.

"Of course babe," she trilled, before cuffing my hands, and tying them to the bedstead. She took her time tying my ankles to the bottom of the bed, seemingly enjoying herself. "Now, I think you've been a naughty boy. Naughty boys get spanked. I think you need a little smack before you get your willy sucked." I wanted to laugh at how ridiculous she was. She seemed to like trying to hurt me, pinching my nipples was a favourite thing. I

scuppered that by only ever fucking her doggy style, keeping her hands firmly held above her head, in case they strayed anywhere near my nipples, or my bollocks for that matter.

Confident that she wasn't strong enough to do any real damage, I decided to humour her, mainly to get my blow job, which was such a rarity, it was almost a birthday thing. "Yeah, I've been a naughty boy. One spank, then my willy'll need a suck," I told her. I was a little puzzled that she wouldn't be able to reach my arse, but decided not to say anything.

I didn't realise the bitch would pull out a fucking flogger, and start raining blows on my stomach and chest. "Take it, take it like a man," she commanded, between blows. It really fucking hurt, each frond seeming to bite into my skin. My erection disappeared in a millisecond.

"FOR FUCKS SAKE, STOP IT NOW," I bellowed. "If you don't stop now, I'm gonna beat seven bells out of you when I get free." The bitch carried on, her eyes glittering, making her look as if she was in some kind of trance. "If you don't stop now, I'll cut up your credit card," I yelled at her. It was like I'd flicked a switch. She came to right away. "Let me out now," I said through gritted teeth.

"You didn't like that?" She said. She looked a little scared. I was beyond livid.

"No I didn't fucking 'like that', you stupid, sadistic bitch. There's something very wrong with you if that's your idea of foreplay." She looked a little pensive as she let me out of the cuffs. I sat and untied my feet, while she disappeared to get dressed, my blow job forgotten. I never went near her again.

I shuddered at the memory. Elle brought me back to the present by telling me that she'd be happy to accompany me, and have a nose around Vlad's mansion. We finished eating, so I figured that the girl's helpings had cooled enough for them, plus their psychologist had told me to always eat first before feeding them, to try and cure their appalling behaviour. We both laughed when they inhaled their dinner in about thirty seconds, Elle remarking that Tania seemed to have got her appetite back.

She scraped her leftovers onto their plates, *no wonder they're devoted to you*, and helped clear our dinner things, loading our plates into the dishwasher. A part of me liked how normal and practical she was, another part of me never wanted to see her lift a finger again.

We went into the lounge, and sat on separate sofas. I flicked the telly on, and found a re-run of one of the comedy panel shows that I knew she liked. We sat in companionable silence for a while, until I heard a small snore. Looking over, I could see she'd fallen asleep, with her hand tucked under her face, and her legs at odd angles. She didn't looked terribly comfortable, and a bit precarious, balanced on the edge of the sofa. One move, and she'd be on the floor. I decided to put her to bed, so picked her up gently, and carried her upstairs, flicking the lights off as I went.

I put her down on the bed in the spare room, taking just her shoes off, before pulling the duvet over her. She didn't even stir. I sat for a while, just gazing at her, fighting the urge to get into the bed and cuddle her. She didn't even wake up when I stroked her hair and gave her a little kiss. In the end, I couldn't resist slipping in beside her, and gently wrapping an arm round her.

I lay there in the darkness, memorising the feeling of her snuggled up against me. It just felt so right, being next to her. I kept thinking '*another five minutes, then I'll go get in my own bed*', but I must have fallen asleep, just too warm and comfortable to stay awake.

I felt the bed shift, and opened my eyes, just as she was sliding out. I apologised straight away, but she didn't seem angry, just curious as to why I was there. "I just wanted a cuddle before I went to bed, so I lay down beside you, and must have nodded off. I'm sorry, are you upset with me?" I asked. She just shook her head, looking amused at my admission, before going downstairs to make some coffees.

I was a bit disappointed that she didn't come back to bed, preferring to sit on the sofa to drink her morning caffeine fix. We decided to go over to Windsor, and check out Vlad's house. I'd been given the keys that week by Lucy, and the news that she'd applied for probate, which should only take a couple of weeks. I wasn't quite sure what to do with it, whether to sell or rent it out. I also wanted to see if there really was a few million in cash hidden there, as I'd been led to believe. I wasn't bothered about Elle knowing of the existence of Vlad's money, hell, I'd even share it with her, I just didn't want another secret between us. I didn't have to explain that he'd been a gun and drug route 'owner'.

She seemed quite excited at the prospect of snooping around Vlad's old house, but announced that she needed to do a quick workout, as she'd missed the gym the day before. She grabbed her iPhone and earbuds, and skipped off to my home gym.

I began to prepare our breakfast, putting on the radio to accompany me as I grilled some bacon, and refilled the coffee machine. I'd left some sausages for the girls in the fridge to save me cooking more for their breakfast, so cut them up, and used them to tease the spaniels a bit, until the three of us were dancing around singing along to the radio. They hopped around on their back legs, enjoying the game, until the song ended, and I noticed Elle in the doorway, watching us. *Ok, that's embarrassing.* She just grinned, and teased Bella about fancying a pop star. I couldn't help but be in a great mood, with Elle by my side, my girls content, and the whole day to look forward to, I was genuinely happy.

We walked the dogs, then set off for Windsor. It didn't take long, as it was still fairly early, and the traffic was light. I knew Nico had changed the code for the gates, but wasn't sure if my old code for the interior alarm system would work. I didn't know if he'd changed things when he'd locked it up, or not. Elle seemed confused, until I explained that there was two different code systems.

She gasped when the house came into view. It was rather impressive, and as large as a small stately home, almost a rival to Conniscliffe, Oscar's castle. The exterior was fairly tasteful, and gave no clues as to the garish horrors inside. I explained that I didn't want to use it, as Windsor was even further away than Sussex, and besides, I loved my bolt hole in the country. It wasn't the biggest place, but suited me, and was extremely tastefully furnished.

My entry code worked fine, and made me wonder why a code that hadn't been used for a couple of years hadn't been changed. I nodded at Nico to sort it. He set about fiddling with the control box, while Elle and I walked into the kitchen. It was probably the least garish of all the rooms, although still rather over the top, featuring lots of pillars and carved woodwork. There was also a bit of a nasty smell, so I set one of the guards the task of emptying the cupboards and fridge of food.

The living room was the worst of Vlad's excesses. He'd taken the oligarch stereotype very much to heart, and liked to gild every surface possible. With hand painted murals on the walls, it made my eyes hurt. Enormous purple and gold sofas finished off the 'look', and added another layer of bad taste to the room. I remembered Vlad being delighted with it when it was decorated a few years previous, showing off about how much gold leaf had been used in just one room. I much preferred my home in Sussex, with its restrained elegance, and modern look. I loved being an Oligarch, but really didn't need to be a cliché.

I grasped Elle's hand, and led her up the ornate staircase to Vlad's bedroom, where I believed the safe to be. It was a large, and rather dark room, decorated in English country castle fashion, with thick, heavy drapes, and the sort of patterned carpet you see in pubs, the total effect being a rather hideous pastiche.

Straightaway, I noticed the old pictures on the walls, musing out loud that they were probably black market paintings. *I know full well that they were stolen, and Vlad bought them off some dodgy bugger in Vienna. I just don't know what I'm meant to do about it.*

Elle suggested that it would be a great opportunity to try and restore them to their rightful owners, so I took photographs, and told her that I'd ask Oscar.

I checked behind every picture, explaining to a puzzled Elle that I was looking for the safe. When I couldn't find it, she suggested that we tried Vlad's study. We made our way down the corridor to the first room in which I'd met him.

It was strange that there was no 'sense' of him there. I'd expected to feel his presence, as he'd been such a huge personality when alive, but dead, he'd just disappeared without trace. Elle wandered around the room, looking at the bookshelves, and stroking her hands along the enormous, carved, desk. I found the safe behind a picture, and pulled out the ring of keys I'd been given to see if one worked.

The second to last one fitted, and I opened the small safe to see a modest stack of cash, and some other papers and items. Elle seemed astonished at the cash, asking why he had so much. I smiled inwardly at her naivety, and explained that it would just be his day to day money, and wouldn't last long, especially with his daughter around. Elle really had no concept of how much it cost to maintain a wealthy lifestyle, and had made a vast fuss about a twenty grand dress, so I couldn't really expect her to understand a life where Dascha had spent at least a quarter of a million a month on clothes alone.

She counted the cash, while I checked out the rest of the contents, slipping a couple of flash drives into my pocket to look at later in privacy. There was a letter to Dascha, which I opened and read.

My dearest Dascha

By the time you read this letter, I shall be departed this Earth, and re-united with your dear Mother. I fully understood the risks involved with the life I chose, and have no regrets, apart from the murder of your Mother.

As you know, my will is lodged at Pearson Hardwick. They will be able to sort out my English assets easily, as it's only my bank account. Everything else is owned by Lortka, and listed in Russia, including my home and offices. There is a substantial amount of cash hidden in a large safe under my bed. The code is 43675479. Don't bank that money, or declare it anywhere.

As you know, the routes are profitable, but dangerous. I have left you two memory sticks full of images, which will provide you with ammunition, and leverage should you need it. Be careful with them, people would kill you for the images they contain. Only use them if you need to. Don't disclose their existence otherwise.

Please make friends with Ivan. He is a decent man, and I would trust him to help you if the need arose. I regard him as family, and wish that you would too.

Take care my little one, and remember that I love you.

Daddy

"This is a letter to Dascha, the safe's in Vlad's bedroom, come, let's look," I said to Elle, before placing the cash back in the safe, and putting the picture back across. I didn't want to discuss the letter with her, or the way it had brought a bit of a lump to my throat.

We made our way back into the bedroom, and I pushed Vlad's bed out of the way. Sure enough, a wooden trapdoor covered a large floor safe. I tapped in the code, and opened it up.

Elle seemed a little scared at the sight of the money, as I began to pull it out to count it. She seemed intimidated, and a bit jumpy, as if she expected Vlad to return at any moment, and catch us. I was less inhibited, probably because I'd actually seen Vlad's coffin, and I was used to seeing large amounts of cash. In the old days, we'd dealt almost exclusively in fifty pound notes, and I don't think I ever saw Vlad or Dascha without a large wad on them. I used a debit card, but then again, I always liked to be different, and to me, using cards was a sign of a certain respectability that Vlad could never attain.

It took us ages to count it all, and there turned out to be around eight million in total, plus the six hundred grand in the little safe, and the million I found in Moscow. I decided it was safe where it was, so, after pocketing a bag of diamonds, and a folder of deeds that were at the bottom, we piled the cash back into the vault, apart from a large stack that I told Elle to keep for her holiday spending. I was pretty sure she'd stay quiet about the money, and I even admitted it was murky, but by being a recipient of it, she wouldn't have an option of blabbing.

The next area we checked out was Dascha's private apartment, which occupied a wing of the house. I debated how to offer Elle her clothes and stuff without causing offence, as I knew Dascha had a vast collection of designer wear, as well as an extremely impressive jewellery collection, most of which I'd bought her. She'd been a similar size to Elle, and it would mean that Elle would be dressed entirely in quality clothing, without the hassle of convincing her to let me shop for her.

Elle seemed to find it rather odd that Dascha had gone back to her father, rather than live alone, after our split. I hadn't really given it that much thought before, but I agreed that it was strange. Dascha had been so fucking hopeless, that she would have either starved, or died of stupidness if she hadn't had a man around to look after her. Well, one that didn't spend all his time being chained up and whipped.

Elle's eyes were like saucers at the first sight of Dascha's dressing room. She stroked a quilted handbag, and wandered along the lines of shoes, taking it all in. "What do you want to do with all this?" I asked.

"That's not my decision to make. It all belongs to you," she replied.

"Ok, I'll phrase that differently, would you like to have any of this? It's no use to me, but it seems criminal to just throw it all away. You're welcome to it, that's if you want it. Some people are squeamish about having things that belonged to someone else." I tried to tread carefully, suspecting that, like me, she'd had a childhood full of cast offs, and might be a little sensitive about secondhand clothes, no matter how beautiful.

"Would you think I was skanky if I asked to keep all this?" *You could never be skanky, whatever that word means.*

"Not at all. It would be criminal to waste it. She may have been a nasty cow, but she had very good taste in clothes. Most of this probably hasn't even been worn. I'll arrange for Nico to get it shipped to your place."

A couple of the drawers contained jewellery. I picked up a handbag, and threw all the pieces into it, before zipping it up, and handing it to her. "You may as well take that home. I bought her most of that, so I'd rather you had it."

"Isn't it a bit weird, seeing me wearing all her stuff?"

I shrugged. "Not really, it's just clothes and objects. I barely took any notice of her at the best of times, so I wouldn't have a clue if you were wearing something of hers or not."

With that issue out of the way, I relaxed a little, and even seeing Dascha's whipping room didn't faze me. If anything, I found it rather sad, and wondered what it was that had driven her to seek her kicks that way. Rows of whips and paddles were lined up on one wall, and various restraints were attached to another. A padded bench was pushed to one side, and in the centre of the room, a sort of examination table with stirrups took pride of place, with a curious mechanical dildo contraption in front of it. I shuddered, and propelled Elle out of the room, telling her it would all be slung out.

I examined the new security system, and satisfied, Elle and I sat in the garden, and had a Starbucks, thoughtfully provided by Viktor. I made the decision to keep the house, possibly for when I had a family. In the meantime, it could be rented out until I needed it. By then, the ghosts would be gone.

When Nico had finished loading up the stuff to go to Elle's, I took the files, handed her the stack of cash, and we made our way back to Sussex.

Chapter 13

Elle insisted on returning to London that evening, which left me feeling a little deflated. I'd tried to change her mind, telling her we didn't need to be in the office until ten the next morning, but she was adamant that she had preparations to make for the following week, and couldn't spare me another evening.

It was even worse when she reminded me that she was out the following Saturday night, then away on holiday the next morning. With not even a sniff of a shag on the horizon, I began to wonder if I was wasting my time with her. I was a bit miffed that I'd just given her around ten million quids worth of clothes and jewellery, and she couldn't even muster up a thank you shag. I got a quick peck on the cheek before she skipped off back to London, driven by MY guard, in MY car, without even so much as a blow job.

When she'd gone, I mooched around indoors for a while, before pulling out my private laptop, and plugging in the flash drives to have a look. The images they contained were revolting, picture upon picture of various politicians, and oligarchs in compromising positions. I recognised the minister I'd met with in Moscow, although in the picture, he had his trousers round his ankles, and a very young girl's lips wrapped round his dick.

There were sheiks, royalty, and even some celebrities. I wondered how on earth Vlad had managed to amass such a collection, although it explained rather a lot as to why he had seemed to be able to get his own way so much. I printed off a copy of each of the pictures, and tucked them all away at the back of my safe, then turned my attention to the folders of deeds.

It appeared that Vlad owned a lot more land than he'd let on, owning swathes of central Russia, and vast tracts of land in the Ukraine, near Odessa. I decided to wait a few weeks to see if his paternity could be proven, before claiming it for myself. In the meantime, I'd get a geologist to check out what lay beneath the surface, quietly, so as not to upset the land values.

With a plan made, I was just tidying up the files, when Elle called, telling me that her flatmate had invited his girlfriend on holiday with them, and asking if I'd like to join them. *So you can 'not shag me' for two whole weeks? I don't think so.*

"I could fly over for the weekend, but not the whole two weeks. I pencilled in two weeks in France in August, I have to organise these things in advance." I'd been a bit pissed at her going away with her flatmate, so had yet to invite her away with me. Petty, I know, but I had every intention of asking her....when she'd started shagging me again.

"Ok, not to worry," she said quietly, and bade me goodnight. Thinking about it afterwards, it was a little strange inviting me, if she didn't plan on shagging me anymore. I was pleased that the flatmate had invited his girlfriend though, as it would ease my concerns about her being alone with him.

The American board all arrived at my offices at quarter to ten the next morning. Galina settled them all into the boardroom, while I waited in my office for Elle, so that we could walk in together. The yanks all seemed quite suspicious of me, and seemed cagey and rather reticent. I'd already looked through their accounts, and found several areas of underperformance that would need to be dealt with.

They sat listening, as I outlined my plans for the new board, and restructuring that would follow. Like their English counterparts, they all sat a little straighter, and looked a little keener. When I turned the conversation to the company performance over the past three years, I was a little surprised that the finance director, a Mr Weintraub, tried to conceal and confuse issues. When he threw out a percentage figure that was clearly wrong, I caught Elle's eye, and saw her write it down in her notepad. We'd both spotted it. When I corrected him, he annoyed me by sighing loudly, and pretending that I couldn't possibly understand the complexities of such difficult accounting, having only just taken over. *Cheeky bastard.*

"Mr Weintraub, can I remind you that I have in fact been running a larger conglomerate than Conde Nast, with far more subsidiaries, and more complex products, for the last fifteen years. Please don't ever assume I'm too stupid to understand a basic accounting procedure."

He looked chastened. "I didn't mean it like that, just that the numbers don't tell the full story, as there can be a substantial lag on payment for image rights, as opposed to the actual sales when they're used. *You're doing it again, I'd stop talking if I were you.*

"What you're describing is a cash flow issue, not a profit issue. I wasn't querying the amounts, I was querying the percentage you quoted. In real terms, your profits fell last year, but you tried to tell me that they'd risen 2%. You can't claim that you've cut costs, because they've risen 3% in the same period, so I'm sure you can appreciate why I'm confused." I fixed him with a hard stare, and watched him shrivel a little. *Good.*

When our meeting finished, Elle announced that she'd get back to her office to finish the paperwork needed for the new company. In the meantime, I took the Americans out for lunch, during which they all jostled for position in a way that I found slightly distasteful. Their head of legal even had the front to suggest that I could get rid of Elle, and he'd take over her role, telling me he had far more experience, and knew all the tricks I could use to stay ahead in the cut throat American market.

One by one, they seemed to prove themselves duplicitous and rather sly. I wondered at the wisdom of trusting them to serve my best interests, and decided to discuss my thoughts with Elle at the first opportunity.

I arranged to take them all to Nobu that evening, and sent them off for an afternoon of sightseeing. I quickly emailed Elle to see if she could join us, but she emailed back to say that she was apartment viewing, and still had a stack of work to do.

I raced home for my meeting with Natalya. She told me that she'd managed to get a sample of Vlad's DNA, and had spoken to someone who had known my mother back before I was born. She swabbed the inside of my cheek, and, rather flirtily, suggested we sit out on the terrace to discuss her findings so far. We sat down, and I poured us both a glass of wine. She'd just begun to tell me about an old neighbour of my mother's, when my phone rang. Seeing it was Elle, I answered it. "Hi, how did it go this afternoon?" I asked, a bit concerned at the amount of work I'd lumbered her with, due to this conglomerate.

"Yeah. Done as far as I can. Are you out with the yanks?"

Now at this point, I should have told her the truth, that I had a meeting to discuss whether or not Vlad the psycho was in fact, my dad, and confess that I'd shagged my own sister. Actually, I should have told her as soon as Kristov had alerted me, but I hadn't. I'd felt ashamed of being even more of a mongrel than I'd first thought. I figured I'd find out the truth first, then tell her. So I lied. "Yeah, just in the car now, heading over to the west end. Are you at home?"

"No. I'm viewing a flat, next to yours, and wondered who that woman is, ya lying bastard." I stood up, and looked across to the next building, to see Elle switch off her phone, and drop it into her handbag, before stomping off. *Shit shit shit. Not again.*

"Is everything alright?" Natalya asked, looking concerned at my scowling face.

"Yes fine. We'll continue this meeting another time. I need to go," I snapped. "NICO," I yelled, he came running, "see Ms Chimneynkov out please."

As soon as she'd gone, I tried to call Elle back, but her phone went straight to voicemail. I was just about to leave for the West End, when Roger called to tell me that she'd gone off with the estate agent, telling him she wouldn't need him that evening. I kept trying during the drive over, but her phone was switched off. I even called Oscar to ask him if he'd seen her arrive home, which he said he hadn't. I quickly sent her a grovelling email, begging her to trust me, and telling her that my meeting was just business, and there was nothing going on between Natalya and I.

It just seemed that Elle and I were having setback after setback, and I seriously considered whether I was cut out for all the 'being a boyfriend' thing. Casual hook-ups were far less complicated, and didn't give me such a sense of failure.

Meeting with the Americans, half of whom were female, reminded me exactly why Elle was so special. They'd clearly all been talking, and the women flirted shamelessly, with that steely glint in their eyes that reflected dollar signs. I played the part, hosting them all graciously, and smiling in the right places, but without Elle beside me, I felt empty, and a bit...alone. I liked having her next to me, catching my eye to show that we both had the same thoughts at the same time, and the way she could put her soft little hand on my knee to instantly calm me when she saw me get agitated.

I left the moment I could, without it being rude. I needed to get home for a sulk, as I'd surreptitiously checked my phone, and read an email from her, calling me a tosser, and telling me that she wouldn't be buying the flat as she wouldn't want me watching her with her new boyfriend. *Bitch*.

Her phone was still off, so, rather than keep pestering, I emailed Carl, and vented to him instead.

To: Carl Verve
From: Ivan Porenski
Date: 8th July 2013
Subject: Screwed up again

Carl

I'd just started to get round her, get us back on track, and tonight I went and ruined it again. I had a meeting with the investigator who is checking out the paternity thing, and hadn't told Elle about it. She saw me with her, while I was on the phone telling her I was elsewhere. I just can't seem to cut a break here. Every little white lie I tell seems to get found out.

I can't bear this distance between us, and I know it's my own fault. I'm seriously beginning to think I'm just not cut out for being a 'partner', and should just be satisfied with hookups instead. I missed her tonight, I was at a business dinner, and I would have much preferred her to have been there. Not one of the other women present interested me at all. I feel stupid and helpless.

Ivan

Five minutes later, his reply pinged into my inbox.

To: Ivan Porenski
From: Carl Verve
Date: 8th July 2013
Subject: re Screwed up again

Ivan

I'm sorry to hear that you are still struggling with your relationship with Elle. As with any major change in life, falling in love can be a rather bumpy ride. As your therapist, I'd counsel you to look inside yourself, and ask the question, "where do you see your life in six months, a year, or five years time?" If the honest answer is that you see yourself working through a series of one night stands, then you have your answer.

If, on the other hand, you see Elle by your side, sharing your life, then you may want to analyse why the two of you are having so many issues. That would be the first step to making the changes necessary to prevent further problems. You may even want to consider some couples counselling to assist the two of you in ironing out these misunderstandings.

A point to remember is that; in loving somebody, it entails giving up some control of your emotions. Having talked at length about your need for absolute control in your life, I can understand why these problems could cause you so much distress. While I can't advise you, I can reassure you that the feelings you're experiencing are completely normal.

Carl

I read his email a couple of times. I quite liked the idea of couples therapy, as Elle had a bit of a tendency to run away, rather than talk out our issues, as if she looked for an excuse to leave, rather than wait to be dumped, or cheated on. The only problem with that idea would be admitting that I talked to a therapist myself.

The rest of his email made perfect sense too. I hated myself for upsetting her, and found it uncomfortable how much of a puppy dog I was becoming. I thought about her almost constantly, and almost craved her approval. All of which was unusual behaviour for me. As for his 'where do you see yourself in five years time?' question, that was easy. I'd be Elle's devoted puppy, being called a tosser on a regular basis.

With my sulk out of the way, I got on with planning the superboard, making the decisions as to which executives would be invited to sit alongside Elle and I. Very few Americans made the cut. With a clear plan in place, I had an idea of the execs I still needed, ready for my meeting with Paul in the morning. I glanced up at the clock, it was nearly two am, and the spaniels had already taken themselves off to bed. I switched off my computer, and padded along to my bedroom, and was amused to see the pair of them stretched out across my bed. I undressed, and squeezed into the inch they'd left me, waking up a rather grumpy Tania in the process. Laying in the darkness, I resolved to make things right with Elle.

Our meeting the next morning was rather uneventful. With Paul present, our conversation didn't stray from professional, and Elle left before I had a chance to talk to her alone. Paul watched us both very closely, but didn't comment. I spent the rest of the day in back to back meetings, finally getting home around six. I tried repeatedly to call Elle, but she wasn't answering. *How the hell am I meant to apologise if she won't talk to me?* In the end, I got Nico to drive me over to hers.

Her flatmate let me in, eyeing me suspiciously. He told me she was in her room, so I went straight along to see her. She was standing in her underwear, and reflexively tried to cover herself when she saw me. "Don't bother, I've seen it all before," I reminded her grumpily. She pulled her robe on, and tied it tightly round her waist, which was a shame, as I'd rather enjoyed seeing her almost naked.

"Hello Ivan, to what do I owe this pleasure?" She sounded sarcastic, and a little miffed at my unannounced arrival. If she'd picked up my call, it wouldn't have been such a surprise.

"Your phone. You're not answering. Yet again."

She rummaged round in her bag, frowning. "It hasn't rung this evening.." She pulled it out, and looked at the screen "It was on silent," she muttered, "what did you want?" *Oh. So you're not ignoring me then.*

"I wanted to discuss Natalya." I plonked myself down on her bed. She came and sat beside me.

"Ok, go ahead."

"It wasn't how it looked. She's a private investigator. I commissioned her to do a job for me in Russia. She needed to see me urgently with some news." I'd decided to go with total honesty, and tell her the entire story.

"I see."

"I asked her to look into the circumstances of my parent's deaths, and a rumour that I heard as a child."

"And that made her all flirty with you?" *I love it when you get all jealous.*

"She was just reacting the same as all women do, except you that is. She came to take a sample of my DNA, and tell me her findings so far."

"Which was?"

"Vlad's henchmen killed my parents Elle, I always wondered why the bastards didn't kill me as well, they could have done. Apparently they were under strict orders to ensure nothing happened to me."

She frowned, "why did Vlad do that, if he really was behind the murder of your parents?"

"That question has bugged me, well, at the time I didn't know Vlad was behind it, but I always wondered why I was spared. The man who took them away said dad was not my father."

"Right..."

"It looks like Vlad was my father, which means Dascha was my half sister, and he wanted us to marry." I could see the shock written all over her face.

"That's sick. Imagine if you'd had kids?"

I shuddered, "I feel sick knowing I had a relationship with my own half sister, that's bad enough, but having a psychopath like Vlad as a father is horrific. I just hope it's not hereditary."

"No wonder he helped you so much, setting up."

"Yeah, he covered that by telling me it was for Dascha. A hospital in Moscow gave Natalya a sample of his DNA from a biopsy they did for him. In a few days, I'll know the truth." I scrubbed my hands over my face. "I was friendly with the man who killed my mother."

"Why were they killed?"

"Vlad basically stole the factory where my father worked. I didn't know until recently who 'the businessman' was. My parents were activists in the protest movement, as all the workers were thrown into even more poverty than under the communist regime. We could barely afford to eat, and it was getting worse. Vlad's men stamped out all dissent quickly and mercilessly. I gave the workers a pay rise, and better working conditions when I was in Moscow the other week, and discovered that the factory was part of Vlad's estate. They were so grateful, it was pitiful." I thought of the factory manager thanking me repeatedly, for what was still a pittance, and cringed inwardly.

"Why didn't you tell me all this before?" She asked softly.

I stared out of the window for a while, trying to find the right words. "You don't like me seeing where you're from, I'm the same. I'm from peasant stock, from the grottiest slums of Moscow. Those people are still there, dying young from the conditions they work in, and the poverty they endure. It so easily could have been me, and if my parents hadn't been murdered, it probably would've been." That was the crux of it. All my success and wealth had come about because they died. The guilt I felt was crushing. Seeing Andrei there had really slammed it home.

"You don't know that, all this could have happened regardless."

I shook my head, "no, I know I would have stayed. I was a bit of a mummy's boy. I watched them dragged out of our tenement, and saw my father executed in the street in front of everyone." I felt the tears fall out of my eyes as I was transported back to that terrible day. I wiped them away, embarrassed at her seeing me so emotional. "I prayed so hard that they'd let my mum go, but they took her and some other woman to the gates of the factory, and killed them there. I heard the shots, and I knew it was her. They left her body there as a warning to the other workers not to get above their position, or cause trouble. I didn't know what to do. I had no other family, or money for a burial. I couldn't even arrange a grave. Almost all the other neighbours were too scared to help me, so I had to dig two paupers graves on some scrubland to bury them. Then I ran away, but you know all that bit."

"So he killed the woman he had a relationship with?"

I nodded. "I don't know if my father ever knew there was a chance I wasn't his. Bear in mind, I was born long before Vlad became successful. I don't know if it was an affair, rape, or anything."

"Baby I'm sorry, this must be so hard for you." She hugged me, holding me tight. "Regardless of who your father is, you're still the same person, that won't change. Neither us are the product of our parents."

"There's only one bright spot. If Vlad was my father, proven by DNA, I'll get my 13% inheritance tax back." *And if I'm right about what lies beneath that land, it's a fucking fortune I'll save.* She smiled, and agreed with me, before pointing out that I still didn't have any family, adding that she wished she had at least some cousins, adding that she felt very alone. I replied that I was used to it, having been alone for so long. It worried me that she felt abandoned though. "You have me," I told her.

"Do I? I bought a flat today. You don't know where, what it's like, anything. You don't know my favourite colour, the music I like, the books I read. I don't 'have' you Ivan. I have the tiny bit of you that you choose to share with me. Is it any wonder we fall out so much when you're so secretive?" *Quite a good point.*

"I wish I was a good boyfriend, and knew how to make you feel loved and cherished. It's like there's a secret that I'm not privy to, you know, how to make a woman happy."

"You are pretty rubbish at it," she pointed out, "unbelievably stingy with the flowers too." She paused, looking pensive. "I need to tell you, I'm not going away with James and Janine now. I'm going to Tuscany with Oscar. He invited me, and I need a

244

break. I did ask you to come on holiday first though," she added hastily.

"And I said no, that I booked August, and didn't invite you..." I trailed off. "I meant to ask you, but you were so intent on not sleeping with me, I just..." She stared at me, her eyebrows raised, "Ok, I'm a tosser."

She went off to make us some coffees. I looked around the room, filled with boxes, and saw that she'd been sorting through them. I encouraged her to carry on while I sat on the bed and drank my coffee. "Yellow isn't your colour," I told her when she tried on a long sundress that made her look like a banana. She added it to a pile in the corner of the room, telling me she'd taken the stuff she wasn't going to use into work for the secretaries, which I felt was very thoughtful of her. With my help, she worked her way through a whole box of clothes, while I'd been stealing glimpses of her nipples through her lacy bra, driving myself mental.

"Tell me about your new flat," I said, "where is it?"

She smiled. "St Saviour dock, just along the river from here. It's beautiful."

"I know that block. Which floor?" I was quite impressed. It was one of the more prestigious apartment blocks in the docklands, with all the latest security features. I approved.

"Top floor," she looked a little embarrassed, "the penthouse." *How the fuck has she afforded that?* Then it dawned on me. Oscar. Fucking. Golding. *What the hell does she have on him?* I decided not to react.

"I can't wait to see it. Do you need to furnish it? Is it a shell or does it already have a kitchen and bathrooms?"

"The kitchen's glossy white, and a bit like the one you've got in France. All the bathrooms are done, and it has a fitted study. I need to get quite a bit of furniture though. It's a big space, and I'll need to take my time, as I've never bought furniture before."

"Would you like me to engage an interior designer to help you?" I offered. I knew how daunting it was decorating a first home. Mine had been a flat in Chelsea, and I remembered feeling a bit clueless. Dascha had been no help, sodding off out with her friends to buy clothes at every opportunity, even though we didn't even have a wardrobe to store them in, and refusing to help, claiming that her nails were too precious to so much as empty a box.

"That'd be great...thank you. It's such a big space that I think I need a bit of help. I want it all modern, you know, sectional sofas and clean lines. I'm just worried that it'd come out looking a bit empty and cold." She pulled a hideous green jumper over her head. I pulled a face.

I changed the subject to her awards do at the weekend, asking her if she'd decided what to wear, mainly to find out if she needed her red dress delivered back. She told me she was wearing the champagne coloured one, as it was a white tie event. It was a shame she'd invited her friend, as I looked my best in white tie. We'd have made a fantastic looking couple. Instead, I offered her the Bentley, and Roger, under the guise of arriving in style, but it would also ensure she got home safely, and alone. She beamed such a lovely smile at my thoughtfulness, that I decided it would be the right time to strike. She was also in just her underwear.

I pulled her onto my lap, and snaked my arms round her. "When can I make love to you? I've been so patient, and I can see your nipples through your bra. It's been driving me crazy all evening." I kissed her neck softly, feeling her soften and lean into me. "Can I at least take your bra off, and feel your tits?" Although I sounded like a stupid adolescent, she didn't say no, so I reached round, and unclipped her bra, sliding it down her arms, freeing the puppies. She shifted slightly, which made them jiggle beautifully. I cupped one, "I've missed your breasts. You have the best nipples I've ever seen." I watched as they hardened into tight little nubs, showing me the effect I was having on her.

I captured one in my mouth, and sucked on it. She arched into me, groaning slightly. "Please tell me when I can make love to you. I can barely control myself." She stroked my erection through my shorts, making it my turn to groan. I thought I'd go off there and then. "Please let me make love to you. I'll beg if you want." Even to my own ears, I sounded needy and desperate. I lifted my face to hers, and kissed her, pressing my tongue into her mouth, in a show of barely restrained animal passion.

"Yes, make love to me now." No sooner were the words out of her mouth, than I had her knickers yanked down, my shorts kicked off, and Elle laying on her back on the bed. I crawled up her body, kissing and licking her soft skin. She tasted divine.

"I need to fuck you hard first. I won't last long, I'm too turned on," I admitted, as I nudged my cock into her, filling her with my thick, iron hard dick. I fucked her at a ridiculously fast pace, completely dominating her body. She could barely move as I pinned her to the bed, totally taking over her body. I just....needed her, and needed to show her physically exactly how much I'd missed her.

As I pounded her, I felt the familiar quickening of an impending orgasm. I kissed her as she called out, swallowing her cries of passion. As she pulsed around me, I stilled, and let go, resting my forehead against hers. "I've missed you so much baby, please don't let's fall out again."

She stretched like a cat underneath me, boneless and languid after her orgasm. "Don't fall asleep, please, I'm looking forward to round two," I said, a little alarmed that she'd doze off before I had another fuck. The first one was just to get me ready for a longer, slower session.

"I'm not going to sleep, not when I've got your big dick to play with," she purred. I rolled off, and lay on my back. Elle licked and sucked my nipples, each in turn, and gently stroked the skin of my torso. I practically arched off the bed in pleasure as she rolled my nipples between her fingers. She kissed her way down to the tip of my cock, which was back to a full strength erection, and leaking pre-cum. Settling herself between my legs, she massaged my anus as she licked my balls, and pressed tiny kisses up my inner thighs. I sighed loudly, giving in to the sensual pleasure she was inflicting on me. It felt amazing.

She slowly licked her way up the shaft of my cock, avoiding the tip, until she had nudged her finger into my anus. I gasped as she massaged my prostrate at the same time as she sucked my cock, swirling my tongue repeatedly over the crest. "Oh god, oh god, don't stop, oh god that feels good," I groaned as she teased and played with me. "Oh no, no, I'm gonna come, stop, stop." She ignored me, and continued her sensual torture until I spurted hotly into her mouth.

"You proved your point, sexy girl. Your turn now, and I'm not gonna show you any mercy." I flipped her onto her back, and lifted her hips, pulling her knees up to her tummy, and pinning her legs open with my arms, so that she was totally open and exposed to me. I began with long, lush licks, before sucking her swollen clit. She groaned with the pleasure, as I lapped and sucked at the most intimate parts of her.

I changed position to slide two fingers into her, and began pumping them in and out. I pressed down on her stomach, just above her pubis. I kept my fingers pumping and rubbing her g spot as I slapped her clit several times, then pressed down again.

"Let go baby," I commanded, as her legs stiffened. She came with a muffled cry, and squirted all over the bed. It was the horniest thing I'd ever seen.

"Oh my god! I'm so sorry, I don't know what happened." She was mortified. I grinned, pleased with myself.

"I gave you what's called a 'squirting orgasm'," I said, "it's supposed to be the most intense a woman can have."

"It looks like I wet the bed," she muttered, going beetroot. I scooped her into my arms, and gave her a deep, lush, kiss.

"No, it looks like you had a giant orgasm. I'll sleep on the damp patch, I don't mind. Now, I think my cock's recovered since your earlier fun. Can we have a slow one? You, on top, so I can see you, and touch those beautiful breasts." I rolled her onto me. She straddled me, and sank down onto my cock, holding still for a moment. I gazed at her face as I stroked my hands over her waist and ribs, reassuring myself that she was real, and I wasn't dreaming her.

She began to move slowly, closing her eyes, as I kneaded and fondled her breasts. She tilted her head back to push them into my hands, revelling in the sheer sensuality of our connection. "Open your eyes, let me see you....please." I murmured. She bent over me, and gazed into my eyes, light blue into dark. "You are so beautiful, so sexy," I whispered, "I could never get enough of you." I cupped her face, and drew her to me for a kiss.

We made it last, moving slowly, just enjoying each other's bodies, with neither of us chasing an orgasm. When she eventually came, it rolled through her in waves, massaging my cock deep inside her, causing me to find my own release. Afterwards, she lay in my arms, neither of us speaking for a while. Eventually she broke the silence, "would you like a drink?"

"Can I have something cold? Water or juice, something like that please." She threw on a robe, washed her hands, and padded out to the kitchen, returning a few minutes later with our drinks, as well as some snacks.

"Brought us some sustenance." She announced. I sat up and took the glasses of juice off her, placing them on the bedside table. She dumped the rest on the bed beside me.

"Great, I'm starving. Sex always makes me hungry," I said, pulling out a breadstick, and scooping up some cheese, taking a bite, before offering it to her. We ended up feeding each other, with Elle licking Philadelphia off my fingers. "Careful, I'll end up hard again. You'll break my cock if you don't let it rest," I warned her.

"I wouldn't want to do that," she smirked as she bent down to give it a little kiss. It twitched, despite being soft. "I agree, no more tonight, anyway, I'm a little sore, and I want to change the sheet before we sleep. It's full of crumbs as well as whatever it was that came out of me."

I helped her change the sheet, before throwing the duvet back over, and sliding in, my arms outstretched. She snuggled into me, giving a contented little sigh. "I will be the man you fall in love with, I'm determined," I whispered.

"You already are," she replied, before dozing off.

Chapter 14

She got me up ridiculously early the next morning, already dressed in the little leggings and vest that she wore to the gym. She even tapped her foot impatiently when I used her bathroom for a quick wee, and to brush my teeth. I took the big bag of clothes that she didn't want, promising to get them delivered to her office for her, to save her lugging them. I went straight home to have some breakfast, and get myself ready.

The spaniels weren't happy that I'd been out all night, showing their displeasure in a dirty protest, as I found a dogshit in my bathroom when I went up to shower. Neither one would own up, so they both had plain dog biscuits for breakfast as punishment, which they turned their noses up at.

When I came down for my breakfast, Mrs Watton had cooked them some sausages, which they were happily tucking into, waving their bums in the air at me. "They were on dry biscuits as punishment this morning," I told Mrs Watton.

"I'm sorry, I didn't realise. Thought they looked a little bit sheepish about something," she replied. The spaniels gazed up at her, adoration in their eyes. She was like one of those grannies who spoiled their grandchildren, then complained about their behaviour.

My day was rather tedious, mainly meetings with grey suited men, most of whom seemed to want to bore me into submission to get whatever was on their agendas. I managed to find five minutes to call Oscar about the paintings I'd found at the Windsor house, and he'd told me about the stolen art register, and agreed that it was an ideal opportunity to restore them to their rightful owners. I gave them a call, and arranged to meet an expert at the Windsor house the following Monday to let him have a look.

One of my other directors had found a lessee for the Knightsbridge offices, who apparently liked the gold leaf decor that Vlad had covered the place in, and wanted a five year lease on the place, which was good news. I also called Sotheby's to put Vlad's car collection up for auction. He'd had a bit of a thing for Rolls Royce's, believing that they made him look rich and successful, and had a collection of seven different ones. They really weren't my cup of tea, so I'd decided to get rid. I preferred my Bentley, with top of the range Mercedes as spare cars if needed. I pondered whether or not I should order another Bentley for Elle's use, as she seemed quite pleased to be using mine for her awards do. Thinking of Carl's advice, I decided to wait until I'd spoken to her, rather than just going ahead, and forcing it on her.

My afternoon was fairly straightforward, and I managed to get home by six. The spaniels seemed to have forgotten their sulk, and greeted me happily as I walked in. Mrs Watton looked a little ragged though. "I'm eating out tonight, so don't worry about dinner," I said.

"Given that I've spent most of today clearing up after these two, that's quite a relief. I've never been so behind with my work. Tania's eaten a toilet roll, and Bella rolled in fox poo on her walk, so I had to call the groomer in, then clean the bathroom after them." She wittered on, listing all their misdemeanours, as I listened patiently. I had to admit that the girls looked thoroughly pleased with themselves, and assured my housekeeper that I'd get their trainer back in at the earliest opportunity.

I called Elle to see if she wanted to go out to eat, and arranged to pick her up. I quickly showered and changed into more casual clothes, before Nico drove us over to hers. I'd let her choose where to eat, mindful of always dictating where we went. She'd called her concierge service, and chosen Hakkasan, which I was pleased about. I'd eaten there before, and really liked it, and was relieved that Elle hadn't let cost dictate her choice.

I'd already warned her that I was waiting on a call that evening, so I was pleased that it came early, so that I could switch off my phone, and concentrate on her. It was only the geologist confirming that he'd arrived in Odessa, and would start his investigations the following day.

I loved taking Elle out, and showing her off. She always looked so demure and classy that it never failed to thrill me that I knew she'd be wearing a skimpy lace thong underneath the ladylike dress. We chatted about her flatmate's girlfriend, who had claimed to be at a job interview at my company that evening. I frowned, telling Elle that the office manager had gone home at around half five, so couldn't have done an interview at six, and Ranenkiov wouldn't have done receptionist interviews.

Elle confided that she didn't trust the new girlfriend, and thought she was a bit sly. I mentioned that she should put her jewellery away in her safe with a stranger around. When she confessed that she didn't even have a safe, I offered mine, and told her that she could rent boxes at Oscar's bank if needed.

We made our way back to Elle's, relaxed from the wine, and more than ready for another shag. I made Nico stay in the car, and practically sucked her face off in the lift on the way up. I loved it when she was all happy and horny.

It all changed when we walked into her flat to find her flatmate sitting in the kitchen with his head in his hands, looking as if someone had died. Elle looked concerned, and asked him what was wrong.

"I don't know. I think she's left me again. She was fine, and asked me to go to the shop for her. When I came back, she wasn't here. No note, nothing. She's not answering her phone either. I don't understand what's happened, we didn't have a row or anything."

We both had the same thought at the same time. Elle turned tail, and ran to her room. She reappeared a few moments later, looking furious. "Did you tell her about that money? It's all gone," she shouted.

"What about the jewellery?" I asked. The money wasn't too important, as there hadn't been that much, but there must have been at least five mil worth of jewellery there.

"Still there, thankfully. That fucking bitch helped herself to the cash, and ran for it," she replied, shooting daggers at her flatmate, who looked even more distraught.

"Elle, I'm gonna call the police. I'm so, so very sorry. I'll replace it." *Oh, that's really not a good idea.*

"Don't call the police. The money was murky. They're going to want to know why you had it, and where it's from. Let me make some calls." I pulled out my phone, and called Kristov, speaking in Russian so that the others couldn't understand. "Hi, it's Ivan, I have a problem I need your help with. My girlfriend's just had some cash stolen by her flatmates girlfriend. Quite a lot of cash, plus the girls gone missing. Happened this evening. I need you to find her, retrieve the cash, and force her to explain herself to Elle's friend."

"Shouldn't be an issue, have you got a mobile number? It'd be helpful if you had a photo too."

I asked James for Janine's phone number, and relayed it to Kristov, followed by a photograph from James' mobile. I explained to Kristov that James would want to talk to her, and while I didn't mind his operatives putting the fear of god into her, I didn't want her harmed. Eventually I clicked off my phone. "Now, have you checked to see if anything else has been taken?"

They both checked their rooms, and after a few minutes, declared that nothing else was missing.

"I'm so sorry Elle, I should've kept my mouth shut. I would never in a million years have thought she could do something like this," said James. He looked contrite, and terribly sad. I actually felt really sorry for him. I'd be devastated if Elle did something like that.

"She left you for your best mate James, she's clearly a sneaky bitch, oh, and she wasn't at Retinski for an interview this evening. I don't know where she was, probably planning this with her next lover," Elle spat at him, still in her rage.

"Elle, come on, it's only a little cash. The poor man's lost his woman over it." I said, convinced that James felt bad enough already, and didn't need a further telling off. I busied myself by making the three of us some drinks, and hoped that Kristov could sort the problem quickly, so that there'd still be time for my shag.

"I don't understand why she didn't come to me, if she needed some money," said James, "I would've helped her. I already invited her to move in here, so she could get a job, and get back on her feet." *So she was telling the truth.*

"Why did she leave her husband?" I asked him.

"I don't know, she wouldn't tell me, just said it had all gone wrong between them, and she'd realised she'd made a terrible mistake, you know, leaving me for him."

"Hmm. Well, we can probably get the money back. What happens from there is up to you." I told him.

"What do you mean?" Elle butted in, "and who did you call?"

"My security company. They'll find her, and if she still has the money, they'll retrieve it. It's what happens after that, whether you want her prosecuted, punished, or just to leave you alone. I suspect that James will want some answers, to get his own closure on this." I favoured the 'leaving alone' option. Trying to prosecute over murky cash wasn't a great idea.

"I want to ask her a million questions," said James. "I want to know if this was a moment of madness, or whether she came back with the intention of robbing me. She knows I'm ok for money. Mind you, her husband wasn't skint."

"Most people who steal have an addiction or problem. Was she secretive in other ways?" Elle asked.

"Yeah, I suppose so. I was never allowed to touch her phone, and she always took her handbag everywhere, even into the bathroom. That's not really normal is it?" We all glanced at Elle's bag laying open on the island with her phone poking out. *No secrets there.*

"No, not really," she said.

"So when they find her, you want to speak to her?" I interjected, looking at James.

"Yeah, if they find her. Who exactly is looking for her?"

"A private security company. They can find a needle in a haystack. They'll track her phone, scan CCTV, that type of thing. They're normally pretty quick, unless she had the nous to throw her phone away." I didn't really want to tell them that I'd put the Russian mafia on her tail. It might have freaked them out a bit, besides, Elle didn't know about my links to them, and I wanted it to stay that way.

We all sipped our tea, and waited, James with his head in his hands. "You know, that was the first time in my entire life that I actually had any money." Elle said sadly. *What?*

"I thought you had money to buy this flat?" I asked, frowning. I knew at that moment that Golding had either given or lent her the money for her purchase, and I really wanted her to admit it.

"I meant money that wasn't earmarked, just for frittering," she said, still not admitting anything. I wondered why she was being secretive about it.

"How much was there?" I asked.

"Two hundred thousand, plus or minus a few quid. I hope they get it back tonight. I need to get some Euros tomorrow."

Was that all I gave you? Oh, that's a bit embarrassing. I thought there'd be at least half a mil in that stack.

"I'll get them for you, don't worry about that." James said. *No you won't. I'll take care of this.*

They both jumped when my phone rang. I looked at the number, saw that it was Kristov, and switched to Russian. "Hey Kristov, that was quick."

He chuckled, "Doesn't take me long. They were at London City, trying to get a flight to Rome, but thankfully not airside, so we have them in a staff room. The flight she bought doesn't leave till the morning. I'll send an operative with the money straightaway. Are you at home?"

"No, Elle's place." I reeled off the address, and fixed a code word for the entry system. "What have you told her?" I asked him.

"Only that there's a contract out on her if she comes back to London. She was with an Italian male, a boyfriend apparently. It would appear that your girlfriend's flatmate was played."

"Hmm, thought so, well, he wants to speak to her, so pass the phone over, and I'll speak to you afterwards." I handed my phone to James. "Ask away." James took the phone into his bedroom. I turned to Elle, "They found her, and her male accomplice in London City airport, trying to buy a flight to Rome. Unfortunately for her, flights are infrequent, and she would have had to wait until the morning."

"What a bitch. I knew there was something shady about her. Poor James, he really did love her. I hope for his sake that he never sees her again."

"I would be devastated. When I think, you had full access to everything, and you didn't even look, let alone take as much as a fiver..." I gazed at her, full of admiration. I'd given her access to everything, and all she'd done was sit and cry because she'd missed me, according to both Roger and Mrs Ballard.

"I'm not a thief, and I know that if I needed anything, I could ask. If anything, I feel a little embarrassed about all the gifts and things that have been showered on me. I love nice things as much as the next girl, but it does make me feel a bit greedy. Plus of course, this has happened, and I can't help thinking that if temptation hadn't been put in her way..."

"She would have stolen from James. She had an accomplice Elle, she meant to steal. Now, in some ways it's better it was you than James, because I can take care of it. James had to work hard for his money, we just found yours. It also gives you an insight as to why I have so much security. I can't bear to be stolen from."

"I've never really been a target before, well, mainly because I've never had anything worth nicking." *I know just how that feels baby, but at last, I've been able to make you feel protected.*

"I'm so pleased that at long last I've been able to fix something for you. It's been rather too much the other way round. I like looking after you." That was a bit of an understatement. As sorry as I felt for James, I'd been delighted that I'd had an opportunity to fix a problem for her, and make her smile again. I'd been quite curious about her reaction to losing two hundred grand. She'd looked as if her puppy had died. She knew how much cash was at Windsor, so if she used up what she had, I'd simply get her some more. What was even more interesting, was that she hadn't even flinched when I'd told her that the money was murky.

I asked her whether she was going on holiday with James now, or sticking with her plans to accompany Oscar. Personally, I felt safer with her going with James. She shrugged her shoulders, and told me that she didn't know, but would've preferred to be going away with me, adding that she'd maybe do a week with each.

We were interrupted by the buzzer for the foyer door. Elle answered, peering at the video showing one of Kristov's operatives. As soon as he gave the code word, I let him in, and waited at the front door for the delivery of cash.

She sat at the island and counted it out, before declaring that it was £700 short. I watched as she stuffed it all back in the bag, looking relieved, and much happier. She was just clearing up our cups, when James reappeared, holding my phone out to me. "The fella wants to speak to you," he said. I took the phone off him, and switched to Russian.

"Hey Kristov, the money arrived about ten minutes ago. Quick work."

"Not a problem. She'll be on the first flight out in the morning, convinced there's a contract on her head. She won't bother you again."

"Thanks." I put the phone away, and listened as James told Elle about their conversation, revealing that his girlfriend had returned with the express idea of stealing from him, as she was pregnant with her accomplice's child.

Elle was sympathetic, and seemed concerned for her friend, until he told her that his girlfriend had been jealous of Elle, saying that everything fell into Elle's lap rather easily. It was how she'd rationalised stealing from her.

Elle exploded, "Easily? Is that what the bitch thought? Up until I moved here, I've had to work my arse off for everything. You saw what I walked into this flat with. I had fuck all to my name. My own mother died penniless so I could go to Cambridge. I came from total poverty, but I never stooped low enough to nick anything. Bitch." She paused for breath, clearly getting worked up. I saw two little red patches appear on her cheeks, coupled with a deep frown. I fought the urge to laugh, as she looked so cute, like an angry kitten.

"Do you know how sexy you are when you're angry? She knew nothing. Don't let her twisted opinions affect you." As soon as I said it, Elle seemed to relax, and let go of her anger.

She just seemed tired, as she fielded questions from James about her holiday.

She looked up at the clock, and announced that she needed to sleep, as it was getting late. I followed her into the bedroom, stripped off, and slid into bed, before she could tell me to go home. She snuggled into me, as I pulled her into a cuddle, for once, feeling as though I was her protector. Unfortunately, she was too sleepy for a shag, and was out cold within thirty seconds.

I lay there, just listening to her breathing, spooning her soft, warm, little body, and thanked the gods for letting me take care of her. The actual money had been nothing, easy to replace, but it had been *her* money, so it had been important that I'd got it back. I held her a little tighter, and marvelled at how calm and content I felt, just feeling her heartbeat, and touching her silky, warm skin. *I love her more than Irina.* The thought popped into my head, an unwelcome one at first, as I'd always regarded Irina as my one true love. I'd been able to leave her, run away from her, as painful as abandoning her had been at the time, my sense of self preservation had won. I wouldn't be able to do that to Elle. Couldn't leave her if I tried. For the first time in my life, I understood why men married, why they wanted ownership of a woman.

I wanted her bound to me, body and soul, in an embrace that lasted our lifetimes. I wanted every Sunday with her, just walking in the woods, enjoying the time together. I wanted to teach her to enjoy our wealth, let go of her poverty, and free herself from the guilt she carried for her mother. With those thoughts in my head, I fell into a deep, dreamless sleep.

She let me have a lay in the next morning, well, her version of a lay in. I peeled open my eyes to look at the clock, and saw that it was half six. It had its advantages, getting up early, as we had a lovely morning fuck in the shower to set me up for the day.

I dropped her off at work, before going home to face the wrath of the spaniels. They hated me staying out all night, so I'd planned for Elle to stay over at mine that night. I also wanted a massive session in my sex room, to make up for not seeing her for at least a week.

The spaniels greeted me with excitement, until they remembered that they were cross with me. Tania even bit me as I fed her some sausage, as retribution for being left with their nanny. Their sulk lasted all of five minutes, before they were clambering onto my lap, and showering me with doggy kisses. I made a mental note to ask the vet to prescribe some breath freshener for Bella.

I asked Mrs Watton to leave dinner for two in the warming drawer, and get some caviar and accoutrements, before kissing the spaniels, and going into work. My day was fairly straightforward, mainly involving the financials of the companies I already owned. I read report after report, and satisfied that revenues and margins were on track with projections, set about reading up on mining equipment.

I'd invited several companies to submit tenders for the heavy duty machinery required to extract more from the three mines, and, as it was going to be a major investment, I made sure I was well informed and knowledgeable about the types and capabilities of the machinery I needed. It was incredibly boring, so I was quite pleased when Joan Lester called to ask if I was happy for Vogue to continue to sponsor London fashion week. I replied that I'd be delighted, and asked if she could get tickets for Elle and I to attend.

My only other respite from the reports was a lunch with Paul, and a stop off at the shops to buy fresh batteries for the vibrator I planned to use on Elle that evening. With the batteries safely tucked into my pocket, I wrapped up for the week, and went home to get ready.

Elle sounded chirpy when I called her to find out what time she should be picked up, calling me 'babe', and replying 'excellent news', when I told her I had fresh batteries waiting for her. I guessed that her flatmate must have been within earshot. I had a quick wank before she arrived, as I wanted a long, slow session with her. I had plans.

She arrived twenty minutes later, kissing me hungrily, before making a fuss of the girls, who were also desperate to garner her attention. I watched as she fussed them, stroking their ears with a kind of maternal gentleness. After a few minutes, I led her into the kitchen, and poured us each a glass of wine. She took a sip, and beamed a smile at me, before asking why we weren't heading down to Sussex.

I told her I'd delayed going until the next day, so that I could have her in my sex swing, commenting that I was going to have two, very boring weeks, so wanted to make the most of her while I could. She rolled her eyes, and told me to hop on my jet and join her, adding that it would save having to go a fortnight without sex.

I pulled our plates out of the warming drawer, and set them down at the table, telling Elle that the spaniels had already eaten, and didn't need any more. "Spaniel eyes are so difficult to resist," she remarked, before eating a slice of chicken, the spaniels watching every mouthful she took.

"That's what they depend on. I wonder if it would work for me too," I mused. I gave her my best puppy look. She just smiled at me, and told me that they needed to be big and brown to have full effect, adding that mine were too blue and sparkly.

She sipped her wine, and looked thoughtful. "Besides, you're going to eat your fill, then have as much sex as you can handle. Exactly what else could you possibly want?" *You, baby.*

I agreed that it sounded pretty perfect, but that I wished I was going away with her. I loved seeing her so happy, and, even though I was confident that she wouldn't sleep with anyone else,

I envied them the simple pleasures of relaxing and reading with her beside them. She told me that she wished we were going away together too, and said she'd like to come to France for the weekend, when I went in August. I decided to speak to her boss, and see if I could get her another fortnight off.

We decided to finish our wine out on the terrace, before we hit the sex room. Elle busied herself clearing our plates, slipping a few scraps to the girls when she thought I wasn't looking. The simple domesticity made me strangely homesick, not for Russia, but more for....family, for a life shared. I scooted round the island to wrap my arms around her, and kiss her. She leaned into me, responding instinctively to my featherlight kisses, "I love you so much, and I want you to be my wife," I murmured, albeit in Russian, so that she wouldn't understand. She looked quizzical, but I just kissed her loudly, and wetly on the lips, before leading her out to the terrace.

I pulled her onto my lap, holding her close, as we sipped our wine. She gazed out over the river for a little while, before setting her glass down, and kissing me, running her hands all over me. Unable to wait any longer, I led her back into my apartment, and along to my sex room.

This time, I made sure that the door was properly closed, before stripping off quickly, and laying on the bed. "Strip for me please," I commanded, before switching on some music for Elle to give me a floor show.

She began slowly, teasing me with a glimpse of nipple, then a flash of pussy, making me wait, turning me on. I made my plans for the session, I wanted her totally mine, begging for my cock. "You look so beautiful," I told her, as I viewed her naked pussy, "tonight will you let me restrain you? Make me feel as though I own you, body and soul?" I half expected her to object, but she didn't, although she seemed a touch nervous, until I reassured her it was for her pleasure as much as mine.

She let me cuff her hands behind her back, and stood watching in the mirror as I gently cupped her breasts from behind. I kissed the silky skin on her back, and she shivered slightly as my hand slid down to rub her clit. I watched her subtly push herself onto my hand. She was soaking, and clearly very turned on, her nipples were like bullets.

I moved slowly, first letting her suck her juices off my fingers, then giving her clit a little suck, stopping before she could come. I played with her body for ages, taking her to the edge, then stopping, until she began to get desperate. When she tried to play me at my own game, by refusing me a blow job, I wanked between her tits until she was straining to get my cock into her mouth.

As soon as I let her suck my cock, I began to lose control, she was just so damn good at it, that I had to give in, uncuff her, and fuck her hard in the swing, by which time, she was begging.

The moment I pressed the vibrator onto her clit, she came hard, screaming my name as she lost control. By the third orgasm, she was shuddering, and almost passing out. I let go, shooting a huge load deep inside her.

I stayed inside her until I softened, and slipped out, totally exhausted. I wiped the sweat from my face, before helping Elle out of the swing, and carrying her to the bed, laying down beside her. She seemed a bit dazed. I kissed her softly. "You are exquisite, beautiful girl. Have you any idea how much I love you?"

"Mmm, I love you too baby," she mumbled, "I am totally wrung out." I held her for a few minutes, basking in our post coital glow, before asking if she was hungry or thirsty, knowing full well that she would be.

Both dressed in bathrobes, we padded along to the kitchen, where we feasted on caviar and blinis. I showed Elle how to make them, feeding her as I prepared them. "Does this remind you of home?" she asked. I smiled at her naivety, before telling her that the only things that reminded me of home were rye bread, salted meat, and pickled vegetables. All of which I avoided. I'd been introduced to caviar when I'd been in London about five years.

I took a big bite of beluga, closing my eyes at the delicious, salty, fishiness. "I was born to enjoy only the good things in life, I think."

"Just a good time boy," she giggled.

"That's me. I make no apology for it," I said, smiling.

When I woke the next morning, Elle was already up. I made us both coffee, and took them out onto the terrace. She looked deep in thought. When I questioned her, she told me that she was daydreaming about her new apartment, then proceeded to tell me all about it. We sat on the terrace most of the morning, discussing plans for when she got back, her new apartment, and the impending trip to the crematorium to scatter her mother's ashes. I found her company so easy that the morning flew past, and before I knew it, it was time for Elle to leave in order to make her hair appointment. She took some jewellery to wear that night, and a little cash for drinks, and said she'd see me the next morning.

The moment she left, I felt strangely bereft. I was used to my own company, so it was a peculiar sensation, missing somebody. I gathered up the spaniels, and headed down to Sussex to begin their weekend. At least they were excited.

I tried to occupy myself that afternoon, tried reading, watching telly, working, you name it, I tried it. Nothing seemed to interest me. I was missing Elle, and dreading the coming week without her, wondering if work would help take my mind off the silly obsession I had with her. Frowning, I even tried a bit of porn to see if it would help, which it didn't really. In the end, I surfed the Internet rather mindlessly, reading the gossip sites to see what they'd written about me, which thankfully, wasn't much.

I had my nose in the fridge, looking for snacks, when Elle called, rather unexpectedly at ten that night. I answered eagerly, hoping it meant she was coming straight down after her 'do', but she told me, without preamble, that there was a change of plan, and that she was going to Spain in the morning with her flatmate, as Oscar had pulled her friend, and was taking her to Tuscany instead. She asked if she could borrow my jet to fly out to see him the following weekend.

I was a little surprised when she admitted that she'd been matchmaking, and confessed that I'd thought that she'd been keeping Oscar as a fallback position. "Don't be silly, Oscar's a great friend, but that's all," she said, brushing aside my suspicion. A tension I didn't even know I was carrying, fell from my shoulders. I promised to arrange my jet for the following Saturday.

"I hope you can come out too, I'm gonna miss you so much next week. Just don't forget that I love you," she said, making me smile. I replied that I loved her too, and repeated my little phrase, 'I love you, and want you as my wife', in Russian, saying that I'd tell her what it meant soon.

After the call, I sat down with a glass of wine, and contemplated the week ahead. I was disappointed that she wouldn't be spending the next day with me, but rather relieved that Oscar had found someone else, and Elle hadn't minded, or been heartbroken over it.

Monday morning, I viewed the apartment below her new one, in St Saviours dock. It was identical to the one she was purchasing, so Nico was able to measure up the balcony for double height ballustrading, and check the area from a security perspective. I put an offer in that day, and had it accepted. I planned to stay over quite a bit, so needed accommodation for the security teams, plus I didn't want her having neighbours.

With that job done, Nico drove me to Windsor to meet the expert from the stolen art register. I showed him the paintings that I thought were dodgy, explaining my logic that if they were legit, Vlad would have shown off about them. He was a strange, beaky looking man, with unfortunate teeth, but he certainly knew his stuff, confirming that the Degas has been taken during a heist from some aristocrat's stately home. The Van Gogh was of international importance, and was believed to have been part of the Nazi art, looted in the Second World War. How it came to be hanging in Vlad's bedroom would always be a bit of a mystery. He thanked me for alerting him, and, satisfied that I hadn't nicked them myself, told me I'd get a substantial reward for 'finding' them, which I thought was ironic.

With that issue dealt with, I went back to work, throwing myself into the numerous reports, meetings, and problems, which made up my daily routines.

Karl called on Wednesday, to see if I was free for dinner. I joined him and Mika at Langhams that evening. Mika announced that he had a new lady, and was madly in love, smiling like a maniac. I felt a little embarrassed admitting that I'd let my lady go away on holiday without me, and I didn't mention that she was there with another man. As it was, the others teased me a little, telling me that she was probably getting chatted up right that minute. *Bastards.*

"So this Elle, you've been seeing her a little while now?" Said Karl. "Is it serious? Or just fuckbuddies?"

"Yeah, it's serious. I'm pretty taken with her," I admitted.

"Never thought I'd see the day, Ivan Porenski, tamed by a woman. Thought you were the ultimate player," he replied.

"Was, being the operative word," I said, "yeah, I guess I've been tamed. Tell me Karl, when you met Ola, how did you know, you know, that she was 'the one'?"

"You just do. You miss them when they're not around, worry about them, and want the best for them. Ola has her faults, believe me, but we have a good time together. I enjoy her company. I know you think it's a strange marriage, being as open as it is, but it works for us."

"Elle's pretty hot in the bedroom," I admitted, "and I really enjoy her company. She's fiercely clever, but nice and normal too."

"I can't wait to meet her. We should have a night out where we all bring our women, " said Mika. Karl and I pulled faces at him.

"I like boys nights," said Karl, "plus Ola'd be all over them, and I hate it when she ogles women's tits." I shuddered at the thought. Other men, I could compete with, another woman was an entirely different matter, although, I didn't think Elle would be remotely interested.

On Thursday, I had lunch with Paul. He'd come up with some names who he thought might fit the bill for the superboard. He handed me a file of CVs, and went through them, telling me about his first impressions of each, and his recommendations. I hand to hand it to him, he was a great recruiter. "These are great, how do you find them all?" I asked.

"I don't do it all myself, my team does most of it," he laughed, "I just do the final sifting when it's a prestige client, otherwise I'd be working 36 hours a day."

We changed the subject to the temps he would be recruiting for me to cover the Christmas rush in the Talk'N'Walk shops. I winced at the cost, knowing full well most of it would be going to him. There was no way we could do it in house, and the infrastructure I'd need in place to sort a few weeks worth of temps made it unviable. He had me over a bit of a barrel, but very few recruitment companies operated worldwide, so I had to acquiesce gracefully. We kept off the subject of Elle, which I was pleased about. I was missing her dreadfully, and apart from a couple of texts, hadn't spoken to her. I'd deliberately kept quiet, not wanting to intrude on her holiday, but she'd been constantly on my mind, and I was fighting the urge to call her. Instead, I called Ms Pearson, and promised her the whole Beltan account, if she would sanction a further two week holiday for Elle in August, telling her I wanted to make it a surprise for Elle.

"Of course I'll sanction it. I'll speak to her manager right away, and make sure he keeps it confidential," she promised. I signed the form for the retainer, and had it couriered over, along with a cheque for the first month.

I'd promised to send my jet on Saturday, and had text to ask the address of the hotel, telling her I'd send a car. Friday morning, I gave in, and swiftly organised another takeoff slot for that morning. I just couldn't stay away a moment longer.

During the flight, I worried that she wouldn't be pleased to see me, or that I'd be intruding on her holiday. I tried to shake the thoughts off, but coupled with my anxiety about flying, it all seemed to magnify, and race around my head. I could visualise her being a bit stony faced and cold when I showed up, which would be devastating. My nerves got worse the closer we got to her hotel.

Chapter 15

"He's just the man I'm in love with, rather than an oligarch." I overheard Elle tell some lanky girl, as I crept up behind her in the pool.

"I'm very glad to hear it. I missed you baby, and couldn't stay away another day," I whispered in her ear, as I wrapped my arms around her. She spun round, and hugged me, beaming with delight. The stupid thought loop had been completely wrong. I relaxed immediately.

"I missed you so much. I'm having a super time, but it's even better now you're here." Her words thrilled me, chasing away my insecurities. She turned to introduce me to her friends, Becca, and Linzi, telling me that they met playing volleyball.

While James ordered the beers, Elle took me aside to tell me that James had hooked up with Linzi, and that she suspected he'd be fine once we'd left. "You've been matchmaking again, haven't you?" I said, smiling at her smug face.

"Not really, James fancied her at first sight, I just got them talking," she pouted.

When I told her the news that I didn't have to get back until Monday night, so could fly over to Oscar's with her, she flung her arms round me, shrieking that it was 'brilliant', and rubbing her tits all over my chest. Unfortunately, my cock decided to get interested, and sprung to life. As soon as I warned her what was happening, she looked down, blushed, and stepped away. "So you're having a good time then?" I asked, smiling at her embarrassment.

"This hotel's lovely, there's no kids, which is fantastic. The foods great, and the people are a real laugh," she gushed. I'd never seen her so animated. *Interesting.*

Once my erection had gone down, we swam back to the bar, where James had lined up bottles of cold beer. Elle and I clinked the necks of our bottles together, and drank. I looked around the pool, noticing the groups of people chatting as they sunbathed, bobbed about in the pool, and sat drinking at the bar. It felt like I'd walked into a large party, one that was varied, and relaxed. I'd seen holidays like this on telly, but had never experienced one, as I'd gone from too poor to afford one, to too rich to mingle with the mortals, in almost the blink of an eye. On the rare occasions Dascha and I had holidayed together, it had always been either her dad's villa, or the villa of another oligarch. I'd never actually stayed in a holiday hotel. Now, I felt as though I'd missed out.

We ate in a tapas restaurant that evening, the five of us ordering far too many dishes, as we wanted to pretty much try them all. The food was surprisingly good, and I watched as Elle dug in, eating as heartily as everyone else. Linzi and Becca were great fun, regaling us with funny stories about the hospital they worked in. With Elle sat beside me, relaxed, and laughing at their jokes, I felt one of those rare moments of contentment.

"Are you staying in my room tonight? Or did you book a room?" Asked Elle, as if somehow I'd insist on separate beds. When I told her that my guards had been booked into the only available room, and that I'd be sharing hers, I saw almost wanton desire written all over her face. She stood up abruptly, scraping the chair. "We're going to head off up to bed," she announced, with a 'fuck me' look on her face. I saw James smirk.

When we got outside, Elle asked if she'd been a bit obvious. *Erm, yeah.* I pulled her into a hungry kiss, pushing my tongue into her mouth to meet hers. She immediately softened in my arms. "Elle what have you done to me? I've been useless all week, counting the hours till I could see you again." *Not strictly true, but 'I've been a bit bored and lonely without you' isn't quite as dramatic.*

She practically dragged me up to the room, and was naked within seconds. I kicked off my clothes, and slid my hands between her legs to stroke her pussy. She was soaked, and as horny as they come. "Hard fuck first?" She gasped, as I rubbed her clit. I pressed her against the wall, and lifted her to position her on my cock, which was as hard as rock, and leaking pre-cum.

I fucked her hard, pounding into her in a show of strength and dominance. Her hands caressed me as I pumped her, sliding over my skin in a sensual massage, which turned me on even more. She came even quicker than I did, soaking me as she shuddered and pulsed around my cock. It tipped me over the edge, and I flooded her with what felt like a bucketful of cum, pressing in deep to feel the last flutterings of her climax.

I set her gently down onto her feet, and she immediately pulled me onto the bed for round two. I took it a little slower, reacquainting myself with her delicious tits, sucking and licking them, until she was squirming in delight. I licked my way down her body, to suck on her clit, feeling her get hornier and hornier, as I lapped at her juices.

When I felt she was ready, I slammed my cock into her, sitting on my haunches, so that I could rub her clit as I fucked her, which drove her crazy. I watched her tits bounce as I fucked her hard, mesmerised by the sight of her nipples standing to attention, as she fought to control her orgasm. "Imcomingimcomingimcoming," she was almost incoherent as she climaxed, her insides contracting violently around me, as I kept up my punishing pace. I rode her right through her orgasm, only letting go as I felt hers begin to wane. I pressed into her as I came, revelling in the feeling of her velvet embrace. Eventually, I softened and slipped out.

Dripping with sweat, I rolled off her, and onto the bed beside her. She seemed to be in a bit of a dazed stupor. "I missed you," I murmured, wanting to say more, but I was a bit dazed myself.

"Missed you more," she whispered back, before snuggling into my arms, and dozing off.

I waited until she was fast asleep before sliding out of bed to pull the covers over her, and put my shorts on. I poured myself a coke, and sat out on the balcony to drink it, and contemplate the day. I watched as people returned from the bars, drunk and giggly, making the most of the knowledge that they wouldn't be getting up for work the next day. For the first time ever, I envied them their normality, being able to go out, make friends, and have no agenda other than a good time. I'd even managed a taste of it myself that evening, apart from being the person with bodyguards trailing about.

I heard James arrive back, shushing Linzi, who was giggling. If he saw me out on the balcony, he didn't say anything. They went straight to his room, presumably to do what we'd been doing. I smiled to myself, knowing that once again, Elle had told the truth, they really were just friends.

Five minutes later, his woman started yowling, a god-awful noise that sounded like she was being murdered. I wanted to laugh. *Must have been a shock when he started fucking her, hearing her screech like that, mind you, must have been a shock trying to sneak back unnoticed, and finding two bodyguards standing outside your hotel room door.*

I drained my glass, and padded back into the bedroom. Elle didn't even stir as I slipped in beside her, and spooned her little body. I lay there, awake, until the yowling stopped, rather abruptly, then turned over, and dozed off.

I woke up to a an empty bed, and a cup of instant coffee the next morning. I pulled on some shorts, and went in search of Elle. I found her on the balcony, drinking coffee with James. I teased him about the noise his girl made, prompting a a rather self-satisfied grin. Elle suggested that we got out of the way, so that Linzi didn't have the embarrassment of facing us all, with us all knowing what she'd been up to.

She took me down to breakfast, held in a large restaurant, and served buffet style. I even had to make my own toast, in a rather baffling machine. While it was toasting, I perused the trays of fruit and cereals, deciding to stick with just eggs and bacon. It actually all looked rather tempting. Elle loaded up with bacon, eggs and toast too, as well as muffins, some fruit, and a pastry. For someone who lived on toast, she seemed to be making the most of the buffet. I grabbed some orange juice, and joined her at the large table that she'd bagged.

As she started working her way through the food she'd picked, she quizzed me on whether I had ever holidayed with other people. I had to confess that I hadn't, but was finding it all extremely enjoyable, commenting that she seemed relaxed and happy.

"I've really enjoyed it. It's a lovely hotel, and I like meeting new people. It feels less.." She paused, "rarefied. I know that if we stayed in a hotel, it would be the presidential suite with a private pool and a posse of guards preventing anyone from speaking to us. I'd love it, because I'd be there with you, but this has been great too. I love seeing you be normal."

I smiled at her, and suggested we should have a hotel holiday every year, as well as my villa. In some ways, she'd opened my eyes to what I'd missed out on, just as I'd opened hers to the world of the super rich.

We were joined by the others, and breakfast became a fun meal, full of laughter and banter. *Actually, this really is good fun.* We spent the day playing in the pool, playing volleyball, and generally lounging around. Even Nico joined in, after I made him rip his eyes away from the topless sunbathers, and help me out on the volleyball court, to save our side from being trounced by Elle and Linzi.

That evening, we went out to a local Spanish restaurant, joining up with a group of Germans, one of whom had hooked up with Linzi's friend. It all started off well enough, they were a friendly bunch, and all spoke pretty good English. When they questioned my accent, I flippantly replied that I was Russian. "Then you must like vodka," one of them called out.

"I do indeed love vodka," I replied...rather foolishly.

"Good, I know this great game..." One of them started, before describing a vodka based drinking game. It all sounded like a real laugh, and as I'd been drinking vodka since my baby bottle, I figured that I'd win. The others were all pretty enthusiastic too, and joined in with gusto.

Three hours later, I was vaguely aware of someone scraping my face up from the table, and throwing me over his shoulder. I guessed it was Viktor, as I looked through bleary eyes to see Elle being carried the same way by Nico. I vaguely recall her being sick on the way back to the room.

The next morning, I woke up with an abominably thick head, to see Elle beaming at me. She was already dressed, and looked like she'd been up for a while, as her case was packed. Thankfully, she'd left the headache pills out, deducing correctly that we'd both need them. She suggested some breakfast before we got ready, saying she'd feel better with some food inside her. I had to agree, and we went down for a full English, accompanied by buckets of coffee and orange juice. I felt much better almost immediately, although I was a touch concerned that I'd be flying that morning, and had a habit of throwing up during take-off.

She'd already packed my holdall, so we said goodbye to the others, and went to the front desk to check out. I couldn't believe how cheap mine was, although only two nights, there was food and drink for eight guards, as well as a room. It came to less than two grand. Elle paid for the food and drink that had been charged to her room, waving my card away, and pulling out cash.

I didn't bother trying to hide my flying issue from Elle this time, although it was pleased that I didn't throw up in front of her, and the flight was too short to need to use a urine bottle. *That's gonna be a horrible one to have to confess.*

Oscar had sent a pair of cars to meet us at the airport, so we jumped in, and made our way to his estate. My first impression, as we pulled in through a pair of iron gates, was that it was all rather dusty and sun-baked. As we drove over a small hill, the villa came into view, along with breathtaking scenery of the landscape beyond. I'd expected it to be beautiful, but hadn't expected it to be on such a grand scale. Oscar, and Elle's friend, Lucy, were waiting at the front door to greet us.

After effusive hellos, Oscar showed us up to our room, which was delightful, telling us that his father had rescued the estate after it had fallen into disrepair. Elle loved it, flopping down on the large, soft bed, and checking out the bathroom.

I wasn't keen on the terrace, as it was predominantly old stone. I much preferred the sleek, clean limestone used around my pools at both Sussex, and my villa. I sipped at the rather good Italian wine which Oscar's butler had served, and listened as Elle asked Oscar what was happening back home. He told her that the LIBOR scandal had escalated, causing the resignation of at least one CEO, with the possibility that another might go soon. He confirmed Elle's suspicion that she'd be looking after a couple more banks when she returned from holiday, adding that in his opinion, she'd be overseeing a couple of rights issues as well, telling her that the other banks would need to generate capital extremely quickly.

"Baby, between Oscar and I, you'll make partner sooner than you think," I told her. *Then with all your ambitions fulfilled, you can crack on with giving me some sons.*

"Nobody under the age of forty has ever made partner before," she said. Her friend pointed out that the boss was rather fond of her, and that the number of prestige clients Elle had pulled in, couldn't go unnoticed. I reminded her that she'd get Conde Nast too, before confessing that I'd called her boss and got her another week off in August to join me in France. I'd actually got her two weeks, but held that bit of info back, not wanting to overwhelm her.

She beamed at me, clearly delighted. I beamed back, pleased that I'd managed to surprise her, and make her so happy, especially in front of Oscar.

After lunch, Oscar took me on a tour of the estate, while the girls sunbathed, and gossiped. He took me down to the farmland, beyond the immaculate gardens, and explained that the farms were all rented to tenant farmers, which allowed them to earn a decent living, while caring for the land owned by the estate.

"Oscar, can I ask you something?" I said, once we were alone, and out of earshot of anyone.

"Of course."

"Have you given Elle the money to buy her apartment?"

He paused, seeming to struggle for the right words. "Yes, I have. She asked if my bank did mortgages. I didn't want her to be in debt, so I offered to give her the money myself. She declined it as a gift, so the agreement we made is that she will pay me back out of her bonuses each year." He paused. "Why didn't she tell you this?"

"I don't know. Embarrassed maybe? She doesn't like anyone knowing that she's poor, but constantly surrounded by wealth. It must be hard for her, with you and I around, trading in billions, yet she didn't have enough money to buy her own home."

"Possibly. Well, it was an easy fix, and will give her a sense of security. I'm sorry if I trod on your toes, but at the time, the two of you had split up, and she had to move out of her rental."

"I quite understand, I'd like to repay the money on her behalf though. Would you take cash?"

"In other words, can I launder a bit of Vlad's cash for you? Sure. It's not such a problem for me. Do it gradually though, a million at a time. I don't want any eyebrows raised."

"Thank you." I was grateful to him. He had stepped in when Elle had needed him, when I'd been busy being a self absorbed idiot, and now was going to do me a favour, by cleaning up some of that dirty money.

He showed me around the 'villa', which was enormous, and although very beautiful, not really my taste, which I was pleased about, as it meant that I wasn't envious. I'm sure Italian Renaissance is all quite interesting, but I much preferred my sleek, modern villa to his ancient, antique stuffed one.

Back at the pool, Elle was happily floating on the surface, while chatting ten-to-the-dozen with Lucy. "I hear you have a villa in France?" Lucy said.

"Yes, although it's quite modest compared to this," I replied, not wishing to offend our host.

"Modest?" spluttered Elle. "It's bloody enormous, and beautifully fitted out, with a view to die for. He's got a white poggenpohl kitchen in there." She said, rather curiously.

"Oo, I love those," Lucy replied, looking impressed, "is it the glossy one with no handles?"

"I'll never understand women," muttered Oscar quietly, while the two girls rabbited on about handle-less kitchens.

"Me neither," I replied, perplexed at what was so great about having no handles on a cupboard.

We had a great afternoon and evening. Oscar was on good form, and seemed happier than I seen him in years. He also appeared to be rather loved up with Lucy. I had to admit that

Elle had done well, introducing them, as they seemed well matched, and very in tune. I was actually a little concerned that Elle would be in the way after I'd gone, being a bit of gooseberry. I contemplated dropping her back off in Spain on my way home.

That night, we lay in bed, discussing Oscar and Lucy. I mentioned that they seemed quite loved up, and asked if it bothered her. She shook her head, and said that it didn't, but added that she was more worried about me, due to the horrible things I'd said to Paul. She was genuinely concerned that with Oscar no longer wanting her, I'd follow suit, dump her, and go after Lucy. I almost laughed, thinking about the braying voice, and slightly horsey features that Oscar found so appealing.

"She's a nice girl, but she's not you. She doesn't have your amazing mind, nor your pretty face. She doesn't have your iron backbone, and she most certainly wouldn't understand my hangups about my background. You have absolutely nothing to worry about. My heart belongs solely to you. I worry more about other men stealing you away because I'm a rubbish boyfriend."

As soon as I'd said it, I felt her relax and soften, replying that I wasn't always rubbish, and there were times that I was wonderful.

I changed the subject, telling her how pleased I was that she hadn't gone topless in Spain. It was a stupid thing to worry about, but I'd actually been really concerned, especially with Nico the pervert around.

"For your eyes only. I figured you wouldn't like it, so I kept them covered," she said, before calling me a cave man. I pulled down the sheet to stare at her breasts, with the little white triangles imprinted onto the skin to remind me that she thought about, and understood me. I repeated my little Russian phrase about wanted her to be my wife, which prompted a poke in the ribs. "Don't talk Russian. What does that mean?"

"I'll tell you soon," I promised, before kissing her deeply, my hand straying down to her pussy to stroke her clit, which was always guaranteed to turn her on. She seemed inhibited by the fact that we were in someone else's house, so I stuck to missionary, quietly making love to her.

As usual, she was up before me, so I showered, and dressed, before trotting out onto the terrace to find her. She was sharing a pot of tea with Oscar, smiling at something he said. She beamed when she saw me, and kissed me good morning as I sat down next to her. "Just lazy Lucy to go, then we'll have breakfast," said Oscar.

The tiny Italian woman had just brought out more lattes, when Lucy appeared. We had breakfast waiting for us on the terrace, she said, in pidgin English, so we headed over to find it. It was truly sumptuous. Fresh pastries, cheeses and breads vied for our attentions with bacon, eggs, and exotic looking sausages. It was a world away from the hotel mass-produced stuff, but Elle didn't appear to notice, and ate with gusto, sampling a little of everything.

We were sitting by the pool later that morning when Elle's phone rang. She was busy swimming lengths with Lucy, albeit at a snail's pace compared to normal, managing to chat and swim at the same time. "Ivan, can you get that?" She called out.

"Hello, Elle's phone," I said.

"Hello, is it possible to speak to Elle please? It's Claire Plant."

I handed Elle the phone, telling her who it was. I heard Elle say 'if you're happy, go ahead', before telling whoever it was that she was with Lucy. She handed the phone over to her, for Lucy to squeal down the phone, and talk rapidly to whoever Claire was. After a few minutes, she handed the phone back to Elle, who listened intently, her smile getting wider with every passing second. "I exchanged on the flat, completing this afternoon. I'm so excited," she squealed, after she'd ended the call. I knelt at the edge of the pool to give her a hug and a kiss, while Oscar called his butler to fetch a bottle of champagne to celebrate. The girls got out of the pool, and Elle did her cute little 'happy dance', which made me smile.

"Bet you wish you were at home now don't you?" Lucy said. *Could you be any more obvious if you tried?*

"Well...yes, I wouldn't be rude enough to rush off though," said Elle.

"Elle, if you want to go and see your new flat, I will understand, and I won't be offended," Oscar told her.

With Elle convinced that she wouldn't be upsetting anyone by leaving, I promised her that I'd take some time off to help her shop for her new home. She beamed a smile at me, and kissed my cheek softly. I squeezed her shoulder, and sat back while she chattered on about sofas and interior designers to Lucy.

Oscar had organised a beautiful meal that evening, serving only the freshest and best food that was grown on the estate. The tomatoes alone were so delicious that I made a mental note to ask my gardener at Sussex if we could grow some there.

We had to leave directly after dinner, I shook Oscar's hand, and thanked him profusely for his hospitality. Elle hugged him tight, and whispered something in his ear, which I didn't catch. I called her to get in the car, as I didn't want to cut it too fine, getting to the airport.

The whole trip took a little over two hours, which I thought wasn't bad. The spaniels flung themselves at me as I walked into the penthouse, desperate for fuss, after being left with their nanny for four days. I made us both a drink, and we sat in the lounge, discussing the plans Elle had made for her flat. I wondered if it was the right moment to confess that I was buying the apartment below, but dismissed the idea, not wanting to steal her thunder.

By midnight, she was exhausted, so I took her to bed, where she fell asleep within thirty seconds. I don't think I was too far behind.

I dropped Elle at the estate agents on my way into work the next morning, promising that I'd do my best to clear my schedule, or that Roger would be at her disposal if I couldn't get away. I watched as she disappeared into the agency, smiling at her enthusiasm. "Nico, can you organise flowers, a vase, and a large Starbucks latte, no sugar, to be sent to her new flat please."

"Sir," he replied, "I'll do it as soon as I've dropped you off."

I strode into my office, fully expecting to be hit with myriad problems, and issues requiring my attention. Galina placed my latte in front of me, and swiped her tablet. "Gail Hayward has sent over all the management reports you will need, flagging up two issues she'd like you to look at. She's prepared a cash report, as of yesterday, and a report on liabilities to the end of the month, as well as projected incomes. I've arranged some interviews with both Mr Ranenkiov, and yourself towards the end of the week, with three potential executives who Mr Lassiter recommended, and the sale of the apartment in Moscow has completed. Is there anything else?"

"Where are the reports?" I asked, flabbergasted. I hadn't even asked Ms Hayward for them, having been away on Friday, yet she'd just done them anyway. *Maybe she could have taught Oleg a thing or two...* Galina placed a file in front of me, containing full management reports for each company, plus a concise, and exact summary of the total cash position, and liabilities of the group as a whole.

"How's my afternoon looking?" I asked Galina. She swiped at her tablet.

"Pretty clear, only a meeting with that venture capitalist who wants you to invest. I can easily cancel," she said.

"Yes, cancel please, and try and keep things clear, if you can." She nodded, and left me to my file of accounts. I read through them carefully, checking out the two issues 'flagged'. One was a query as to where to place the proceeds of the Moscow flat, the other where to place the proceeds of the car auction. Vlad's horrible Rolls Royce's had obviously appealed to someone. I quickly called her, and gave instructions as to where the money should be held. I was beginning to like Gail, finding her straightforward, and quick witted. She also mentioned that she was concerned with the interim figures, or lack of, that the American Conde Nast were failing to provide, telling me that they should have been done by the middle of July, and were now overdue.

"Tell Weintraub to get his finger out. I expect them on my desk first thing in the morning."

"Will do," she replied cheerfully.

I called Nico in, and asked him to take fifty grand out of the safe for a shopping trip that afternoon. He nodded, and set off. I had a brief conversation with Ranenkiov about the interviews we'd be holding that week, but he'd already checked out the CVs, and had a list of questions prepared for each candidate. I was actually at a bit of a loose end, until Nico returned.

Despite stopping off for more Starbucks, I was still early. I called Elle for the code to get into the building, which she reeled off happily. She was waiting at the front door when the lift doors opened, grinning from ear to ear. "Everything alright at work?" She asked.

"All fine, I think they work better without me there," I replied, "more importantly is everything alright here?"

"Totally, utterly, brilliant," she gushed, which made me smile. She caught sight of Nico with a briefcase chained to his arm, and gave me a quizzical look.

"Case full of cash. Thought we'd go shopping. I'm sure you have a list."

"You really do know me too well, " she laughed. "Anyway come on through to the kitchen, I want to show you all the gadgets. I placed our coffees on the island, and checked out the pantry and laundry rooms. I was intrigued by the internal vacuum system, and very impressed by the concealed safe in the study, as it had an undetectable false wall covering it. *Ingenious.* I found out that she'd already checked to ensure she could have animals in the apartment, and was perfectly happy for me to add to all the security systems for her. When I broached the subject of raising the height of the railings around her terrace, she told me to do whatever I wanted, saying it was important to her that I was happy there. *Yes!*

She seemed a little reluctant to leave the apartment to go shopping, but practicality won the day. It was no good her having a beautiful shell, with nothing in it, so we locked up, and hopped in the car to go to Harrods. "Here, you take these," she said, handing me the spare keys. *I didn't have to even copy them, she just....gave them to me. There really is no hassle with her, just easygoing.*

Harrods was enormous fun, we worked our way through her list, buying outrageously beautiful crockery and cutlery, chef quality cookware and knives, and even little basic things like tea towels, and mugs. To buy an entire home from scratch would have daunted anyone apart from Elle, who just ticked things off her carefully prepared lists.

She insisted on an enormous telly, choosing one that had HD and smart capabilities, telling me that it meant we could have Netflix. I then insisted that we have a serious sound system, as I loved my music, dropping the 'we' in, unnoticed. I settled on a fancy Bang and Olufsen system, that would send music wirelessly around the apartment. By the time we finished, we'd cleared the cash, and had started using my card.

Back at Canary Wharf, I suggested visiting the huge Waitrose to fill up her pantry and fridge. While we pushed two trolleys around, Nico was despatched to get more cash, and another car. I made sure Elle bought the best of everything, filling her trolley with some superb wines and champagnes, as well as cleaning stuff, and normal food. The pair of us had a real fun afternoon, laughing at Viktor's discomfort at pushing a trolley, as opposed to just posing as a hardman. We both giggled at the checkout when Elle realised we had forgotten milk, and dispatched a huffing Viktor to go and get some, snickering that he looked like he'd lost the will to live.

How we managed to spend nearly ten grand in Waitrose was beyond me. But I counted out the fifties, and kept a straight face while Elle sniggered at the disapproving stare of the checkout girl. Viktor was then told to load it all up in the spare car that Roger had brought over, much to his dismay. "How on earth did we manage to spend that much?" She whispered when we were back in the car.

"I bought some good Whisky, brandy, and other drinks. One of those bottles of champagne was seven hundred quid," I explained.

"That's so naughty," she admonished.

"No, that's so much fun," I told her, "it doesn't matter what you spend baby, I'll always make it faster than we can spend it." I kissed her nose. I'd enjoyed every minute of it.

Chapter 16

We had to go back over to my place that evening for my meeting with Natalya. I was glad Elle was with me, as it put a stop to all the tiresome flirting, and saved any suspicion or arguments later. I poured us all glasses of wine, as we sat down out on the terrace. "What news do you have for me?" I asked. My stomach was churning slightly, so I wanted to get straight to the point.

"Vlad was definitely your father. The DNA proves it beyond doubt. The details of your conception are sketchy, but I managed to trace a man who was a neighbour of your mothers at the time. He thinks it was a brief affair, which ended as soon as she knew she was expecting. He seemed to think she met your father straightaway, possibly passing you off as his. He was named as your father on your birth certificate, of which I purchased a copy." She handed me a file. "Inside is the DNA report, your birth certificate, and the report from the neighbour. Is that everything you require?"

She was so matter of fact, that I almost wished she'd stayed coquettish and flirty. I was gripped by an intense sadness for my parents. I managed a simple "yes it is, thank you," before lapsing into shock. My gentle, kind mama had possibly duped my father, my placid, hard working father, into taking on a bastard child. I wanted to cry for him. He hadn't deserved that.

"Are you ok?" Elle asked in her soft voice. I looked up, to see that Natalya had already left.

"Yeah, a little shocked, a little sad. Sad for my father that he never had his own child." My mind was racing back to the childhood memories I'd had.

"Higher daddy, throw me higher," I'd yelled, as he played a game of throwing me into the air, catching me in his big, sturdy hands, as I giggled happily.

I recalled him patiently teaching me how to mend our shoes, showing me how to tap the little nails into the new soles so they wouldn't let the water in. I recalled him loving me, as his son. Neither of us realising that I wasn't.

Elle brought me back to the present. "How come they never had any further children?" She asked.

I remembered the horror of sharing a bedroom with my parents, and accidentally waking up while they were making love, hiding under the covers to block out the sounds, and the horrible image of Dads back humping up and down. "I don't know. Most of the families were huge. I suppose it was a little odd, there being only me. I never really thought about it before."

Elle's theory was that my father had been infertile, which was certainly a possibility. It was also possible that it had been caused by the chemicals he worked with at the factory. He'd mainly worked with the ore they extracted lithium from, so I decided I'd do some I research at a later date.

To cheer me up, Elle suggested an evening in my sex room, to explain what all the toys were for. It started off innocent enough, but quickly degenerated into a serious fucking session on my swing, we really couldn't keep our hands off each other. I loved how much she desired me, how unashamed she was about the effect just the sight of my cock had on her.

Next morning, I dug her jewellery, and some more cash, out of my safe, and handed it to her to put in hers, before dropping her off there on my way to work. She had a meeting with my interior designer, as well as a load of deliveries arriving. She kissed me goodbye, and happily skipped off to do more sorting out.

I had a few meetings first thing, then sat in my office to read through the notes Ranenkiov had prepared ahead of our interviews. I had the bank of televisions switched on, showing market data, and the Sky news, and glanced up at the moment there was one of those 'breaking news' banners across the screen. ***Recruitment tycoon found dead in tragic sex game accident*** I turned up the sound just at the moment they said the name 'Paul Lassiter'. Grabbing my phone, I speed dialled Elle.

It turned out she already knew, seeing it on her new telly the same time as I did. She seemed quite upset, telling me that she'd liked him as a client.

"He was a good recruiter," I told her, "I wonder what'll happen to his company now? Did he put a contingency in place?" *I wonder....*

Elle seemed to think he'd left everything to his sister, and told me she'd try and find out if her firm held his will. She also seemed to think I should leave things for a few days. *No baby, sod niceties, I'd rather jump in before anyone else gets a sniff.* I told her that I'd like to buy it, adding that it would be a great fit with all my other companies. "Find out as much as you can please," I barked at her, a little more aggressively than I meant to.

"Sure," she said, sounding just a touch annoyed.

I called Mrs Restorick to move some funds around. If an opportunity was going to present itself, I wanted to be ready to strike. As soon as I'd got off the phone to her, Elle called me back to tell me that Pearson Hardwick held the will, and everything would go to Paul's sister. I quizzed Elle about the company setup, and found out she'd listed everything in the Cayman Islands, as she'd done with mine. Once she confirmed that the inheritance tax rate was zero, I set about forming a plan.

That evening we discussed Paul's company over dinner. Elle seemed to think I should leave things a little while, out of respect. I argued that the sister may not want to keep it, and I'd pay a hundred mil for it.

"It's worth way more than that," said Elle, wrinkling her nose.

"Not without Paul it's not," I countered. I figured that the sister would be more than happy with a hundred mil with no tax to pay. I also figured that other interested companies would take a while to come up with that sort of money, so it was better to strike quickly.

The very next day, I got a call from Elle telling me that the sister had contacted her, and asked to see her. She was on her way over to the tower. I rubbed my hands together in expectation.

"Cancel the next two meetings please," I told Galina. "I need to be available for the next few hours." Ranenkiov could do the interviews.

About an hour later, Elle called to tell me she was bringing Julie Lassiter up to see me, but Lewis would be negotiating on her behalf. It was a little odd, but I didn't comment. Five minutes later, Elle walked into my office. "Babe, I couldn't shark her, I'd get struck off. You do understand don't you?" She seemed nervous. I reassured her that I'd be fair, then asked what Lewis' opening bid would be. I nearly fell off my chair when Elle said that the girl only wanted a few million, then begged me not to rip her off, but to pay her a decent amount.

I promised her I'd be fair, and asked her to start the sale contract, letting her sit at my desk to use my computer, while I went along to the meeting room. Miss Lassiter and Lewis were deep in conversation when I walked in. I shook their hands, and introduced myself to Paul's sister, telling her that she should call me Ivan. "I understand that you are keen to sell Lassiter recruitment, as opposed to running it," I said, after expressing my condolences about her brother.

"Yes, I know other people think I should keep hold of it, but I'm keen to get rid of it." She shot a pointed look at Lewis, then dabbed her eyes.

Lewis opened with a price of 150 mil, which I declined, telling him that without Paul, and without seeing the books, I couldn't pay that kind of money for it. I offered to wait until Julie had prepared management accounts, which made her look panicked. "What would you offer on the basis of no Paul, and no accounts," asked Lewis, eyeing me suspiciously.

"I'm a generous man, so, while in these circumstances, other companies would be offering the forty to fifty mil mark, I'm prepared to go up to seventy mil for a very fast sale."

"Not good enough Porenski, I had a quick look on companies house, and the GP last year was fifty mil. The absolute minimum would be a hundred and twenty mil," said Lewis, sounding annoyed.

"Yes, the GP with Paul at the helm. I have to assume that's going to drop substantially. I really can't go as high as that Lewis. Perhaps this deal is too rich for me." Julie looked panicked. "Did Elle tell you that she listed the company in the Caymans? Julie would be getting the full amount, with no tax, no squabbling over liabilities or arcane accounting principles. Just a sale, a contract, and the money...today. That has to be worth something." I watched as Julie gave Lewis a pleading look. *I'm winning.*

"A hundred and twenty mil is the absolute minimum, " Lewis repeated, despite a horrified glance from Julie.

I sighed. "I'm not going there Lewis. Forgive me Ms Lassiter. Ninety five mil, or there is no deal. That's my best and final offer."

"It's a deal," said Julie, taking Lewis by surprise. He scowled at me as Julie and I shook hands.

"Well done Julie. We have a deal." I took her back out to my office, where Elle was typing at the speed of light."Galina, we need champagne, Elle, the sale price is ninety five mil, and we would like to complete the sale as fast as possible please."

"Well done Julie, Lewis. I'm preparing the sale document now," she said, not even slowing down.

"I'll proof as you type," said Lewis, pulling some pages off the printer. I went into Galina's office to call Mrs Restorick to action the funds transfer. I was shocked to discover that Julie Lassiter only had a basic bank account, one that people in financial trouble have. It seemed that Paul hadn't been free with his money towards her either. *Such an odd man.*

An hour later, contracts were signed, and the deal was done. Elle went off with a rather shell shocked Julie, and said that she'd see me later on. I sent a memo to the board to inform them that we now owned Lassiter recruitment, and all hiring should now be done through them, worldwide.

Galina cleared my schedule so that I could go down to their offices, and introduce myself, and meet the staff. Rather understandably, they were in shock over Paul's death, and rather nervous as to what the future held. I was able to reassure them that it would be business as usual, and I wouldn't be making any significant changes. I'd called Andrea Mills, and asked her to come over for a meeting. I'd promoted her to the superboard at Beltan, in charge of administration, but to be fair, she was a little wasted in the role. I offered her a managing directorship of the new recruitment company in addition to her role on the Beltan board. She was delighted, and agreed immediately, as HR was her real skill, and I knew she'd been missing it.

We toured the company together, and introduced her to all the senior head hunters employed there. As soon as they knew she'd been the director of HR at Conde Nast, they seemed to relax a little, and warm to her. I looked closely at all the management accounts to date, and saw that profits had been tipped to reach over seventy five mil that year, mainly generated by the temp arm of the business, which Paul had little to do with. Satisfied that I'd made a killing, I said my goodbyes, and headed home. It was nearly nine. *Elle's gonna go nuts at me.*

I fully expected her to be furious at me for squeezing an extra five mill out of Julie Lassiter, but she seemed quite perky when I walked in, joking that she'd made dinner, which meant pulling Mrs Watton's creation out of the warming drawer.

She dismissed my worries about the five mil, telling me that she felt Julie had got more than she wanted. She went on to admit that she recorded her conversation with Ms Lassiter, which saved her from losing her job, after Lewis accused her of helping me get the company on the cheap.

I listened to the recording while we ate, hearing Elle counsel Julie against a quick sale, telling her it could be put out to tender for the best price, and Julie stating that if she got a few mil, she'd be happy. "Well played baby, got you right off the hook," I said when it had finished. "I looked at Paul's accounts, and I'm happy I got a bloody good deal. She's happy to be out of it, and rich, and you're happy that you won't get struck off. A good day all round." I clinked my glass against hers. Elle just muttered something about it being her holiday.

I pointed out that I'd taken the following day off to accompany her to the crematorium for the final goodbye to her mother, then on to Windsor to clear the house. It had been better to get business done and out of the way to leave our schedules clear for those things.

I accompanied her to the crematorium the next morning, holding her hand as her mother's ashes were dropped into the ground. She seemed pale and shocked when it was all over, and sobbed into my chest all the way over to Windsor.

"Baby, let it all out, let the tears fall," I told her, holding her tight. I stroked her hair to comfort her, my poor girl seemed in so much pain. I wished I'd been there to help her at the funeral.

When she finally stopped crying, I licked a tissue, and wiped her face, cleaning away the mascara streaks. "I bet I look a sight," she croaked, hoarse from all the tears.

"Baby, you just look like you've been crying. Now, would you like a Starbucks? There's one on the way." She nodded.

She seemed to have recovered by the time we got to the house. Nico had organised a large team to pack and move everything that had to be removed. The house was being rented fully furnished, so only personal items had to go, ready for the inventory company to come and do their thing. We worked our way through the rooms carefully and methodically, sorting everything into throw, donate, and keep boxes.

Elle saw me tell the men to throw out everything in the sex room, before she moved on to Dascha's room to get more stuff for the girls at work. She didn't see Nico sidle up, and ask if he could have it all. He really was a pervert. God knows why he wanted a mechanical dildo.

The last thing we tackled were the safes. We piled the cash into boxes, and stuffed them into the boot of the Bentley. I locked up the house, and we made our way back to London. I got Roger to stop off at Elle's place to fill up her safe, explaining that the cash wouldn't all fit in mine. Opening hers up, I wanted to laugh at the jewellery all neatly arranged, and her measly little pile of money stacked up at the back of the rather cavernous safe. She sat quietly as I shoved at least a few million in there, possibly more. I replaced her jewellery a little haphazardly in the remaining space, and we locked up to go back to mine.

I took her out to eat that evening, choosing a great little curry place south of the river in St Katharine's dock. It was all part of my 'cuisines of the world' plan for her. We chatted about the events of that week, while working our way through a basket of popadoms. I told her about Vlad and Dascha's funeral, she told me the things she'd ordered for the new flat. I found out that she was planning to move in next week, as soon as her flatmate got back from his holiday. She was animated as she described the new furniture she'd ordered. "Whatever you need, just use the cash in your safe," I told her. She pulled a bit of a face, and reminded me that she was well paid, and could use her own money.

I told her again that the money was dodgy, so should only be used for untraceable items such as food, furniture, and household things. "Don't you worry that I'd spend it all?" She asked. I wanted to laugh.

"Baby, I'd be delighted. It'd mean that you had a good time, which would please me."

"You're very trusting."

"I think you're the only person on the planet that I truly trust, and that's the truth. You've proved yourself again and again." I switched to Russian, "Ya lublu tebia ee hotchu zhenitsia na tebe."

"You keep saying that, come on, what does it mean?" Her eyes bored into me.

"It means 'I love you, and want you to be my wife'."

She looked stunned. "Is that a proposal, or a statement of intent?" She demanded, which made me laugh. Only a lawyer could dissect a sentence to ensure there were no ambiguities. I confessed that it was just a statement of intent, to make her feel secure. She made me teach her how to say the same back to me.

That night, after making love, I confessed that I'd bought the apartment below hers for the guards, expecting her to be cross about my 'control freakiness'. I was pleasantly surprised when she said 'good'.

I had an early start the next morning, having a breakfast meeting booked with Andrea Mills. I dropped Elle off, and made my way to Smollenskis. Andrea was waiting in a booth for me, notepad at the ready, looking a little nervous. It reminded me a little of how Elle used to be, when we first started working together. I ordered our breakfasts, and got straight down to business, outlining what I already knew from Elle on the structure and functions of the three arms of the company. I was delighted to discover that she'd been researching too, and was pretty much up to speed. She'd also spent the previous day meeting all the senior people to discuss their current projects, and how they would need her assistance to ensure the results we all wanted. She'd also liaised with Ranenkiov to ensure the payroll would be in line with the rest of the Beltan companies, and, rather apologetically, organised some decent office furniture.

"Paul didn't like to spend money did he?" She said.

"I know, he was a very strange man when it came to things like that. His personal office looked as though he'd furnished it from a secondhand store. He never paid bills on time either, just squirreled his money away in offshore savings accounts."

"So me upgrading the furnishings and equipment isn't a problem?" She asked.

"Not at all. It's a Beltan company, so I'd prefer it to look like one. Call IT if you need to upgrade the computer systems, and Ranenkiov can guide you with all our staff systems. Gail Hayward will assist you sorting out the bank accounts, along with all the reporting procedures that we use." I watched as she made copious notes in neat handwriting.

The rest of the day became a blur of meetings and hassles. Eventually, I got away at six, and went straight to Elle's flat to pick her up. She'd had a load of deliveries that day, as well as workmen fixing the new balcony, and upgrading security. I looked at the new furnishings she'd bought, and complimented her on her choices.

She was back at work the following week, working punishing hours, often still at her desk at nine at night. She was apologetic about not seeing me too much, but following the fallout from the LIBOR scandal, she had three more banks switch to Pearson Hardwick as their legal firm. Her company were recruiting furiously, through Lassiter recruitment, naturally, but in the meantime, they were all having to work ridiculously hard.

In September, after she returned from her holiday, she was called into see Ms Pearson. I'd never seen Elle so nervous, so convinced that she was going to be sacked for taking her annual leave. No matter how much I tried to convince her that she wouldn't be dismissed, she set off for the city looking like the condemned man. I went into work, almost convinced, myself, that she'd be spending the evening in floods of tears. An hour later she called me.

"I have some great news," she squealed, "I've been promoted to associate, and four of those lawyers that Andrea nicked from Odey and Corbett will be working under my direction. How brilliant is that?"

I relaxed immediately. "That's wonderful news darling, next step is partner isn't it?" *Then sons.*

"Junior partner, then equity partner." *Bugger, could take years.*

"Associate by the age of 24 is quite something baby. We should go out to celebrate."

"Great, I'll book a table somewhere, and try and get away at a decent time."

She must have called her concierge, because they got us a table at The Ivy that night. Elle was grinning like a Cheshire Cat as we toasted her success with Krug. I decided it would be a good time to broach the subject of moving in together. "I have something I'd like to ask you baby," I started.

"Sure, ask away."

"Would it be okay to plant a patch of grass on your terrace, for the girls? Only Bella had her legs crossed the other night, and only just made it out of the foyer downstairs."

"Sure, tell whoever does that type of thing to go ahead."

"It would mean that we could all stay over whenever you like." I looked at her expectantly.

"I'd like you to stay over all the time, you know that."

"Great, I'll get my clothes moved tomorrow. Can I share your study? Or would you prefer me to set another one up in the spare room?"

"You can share mine, it's big enough."

"I'll tell Mrs Watton she'll be working at yours from now on. Is that ok?"

She sighed, "Yes, I suppose so. Whatever makes you happy baby. What'll you do with your apartment?"

"Rent it out I think. It's a shame to just leave it sitting empty. I'll get Andrei onto it tomorrow." I beamed at her. *That wasn't too difficult.*

"Good, at least I'll be able to see you a little more. This rights issue we've got coming up is fiendishly complex, one alone would be hard going, but overseeing three at the same time is pretty horrendous. We'll all be working every night to try and get it done."

"Better then that we have Mrs Watton around to help out," I remarked. I knew Elle liked taking care of her apartment herself, but it was pretty big, and I could see she was struggling. It was time for her to accept some help.

Elle wasn't exaggerating about the long hours she'd be working. Every night for weeks, she'd been at the office till gone eleven, arriving home almost delirious with hunger and exhaustion, eating her dinner in bed, then pretty much passing out, until it was time to start all over again the next morning. I barely saw her during September and October, apart from Sundays, when she tried not to work, and concentrate on the girls and I instead. The rights issue was scheduled to complete in mid November, and it couldn't come soon enough.

Elle was getting dangerously thin, and looked tired, complaining of being cold a lot of the time. I tried to talk to her about it, begging her to speak to Ms Pearson, and get her workload reduced.

"I know baby, but this is my big chance. If I can deliver this on time, and exact, it stands me in great stead for the next step up," she argued. "Just bear with me a little longer, it should all calm down soon."

"I hope it does. I miss you being around," I muttered. I sounded petulant, even to my own ears.

"It's Mr Carey and Lewis who are really bearing the brunt. Lewis even pulled some of the staff from New York to help us out. Poor Mr Carey practically lives there at the moment. It'll all wind down after the cut off date, until then, I'm at the mercy of every twat who rings me up to tell me they've had a great idea for a new clause, with no idea it means checking against every other clause they've thought up, to see if there's a conflict, which there invariably is, so we start again."

I kissed her gently. "Baby, don't let it get to you. I'm going to ask Roger to make sure you have food during the day. I'm worried about you."

She smiled, "I'm sorry baby, it'll all be over soon. Another week. What'll we do for Christmas?"

"Whatever you like, I don't mind."

"Can we spend it in Sussex? I'll do an English one, then maybe next year you can show me how the Russians do it?"

I laughed, "Whatever you like. Russian food is pretty rank, so on your own head be it."

The final week before the rights issue was mad. Elle was getting home around midnight, and back in at six next morning. Even her old flatmate, James was concerned, and took to dropping in cakes for her, trying to fatten her up. I just worked as normal, and tried not to add to her stress.

It was quite odd, having to work around somebody else's job, but I took it in my stride, and concentrated on keeping Beltan on a reasonably even keel.

As I left the tower on the Wednesday evening of her final week, I saw the ambulance pulling up outside, but didn't give it another thought. I hopped into my car for the thirty second drive home. As soon as I walked into our apartment, my phone rang. "Hi babe," I answered, seeing it was Elle.

"Mr Carey, he's had a heart attack, we think," she spluttered, sounding distraught. "That leaves Lewis and I as the only ones with banking expertise."

"Calm down, we don't want you in the same boat." I replied, concerned. She sounded panicky. "You're more than capable, and so is Lewis. You worked closely with Mr Carey looking after Goldings. I'm sure you know what needs doing. What about Ms Pearson?" As far as I could see, she'd been leaving them all to it.

"No banking expertise, that's why she looks after head office, and not corporate." I heard her take a deep breath. "I've never done a rights issue for a bank before, it's such specialised work that very few lawyers ever even experience one. Lewis is as clueless as I am."

"Well then, nobody will know if it's not done properly then. Fake it baby. Tell all the twatty accountants that it's too late for alterations, and just go for it. If you fall, I'll catch you."

"You're right, as usual. Ok baby, I'd better go. See you when I see you."

I called Oscar to see if there was anything he could do to help. He was shocked to hear about Mr Carey. "He's an absolute expert in the sector. Let's hope the bulk of the work's already completed, otherwise Elle'll have a major problem on her hands. If this rights issue doesn't go well on Friday, the banking sector will suffer another massive shock, possibly needing another bailout. Whether the government has the stomach for it is another matter." *Yeah, ok, I don't need to know the worst case scenario, I asked if you could help.* "If she can keep Goldman Sachs on a tight rein, and not let them dictate terms, she might be in with a shout. They'll always try and manipulate situations to suit themselves, often not their clients. I'd guess that they've hedged massively in favour of this rights issue flopping. Communicate that quietly to Elle, if I were you," he said, being a bit cryptic about it.

The girls bounced at my feet as I called Elle to pass on Oscar's message. "I get what he means," she said.

"I'm glad you do, because I don't have a clue," I confessed.

"They're trying to twist things, tie us in knots. Ok, gotta go, thanks baby." With that, the phone went dead.

I didn't see Elle until Friday evening, by which time the rights issue was over. I'd followed proceedings at work, nervous for her. The commentators on the news channels had cautiously declared it a success, pointing out that failure could have led to three retail banks going bust, taking everyone's money with them. It appeared that disaster had been averted.

Elle arrived home about half eight, and promptly burst into tears as soon as she walked through the door. "Baby, what's wrong?" I asked, worried that things hadn't gone as well as had been reported.

"We did it. I don't know how, but we did it, and it worked," she sobbed, "and I'm so very tired." I pulled her into a hug, and squeezed her tight. "I'm so sorry I neglected you," she sniffed.

"Don't be silly, I'm still here, worried about you, but still here. You pulled it off baby. I'm proud of you." I felt her shoulders shuddering. "How's Mr Carey?"

"He should recover. Poor man, he was so angry with himself for getting ill. Kept apologising for having a heart attack. Mind you, all of us look like we've been through a mangle this week. The Americans'll run for their lives I think." She managed a wan smile.

I sat her down on the sofa, and poured her a large glass of wine. Mrs Watton had left some casserole in the oven for her, so I dished it up, and set it all on a tray for her. "Let's get you fed," I said, placing it on her lap. She practically inhaled it, while watching sky news for the pundit's verdicts on the day's events.

"Any afters?" She asked. I pulled out the chocolate cake that James had brought round the day before, and cut a large chunk off. Thirty seconds later, it had disappeared, not having touched the sides.

"Elle, did you not eat for a few days?" I asked, while cutting another slice.

"Not really, it was too difficult. I was either on the phone, in meetings, or typing. I barely had time for a wee, let alone food." I noticed that she was still in the same clothes she was wearing on Wednesday. "I need a shower, and some sleep," she declared, kicking off her shoes.

She slept in till nine the next morning, unheard of for Elle. I'd purposely kept the day free, and was determined not to let her go into work. "Shall we go to the gym together?" I suggested when she finally surfaced.

"That sounds like a great idea. I'm still tense from the week, a good run, and a swim would help." *Plus you won't have that blasted phone in there with you,* I thought. She threw her gym bag together, and we set off across the road. Elle seemed to relax almost instantly as soon as she began her run, pushing herself at a punishing pace, that even I couldn't match.

"Needed that," she said, wiping the sweat from her face at the end of it. We moved on to the machines, watching each other work out, enjoying the time together. We finished with a swim race, which as usual, she won. "I feel about a million times better," she exclaimed, beaming. "Shall we go down to Sussex after this? Or is there anything you need to do in town?"

"I think straight to Sussex. I have the overwhelming urge to fuck you senseless, after you've been waving your little booty at me for the last hour." I smiled at her.

Apart from a couple of calls to congratulate her, she was left alone all weekend. She needed some time to unwind, sleep, and fatten up a bit. I needed a bit of attention too. My reward for being a good boyfriend, and not a tosser while she was busy, was a stupendous blowjob, with a well lubed butt plug tickling my prostrate. It made it all worthwhile.

Monday came a bit too quickly, and Elle was quite nervous about what lay ahead. She went in a bit early, in case there were any problems left over from Friday. My day was fairly straightforward, dealing mainly with issues relating to the mines. The new machinery I'd purchased had been delivered, and was busy gouging its way through the mountains, much to the dismay of the locals, who were the fuckers who'd tipped off my kidnappers as to my whereabouts. *They should have thought about the consequences before they chanced their arm at getting fifty mil out of me.* I simply asked Kristov to put together a militia to guard the new machinery, and stamp out any dissent amongst the locals. *I learnt a lot from Vlad.*

After claiming the land in Odessa and Central Russia, we'd begun exploratory drilling to see if the geologists were correct, and rich seams of coal were laying beneath the surface. I spoke to the drilling teams, after they announced that they'd hit coal, and the early indications were that they were huge seams, well worth mining.

I glanced at the clock, concerned that Elle hadn't called. I picked up my phone to see if she was free for lunch at the same moment that she chose to call me. "Hi baby, I was just about to phone you and see if you were free for lunch," I said.

"Yeah, I'm free. I'll meet you in the bistro in ten."

She was already there when I arrived, sitting in a small booth looking a little pensive. "So how was it this morning?" I asked, making her jump.

"Hmm, sit down, and I'll tell you all about it." I frowned slightly, but sat myself down, and nodded to my guards to seat themselves at the table behind. I looked at her expectantly. "Mr Carey won't be coming back to work. He's decided to retire on health grounds."

We were interrupted by the waiter coming to take our order. When he'd left, I turned my attention back to Elle. "So, Mr Carey's retiring...?"

"Yeah. Lewis had been asked to take over as equity partner. That left a gap at junior partner level. I thought they'd offer it to me, especially after the work I did last week, pulling it out of the bag like I did." She gazed at me with hurt eyes. "They offered it to Peter instead. I wasn't even considered."

"Baby, you only recently became an associate. Has Peter been there longer than you?" I was scrabbling to find something to make her feel better.

She nodded. "A few years. I know he's overdue a promotion, but he was pretty useless last week, sucking up to those bastards from Goldman's, who were doing their level best to derail us. I just....I don't know....I thought I'd get rewarded for putting the company's interests first."

"I'm sure you will, but you said yourself, it takes years to make partner. Don't be so hard on yourself. What you did last week was a triumph. You took on the vampire squid, and won. Those men at Goldman's are the finest financial brains in the world, and you beat them. You should be whooping right now, not sulking because you didn't change your job title."

"Sulking?"

"Yep. I know a sulk when I see one. I am the expert in sulking you know."

The corners of her mouth twitched. "Spose.."

"No 'spose' about it. Just get the sulk out of your system, then move on. Bear a grudge if you want to, but don't allow it to eat away at you." I spoke from experience. I'd long ago made the decision to forgive my past for the injustices I'd suffered. They'd made me into the man I was.

"You are totally wonderful, you know that don't you?" She smiled at me.

"I do my best." The waiter interrupted us with our lunch. "Now will you please eat? You're getting too thin."

"Yes sir," she giggled, digging into her chicken.

She went back to work much happier, but for the next few days, came home at six, rather than staying late to try and impress anyone. We settled into a more balanced routine, and Elle had more time to give her exec position at Beltan a bit more attention. Life got back to normal.

The following week, I was delighted that she seemed to have forgotten all about her disappointment, and was her normal, happy self.

Chapter 17

James and Linzi came to dinner Tuesday evening. We cheated a bit by asking Mrs Watton to organise the food, rather than risk Elle's cooking. I knew I'd struggle to get away early enough to prepare anything worthwhile.

Elle had experimented with cooking when we'd first moved into her apartment, even buying a stack of cookbooks to help her. I'd tried to be polite, and not gag on some of the horrible meals she'd served, as I hated seeing her disappointed little face when even the spaniels turned their noses up at some of her offerings. I was quite relieved when she snapped out of her 'domestic goddess' phase, and let Mrs Watton take over the catering. I think the spaniels were relieved as well.

James guessed immediately that Elle hadn't cooked that evening, teasing her about her lack of culinary skills. We ended up having a great evening, enjoying their company, laughing at Linzi's jokes, and hearing all about the latest game that James had dreamed up.

I had Elle all day, on Wednesday, as she attended a board meeting at my offices, then joined us all for a long business lunch in Nobu. In the afternoon, we both attended a negotiation for a small engineering company I was looking to buy. She sat beside me, taking notes as I negotiated with the three owners, getting the company for well under what I was prepared to pay. It turned out to be an extremely good day, except for an email I'd received with the interim report for the American Conde Nast, showing a distinct lack of profit. I'd mentioned it to Elle, who had read it through, and frowned at the final figure.

We sat discussing the lack of profit at the American arm of Conde Nast at dinner that evening. "Maybe Joan should take a look at it for them," Elle said, frowning slightly.

"Not sure. I looked at their management accounts earlier. There seems to be a couple of one off payments made under 'other' that's eaten away at their profits this year. I'm waiting for Weintraub to call me back with an explanation." I watched as she slipped some chicken to the spaniels, who gazed at her with total adoration.

"There's something about that man that I just don't like," she said, shuddering slightly, "and I've got no idea what it is, apart from the feeling that he's a bit slippery, and I don't trust him."

"I know what you mean. I don't like all this huffing and puffing when I ask him to explain himself, as if I'm some sort of retard. Makes me wonder what he's trying to cover up. The exceptional payments come to over ten million in the last six months alone, so it's not small change. He's behaving all affronted that I want to know what the exceptional expenditure is, so there's something not right." I glanced at the clock, it was still quite early. Plenty of time for an early night, and some fun.

We were interrupted by my phone. I glanced at the screen, and saw that it was Weintraub. "Hello Jonathan, have you got that information ready for me?"

"Yes. The exceptional payments were settlements of some lawsuits that went against us. Three of them, but they're all paid in full now, and finished. One was before you took over, the second and third were before your time too, but judgements were handed down about a month ago."

"You're telling me that you had to go and look that up?" I was incredulous. "Surely something like settlement of a lawsuit would stick in your head? Especially when you're losing to the tune of 10.65 million dollars." I glanced up to see Elle frowning. *How come she wasn't told about this?*

"As I said, they were lodged before your arrival. Were they not disclosed in the list of liabilities?"

"No, they most definitely were not. Which cases were they?"

"Oh, just staff ones, a wrongful dismissal, a sexual harassment, and an accident at work. Like I said, all put to bed now. There's no more on the horizon."

"10.65 mil on three domestic cases? That doesn't sound right. Can you email me the case notes please?" I asked.

"They're with our lawyers. I don't have them." *You're bullshitting.*

"Ok, I'll get Elle to look them up on the court systems. I'd like all the notes and correspondence from our legal representatives emailed to me straightaway. It's still early enough that you can call them."

"Will do." He sounded sulky. I ended the call.

"Did I just hear that right?" Elle exclaimed. "So there've been two judgements made against the company, and I wasn't told?"

"That's what he's saying, although it felt like I had to drag it out of him. Have they changed over to Pearson Hardwick yet?" I knew Elle's company had a New York office, with an even more fearsome reputation than their London office, which was widely regarded as the very best in Europe.

"No, not yet. They keep delaying for some reason. Maybe they were waiting for these lawsuits to complete."

"He just told me they completed a month ago. Can you find out what's going on?"

Elle picked up her phone, and called the New York Pearson Hardwick office. After a ten minute conversation, she walked through to her study, and wiggled the mouse on her computer to bring it to life. I watched the complicated log in procedure, fascinated by the layers of security in place to prevent unauthorised access to the American's systems. She asked whoever was on the other end to do a search through the recent court cases, to find anything to do with Conde Nast.

Within half an hour, she had all the documents downloaded, and was reading through, while discussing the cases with her American counterpart, jabbering away in legal jargon, and querying dates and clauses. I sat on the sofa and watched, enjoying the spectacle of seeing her in action. "Can we do a search on Linda Yentob, as she seems to be the link here," I heard her say. She waited, clicking through the pages of what appeared to be court papers, on the screen. "Thought so. That makes things a bit clearer. Oh well thanks for your help on this. I'll be in touch soon."

When she'd ended the call, she swung round on her chair to face me. "There's been some fuck ups by the looks of it. The Americans have been using a firm called Wiseman, Overy and Kaufman. Their contact there is a Linda Yentob, who co-ordinates all their cases, rather like I do for Retinski and Goldings, only she seems to have a habit of screwing up. One of these cases was lost because the paperwork was wrongly filled out, and the other two because Ms Yentob didn't present a defence in time. Stupid, basic mistakes which cost over ten million quid."

"Right, so why are they still using the firm? At a retainer of a million a year, they should have moved to lawyers who know what they're doing." It didn't really make sense, sticking with such an inept legal firm.

"That's where it gets interesting. Yentob is her maiden name, used for professional purposes. She is Linda Weintraub in her personal life."

"Oh for fucks sake," I sighed, "so the company was paying a million a year for a shit lawyer, just because she was Jonathan's wife? Wonder how much she was getting out of it."

"About 25% is the going rate for a lawyer with that sort of client," she replied, "no wonder he wasn't keen to give that up to someone more competent."

"I don't mind people earning good money, when they actually earn it, but this seems to be a series of us paying out, and getting nothing in return. Not only do we need to change lawyers, but he needs sacking, and she needs suing." I hated being ripped off, and could feel myself getting irate.

"Do you want me to fly over and sort it?" Elle offered. "I can email Ms Pearson, and get over there tomorrow." It was tempting. She didn't mind flying, and could sort the issues easily. I had a packed schedule all week, with people flying in from China to discuss the production of a new handset we'd developed, so couldn't really go myself.

"Ok, but take Roger with you. I'll worry about you being in New York on your own."

She smiled, and kissed the tip of my nose. "You are such a worry guts. I'll be fine. I might even do some Christmas shopping while I'm there." She turned back to her computer to email her boss, while I went to the kitchen to pour us both fresh glasses of wine.

By the time I returned, she was on the phone to Ms Pearson, discussing the visit to New York to deliver the Conde Nast contract to the American arm of her company. As expected, her boss was more than happy to sanction the trip. I pulled out my phone to organise my jet for an early take off slot, followed by a call to Roger to inform him of the plans.

With business issues out of the way for the evening, I turned my attention to romance, wrapping my arms around Elle's shoulders as she tapped out a quick email to Lewis to tell him what was happening. I nuzzled her neck as my hands slithered down to cup her breasts, kneading them gently as she finished typing. I watched as she pressed 'send', and swivelled round so that we were face to face.

"Yes sir, can I help you?" She teased in a soft voice.

I smiled at her, " you could certainly help me relieve some tension. I booked your flight for eight tomorrow, so we have plenty of evening left for fun." I glanced at the clock, it wasn't even nine, plenty of time for a nice, long session. She followed me into the bedroom.

I got her to do a slow striptease, flashing glimpses of her nipples, teasing me with her delicious body, while I sat naked on the bed, stroking my erection. My breath hitched, as her lacy knickers finally hit the floor, and she was gloriously naked, and clearly as horny as ever.

She crawled up the bed towards me, a naughty gleam in her eye, and leaned down to give my balls a long, slow lick, which made my cock iron hard, and begin to throb. I groaned as she captured it between her lips, and began to roll her tongue over the head, while her soft lips worked the shaft, and her hand gently stroked my balls.

I should've stopped her, and made her come first, like a gentleman, but I was effectively helpless under her onslaught, unable to stop even if I wanted to. The best I could manage was reaching down to play with her nipple, while she gave my cock her full attention.

I spurted straight down her throat, crying out with the intensity, and watching with fascination as she swallowed the lot, then licked me clean. Even after months of this wonderful treatment, it never failed to turn me on even more.

I pushed her onto the bed, onto her back, and dived down to lick her pussy. She was soaking, her clit pulsing wildly. I lapped and sucked at it, desperate to feel her orgasm. As soon as I slipped two fingers inside her, I felt the quivering start. I sucked on her clitoris while she orgasmed, screaming my name over and over, her hands grasping at the sheets.

Before she'd had a chance to come down, I plunged my cock into her, riding her hard and fast. As I pounded into her, she came again, her pussy greedily pulling me into her. I leaned down to rest on my elbows to kiss her hungrily, swallowing her cries of passion.

I let go, flooding her with cum. I could feel her insides still twitching and pulsing around me. I kissed her again, a deep and grateful kiss. Only Elle could make me feel like a demi-god, simply by making me the man that she chose. Only Elle could come repeatedly from just my cock alone.

She lay back to catch her breath for a moment, before disappearing into the bathroom to clean up, while I let the spaniels in. They were waiting patiently outside when I opened the door.

Next morning, she was up and packed by the time the spaniels and I had even woken up. I suspected that she'd even done a quick run as well. She placed my coffee on the bedside table, and sat on the edge of the bed to drink hers, stroking a very sleepy Bella. "I'm gonna miss you baby. I hate being away from you," she admitted.

"It's only two days. One sleep, that's all. Not too bad." Her itinerary didn't leave much time for shopping, but she only had to chair a board meeting, and meet with the new legal team to instruct, so didn't need any longer. It would be late on Friday when she got back, but I'd arranged for her to land at Gatwick, so she'd be home in just twenty minutes. We'd still have our full weekend together, although I needed to visit my tailor in the West end, and get my hair cut. I loved London in December, so spending a Saturday in town didn't seem too much of a hardship. We could also look at Christmas decorations while we were there, as Elle had planned to decorate the Sussex house, and have the holiday there.

"One night away seems too much these days. I don't know how I ever slept alone," she admitted.

"What? Without snoring spaniels kicking you in the face, and taking up the whole bed?"

"Yeah, something like that, although Tania let me have a whole inch of the edge last night." She smiled fondly at the spaniel, who was fully spread out. We had an emperor sized bed, and still both ended up teetering on the edges. "It's amazing how much space a spaniel requires."

She left at seven to catch her flight, giving me a passionate kiss goodbye, "love you," she called out as she disappeared through the door.

"Love you too," I yelled as she pulled the door shut.

I threw myself into my work that day, with almost back to back meetings. We were launching a next generation smart phone which had taken a vast amount of research and development. With some truly groundbreaking technology, I was confident that Apple would be scrabbling to keep up. My policy of investing in brilliantly creative tech entrepreneurs had really paid off. I listened intently as they listed the key features, and potential of the new handset, turning it over in my hand to get a feel for it. It really was far in advance of the iPhone, as well as being more tactile. I was excited.

I met with the Chinese, who would be manufacturing it for me. We discussed time frames, costings, and shipping. We were getting enough lithium out of the ground in Russia to be able to guarantee a supply, and drive the costs down significantly. It felt like one win after another. If Elle had been around, I'd have gone out to dinner to celebrate, but as it was, I had to make do with one of Mrs Watton's creations, and the company of the spaniels.

They played as I sat in the lounge, working on my laptop. I worked out the costings of the new handset down to the nearest penny, then checked it all again to make sure. Satisfied that I was correct, I was just about to work out the potential profit margin, when I was interrupted by Nico bursting in, looking distraught. "Boss, just had a call. Elle's been shot."

I didn't hear the rest of what he said. My entire body went cold, my spine prickling in fear. "Shot? Is she..." I couldn't say the words.

"Still alive sir, injured, but alive. We need to get you there."

"My planes in New York," I said weakly. I wasn't really thinking straight. *Not Elle. What did I send her there for?*

"Sir, either borrow a plane, or I'll get you on a scheduled flight." Nico snapped me out of my trance. I pulled out my phone and called Karl. As soon as I said what had happened, he told me to 'get my arse' to London city, and that he'd bribe a takeoff slot. Nico had already assembled the guards from the apartment downstairs, assigned four to the spaniels, and briefed the rest. I quickly threw a change of clothes into a bag, and we made our way to the airport.

Details were sketchy, but it seemed that Weintraub had pulled his gun when Elle had tackled him about the legal issues. Roger had shot him dead, but only after he'd been able to inflict some serious damage on Elle. As soon as I'd ended the call to a rather hysterical Ms Hogan from the American board, Oscar called to find out what had happened, telling me he'd seen it on the Sky news.

"I'm just on my way to the airport. She was shot by the finance director during a board meeting. She'd uncovered a scam, and had gone over to tackle it. Her guard shot him dead, all I know is she's alive, but injured. Can you pull any strings to make sure Roger doesn't get arrested please?"

"Certainly, I'll call the American Ambassador now. If there's anything else you need, just ask."

"Just make sure I get a takeoff slot at City airport, I'm cutting it really fine for the curfew. My friends lent me his plane, but I'm not confident they'll let me take off so late."

"I'll see to it. Call me when you have some news."

I threw up twice on the flight. Six hours of horrific fear, coupled with not being able to communicate by phone, and my mind playing a grotesque tape of being told she was dead the moment I landed. I was desperate for the loo, and, with no urine bottles on board someone else's jet, for the first time, I was forced to get up, and use the toilet on board, which I was convinced, would make us crash.

It must have looked quite funny, Nico holding my hand, as I edged my way to the back of the plane, and I must admit that with an empty bladder, I was able to get back to my seat a whole lot easier, and without his help.

I was grateful to Karl for thinking to send two cars to meet us at the airport, and whisk us straight to the hospital. His driver informed me that we would be staying in Karl's Manhattan apartment during our stay, as it was conveniently situated, and fully staffed.

Nico had been trying to contact Roger, without any luck, deducing that he was either in the hospital with Elle, or under arrest somewhere. I wasn't used to such a lack of information, and could feel my blood pressure skyrocket as the minutes ticked past.

I called Oscar as we drove away from the airport, to see if he had any information. He was only able to confirm that Roger was at the hospital with Elle, and that no charges would be brought, adding that he wasn't able to find out about her condition, as he wasn't family, and the hospital were guarding her privacy from the press.

It was late at night by the time we finally got there, a full eight hours since the incident. It crossed my mind that they might not let me see her, as I wasn't related, but with no living relatives, they had to let someone in, and I was almost her fiancé. I cursed myself for not marrying her quickly enough. I strode up the steps, past some waiting press, and into the foyer, looking around for the information desk, only to be met by a white coated doctor. "Mr Porenski? I was informed by the British consulate that you'd be arriving. Follow me please, and I'll update you on Ms Reynolds' condition on the way." *Good old Oscar, thinking to alert the ambassador.* My entourage and I followed along behind him.

"She sustained a gunshot wound to her shoulder, damaging her scapula. Thankfully there's no nerve damage, nor was there any major arteries involved. What's slightly more worrying is that the force of the bullet sent her flying, hitting her head on the wall behind. Her skull has a fracture, and there is some brain swelling. We don't know at this stage how long she'll be unconscious for. It could be a day or two, or longer. On the plus side, she's young and fit, so has all the best chances possible."

I reeled with the news. "Tell me doctor, this brain injury, could it cause permanent damage?"

"It's impossible to say at this stage. Everyone is different. I've had patients with this type of injury recover completely, others have lost their sense of smell, their sight, or cognitive skills. We can't know until she wakes up."

"But she won't die..right?" I said.

"It's unlikely, as I said, she's young and strong, but her head injury is quite serious, and there is always a possibility that she may not wake up." I went cold. "It's called PVS, or persistent vegetative state." He pushed open the doors of the ITU ward. I could see Roger through a window at the far end, looking pensive, chewing on his thumbnail.

"Guards remain in the corridor please," I barked. They all halted, and let me go in alone with the doctor. My poor, beautiful Elle looked tiny, laying in the bed, all hooked up to machinery. Her shoulder was in a sort of cast arrangement, holding it still, and her head was bandaged. "Did you shave her hair off?" I asked.

"Only a small bit around the wound where we stitched it. She won't even notice it," the doctor replied, before leaving me alone with her, and Roger.

"Boss, I'm so sorry," he began, the moment we were alone. I held my hand up to stop him.

"Not your fault Roger. Nobody would expect a finance director to pull a gun. I'm just glad you killed the fucker before I got my hands on him. You won't face any charges by the way." I watched him let out a breath. "We're staying at Karl's place. Why don't you go and get some rest?" I knew he'd been up 22 hours.

"Thank you sir." He walked out of the room, and spoke briefly to Nico, before walking off down the corridor. I pulled a plastic chair to the side of Elle's bed, and sat down, taking her soft little hand in mine, and marvelling at how warm it was. Her poor face looked swollen, and a bit battered, and I could see blood around her nails on her damaged side. My heart broke for her. My beautiful, healthy, sporty girl looked so small and helpless laying there. I carefully leaned over to kiss her gently on the cheek.

"Hey baby, I'm here," I told her, "I'm going to stay here till you wake up, and kiss me back." I scanned her face for a flicker of recognition, disappointed that she didn't even stir. I sat, talking to her for hours, reminiscing about meeting her, our first weekend, anything I could think of. I sat while the nurses took her vitals, doctors checked her over, and made their notes.

The wound on her shoulder looked horrific. They'd had to get the bullet out, and piece together her shoulder blade. I thought of her slicing through the med to save Bella, and wondered if she'd ever be able to swim again.

I must have dropped off, because I was woken by Nico shaking my shoulder. "Sir, there's someone here from Pearson Hardwick, says he's been sent by Ms Pearson to offer his assistance."

"Ok, can you stay with Elle in case she wakes up?" He nodded. I went out to the corridor, and saw a man waiting by my guards. He introduced himself as Oliver Fitch, senior partner in the corporate division.

"I was contacted this morning by Valerie Pearson. They're all frantic for information over there. I know you had to switch off your phone in here, so I said I'd drop by, to get some news of her condition, and to offer any assistance that you need."

"The doctors are telling me that her condition is serious but stable, whatever that means. She's got a broken shoulder, and more seriously, a fractured skull. They can't give me a prognosis as yet."

"I'll relay that to our London office. Is there anything you need, accommodation, transport?"

I shook my head, "One of my friends has provided his apartment, cars, and drivers. I will need you to look into some circumstances for me though. People don't normally get shot for sacking a law firm."

"Let me look into it for you. I agree, it doesn't ring true. I'll make a start with the board at your company, and dig around a bit."

I was grateful to Roger for thinking to bring a change of clothes, and a wash bag when he later returned. Leaving him with Elle, I was able to get cleaned up and changed. I went down to the foyer to make some calls, phoning Oscar, James, and Elle's work, relaying the small amount of information that I knew. Oscar informed me that Weintraub's wife was in custody, suspected of fraud, and he had sought assurances that she wouldn't be released until everything had been properly investigated. I called Galina to put everything on hold for at least the next week. "Already done," she said, "Mr Ranenkiov called me in early this morning, and asked me to clear your diary. How's Elle?"

I told her the news, listened to her sigh, and promised to keep her updated.

At some point, I'd have to speak to the Conde Nast board, and the press, but they could wait, Elle was far more important. I went back up to the room, and sent a guard out for some food, settling myself into the chair beside her, I figured I'd be there a while.

The hours ticked by slowly, punctuated by the beep of machines, and the periodic visits from the healthcare professionals. I watched as they checked her over, flinching as the nurses changed the dressings on her shoulder. Nico and Roger took turns waiting outside in the corridor, sending their assistants out for food and drinks. I drank so much coffee that my eyes were pretty much on stalks.

I asked the doctors if there were any scans they could do, any tests that would tell me what was going on in her sleeping body. They'd done CAT scans, and various tests, and could only tell me, in sympathetic tones, that it was a waiting game, that she'd wake up when she was ready.

I paced around, mentally bargaining with the gods. I promised to donate to charity, help the poor, anything, if they would just deliver her back to me. I even asked my Mama to help me. As Saturday dragged on, I began to despair. I held her hand, stroking her slender fingers, remembering them flying over a keyboard, as she whipped up a contract, or stroking the spaniels in just the right way, turning them into her devoted slaves.

"Baby, come on, come back to me," I begged, "it's almost Sunday. I want to make you bacon sandwiches, and take the girls into the woods with you. You need to wake up." *Nothing.* I even considered sending someone out to buy me a laptop so I could email Carl, I was so desperate for the pain to go away.

Chapter 18

I fell asleep in the chair beside her, in an uncomfortable position with my head and arms resting on her bed. I woke up stiff and sore after a few hours, and stretched, yawning loudly. Out of the corner of my eye, I saw her hand move.

"You're awake!" I exclaimed, pressing the call button for the doctor. Her eyes were still closed, but her hand moved, grasping at the sheet. "Can you open your eyes?"

Her face screwed up a little. She couldn't speak as she had a tube down her throat.

"Hey baby, it's Sunday morning, lazy girl. We're wasting the day." I hoped that my words would jolt her out of her doze. The door opened, and her doctor came in to see why I'd pressed the button.

"She's woken up, ish," I told him. "She's not opened her eyes yet though." I turned back to her. "The doctor's here. You need to open your eyes baby." I grasped her hand, feeling her fingers move around mine. Her eyes flickered as she fought to open them. She frowned slightly, and opened one, peering at me, then opened the other. Her eyes were as blue and beautiful as ever, if a little bloodshot. She looked panicked when she realised that she had a tube down her throat.

"Morning," said the doctor. "I'm going to remove your breathing tube Elle. Your throat will be a little sore, but you'll be able to speak." He called her nurse in.

I held her hand while they removed the tube, and checked her over. "Where am I?" She demanded in a husky voice the moment the tube was out.

"You're in hospital in New York. You were shot. You've been out cold for a while," I told her.

"What day is it?"

"Sunday. You've been asleep since Thursday."

"I'm really sorry. You look exhausted," she said.

"Don't be silly. Not your fault...so you can see me ok?"

"Of course I can. I hurt all over though. I've got a stinking headache," she whispered. I wanted to whoop and cheer, but instead, I just held her hand as the doctor carried out a load of tests.

"In about half an hour, when she goes back to sleep, we'll do another brain scan, but, without wanting to be too optimistic, it's looking good."

"Who's looking good?" A little, hoarse, voice demanded, sounding annoyed that we were talking about her. *She's definitely back.*

While she was off having her scan, I used the opportunity to call everyone who needed an update, that she'd woken up, and the early indications were good. I'd sent Karl's plane back to him, and called to thank him for his kindness and hospitality. "Glad to help Ivan," he said, " gives the staff something to do as well. Think they get a bit bored there." His staff maintained an enormous apartment in Manhattan, which he used about half a dozen times a year at most. My security team had never been so spoilt.

I listened to a voicemail from Oliver Fitch, saying he needed to speak to me rather urgently. I called him back straightaway, telling him the news that Elle had woken up.

"Oh, that's great news, does Valerie Pearson know?"

"I called Elle's work, her manager said he'd relay the news."

"Good, now, as for the other matter. I've been doing some digging. You were done out of 10.65 million dollars. I don't know how much Elle had uncovered, but Linda Yentob was Weintraub's wife."

"Yes, Elle had found that out. It was the reason he shot her. She'd come over to confront him."

"Did she know that the three plaintiffs who were awarded those settlements were Jonathan Weintraub's three sisters? All using their married names of course. All three cases were what you Brits would call 'vexatious claims', only lost because Linda Yentob sabotaged the defence paperwork." I smiled while listening. I'd never been called a 'Brit' before.

"No wonder he shot her. She probably uncovered it. It's the type of detail Elle would look at...did the rest of the board know?"

"They're all denying, saying that Weintraub dealt with the lawsuits himself, but, you know, that seems unlikely. At the very least, the HR director must have been involved, or had knowledge of staff legal action, otherwise why have an HR director?"

"Quite. Have you reported all this to the police?"

"Yes. This case seems to be a top priority for some reason. They've pulled everyone in for questioning, and frozen the assets of everyone accused. Is Elle some kind of superstar back in England or something? Things don't normally happen that fast for a bit of fraud." *Oscar's at it again.*

"You just wait till you meet her when she's back on form. You'll end up her devoted puppy too, I promise. She had every billionaire in Canary Wharf trailing around after her like ducklings following their mother." *And she chose me.*

He chuckled, "I can't wait. In the meantime, I've taken the liberty of issuing lawsuits against the three sisters, Linda Yentob, and also the firm she worked for, as they were the retained company, and failed to supervise her properly, leading to this disaster. Pearson Hardwick looks after their own."

"Can you prepare the paperwork to become the Conde Nast preferred legal firm please? I'll sign and action it before we leave."

Over the next few days, Elle went from strength to strength, able to stay awake longer each day. The gunshot wound was deemed healed enough to put a cast on her shoulder, which would help the bones to knit better. I think the doctors were astonished at how quickly she bounced back. I put it down to her general good health and exceptional fitness. She fretted about her shoulder, wondering if she'd still be able to swim, and do sports. The doctors seemed optimistic, and advised intensive physio once the cast was off.

She managed to retain her dignity even while ill, being undemanding and grateful to the nursing staff. She was mortified that she had a catheter though, and horrified that I'd seen the bag of wee, telling me that she hated me being aware of her bodily functions. When I whispered that I knew her bum was for more than just a well lubed butt plug, she went bright red, and laughed, which I thought was adorable.

By the Tuesday, she was out of ITU, and in a private room. Roger had thought to grab her handbag and phone in the confusion after the shooting, so she charged it up, and played me the recording. It was quite clear that Roger's shot was a millisecond after Weintraub's. I was confident that nobody else could've reacted any faster. I listened to the rest of the board behaving like headless chickens after the shooting, and Roger calmly taking control, and administering first aid while waiting for the paramedics, angrily telling some stupid woman that sitting Elle up and giving her a glass of water was not the best idea. *Thank god he was with her.*

I held a board meeting on Thursday, with Nico frisking all the directors for guns before they entered the room. Despite a directive stating that there were no firearms permitted in the building, three of them were caught, and sacked immediately, and publicly. Out of the remainder, another three were suspected of having knowledge of the scam, with one confessing, claiming Weintraub had threatened her if she didn't keep quiet. She was sacked on the spot, swiftly followed by the other two. I'd have to pay severance, unless it could be proven that they had knowledge, and I warned them that if this was proven, they'd be sued for everything they had, so it was better to confess now, and walk away quietly. They both confessed that they too had known, and kept quiet.

I went around the table, asking the remaining directors in turn. In all, seven directors knew about the crime, and had taken no action. All were sacked on the spot. My new recruitment company was going to be busy. I comforted myself in the knowledge that Elle hadn't really liked many of the American directors, so sweeping out the disloyal ones would be a real positive. The fraud had actually been perpetrated against the previous owners, and Weintraub wouldn't have known that the company would be sold prior to his plans completing. For all we knew, he may have been doing this kind of thing for a while.

The rest of the day was spent dealing with the police. Both Elle, and Roger gave statements, and the recording was emailed to the investigating officer. They seemed pretty efficient, confirming that Linda Yentob, and her three sisters-in-law had been charged with fraud. Elle was pleased that her colleagues had sued Wiseman, Overy and Kaufman for their lack of supervision.

The doctors gave her clearance to return home on Friday. She was still quite weak, and tired quickly, but we were both keen to get back to England, and the girls, so, taking a nurse, and doctor for the flight, we made our way home to Sussex.

Funny enough, I was a lot better on the flight home than usual, even able to walk to the loo by myself, much to Elle's astonishment. Well, I couldn't really pee into a bottle with an audience, so, emboldened by my previous trip, I managed the walk there and back with no assistance.

Nico had organised a private ambulance to meet us at Gatwick, so that Elle would be comfortable during the short drive home. We both relaxed the moment the house came into view.

"It's lovely to be home," she said, squeezing my hand, and beaming a smile. I loved her calling our Sussex house 'home', just as I called her apartment home too. Mrs Ballard stood waiting in the doorway, holding the girls on their leads, until the ambulance had stopped, and we'd got out. They were overjoyed to see us, bouncing about at our feet, begging for fuss.

Once Elle was settled onto the sofa in the lounge, both spaniels vied for her lap, almost coming to blows. "Girls! One at a time please," Elle laughed. They settled for a leg each, draping their paws over her knees, while she stroked each in turn. They both ignored me.

"There's a roast in the oven, ready in about half an hour. Just switch the veg on. It's so nice to see you both back, I've been so worried," said Mrs Ballard, "the fridge is full, and the girls have been fed this afternoon. Is there anything else you need?"

"No thank you. You get off home, we'll be fine." I replied.

I busied myself in the kitchen, while Elle called her office to tell them that she was home, and catch up on the gossip. She'd been advised to take a few weeks off, which took her up to Christmas. Her boss ended up telling her to come back to work in the middle of January, which gave her four whole weeks.

"We could go away somewhere, take a little break in the sun," I suggested when she'd finished her calls.

"In my cast? Besides, I want to spend Christmas here," she replied, staring at the open fire blazing in the fireplace.

"We could go just after Christmas, fly out on Boxing Day. You'll still be in your cast, and sling, but hopefully a lighter one by then." I was forming a plan.

"Ok, where would you like to go? France?"

I shook my head. "It's a bit chilly there in winter. I'll book us a surprise baby, somewhere hot. You can still paddle." She beamed a smile at me, and agreed it would be lovely to get away together. I understood her desire to spend Christmas in Sussex. It would be her first one with no 'home' to go to, and I knew that had played on her mind. I also knew that she'd been shopping quite a bit, and sneaking around, hiding things.

"So, are you going to stay down here and recuperate, or come back to London with me next week?" I asked.

"I'll come to London. At least I can shop, watch telly, and see friends. I might be a bit bored over the next couple of weeks, while you're at work, plus we have rather a lot of Christmas functions to attend." She sank back into the sofa. I noticed that she looked a little pale and tired.

"Ok, but I need to know that you're resting, not racing around London, and sneaking into work. You've already scared the life out of me once."

She looked quizzical. "It must have been quite frightening, but surely they told you I was only shot in the shoulder?"

"No, I was just told that you'd been shot. Bear in mind, my mother was killed by a shot to the head, I nearly had a meltdown." I took a deep breath. "I get these tapes playing in my head, things like 'everyone you ever loved dies', things like that. They taunt me." *There, I've admitted it.*

"Oh I get those too. I think everyone does. It's why I did the relentless swimming. It was the only thing that cured the 'I'm not good enough' that used to play in my head over and over."

I gaped at her. I hadn't expected her to say that. I struggled to believe that my strong, clever, Elle suffered the same affliction as I. "I thought I was the only person it happened to." *Another deep breath.* "When I had my breakdown, I started talking to a therapist about it. I still talk to him by email. He never said that other people get the same thought loops."

"Well he won't if you're paying him to listen will he?" She rolled her eyes. "What therapist is gonna say 'yep, you're cured, and completely normal'? They want you to need them for as long as possible so they can keep getting paid, don't they?"

As had happened before, her simple explanation floored me. Her easy acceptance of, what I thought were the secret, and rather shameful inner workings of my mind, just made me feel...relaxed, loved, and...normal.

"Do you still get thought loops?" I was curious.

"Oh yes. I often get 'he'll get bored with you'. I sometimes get 'they're just kind because you're poor', and occasionally 'he wants to own the world'. I do think everyone gets them though."

"Well, for a start, I'll never get bored with you, you're not poor anymore, and you're right about me wanting to own the world." I smiled at her, relieved that we'd talked about it. She'd be able to use the study after all. I decided against suggesting couples counselling.

Oscar and Lucy called round after dinner, just to say hello, and see how Elle was. I asked Oscar to help me choose a bottle of wine, while the girls had a talking competition in the lounge. "Those two can talk for England can't they?" He said, as he followed me out to the kitchen.

"I know. I can't follow their conversations, there's not many people who speak too quickly for me to understand," I admitted.

"I'm a native, and I can't follow it either." I grinned at him, and grabbed a bottle of apple juice from the fridge, before pouring some into a large wine glass.

"For Elle, she's on strong painkillers and antibiotics. No alcohol."

"She'll be a grump then." Oscar replied.

We went through to the wine store. Oscar looked at several bottles. "You've been buying some great vintages. This one is particularly good." He held a bottle of red aloft.

"I'm going to propose to Elle at Christmas," I blurted out, "I'm planning to take her to Mustique on Boxing Day for a fortnight, maybe get married out there." I watched as his mouth dropped open.

"Well, I'll be blowed. I thought you were the most confirmed bachelor, after me," he said, smiling.

"So did I," I admitted, "but things change sometimes. When Elle got shot, I panicked that I wouldn't be able to see her, not being next of kin. She's got no family, so there was nobody to make decisions for her, you know, with life support, and nobody to give her away at her wedding, if we held it in England. I want more for her than that." I busied myself with the corkscrew.

"Would you like Lucy and I to come to Mustique for a few days? I can give her away, walk her down the aisle."

"Would you mind?"

"Not at all. Delighted to help. I take it she doesn't know about this yet?"

I shook my head. "She might say no, so don't book a flight just yet."

He grinned, "I can't see her refusing. I will keep it from Lucy though. She can't keep a secret for the life of her. I'll just tell her I'm planning a couple of days away."

"Do you think I'm mad, getting married?" I asked.

"I'd think you'd be mad not to," he replied. "You and Elle seem very....in tune. She seems to have humanised you, turned you into a one woman man."

"Nothing like the risk of losing someone to make you value them, and there's been times that I've held on to her by my fingertips." I carried the wine bottle, and three glasses into the lounge, Oscar brought in Elle's apple juice, and placed it in front of her.

"Ivan said you were on meds," he said apologetically. She pulled a face.

"I'm gonna be on these tablets for another week, we've got three Christmas parties to attend where I'll have to bypass the champagne. It's really not fair," she complained.

"Have you given a press conference yet?" Asked Lucy.

"Ivan did, after I woke up. There were press camped outside the hospital. I haven't yet though, I'm putting it off as long as possible."

"Might be an idea to get it out of the way, if you're planning to be out and about in London, especially with that cast on. How on earth will you find dresses to wear with it?" Lucy asked.

"I'll take you to Harrods, the consultants there will have some ideas," I interjected, *and I can get them to organise some dresses for a wedding without you knowing.*

"Good idea," said Lucy, "strapless with a shawl would work ok."

"Well, I'll never be able to wear strapless without one again," Elle said rather sadly, "my shoulder's a bit of a mess, I'm going to have quite a scar." I squeezed her hand.

It was bliss to sleep in my own bed that night, in any bed for that matter. I'd barely slept for the past week, catching odd hours here and there in the chair beside Elle's bed. Thankfully, I slept on Elle's 'good' side, so didn't worry that I'd roll over and hurt her in my sleep. I helped her out of her clothes, quickly shed mine, and slipped into the covers. I wanted to lay awake for a while, make sure that she got off ok, and enjoy the feeling of the girls and her all snuggled up to me. Unfortunately, I was asleep before the spaniels even had time to stretch their legs out, probably giving them the most cramped night's sleep they'd ever had.

I woke up unusually late the next morning, and rolled over to see an empty space beside me. I padded downstairs to find Elle sitting in the kitchen with her laptop open, seemingly engrossed in something. She shut it before I could see what she was looking at. "Morning baby, you must have needed that. I've never known you sleep so long," she said, before wandering over to pour us both fresh coffees.

She put mine down in front of me, and gave me a kiss. She tasted of coffee and mint. I breathed her wonderful scent, and pulled her onto my lap. "I'm sorry I went out cold last night, I meant to make slow but passionate love to you."

"Mmm, might be a bit tricky to do a hard fuck against the wall for a while," she teased, "I'd really like a nice bath first though, get nice and clean. I might need you to wash my hair for me though. I'm not sure if I can do it one handed."

"I'll give it a try," I said, rather doubtfully, "otherwise I'm planning to get a haircut later on, you could come with me, and get yours done there." I didn't mind helping her, but worried that I'd hurt her, or get her cast wet.

After breakfast, she ran a shallow bath, adding loads of that foam shit that women like. I helped her in, and sat at the side to assist her. In the end, I only had to wash one armpit that she couldn't reach by herself. "Why don't you join me?" She murmured seductively.

"I think I just might." I clambered in the opposite end, and rested my legs outside hers. Thankfully, it was a large, double ended bath, with the plug hole, and taps in the middle. In the two years since the bathrooms were fitted, I'd never used it, preferring the huge wet area, and power shower.

Baths have their advantages though, and I sank down into the foam, feeling the tension ebb from my shoulders. I closed my eyes to enjoy the sensation, just as Elle leaned forward to gently stroke my dick. I sighed in appreciation, desire unfurling as she gently caressed me. "Am I making you horny?" She purred.

"I'm always horny for you," I murmured, reaching to play with her clit. I heard her breath hitch as I rubbed little circles with the pad of my thumb.

"I really need to be fucked," she admitted, grasping my dick a little more firmly. I took the initiative, and helped her out of the bath, noticing that she seemed a little wobbly on her feet. I picked her up, and carried her, still wet, through to the bedroom, and laid her gently onto the bed.

"I don't think I'll last too long," I admitted, pushing her legs open, and diving down to give her lush, soft, licks. I teased her clit with the tip of my tongue, taking her to the brink, before plunging my cock into her, making her cry out as I stretched her inside.

I stayed upright, and caressed her breasts as I rode her, pushing her into a deep, intense, orgasm, watching as a flush spread across her chest, and her lips darkened. I let go, flooding her with cum, releasing a week's worth of tension and fear, as I reaffirmed our connection.

"I needed that," I admitted.

"So did I," she replied, beaming a smile, "but now I've got a taste for it again, you'll have to be a bit inventive to work around this cast."

"I do love a challenge," I told her. I looked at the cast and sling arrangement closely. It had been designed to hold her shoulder immobile for three weeks, when it would be removed, and either replaced with a smaller, lighter one, or left off altogether, and her arm held in place with just the sling. Either way, we could use a sex swing, as long as she was fastened in securely. I decided to give it a try later on.

She came with me for my appointments that afternoon, sitting quietly while I had fittings for the three suits I was having made, smiling at the pernickety tailor making minute adjustments. I'd called the Urban Retreat to see if they could do her hair at the same time as mine, and they'd managed to get her a slot with a stylist.

She said that she felt a whole lot better with her hair clean. I took her down to the occasion wear department to get her some dresses for the dinners we had coming up. The same assistant served us who had picked out the red dress previously. She looked at Elle's cast, and came up with a few suggestions, bringing in a rail of dresses for Elle to try.

"I just need to use the gents," I called out to Elle while she was behind the curtain.

"Ok, see you in a bit," she replied.

I indicated to the saleswoman to come outside. Once we were out of earshot, I said; "I need you to find me a selection of dresses, suitable for a tropical wedding, that will work with her cast. I'm going to need you to keep this secret from Elle, charge them to my account, and have them sent to my office."

"Her wedding, or someone else's?" She asked.

"Hers, white I think, but not too formal. I'm planning to marry her on a beach." I handed her my business card. "This is my office address. Have them sent there please. Make them extraordinary. There's no budget limitation. Pick about five, so she can choose."

"Will do sir. They'll be with you in a few days. Is that ok? Or do you need them sooner?"

"A few days is fine, but make them extraordinary please." I went back into the fitting room. Elle popped her head around the curtain.

"Great, you're back. What do you think of this one? I was thinking it would be good for the Conde Nast do." She stepped out wearing a shimmering blue dress, which showed off her amazing, lithe figure to perfection.

"I like it," I said appreciatively, "the colours great on you." The saleswomen bustled in, bearing a selection of scarves and shawls to cover the unsightly sling. Rather artfully, she draped a matching wrap around Elle's shoulders, covering her sling completely. "Oh yes, that works brilliantly," I said, snapping a picture with my phone so that I would be able to recreate it.

We managed to find enough dresses to see her through the party season, and probably beyond. I actually enjoyed shopping with Elle, she wasn't overly picky, was never demanding, and liked my opinion on everything. If I screwed up my nose, or shook my head, she didn't argue, just tried on the next thing. I liked that she trusted my good taste, and allowed herself to be guided.

By the time we'd finished shopping, Elle was too exhausted to eat out, so we headed back to Sussex for an early dinner, and some relaxation.

Sunday was spent walking the dogs, eating, and making love. I'd installed a swing in one of the bedrooms, so taking care, I gingerly strapped her in. I needn't have worried, the swing supported her completely, and I was able to fuck her really hard and fast, without hurting her.

"Again?" I asked. I was slicked with sweat, and a bit out of breath.

"Please...it makes me feel so alive. I need to chase away the flashbacks," she admitted. I frowned slightly, vowing to discuss it afterwards, before plunging into her once again, with her favourite vibrator pressed onto her clit.

"Yes..yes...yes," she called out, in time with my balls slapping her arse, as I pounded into her. "Ivaaaan, fuuuuck," she yelled as I fucked her into another orgasm, her pussy spasming around my cock. With one last thrust, I let go, and somehow managed to shoot another load into her. My poor cock felt a bit sore and over used, as I stilled the swing, and caught my breath.

"Life affirming enough?" I asked, when I was finally able to speak.

"Oh yes, definitely chased the cobwebs away," she grinned. I helped her down from the swing, and the pair of us wobbled over to the bed to lay down. I rolled onto my side, and traced little circles over her breasts.

"Are you having flashbacks then?" I asked. I was genuinely concerned. Being shot must have been a terrifying experience for her. Waking up with a tube down her throat couldn't have been much fun either. She stared up at the ceiling for a little while.

"When I was questioning him about using his wife as the company lawyer, and her failure to defend those lawsuits, he looked at me with such hatred..." She trailed off for a moment. I stayed silent. "I've never been hated like that before. It was...shocking. I mean, I've had people dislike me, or be irritated by me, but not hating me, and certainly not enough to want to kill me," she paused, "have you?"

"Yes. It's something I've lived with for years," I admitted, "nobody can become as wealthy as I am without upsetting anybody. Sometimes it's people I've not even dealt with, who are just envious. I've never been shot though."

"It really hurts," she replied, "I wouldn't recommend it." She paused. "Can I ask you something, and you tell me honestly?"

"I'll try."

"Have you ever killed a man?"

"Nope." I was able to say it with total sincerity, as I'd only ever killed a woman. *Karen fucking Hodges.*

"I'm glad. I thought, what with Vlad being such a gangster, that you'd have been dragged into stuff." *So she knows. Seems quite calm about it too.*

"He was originally involved in what was known as the Bratva, controlled a tribe in one of the Gulags, he once told me. I don't know whether that was true or not, but he was a brutal man. I was part of his 'team', but the others used to tease me because I was too squeamish to kill a man. I saw men being killed though, saw Vlad kill three altogether. I'm a good shot though," I added.

"How come you ended up legit?" She asked.

"I bought legit businesses, grew them, added to them. I've done my fair share of sharking and intimidating, I'll admit that, but all the really seedy stuff was never my style. I take a lot of pride in being an upright and law abiding business tycoon," I stated, rather primly.

She laughed, "there was me thinking you ran the criminal underworld..." She said in a teasing tone.

"Can I ask you something?" *It's been bugging me.*

"Sure."

"When we discovered that money in Vlad's house. I told you it was murky. You didn't even flinch. As a lawyer, and super-honest citizen, I was surprised that you didn't ask questions. Why was that?"

She stared at the ceiling for what seemed like ages. "I am from South London you know. Everything I ever had fell off the back of a lorry. You knew to never ask questions. Plus, I didn't want to embarrass you by being priggish about it." I pulled her into a hug, and kissed her cheek, relieved that she hadn't judged me. "So has the source of the cash dried up?"

"Yes." I took a deep breath. "Vlad controlled routes through the Ukraine that were used by gun and drug smugglers, hence the cash. I didn't want that in our lives, so I gave the routes to his head of security."

"Good call....will you miss the money?" She asked the question so innocently that I wanted to laugh. She really had no idea how much I was worth.

"No baby. We'll be fine for money, don't you worry."

"I'll never worry with you around, Mr Goldfinger... Now has your cock recovered yet? I could go again." She looked hopeful.

"Christ Elle, I've come three times already, you'll break my cock if you're not careful." I bent down to suck her nipple, before licking and sucking her into another climax. *Greedy girl.*

We left for London early the next morning, the spaniels sitting on our laps all the way, which meant I had to change again before I went to the office, as Tania had covered my suit with dog hairs. I left Elle in our apartment, with a promise that I'd try not to be too late home that evening. Having been off for a week, with nothing but email communications, had left me scrabbling to catch up.

I barely drew breath all day, with meetings scheduled for every available minute. I barked instructions at Galina between visitors, instructing her to find me a house to rent on Mustique from Boxing Day. It needed a private beach, total security, and full staff. She solemnly noted it all down, before handing me a list of people I needed to call.

My recruitment arm had to be briefed on the replacements I needed for the directors dismissed the previous week. I quickly typed out a list, adding the CV's of the sacked execs, so that they could compile a list of the skills and experience we required.

Andrei had taken over the details of the handset launch in my absence, and quickly brought me up to date with developments. It all seemed to be in hand, and the Chinese had been instructed to produce prototypes on a larger scale for testing.

I ended up getting home around eight that night, walking into to marvellous cooking smells. *Has she learnt to cook? I thought it was Mrs Watton's afternoon off.* I smiled at the sight of James and Linzi sitting on the sofas, sipping glasses of wine. "Hi everyone, something smells good in here." I kissed Elle on the cheek.

"James brought a beef Wellington over. Thinks I might need feeding up," she told me, "as if I've not spent a week in the states, with their conservative portion control."

"Yes, but you're recovering, and the good doctor here recommended hearty food, as well as plenty of rest," James called out.

"Quite right too. You go sit down, I'll dish up," I offered.

"You just walked in," she scolded, handing me a glass of wine. I took off my jacket, and pulled off my tie, flinging them over the back of a chair.

The beef Wellington was fabulous. "Wonderful to walk in to such a lovely meal," I said, finishing the last morsel.

"Is that a dig?" Elle laughed. "Whenever I try to cook, he ends up having to rustle up something else. I even bought cookbooks, and tried really hard," she said to James.

"It's not one of your talents, " he agreed, "but you do a great slice of toast."

"Cheeky bugger, I can make more than toast," she said, pouting. I enjoyed watching James tease her in his good natured way. I'd long got over worrying that she was too close to him, and was relaxed about their friendship. His girlfriend was a delight too, being humorous and entertaining company. I always enjoyed their visits.

The rest of the week was a blur of meetings, conference calls, and spreadsheets. The only high point being a meeting with a jeweller from Van Cleef to discuss the engagement ring I wanted to commission for Elle. He came to my office, flanked by security guards, and showed me a selection of diamonds for me to make my choice. I'd borrowed one of Elle's dress rings for the size, and carefully examined each diamond in turn, listening to his explanations about cut and clarity.

I chose a large, brilliant cut, white diamond, which he said had once belonged to a Maharajah. It was large enough to be extravagant, but not too big for her slender fingers. I asked for a gold setting, as I knew she preferred gold to platinum.

I had to let Nico, Roger and Galina in on the secret, what with ring buying, wedding dresses arriving, and my instructions for Galina to organise a minister on Mustique, and book another villa for Oscar, it was impossible to keep it secret. Galina sighed wistfully, and said it was 'so romantic', Roger just nodded in his inscrutable way, and Nico sniggered. *Bastard.*

Elle had taken to visiting her local salon every morning after the gym, to get her hair washed and dried. She seemed a little sheepish about it at first, feeling that she was being rather profligate, until I pointed out that she was happier with her hair looking nice, and given the amount of functions we were attending, almost every evening in December, she would have been having it done almost every day anyway.

She spent her days shopping, doing a little work from home, and reading. She also bought a load of Christmas decorations, after finding out that I didn't have any. I came home from work one evening to find the apartment adorned with fairy lights, a gigantic tree, and carefully colour-schemed baubles. "You realise that the girls will enjoy destroying that don't you?" I said, laughing.

"They've already been told off for touching it. I gave up on chocolate decorations. They drove Bella mental. Do you like it?" She looked a little anxious.

"It looks wonderful. Please tell me you haven't been climbing up to decorate it though?" I eyed the star at the top, well out of Elle's reach.

"What, one handed? Don't be silly, I made Roger do it. I just supervised."

She did the same at our Sussex home, travelling down early Friday morning with the girls, so that it would be ready for me when I got back that night. I saw the tree, all lit up in the hall window as soon as I pulled in through the gates. Even I had to admit it looked homely and welcoming, especially with Elle waiting eagerly at the door for me, the girls at her feet. I had barely kissed her hello, when she was dragging me through to the living room.

She had a real tree set up in the lounge, covered in lights, and gold ornaments, set next to the open fire, which was roaring away, loaded with logs. Even the mantelpiece was decorated beautifully, with more pine fronds, and ornaments. "Doesn't it smell wonderful?" She said, almost childlike with glee. "I've never had a real tree before, we never had enough room at home." I eyed the pile of presents underneath it.

"It smells delightful. Looks wonderful. Very homely." I kissed her, smiling at her excitement. "And those gifts?"

"Oh, most of them are for you, there's some there for the girls too," she replied.

"It's a week and a half until Christmas. Did you put them there to tease me?" I asked. I'll admit I was quite interested to see what she'd bought me. *Ok, more than a little interested. I'd snoop after she went to bed.*

"They look nice under the tree," she pointed out.

"I'll have to put all of yours under there as well," I lied, panicking slightly inside. I'd have to count up how many she'd bought, and get her the same. So far, I'd organised a ring, that was all. My mind was a bit of a blank as to what to get her. She had enough clothes, lots of jewellery, and enough money to buy whatever she wanted. It wouldn't be easy. I vowed to ask Galina on Monday for some advice.

We had to drive back to town on Saturday night for the Beltan Christmas party, which was a bit of a nuisance. Elle insisted on visiting her usual salon for hair and makeup, which meant leaving Sussex early. She wore the shimmery blue gown, and I found the picture on my phone to help arrange the shawl in the same way as it was done in the shop.

We arrived outside Battersea Evolution, where our Christmas party was being held, to a bank of photographers. "How's your shoulder after the shooting?" Yelled one.

"Healing nicely, thank you for asking, " Elle replied, beaming for the cameras.

"Is it true that the two of you were having an affair while he was seeing Dascha Meranov?" Yelled another. Elle didn't let her smile slip.

"Not true at all."

I glared at the journalists, and whisked Elle into the venue. "Where did that come from?" She asked, frowning.

"God knows. Probably just want a bit of dirt to dish. Anyway, switch your smile on, we have staff to entertain."

Chapter 19

"What do women like for Christmas?" Was the question I asked Galina, Ranenkiov, Oscar, and Gail Hayward, during meetings the following week. I carefully noted down their ideas, and sent Nico out on a few missions. Galina even managed to source a 'professional present wrapper' to make the numerous parcels look picture pretty, and fit in with Elle's festive colour scheme.

It was a manic week, mainly due to me taking two weeks off after Christmas. Normally, in the UK, business winds down a little in December, but I seemed to be as busy as ever. Even Elle's work, which she'd been doing from home, seemed to stop for the holidays. The team that she managed had a long, boozy lunch, after which, Elle had to be scraped up, and carried home by Roger, much to my amusement. *She won't dare tell me off anymore when I do it.*

Her ring was delivered to my office the day before Christmas Eve. I opened the little box, and stared at it. The little piece of metal and stone that would bind her to me forever. I'd put the two wedding rings in with the rest of the wedding stuff that was in my office storeroom, ready to be put on the plane.

The diamond glittered at me, almost insolent in its beauty. "Is that the ring?" Galina whispered in hushed tones. I hadn't noticed her coming in.

"Yes. I hope she likes it," I replied.

"She'll love it," she asserted, "it's beautiful. Such a lovely design."

"I think so too." To be honest, seeing the ring, and finally holding it, made me extremely nervous about what I was planning to do. *What will I do if she says no?*

"It's so romantic, proposing on Christmas Day," she went on, "like something out of a Mills and Boon novel." She sighed loudly, and went back to her office with a dreamy look on her face. I almost laughed. Galina was a plain, dumpy, and rather sensible woman, and I'd never have put her down as a reader of romance novels.

I closed the ring box, and tucked it safely into my pocket. I could feel it pressing against my chest, taunting me with its promise to change my life irrevocably. As soon as I got home that evening, I hid it in my underwear drawer.

I took Elle out to dinner, as it was our last night in London for a while. She booked Gordon Ramsey, in Hospital road, as a special treat, musing that Quintessentially never seemed to have a problem getting us a table anywhere. I smiled at her naivety, knowing full well that the moment my name was mentioned, any maitre'd worth his salt would accommodate us.

I loved the food, having opted for the tasting menu, and a bottle of Cristal to accompany it. Elle was on good form, telling me that she felt a lot better having had the heavier cast removed that day. With just a sling to contend with, she was a lot more comfortable. "Have the flashbacks stopped?" I asked.

"Pretty much. I've been enjoying being off, although I feel a bit of a fraud, as I really could have gone into work."

"You worked from home though," I pointed out. The lawyers she managed could easily cope with the work she set for them, and Lewis had helped by overseeing them for her.

"I know, but nowhere near the amount of work I'd normally do. I feel a bit of a fraud, still getting paid."

"Your clients are still being looked after, so you should still be paid, besides, you were told to rest, not race around the Canary Wharf Tower." I gave her my 'stern' look. She just beamed a big smile, disarming me completely.

"Bossy boots," she teased. "I'm pretty much fine now, apart from shoulder ache, a scar, and a tufty bit of hair at the back."

"I like taking care of you," I told her.

"You always make me feel very protected," she admitted, which got her a big smile from me.

"Ya lublu tebia ee hotchu zhenitsia na tebe," I said, prompting her to reply that she loved me too, and wanted me to be her husband, in possibly the most badly pronounced Russian I'd ever heard. "Languages are really not your thing are they?" I smirked at her.

"Didn't I say it right?" She asked, all embarrassed. I just smiled, the sentiment had been there, and had thrilled me.

"You sound like a cockney, trying to speak Russian, but I get the gist," I teased.

"Says he who says 'pliz', rather than 'please', when you get agitated," she countered, "and I'm sure you said 'vant' rather than 'want' once, when you were in the middle of an orgasm."

"Oh come on, is that the best you can do? Besides, you probably misheard me, if you were getting fucked at the time." I grinned at her.

"I'm gonna get you to recite a poem or something, next time you fuck me, so I can hear your accent get thicker and thicker, the closer you are to coming." *she's got that sexy gleam in her eye..*

"We could try it on the way home if you like. Pick a poem."

"Ok, get the bill," she demanded, winking at me.

She practically dragged me out to the car, and immediately slid the privacy screen up. "You are so fucking sexy, she growled, looking as if she wanted to rip my clothes off. She quickly undid my trousers, yanking them down my legs, swiftly followed by my boxers. Within moments, she had her lips wrapped around my cock, sucking and licking, as if she was sex starved.

"Let me fuck you," I murmured, excited by the close proximity of pedestrians, and other drivers, as we sped through the west end. She hitched up her dress, and slid her knickers off, before straddling me, sinking slowly down onto my iron cock. *Oh god, I'm outside, being shagged, and none of these people know what's going on under their noses.*

She began to move, holding onto the headrest with her good arm, slamming her body down onto mine, leaning back so that the crest of my cock rubbed against her spot. I cupped her breasts over her clothes, feeling how erect and hard her nipples were. I was turned on beyond belief.

"Just think, all those people out there, seeing you fuck me like this. Does it turn you on?" She whispered, increasing her pace slightly. I felt helpless in the face of her onslaught, and the sheer horniness of what we were doing. Turned on beyond belief, I was almost mindless with the need to come.

"Elle, I need to come, pliz, pliz, I need you to come," I begged, hearing my accent thickening, as I lost concentration. She let go, gasping as she came around me, sagging into my embrace. I followed suit, pouring myself into her, lapsing into Russian expletives as I gave way to intense pleasure.

We stayed silent for a moment, clinging together, as we both recovered from our climaxes. I could hear her breathing heavily, and felt her relax. After a few minutes, she peeled herself off me, and rummaged round on the floor of the car to find her knickers, and restore them to their rightful place. I sat there for a moment, with my dick still hanging out, marvelling at just how sexy she was.

"Think I proved my point," she said impishly. I grinned at her, and righted my clothing.

"You are so fucking sexy that it makes me lose my mind," I said, "and I won't apologise for it."

Roger drove us down to Sussex the next morning, while Nico took our cases, and all the wedding stuff to London city, before accompanying the plane down to Gatwick, ready for us on Boxing Day. I called him before takeoff to make doubly sure he had the dresses and rings, speaking in Russian so that Elle wouldn't hear what I was up to. "Yes boss, of course I've got the dresses and rings, as well as your cases. I've also made sure you have champagne on board, as well as urine bottles." *Cheeky bastard.*

"They won't be needed," I snapped.

"The caterers at Gatwick will stock the plane with food on Thursday morning, they can accommodate all your requests."

"Good," I replied, clicking off my phone.

We arrived at Sussex in time for lunch, which Mrs Ballard had already prepared. Elle handed her a small gift, and thanked her profusely for everything she'd done for us. I watched as my housekeeper unwrapped a pair of earrings, declaring that she loved them, and thanked Elle for her thoughtfulness. I opened a bottle of champagne, and poured three glasses for a toast, raising mine aloft. "To good health, happiness, and a merry Christmas," I stated. We all clinked and drank.

Mrs Ballard said her goodbyes shortly afterwards, and disappeared home to her own family. After lunch, we took the girls into the woods for a walk, both enjoying the change of pace. London had been rather frenetic, and Sussex seemed peaceful, and silent. The girls bounced about, oblivious to the cold, as they snuffled at the twigs, and rotting leaves. Elle hooked her arm though mine, and snuggled into my side, as we strolled along. The tension leaving my body with every step.

"What's the plan for tomorrow?" I asked. I'd been wondering how we'd be spending the day itself.

"Eating mainly. Telly, probably a shag or two, opening presents, that's all I've got planned," she said.

"Sounds good. What did you do at Christmas as a child?"

She smiled. "I thought it was magical. I fully believed in Father Christmas. I used to put out a pillowcase on Christmas Eve, and go to bed early, so that he could come. I'd get up outrageously early, and be all excited, waking mum up so I could rip them all open. When my Nan was still alive, she used to come to us, so I'd sleep in with mum. I'd spend the day playing with my new things, while they watched all the soaps on the telly. My Nan used to make the dinner, always at one o'clock, then turkey sandwiches for tea. What about you?"

"We used to go to my dad's parents for the day. They died when I was around twelve. Nana was a great cook, and the meal was always the most important part. There were loads of dishes, and she used to serve everyone, never sitting down to eat herself. I think she used to collect food over the last few months of the year, so that we could have a feast. We had another celebration in January too, for the 'old Christmas', which was fun. My presents were usually quite practical, like a new coat, or new gloves, although I remember the last Christmas, getting a bottle of aftershave, which I was delighted with. We watched telly too, during the day, but in the evening, we usually visited neighbours for parties."

Back at the house, Roger had placed the gifts I'd bought, under the tree. Elle's eyes widened at the sight of them. I had to admit, it all looked rather lovely, and I was getting quite intrigued as to what was in mine. I'd already had a rootle through them while she'd been asleep, the weekend before, squeezing and shaking them to see if I could guess what they contained. One had felt like a book, but the remainder were indistinguishable. I thought about the ring, now hidden upstairs, and silently congratulated myself for my thoughtfulness.

We spent the evening relaxing, sharing a bottle of fine wine, and watching a film. Mrs Ballard had stocked the fridge with a fabulous array of food, so, after checking it all out, I made us caviar and blini, topped off with smoked salmon, and hard boiled quails eggs. She'd even provided turkey sausages for the girls.

I was woken up early the next morning by Elle, placing a coffee beside me, and declaring, "it's Christmas Day baby. Santa's been, and you have a stocking to open. I peeled open my eyes, to see her beaming at me, clearly excited.

"Ok, I'm awake, just let me drink my coffee." I struggled up onto my elbows, and glanced at the clock. "Elle, it's quarter to six."

"I know, but I've been waiting patiently so that you could have a lay in. The girls are up too, and are waiting by the tree." Her excitement was infectious, so I took a quick sip of coffee, and swung my legs out of bed. She handed me a robe, and carried my coffee downstairs while I quickly used the bathroom, and slipped the ring into the pocket of my robe.

I laughed at the sight of the two spaniels sitting, staring at the pile of gifts, and wondered if they'd copied Elle, who'd probably been doing the exact same thing. She'd already sorted them into piles of hers, mine, and the spaniels.

"So how do you want to do this? One at a time? Spaniels first? Or a big rip fest?" I didn't want to admit that I was extremely excited myself. It wasn't terribly manly to bounce up and down over a pile of presents. I noticed that my pile had gotten bigger overnight.

"They look so pretty that we really should take our time, and fully savour each one....." She trailed off.

"Rip fest then?" I grinned at her.

"Go for it."

Like a pair of kids, we tore open our gifts, with the spaniels leaping about in the paper, having a good time too. I loved all my presents, some were jokey, some useful, and some extravagant. Elle loved hers too, piling them up by the side of her to have a closer look at later. When we'd finished, she launched herself at me, planting kisses all over my face. "Thank you baby, I love all mine." She squealed between kisses.

"I love mine too," I said, pulling her into a hug. "Thank you. It's the first time I've ever done that." She looked quizzical. "Ripped open a big pile of presents," I clarified, "and it was great fun."

She kissed my nose. "Every year, we should do this. I don't care what you buy me, as long as I get to do a ripfest."

I laughed, "I'm sure I'll always buy you nice things, that'll never change. So, did I get it right?"

"Perfect, totally, utterly, perfect." She almost glowed with happiness.

"There's one more gift." I stated. My stomach began to churn with nerves. *Maybe I should do this later, when she's had a drink? No. Man up.*

"There's more? I am spoilt."

"Yes, but in order to have it, you need to answer a question first." *Here goes.* I pulled the little ring box out of my pocket, and opened it, to show her the glittering ring. She must have caught on, because her hand flew up to her mouth, and she gave me a searching look.

"Is this what I think it is?" She murmured, giving nothing away. I nodded.

Deep breath. "Elle, will you marry me?" *This is fucking terrifying.*

She smiled, a soft, shy smile. "Of course I will." My heart stopped. Relief, and elation flooded through me. With shaky hands, I pulled the ring out of its little slot, and slipped it onto her finger. She held it up to stare at it. "It's beautiful, perfect."

"I helped design it for you," I told her proudly.

"It's gorgeous, like you...I can't wait to show it off."

"Well, you'll have to wait another fortnight, it looks beautiful on you, you'll have to take my word for it."

She stared at it a bit more. "I'm gonna be flashing it around everywhere. I want the world to know that I'm yours, and you're mine."

"They'll know soon enough," I reassured her, "I'll do a press release when we get back from holiday."

"Elle Porenski," she mused, "I'll have to practice my new signature."

"You're going to take my surname?" I asked, slightly surprised. I'd half expected her to keep her English surname for her professional life.

"Of course," she said, "I think it would be weird to have different surnames." A worry that I hadn't even been aware of, disappeared. She'd be mine in every way. I kissed her softly.

"Thank you," I said. She looked quizzical. "For being mine, for taming me."

"Did I do that?"

"Oh yes. Now, changing the subject, I really need some coffee."

"Surprised you don't need anything stronger after that," she giggled.

The rest of Christmas Day was rather lovely. We ate fabulous food, walked in the woods, made love several times, and played with the spaniels until they conked out with exhaustion. That evening, we lay on the sofas watching telly, and drinking wine. Elle was scoffing quality street, which she claimed were 'traditional'. "So, have you thought about where you'd like to get married?" I asked, nonchalantly.

She shook her head. "I don't mind at all, it's not as if I've got family to please. I'll leave where and when up to you."

"Ok. I'll give it some thought," I lied, secretly delighted. My insides fizzed with excitement.

The next morning, we made our way to Gatwick for an early take off slot, after kissing, and hugging the spaniels goodbye. It was a shame they couldn't join us, but Mustique had strict rules on animals being brought in from abroad, so we left them at home.

I was getting better and better with each flight, managing the take-off without throwing up, and even being able to relax, and eat the breakfast that was served on board, washed down with plenty of Krug. "So how come you can walk about now?" Elle asked after I'd returned from the loo.

"When you were shot, I had to borrow Karl's plane, which didn't have anything for me to pee into, so I was forced to get up and use the bathroom. I suppose once you've done it once, it's not such a big deal."

"Does that mean we can have a mile high?" She looked all hopeful.

"Not sure about that. I doubt if my dick would co-operate. I'm still scared of flying."

"Hmm, might give it a try one day. Did you know there's a bedroom at the back of the plane?"

"Yeah. Nico's probably snoozing in it as we speak."

She looked down the plane to where all the security detail were seated. "Yeah, he's not in his seat."

Mustique airport was basically a landing strip and a large shed. The heat hit us as soon as we stepped off the plane. "This is just what the doctor ordered," said Elle, stretching her good arm. The villa Galina had rented was delightful, right on the beach, and beautifully appointed. It came with a chef, a butler, and a housekeeper.

"This place is so beautiful," sighed Elle, "how did you find it?"

"I didn't, Galina did. I gather it belongs to a computer billionaire."

We changed into swimwear, and took a walk around the grounds, and along the beach. It really was paradise, with its crystal waters gently lapping at the white sand, and the sun caressing our winter pale skin.

We spent the first few days exploring the island, and relaxing in the pool. I'd sneaked off to speak to the minister, and double check that everything was set for our wedding day, which would be New Year's Eve. He assured me that everything had been taken care of, and all we had to do was turn up. Galina had organised a wedding planner to set it all up, and look after all the details. Oscar and Lucy would arrive the day before.

"I have a little surprise for you," I told her, after reading a text from Oscar telling me they'd arrived, and were on their way over.

"I love surprises," she said, "go on."

"We have some visitors coming."

She looked quizzical. "who?" Just then, Oscar and Lucy walked out onto the terrace. Elle squealed, as did Lucy, and they all hugged each other. I motioned for the butler to bring some champagne.

"How come?" She asked, her eyes boring into me.

"Well, we need some guests at our wedding," I said.

"And you need someone to give you away," added Oscar. Elle stood open mouthed.

"Did you know about this?" She asked Lucy, who looked shocked.

She shook her head. "No, Osc only told me we were having a few days away." She turned to him. "How on earth did you manage to keep that quiet?"

"Pair of sneaky beggars..." began Elle, smiling happily. "I haven't got a dress or anything though."

"All taken care of," I said, smug. "There's a selection hanging up in the spare room. Just choose the one you like. I took care of everything baby."

"You are bloody wonderful, you know that?" She said, beaming at me. "Come on Luce, let's check out these dresses." The pair of them skipped off into the villa to see what was there.

"That went well," Oscar remarked, flopping down on a sun lounger, and pulling off his T-shirt.

"Yeah, she's pretty difficult to faze. Takes everything in her stride. She's going to take my surname, she's already told me that," I said proudly.

"Quite right too. I don't like all this 'keeping the maiden name' business. I fully expect Lucy to become a Golding." I caught his eye, and grinned at him.

"Your turn next." He rolled his eyes at me.

"Maybe, but I'll have to do it at the castle, with full rigmarole, a dozen bridesmaids and page boys, and my mother done up like a wedding cake," he pointed out. "I envy you being able to do this so easily. No foreign dignitaries to invite, no protocols to adhere to, and no hassles. You're a lucky man." I glanced over at him, a new understanding dawning. For all his wealth and status, he was tightly bound by the chains that his position in life entailed. *He envies me.*

I might be a Russian mongrel, but at least I was a free one. I could marry the love of my life barefoot on a beach, live where we wanted, and spend my money recklessly if it pleased me. The good lord had expectations to live up to, and his social status depended on that. His wedding day would be like a military operation, mine would be happy and relaxed. *Yeah, I'm lucky, they don't come more free than Elle and I.*

"You can do what you like, surely? You are head of the family after all." I only said it to make him feel better. We both knew it wasn't true.

"Can you imagine facing my mother to tell her she'd missed out on being queen for a day?" He pointed out.

"Hmm, I see what you mean," I agreed, secretly thrilled that at last, I had something that he couldn't ever have.

"The press will be going nuts when you announce this back home. You realise that? One of the world's most eligible bachelors off the market. 'Hello' will be pissed that they didn't get wedding pictures."

I shrugged, "I didn't want pictures splashed everywhere. This is about our marriage, not just a wedding day. The papers and gossip rags can have a press release, but that's all. I don't want our life dissected by the public."

"I'll make sure Lucy stays off twitter and facebook then, I know what she's like. Is everyone else involved sworn to secrecy?"

"Oh yes. All signed non disclosure agreements. I don't want any press showing up."

"Have you done a pre-nup?" He asked.

I shook my head. "No. I want her to understand that she's rich. It's a big hang-up of hers, being poor. I'd trust her not to fleece me in the event of a divorce."

The girls returned, Elle declaring that all the dresses were gorgeous, but she'd made her choice. Oscar checked that Lucy hadn't tweeted or facebooked anything, and impressed on her the importance of keeping quiet, pointing out that an influx of press would easily spoil things.

Our wedding day went without a hitch. Nico had guards patrolling the perimeters of the property, but nobody tried to gatecrash. Elle looked perfect, as she was brought out to the beach on Oscar's arm, to be 'given' to me, as her new husband, and Lucy daintily cried into a hanky as we said our vows, promising to love each other until death do us part.

I'd never really given much thought to what my wedding day would be like, men don't tend to dwell on such things that much, but I'd expected to be nervous, even sad to say goodbye to my bachelor days, but as I slipped the ring on Elle's finger, I simply felt a sense of calm. It was like owning my very own angel.

Chapter 20

Oscar was correct, the press went nuts when we returned from Mustique, hounding Elle everywhere she went, and inundating my PR team with interview requests. Her return to work was a bit rocky too. The new junior partner was doing his best to sideline her, and take all the credit for the clients she was pulling in. She seemed to concentrate more on our companies, as I kept pointing out that they were hers too.

I broached the subject of her taking over as head of legal rather carefully. I knew her big ambition was to be a partner in Pearson Hardwick, and I was wary of dismissing her big ambition, but I was also concerned that her colleagues had an issue with her being my wife.

"I really don't want to allow Peter to get to me. I'm made of stronger stuff than that. I'm just fed up with all the snide comments about not needing to work. He can go swing if he thinks I'm handing all my clients over to him, just because he has a job title." She pulled our dinner out of the warming drawer, sniffing Mrs Watton's creation appreciatively.

"Just don't put yourself through the wringer unnecessarily, you don't need to work there. We own a vast company, which could do with a head of legal, if that's what you want. I just hate seeing you unhappy," I told her as she put my plate down in front of me.

"What would you like me to do, husband?" She teased.

"Well, wife, what I'd like you to do is build a dynasty of sons for me to pass on all these companies to, failing that, I'd support you in whatever made you happy." We'd become close enough for me to be upfront about my desire for a family, preferably a large one. We were both young enough to take our time though, and I wasn't about to pressure her.

"What'll you do if we had a load of girls?" She asked, smiling.

"I'd keep going till we had a boy. I'm Russian, remember. We like having sons."

"Bloody caveman."

"That's me," I quipped, grinning at her, "what do you say to getting a bit of practice in this evening?" She looked quizzical. "Practice, you know, in how to make babies."

"That sounds like a plan. I might shock you one of these days, and forget my shot. You'll soon change your tune."

"I won't be shocked. We're married, rich, and young, perfect for having a family." I sipped my wine, and gazed at her. My beautiful, clever wife was unfazed. She slipped the spaniels some lamb, prompting adoring looks.

"Changing the subject," she said pointedly, "Joan Lester asked me for an interview today, to give Vogue an exclusive story. I told her I'd ask you first."

"If you're going to do any interviews at all, better to give our own magazine the exclusive I suppose. Just make sure that we ok it before it goes to press. I don't want any of our personal details discussed, and I don't want to give your colleagues any ammunition."

"I'm over giving a shit what they think," she asserted, surprising me. *Eight months ago, you were terrified of them finding out you came from South London, now you don't give a shit. You've come a long way baby.* "If they want to be snotty, then they can. I won't apologise for getting married." She paused. "Just because I married a drop dead gorgeous billionaire, that's no reason for them to be jealous." She smirked. *I think you'll find they're shitty because you got taken off the market, and all those devoted saps realise they're never going to be in with a chance.*

"I doubt very much they're jealous because they like my smile baby. The women maybe, but not the men."

"Funny enough, the women at work aren't so bad. Priti and I went out for lunch today. She just thought it was all very romantic. Wasn't arsey about it at all." I was quite gratified hearing about how wonderful my big, romantic gesture had been. I wasn't a naturally emotional man, but for Elle, I made the effort. Our wedding had been perfect, especially for two orphans. She still struggled to get her head around how wealthy she was though. When we'd had the conversation, shortly after we tied the knot, it had floored her when I spelt out to her the full extent of our net worth. As soon as we got back, I presented her with a debit card for our new joint account. She'd been slightly overwhelmed, and a bit reticent about using it, until I pointed out that I'd put twenty mil in there for her use. I'd loved all the sexy lingerie she'd brought home after her first shopping trip.

"Your real friends won't be nasty, but there will always be people with an agenda, especially when you have something that they can't have. Don't forget that this Peter will work hard all his life, and never amass even one percent of what you currently have. I'm used to the envy, and actually enjoy it, but it's all new to you. Don't forget that it was a problem for them when you were poor as well."

"True. It's odd being too rich though." I smiled at her as she said it. *No such thing as too rich.*

"They should be more careful. If they drive you out, they'd lose a lot of clients. Peter shouldn't let his envy cloud his judgement like this. What has Lewis said?"

"Not much. He's so tied up with his workload at the moment, I don't think he's terribly aware of how Peter's behaving."

We snuggled up in bed early that evening, after a lovely fuck on the sofa. Getting married hadn't caused our sexual fascination with each other to wane at all, if anything, we'd achieved a new closeness which hadn't been there before. I was able to show her my slightly pervy side, while she was allowed to be wanton and insatiable. I'd never had so much sex in my life. I think I fucked her on just about every surface in our apartment. We were working our way through the Sussex house too.

A few days later, Elle called me mid morning to see if I was free for lunch. "I have news," she said.

"Ok, I'll meet you at the bistro at twelve," I told her, intrigued. I was busy going over the figures for the new handset. It had been a great success, lauded by the critics as the best handset on the market. Apple had been knocked off the number one spot that week, and were probably taking it apart to look for patent infringement. I was happy that our technology was so new and innovative that they wouldn't have a hope of finding something of theirs. Needless to say, we'd be checking their next handset to see if they'd copied us. I'd quietly won the last lawsuit they'd brought against me, so was confident they wouldn't take me on again in a hurry. The new handset was also making our App Store a shedload of money. Elle's friend, James, had devised a game which had been a massive hit, and was exclusive to us. Furious frogs was earning him an eye watering royalty, and driving sales of the Bel phone through the roof, exceeding all our expectations.

Elle was already in the bistro when I arrived, with Roger seated just behind her. She'd had to accept having 24 hour security when we married, which she struggled to get used to. "Hey baby, how was your morning?" I asked, before giving her a soft kiss.

"Interesting," she replied, being rather cryptic. I settled myself into the booth, and we ordered.

"So come on then, what's this news?" I asked.

"Odey and Corbett have approached me, via a head hunter, to offer me a junior partner position in their corporate division."

I stared at her, "Baby, that's fantastic news. What did you say?"

"I told them I'd think about it." She gazed into her wine glass, not meeting my eyes.

"What's there to think about? I thought this was your ambition? I know that Pearson Hardwick knocked them off the number one spot when you gained Beltan, and all the banks, but if you moved to them, it would put them back there."

"I'm aware of that."

"So, why are you hesitating? Please don't tell me it's loyalty to Pearson Hardwick, when they passed you over for promotion, and put a dickhead in charge of your department."

She took a deep breath. "I'm not sure it's what I want anymore, but I worry that you fell in love with me because I'm a clever lawyer, and if I stopped being ambitious, you'd get bored with me."

"You have a thought loop?" I asked. She nodded.

"Ok. Let's clear this up. I fell in love with you, not your job. Your intellect would remain, even if you weren't a lawyer. Second, I would dearly love you to give up work, and concentrate on building me a dynasty, thirdly, you made partner, even if you don't accept it, you made it. That's an amazing achievement, and you should be proud of it. I'll support you in whatever decision you feel is right for you."

"Who would have thought you'd make such a good husband?" She teased.

"I know, I surprise myself at times."

"They've asked to meet with me this evening. I think I'll go along, and see what they have to say. Maybe I need to get this whole 'partner' thing out of my system once and for all. I mean, my mum sacrificed a lot to get me there, so I feel like I owe it to her to make it."

"I can understand that," I said, secretly thrilled with the way things were going. She could reach her ambition, then give it up and have a family. I'd been thinking about it a lot, reasoning that we should have lots of children, rather than inflict our 'only child' status' on another generation.

"I'll be home a bit late then tonight. I'm meeting with the partners at half six."

I was home long before her, the spaniels greeting me with excitement. Mrs Watton told me that they'd had their trainer in that morning, who had managed to get Bella to sit and stay, and had their groomer in that afternoon for fur-dos. "Bella forgot all her lessons from that morning, bit the groomer, and did a dirty protest in the lounge," she said. "Tania's been a good girl today though."

"You both look very pretty," I told them, they wagged their tails happily. "Elle's got a meeting, so can you put our meals in the warming drawer please? I'll wait and eat with her."

I got on with some work while I waited, ok, I surfed the net, reading reviews of the new Bel phone. I checked my personal emails, grimacing when I saw one from Carl, telling me he'd seen the news that I'd married, and asking why I hadn't been in touch for so long. I didn't bother to reply.

She got home around eight, and told me all about her meeting during dinner. They'd been willing to give her a 'golden hello', to move to them, a junior partnership, with guaranteed promotion to equity partner in two years. Her salary and bonus percentage would be higher as well.

"So? Are you going to accept?" I asked.

"I already have. I'll be starting there the first of April. I have to give three months notice, although my guess is that they'll put me on garden leave to try and cut me off from my clients."

"All your clients came from Oscar and myself, so there'll have a bit of a hopeless task on their hands. Anyway, congratulations,

Mrs-partner-in-a-law-firm." I raised my glass, and toasted her success. After dinner, she typed out her resignation letter.

I had a phone call the next day from Ms Pearson. "Is this your doing?" She asked.

"Nothing to do with me at all. She was approached by a head hunter, and after being so badly treated at work, and so unhappy, I encouraged her to explore the offer, but I didn't instigate it, and neither did she," I replied, rather angry that Ms Pearson had spoken to me about it, rather than take Elle's word for how events had occurred.

"Badly treated? How do you work that one out?"

I let her have it with both barrels. "I watched her work 48 hours with no sleep during that rights issue, tackle an extremely difficult and complex case, coming out on top against Goldman's, then get passed over for promotion, with her wanker of a colleague trying to take credit for her hard work. I'm witnessing her being bullied and sidelined at work by the tosser that you promoted instead of her, and quite frankly, she's had enough. She didn't look elsewhere, they came to her. Her new boss appears too stupid to realise that all those new clients are with your firm because of her. Pretty much all of them came from either myself or Oscar Golding, who gave her away at our wedding. On all the retaining contracts, we all insisted that Elle was our co-ordinating lawyer. No Elle, no retaining contract." *Suck on that.*

"Peter's a talented lawyer. He'd be able to look after your legal requirements." *Oh please.*

"He's bullying my wife. Would you trust a man who did that? Come on Ms Pearson, you're not a stupid woman. Did you really think we'd all stick around when you'd run Elle out of the company? I see firsthand how hard she works, her work ethic is astonishing. I'm not surprised that Odey and Corbett have offered her the moon on a stick."

The Taming of the Oligarch

"Odey and Corbett? She didn't tell me that bit." *Oops.* "I thought she'd be taking over the legal dept at your company."

"Her company you mean? No, sadly, for me, she still has ambitions far beyond a mere legal department. I'm not sure why she didn't tell you, but she's been offered a partner position by them. Probably didn't want to be seen to be offering an ultimatum. She's got rather a lot of integrity you see." I was getting bitchy, and knew it, but I was enjoying myself.

"I see, well, thank you for the insights Mr Porenski. I'll be meeting with Ms Reynolds this afternoon."

"Mrs Porenski, you mean," I corrected her. The line went dead.

I wrapped up early that day, and went home via the florist, picking up some nice flowers for Elle. I fully expected floods of tears, and a picture of misery to walk through the door.

She seemed quite alright when she arrived home. Kissing me hungrily, and pulling me into a tight hug. "You told Ms Pearson about Odey and Corbett, didn't you?"

"She thought I'd nicked you to head up Beltan, called me to accuse me of luring you away to work in your own company. I didn't realise she didn't know. Sorry."

"She matched their offer. I wouldn't have been able to tell her the offer that was on the table without it looking like a Dutch auction, so it worked out well that you did."

"And?"

"And I turned her down, Odey and Corbett too. I hope you don't mind."

I was a bit lost for words. "Why?"

"Because I want....more from life. My mum might have died poor, but she had lots of friends, people who cared about her. I love you more than I ever thought I could, and I want to make you happy. My education won't be wasted, as our companies will always need a head of legal, and we can have a married life that doesn't just consist of an hour together of a night because I've worked so late." I stood open mouthed. "You're not disappointed are you?"

I pulled her into an embrace, and kissed her softly. "No, I'm delighted. I'm happy that this is your decision, and that you made partner at Pearson Hardwick. Only for your own sake though. You won't spend your life wondering 'what if'."

"I cancelled my shot too," she murmured, "I'm on garden leave now, so....that's it. I'm free to build a dynasty."

Four months later, we sat on the edge of the bath, side by side, my beautiful wife and I, watching as a little stick developed a thin, blue line. "That's it," she squealed, we did it! We started our dynasty." I smiled at her beaming face, and kissed her softly.

"Now I don't want any thought loops thinking I won't want you when you're pregnant. I'll always want you."

"Even when I'm fat and my ankles are swollen?"

"Especially when you and your ankles are fat. I can't wait." I wanted to fuss over her all through her pregnancy. At least with her working alongside me, I could keep an eye on her at work. When the time came for her to stop work, I planned to take some time off with her and the baby.

"You carry on like this, they'll kick you out of the Russian caveman club."

"Good. I'd rather be right where I am now. I love our love."

"I love our love too." She kissed me again, this woman who had taken a sledgehammer to my barriers, and taught me how to be 'in love'.

The End

Other Titles by D A Latham

The Beauty and the Blonde

A Very Corporate Affair Book 1

A Very Corporate Affair Book 2

A Very Corporate Affair Book 3

A Very Corporate Affair Book 1

Chapter 1

I stood on Welling station shivering in the cold, and trying to calm the butterflies fluttering around in my stomach. Today was the day of judgement at work. The day I would find out if my training contract would turn into a fully fledged job at Pearson Hardwick, one of the big four law firms in London. If today went well, I would become a qualified, and gainfully employed, corporate lawyer. If today went badly, then six years of studying would be down the drain.

It had been a real slog to get this far. I came from a working class family, who didn't believe in social mobility, and thought I was wasting my time. I had worked hard at Bexley Grammar to get top grades and secure a place at Cambridge to study law and business. I had kept my head down through university and had put in enough effort to gain a first. A year long legal practitioner course led to my traineeship, and another two years of intense concentration at Pearson Hardwick had followed, as I threw myself into the opportunity they had given me.

I looked around the grey, featureless platform. At six thirty in the morning, only the early bird commuters were present. Pale, pasty looking men in badly fitting suits looked resigned to another miserable day in mundane jobs. There was not one exciting or interesting looking person there. Suburbia doesn't really breed the people who make you sit up and take notice, I thought to myself. All the more reason to escape as quickly as possible.

I'd enjoyed Cambridge as it had been a huge relief to be around intelligent, informed people who had been passionate about academia. My mum had never understood a thirst for knowledge, and had tried to get me to lower my aspirations and take a 'nice shop job' at sixteen. The thought of returning home tonight unemployed and a failure, confirming all her warnings about 'getting ideas above my station', made the butterflies ten times worse.

I arrived at the offices at quarter past seven, pausing in the stunning wood panelled lobby of the ancient law firm, and wondered if it would be the last time I would walk through on my way to work. I ducked into the cloakroom to change into my heels and shed my coat.

"Good morning Elle," said Roger, the security man who was based in the lobby, as I waited for the lift up to my floor.

"Morning Roger, today's the day."

"I wish you the best of luck. I'm sure you'll be fine, the time you get here every day must have shown them how conscientious you are."

"Thanks. Hope so." I smoothed the front of my neat pencil skirt, and gripped my handbag a little tighter.

Once I had reached my floor, I made my way straight to my desk to switch on my computer, check my emails, and just wait. All the cases I had been assigned to work on had been completed, and as my traineeship had been near its end, they hadn't given me any new ones. For the last week or so, I had just been assisting the other trainees with their cases, doing their drudge work, and helping out in the filing room. I had felt that the lack of new cases being put my way was a bad omen, and if they were keeping me, they wouldn't have worried about giving me fresh work.

Checking my emails, I saw one from Mr Lambert, my line manager. I opened it.

From: Adam Lambert
To: Elle Reynolds
Subject: Interview
Date: 28th March 2013

Dear Ms Reynolds,
  Your interview today will be held at 11am in room 7 on the 4th floor. In attendance will be Ms Pearson, Mr Jones, and myself.

Kind Regards
Adam Lambert

I stared at the email for a minute or two. It wasn't giving anything away. I decided I need a cup of tea. In the small kitchenette area, I realised that my hands were shaking as I filled the kettle. I needed to get a grip. The last thing I wanted to do was show nerves or weakness when the rest of my workmates arrived. Cool, calm and collected was the image I wanted to project at work, not needy, insecure or scared, no matter how I felt inside.

As the other trainees filed in, I could see how rattled they were. It was interview time for all of us who began in 2011, and usually only a quarter of the intake would be offered permanent jobs. Scanning the faces, I tried to figure out who had screwed up, who had excelled, and who would be a tough call.

"Why are you looking so pensive?" Lucy demanded, standing in front of my desk, "we all know you'll be ok, miss perfect," she teased.

"I don't know about that, they could easily decide I'm not posh enough to fit in," I said, fully aware of my lack of private schooling and accompanying posh accent.

"Don't be daft, the fact that you have a perfect record and are a bloody genius will easily outweigh the problem of a glottal stop." She smiled to let me know she was teasing.

"Wha times yuh mee-ing?" I said, in full south London accent, taking the piss.

"11.30. You?"

"11. Good luck."

"You too. If it's good news, I'll treat us both to lunch in Bennies." Lucy came from a wealthy background and didn't have to watch the pennies as I did. She sauntered off, seemingly unconcerned about her fate being decided upstairs.

At ten to eleven, I rinsed my hands in cold water to avoid a sweaty handshake, and made my way up to the floor above. The secretary directed me to take a seat just outside the meeting room to await my turn. The door swung open, and a fellow trainee, John Peterson, came out looking as white as a sheet. I caught his eye, and he gave an almost imperceptible shake of his head. He had been one of the 'sure things' I had judged earlier that morning. My stomach sank into my boots.

"Miss Reynolds, you may go in now," said the secretary. I plastered on my best fake smile and entered the room. The three interviewers sat behind a long table, with a single chair placed in front of them. Mr Lambert smiled at me, and asked me to take a seat. I shook their hands, and sat down.

"Good morning Miss Reynolds, I'm sure you must be nervous, so I won't waste time on pleasantries," began Ms Pearson. My heart sank. "You have the highest work output rate of your year group, the best attendance and punctuality rate, and the best report from your superiors." My heart hammered, and I tried to stop myself blushing at her compliment. Ms Pearson was a managing partner, so remaining in control in front of her was extremely important.

"So I'm delighted to be able to offer you a permanent position at Pearson Hardwick. Now your report states that you would like to specialise in corporate law, is that correct?"

I pulled myself together quickly enough to answer her, "yes, that's correct."

"Good. We have an opening in our corporate department at Canary Wharf. You can begin there on Monday. For the rest of this week you will be on paid leave, as Mr Lambert has indicated that you have taken no holiday at all this year. The salary will be eighty thousand per year, plus the grade 3 benefit package. Do you have any questions?" Ms Pearson looked at me intently.

"No questions, and thank you Ms Pearson, I won't let you down," I said, barely able to take it all in.

"I'm sure you won't. Now, please head over to HR, where they have your new contract ready for you to sign, and sort out your package, then I suggest you have some rest until Monday."

I smiled widely at the panel, "thank you for this opportunity," I said before heading out.

Over at HR I signed my new contract, collected the details of my new workplace, and perused the list of benefits I could choose as part of my package. As I didn't have a car to be subsidised, I chose gym membership, private health care and an enhanced pension. The HR lady assured me that the gym at the Canary Wharf building was superb, and useful for showering and changing facilities if I needed them. On my way back to my floor, I bumped into Lucy, who was sporting a wide grin

"Great news Elle, I got family law, just as I wanted. What about you?"

"Good news for me too, I got corporate, so Canary Wharf here I come," I replied with an equally big smile.

"Wow! They are the most prestigious offices in the firm, you must have done really well. I'll come and visit you there. Now, shall we meet by your old cubicle as I have to see HR before we go to lunch?"

"Great, see you in a bit."

I went back to my cubicle with my shoulders back, and a lightness I had never felt before. Success felt fantastic, and for the first time ever I could escape my background.

Bennies was a bistro type bar tucked away down one of the tiny passages that characterised the city. Lucy ordered a bottle of Moët while we waited for our overpriced sandwiches. We clinked glasses and gossiped about who got kicked out and who was kept on. It turned out that out of a hundred who began the training contract with us, only fifteen had been offered full contracts.

"So, what's your next plan? Are you moving nearer work?" Lucy asked.

"Sure am, I have the rest of the week off, so it's a good opportunity to look for a flat share or a studio. Mum's boyfriend wants to move in, and it's too small a flat to have all three of us there, so it's time to move out." I hugged myself with glee. Escape from the moaning about my getting up early, use of hot water and aversion to junk food.

Lucy broke my reverie, "my brother's friend is looking for a flatmate, he lives near Canada square. Would you like me to call him?"

"Oh yes please, that would be great." She pulled her phone out of her bag and prodded the screen.

"Hi James, it's Lucy Elliott. Have you still got that room available? Only one of my friends is looking for a flat near Canary Wharf." She listened to the other person, injecting a 'mmm' every now and then. "Yes it's a she, and she is a nice, hardworking, quiet, corporate lawyer. Yes I work with her.....yes.....no......ok I'll send her along this afternoon. Text me the address yeah." Lucy ended the call.

"Room's still available then?" I asked.

"Yep. He's a bit fussy about who he shares with. James is a nice guy, and likes a quiet life. He works from home, so needs a flat mate who goes out to work, and isn't too noisy." Lucy's phone chirped as a text arrived with the address, which she forwarded to me.

A couple of other trainees from our year arrived to celebrate with us, nicking our champagne, much to my relief. I didn't want to view a flat half cut.

After lunch, I headed over to the docklands, taking the DLR. I had to double check the address, as the building looked way too swanky to be a flat share type of place. Pressing the buzzer, a voice came through, "who is it?"

"Elle Reynolds, Lucy sent me."

"I'll buzz you in. Take the lift to the fourteenth floor. My door is right in front of you." The buzzer sounded, and I pushed my way into a marble and glass lobby. I took in the silence, the deep carpet, and sense of restrained opulence. The lift was large, mirrored and silently sped straight up to floor fourteen, which I noticed, was the highest floor.

The door in front of the lift was open, and what could only be described as a bear was standing in the doorway. It was hard to gauge his age with all the facial hair, but I took a guess at early thirties. He was tall and broad, dressed in jeans and an old t-shirt which showed off muscular, hairy arms. Through all the long, curly hair and copious beard, a pair of twinkly blue eyes reflected a smile. "You must be James? I'm Elle," I said, extending my hand out to him. He shook it warmly and invited me in.

"Did you find it alright?" he enquired, "and would you like a coffee?"

"Yes it was easy to get here, and yes I'd love a coffee if you're having one." He showed me through to what could only be described as a state of the art kitchen. James pulled two cups out of a cupboard and pulled two pods out of a drawer.

"What sort of coffee? I can do americano, espresso, latte or cappuccino."

"A latte would be lovely," I said, awed that there was a choice. If my mum remembered to buy fresh milk it was an event, and yet this hairy, bearded, bear-person had fresh coffee and fresh milk. I was impressed.

I found out that James was an app developer, and had built a few hit apps, which had enabled him to buy the apartment. He was working on a new app, and worked from home, so needed some peace during the day. I told him all about my promotion, and we toasted my success with fresh coffee, which made me giggle. He explained that Canada Square was quite literally round the corner, and my walk to work would be around five minutes.

"So why do you want a flat mate?" I asked.

He squirmed slightly, "I work from home, and sometimes barely speak to a living soul from one day to the next. I guess I get a bit lonely here on my own." He looked a bit sad.

"No girlfriend?" I wanted to make sure there was nobody to get jealous that a woman was moving in. The last thing I wanted was to put anyone's nose out of joint.

"Nope. My last girlfriend went to live in Australia, so don't worry, nobody to get arsey about a girl living here. I have to ask, any boyfriend?"

"No. I've been working like a demon for the last few years. No time for a man." Much to my mother's disgust, I thought.

"Well, I have no issue with you bringing friends back, but I'd rather not have a man move in here, so if you get serious with anyone, please bear that in mind."

"Will do. Can I see the room?"

"Sure, this way." James led me down a short corridor and opened a door. The room was enormous, with floor to ceiling windows covering one wall. There was just a large bed and a cabinet with a TV in the room. It looked a bit sparse. I walked over to the windows and stared at the view of the Thames.

"There's a dressing room through here, and an ensuite through that door," said James, pointing at two doors. Looking in the first one, I found a beautifully fitted out walk in wardrobe, with acres of hanging space, shoe racks and a dressing table. My paltry clothing collection would take up about a tenth of the space.

The ensuite was lovely. It had a large, deep bath, a separate shower, and a heated towel rail. It all looked brand new and pristine.

"How much is the rent?" I asked, suddenly nervous that I wouldn't be able to afford to live in this luxury.

"A thousand a month, but that includes all bills. Does that suit?" I breathed a sigh of relief.

"Fantastic, it's a deal." We shook hands. I arranged to pay the deposit and first month's rent into James bank account via my laptop, and he gave me a key.

We bonded over another cup of coffee. I really warmed to James. He was just the right mixture of intelligence, geekiness and humour. We had thrashed out some basic house rules which, thankfully, didn't include hot water usage or rationing the gas. He also mentioned that he was an early riser, and hoped that it wouldn't be an issue for me to be quiet late at night. We both laughed when I pointed out that ten pm was staying up late for me.

I headed back to Welling with a spring in my step, eager to begin my new, London life. As predicted, my mum could barely contain her excitement at my moving out. She dug out the News Shopper and found an ad for a 'man with a van' who would be able to move all my belongings at short notice. He was able to do Thursday, so that left Wednesday to pack up, and get everything ready. I would still have a few days to unpack, settle in, and explore before starting work.

Mum was eager to help pack my belongings, and I actually didn't have much. The whole lot took us a morning to box and bag up. I had invested carefully in good work clothes, but apart from that, I didn't really buy a lot. Plus I had used the money I earned during my training contract to pay off my student loans, and build some savings, rather than blow it on clothes and makeup.

That afternoon, I decided to hop on a bus to Bluewater and treat myself to a haircut and some new work outfits ready for Monday.

I went into the swankiest salon there, and booked in for a trim. I kept my hair long, but the stylist added layers, and the whole effect was classy and grown up. Delighted with my new hair, I wandered round the boutiques trying on clothes until I found a fabulous navy dress and jacket combo which fitted like a dream, and projected just the image I was aiming for. I stocked up on tights and toiletries and bought a pair of navy heels to match my new dress. In a mad moment of optimism, I even bought a box of condoms before heading home.

The next morning a slightly grubby van pulled up outside the flat, and an even grubbier, skinny man got out. He wasted no time flinging my stuff in the back while I wrote out my new address for mum.

"You have fun, and don't work too hard," were her parting words of wisdom. No doubt Ray, her boyfriend was waiting round the corner for my van to pull away before rolling up with his bags.

As we pulled away from Welling, the excitement rose in my belly. This was the moment I had worked towards for six long years. My life could finally begin.

James helped van man with my bags and boxes, so with the three of us, it didn't take long. It took a further two hours to unpack and neatly hang my clothes in the closet.

"You don't have much stuff for a girl," said James, wandering in with two glasses of wine.

"I'm not a great shopper, and I've not had much spare cash to spend on clothes and stuff," I replied, a bit embarrassed by my meagre use of the dressing room. I aimed to spend 10% of my new salary on clothes every month to make sure I looked the part.

"Not criticising, just saying. I've got even less clothes than you," he said in a good natured way. He sat on the dressing table seat sipping his wine as I checked all my shoes for dirt before stowing them on the rack. He told me all about the new app he was working on, which sounded great, and described the other occupants of the building.

"The only unfriendly one is the fella on the floor below. Never says hello, and seems to bring lots of different women back. I saw one crying in the lobby once, said he threw her out. He's definitely one to stay away from."

"Thanks for warning me. He sounds delightful, not. Now is there a grocery store around here? I need to pick up a few bits."

"There's a small mart round the corner. What do you need?"

"Milk, bread, that kind of stuff."

"I had it all delivered today. There's loads in the fridge. I get everything ocado'd in. I have everything sorted for dinner tonight, thought you might be too busy with the move to worry about it."

"James, that's really kind of you, thank you. I'll pay you back."

"Nonsense, it's only a few groceries, and besides, I love to cook, but I never have anyone to cook for, so indulge me and let me prepare something." He smiled warmly, and wandered back to the kitchen area.

I hugged myself with glee. Sipping wine in a gorgeous apartment overlooking the river, with a new friend, and a new job. It was everything I'd imagined it would be.

"Elle," James yelled, "foods ready." I hurried into the kitchen as he dished up a pasta and tiger prawn concoction. He poured another two glasses of wine, and pushed one over to me.

"Bon appetite little Elle, and welcome to Canary Wharf. I hope you'll be very happy here." We clinked glasses.

"Thank you big James, and I'm sure I'm gonna love it." I took a bite of my pasta, it was all lemony and buttery, and delicious. "Wow, you are a great cook, this is gorgeous."

"You look like you need a bit of feeding up."

"I'm not a great eater. My mum only ever heated stuff up out of the freezer, so it was often better to go without than suffer the nightly unidentified breadcrumbed fare."

James laughed, a rich, deep, hearty laugh, "no wonder you're skinny. You need good, healthy, hearty food, especially with a pressurised job. Will they have you working all hours of the day and night?"

"Probably. I'm going in there as the lowest in the pecking order, so I'm in no doubt that I'll get the donkey work. Law is like that, hierarchy is everything. I'm pretty certain that I'll be given a cubby hole next to the bogs for my office, and the secretaries will be sly bitches. I don't mind though, I'm prepared to earn my stripes."

"I hated corporate life," James confided, "glad to be out of it. Hated sucking up to a useless wanker of a boss, and attending endless meetings. If I need a status meeting nowadays, I just look in a mirror."

"Do you always work alone? Or do you sometimes collaborate?" I asked.

"Always alone. I did one app a few years back with a designer, and it was a bit of a disaster, all style over substance, so since then, I do it all myself. So what made you go into law?"

I pondered his question. "Money really. Corporate law is a well paid profession, and I wanted to escape my background. I wanted to aim high, and I enjoy the intellectual rigour of law. I didn't want to be involved in criminal law because I hate grisly stuff, and family law is often emotionally draining. I like the detail of contract law, and the fact that its usually done in shiny, neat offices rather than police cells or prisons."

James smiled at me, "I admire your ambition, I wish I had more of it. I'm happy just sitting coding apps and dreaming up games."

"You did ok out of it," I said, sweeping my hand to indicate the apartment, "this place is fantastic."

"Yeah, I'm pretty lucky," he agreed.

I spent the first evening in my new home watching telly on the big flat screen in the living area. James had shown me how to use the coffee maker, and dishwasher, so I insisted he sat down while I cleared up after dinner, and made us both coffee. By nine, I was yawning, so bade him goodnight, and went to bed.

The next morning I was up at my normal time of half five. I wandered through to the kitchen to make tea, and discovered James boiling a kettle.

"Morning Elle, sleep well?"

"Morning, yeah great thanks. Is there enough water in the kettle for two?" James nodded. He looked even more dishevelled in his dressing gown and pyjamas, with his beard sticking out like bed hair. He pulled out another cup and threw a tea bag into it.

"So what's your agenda for today?"

"I'm gonna check out my new gym, pop into my new office to say hi, and explore my surroundings. Anything you need me to bring in?"

"Don't think so, I'll text you if I think of anything. I've got stuff in the fridge for dinner tonight, so don't worry about food."

"Ok, thanks, just let me know. I'm gonna take a shower now and head out." I took my tea back to my room and drank it while staring at the view from my window. After a luxurious shower, I dried my hair as I watched the stylist do, and applied a touch of makeup. I decided that trousers and flats were best bet for the day I had planned, so dressed in neat but trendy trousers and a simple cashmere jumper. As I wasn't sure what time the gym would open, I went back to the kitchen and made another tea. James wasn't around, so I sat quietly at the island and read through the bumf on the gym that HR had given me. It all looked pretty straightforward. I would have unlimited use of the facilities, and only pay for personal training. I checked the opening hours, finding that it opened at six. I would be able to do a workout in the mornings and still be at my desk by seven thirty, perfect. I finished my tea and placed mine and James cups in the dishwasher before heading down.

The lift stopped and the doors slid open while I was looking at my map of the area, and I automatically began to walk out, bumping straight into someone stepping in.

"I'm so sorry," I began, before noticing we were not in the lobby, and I had just bumped into Adonis himself. "I thought I was on the ground floor." I said lamely.

"Just be more careful," he snarled, before studiously ignoring me for the rest of the journey down. Must be the man James warned me about I thought. James didn't tell me he was sex on legs though. I surreptitiously studied him as he exited the lift. Short dark hair, bespoke suit, and a face that would be handsome if he smiled.

I was indeed five minutes away from the Canary Wharf tower, which rose majestically to top the surrounding skyscrapers. I followed the directions to the gym on the lower ground floor. It was a health enthusiasts dream, row upon row of state of the art equipment, complimentary towels, pristine changing rooms, and a full list of fitness classes. I booked in for an orientation session the following day, and picked up a class timetable. I exchanged my voucher from HR for my gym pass at the desk, and wandered around for half an hour, checking out the changing room and the machines.

My new office was based on the 34th floor of the tower, so at nine, I went up there to introduce myself. The receptionist was a pretty Asian girl, called Priti, who seemed efficient and welcoming. She introduced me to a few of the other lawyers, all of whom seemed friendly enough.

"I can show you where you'll be working," said a geeky, skinny man who introduced himself as Peter Dunn. "They told me you were starting Monday, so your desk is all ready."He showed me through a large open plan office full of people to a corridor of glass fronted offices. Pushing a door open, he revealed a large office with four desks. Two desks were occupied by men. Peter explained that he sat at the far end, and the final desk was earmarked for me. I introduced myself to the other two.

"I'm Adrian Jones, and he's Matt Barlow. So you're the ex trainee we have to get up to speed then?"

"That's me. I hope you don't mind having a newbie around," I said, hoping to disarm them. I knew that nobody liked babysitting newbies.

"I'm sure we'll cope, and it'll be nice having a bit of eye candy around, eh boys? This firm has an ugly secretary only policy," Adrian sniggered.

"I'll do my very best to look pretty gentlemen, just don't forget I'm not a secretary." I smiled to make them think I was teasing.

"If you wear a tight blouse I promise I won't get you making tea," quipped Matt.

"I'll see what I can do," I laughed, "as long as you'll be able to concentrate on your work if I'm in here with my cleavage on show."

"She's gonna have every hotshot in the tower salivating over her, you have no chance," laughed Peter, looking amused at the adolescent behaviour of his colleagues. I had fully expected sexist banter, and it all seemed quite harmless. Certainly my office mates seemed friendly enough, and I was confident I'd be able to handle them.

I didn't hang around long, as I wanted to explore the whole area. I discovered the vast shopping complex beneath the tower, looking out for decent lunch places and a dry cleaners. I found wine bars, restaurants, and pubs for evenings out, and a gorgeous deli for supplying food for evenings in. I stopped off at a Starbucks for a coffee, and settled into a sofa to check my map.

"May I join you?" My head snapped up at the masculine voice. Adonis from the apartment block was standing in front of me.

"Sure," was all I could manage. I went back to my map. I could do rude too. He coughed slightly, which made me look up. He was staring intently.

"You just came out of Pearson Hardwick," he said.

I stared back, "yes," I replied, giving nothing else away. He unnerved me, which I didn't like. I hoped he didn't work for them as well. He blew on his coffee before sipping it. I watched his mouth. He had the sexiest mouth.

"So what were you doing there?"

"I beg your pardon?" How rude was this man? Out of all the ways to frame a question, he had to pick the worst.

"Are you a secretary?" I almost spat my coffee at him.

"No I'm most certainly not. It's none of your business why I was there." I watched as his eyes flashed. I couldn't work out if he was laughing at me or angry.

"I suppose it's not, I just saw you in their offices. I was in there signing a contract," he said.

"Are you a client?" I asked, suddenly wary of upsetting him.

"No, I was there with my own legal team, they had drawn up a contract for the other party. So are you going to tell me why you were there?"

"I start work there Monday, I'm a lawyer for Pearson Hardwick, just moving over to corporate. Went there today to introduce myself."

"So are you going to introduce yourself to me? Seeing as you nearly knocked me over at home and work two floors below me in the tower?"

"I'm Elle Reynolds. I just moved into the apartment, James' new flatmate. Have you lived there long?"

"About two years. I'm Oscar Golding, and it's very nice to meet you Elle." He leaned forward and shook my hand. His hand was surprisingly warm and soft for such a harsh looking man. I wanted to get a smile from him to see if I was right about him being more handsome. I gave him my best beaming smile, hoping he would reciprocate. He just about managed to turn the corners of his mouth up when his phone rang. As soon as he saw the screen, he scowled and excused himself. I went back to my coffee and my map.

I picked up a box of Krispy Kremes before heading home. James came out of his study when he heard the front door.

"Thank god you're back. I was going boggle eyed at my screen in there. What you been up to?" He made coffee and set out the box of doughnuts while I told him about the gym, my office, and the shopping mall.

"I bumped into our downstairs neighbour this morning, quite literally. He really is a strange one. Snarled at me in the lift, saw me in Starbucks this afternoon and managed to piss me off again."

James laughed, "how did he manage to piss off a jolly little thing like you?"

"Said he saw me in the Pearson Hardwick offices and asked if I was a secretary." James' eyebrows shot up.

"Why did he assume you were a secretary? Stupid man."

"Quite. He really is quite unpleasant. Never smiles either." I sipped my coffee, and smiled at James demolishing the pile of doughnuts. "I did make sure he wasn't a client though."

"Clever move. Never a good idea to make a client feel like an idiot." We both laughed.

James made fajitas that evening, which were delicious. Afterwards I had a long hot bath before putting my pyjamas on and joining him for a bit of telly and a glass of wine before I turned in.

Thank you for reading the little taster of A Very Corporate Affair Book 1, the story of Elle's rise to corporate lawyer at Pearson Hardwick's Canary Wharf department, her affair with Oscar, and the truth about their infamous break-up.

18428300R00214

Printed in Poland
by Amazon Fulfillment
Poland Sp. z o.o., Wrocław